Poison Makers

Also by Jimmy Olsen

Novel

Things In Ditches
(paper and eBook)

Short Stories

The Private Eye
Wormwood
(eBook only)

Poison Makers

A Novel

Jimmy Olsen

505 Fourth Street South
P.O. Box 161
Hoffman, MN 56339

This is a fictional work. Names, characters, places and occurrences of plot are imaginary and bear no resemblance to any person alive or dead, except by coincidence.

First Hoffman House Press hardcover edition June, 2011

This book is also available as an eBook on Kindle, Nook, and iPad
Go to www.hoffmanhousepress.com for further information.

Dust cover photo by author.

Manufactured in the United States of America

Olsen, Jimmy

Poison Makers: a novel/ by Jimmy Olsen
First Hoffman House Press edition

ISBN 978-0-9801835-4-2
ISBN 978-0-9801835-5-9 (eBook)

Dedication

In Memory Of

Jacqueline Jacobo

February 18, 1968 - January 22, 1978

Author's Note

One cannot write about voodoo or Haiti without incurring skepticism from some, displeasure from others. Since it's not for an author to question such reactions, it is this author's desire to express a great affection for every Haitian I met during the years we lived on the Island of Hispaniola. They may be the poorest people in this hemisphere, but also some of the most open-hearted. Beaten by the winds of countless hurricanes, two centuries of political repression, and devastating earthquakes, they survive. Many of them were hungry before these disasters and few of us have noticed. Billions of dollars spent to save a nation from poverty, but like water over a stone, it grows nothing but slippery moss.

In writing about the people, place, and the poison makers, I wasn't seeking solutions. The resilience of so many Haitians will eventually win out and preserve the nation. In recent years a growing revival has begun in Haiti, and I'm encouraged by the efforts of fair-minded men like Franklin Graham and staff of the Billy Graham Evangelical Association (BGEA) to offer the essential hope that is awakening in thousands of Haitians. No nation, including the most powerful on earth, survives long on a foundation of power and money. Our mission to Haiti must be hopefulness, not a fistful of greenbacks.

There may have to be a "poorest" nation in this hemisphere, but no nation should be this poor.

Poison Makers

Prologue

The world is rife with clever men, but some are more clever than others and Adam Quist thought he was one of those. This opinion was reinforced by many who knew him - most of his colleagues, scores of beautiful women who curried his favor, the rich and powerful, even the President of the United States, who'd appointed him Ambassador to the Dominican Republic. Strolling along a hallway of the official U.S. Ambassador's Residence in Santo Domingo on an exceptionally fine tropical morning, he felt himself to be the luckiest man alive.

In a kitchen thirty-five feet away, three Vodoun bokors sat around a table drinking tea, waiting to kill him. The two men and one woman had no opinion about Adam Quist's value to the world, nor his cleverness or power. They were simply Vodoun poison makers doing what the spirits demanded. Spirits rouse believers to do what seems illogical to mind or heart, but denying spiritual supremacy was to live in hopelessness instead of harmony. Bokors, the chosen priests, knew this better than anyone and knew how to kill in the ancient manner of their red sect. Secret methods handed down over thousands of years. In a matter of moments this magic would reap another soul for gehenna.

Ambassador Quist was in his early sixties and fit for a man of his years. He swam in the Residence pool daily, played golf twice a week, some tennis still, though his shoulder bothered him now, and even lifted weights in a small gym downstairs. His movements were fluid as he turned into the Haitian Room to pick up a folder he'd left there after breakfast. An ex-marine, he wasn't an easy fellow to overpower. On Iwo Jima he'd fought a Japanese soldier hand to hand and split the man's skull by striking him repeatedly with a live grenade. This so impressed the others in his platoon they began calling him Sapper. A few people still used the nickname but often now the meaning was lost. Diplomats stood aside from the world of war and physical contention, preferring wit to force, but Quist was proficient in both worlds.

The three bokors received their signal and put the tea things carefully in a sink. One of them spun three feet of paper towel from a roller and wet it. The female, who had painted her face with white dots, withdrew a small pouch from the waistband of her skirt. None of them spoke. All were barefooted and their cotton clothing made not the slightest sound as they crossed the kitchen, slipped out the door and along the hallway toward the Haitian Room.

Adam Quist was also barefoot. He'd dressed earlier for breakfast but since he wasn't going out until later he wore chancletas on his bare feet. Now he wanted to refresh himself on several items contained in the file and dropped into a Kennedy rocker, a gift from the President of the Dominican Republic. He slipped the sandals off and placed the soles of his feet on the cool marble floor. It, and the rocker, were the only things in the room not Haitian, besides Quist himself.

Haiti was Quist's previous post and he had a fine collection of art, both painting and sculpture. Primitive art was virtually worthless at that time, but he was sure his son and two daughters would someday thank him for his foresight in buying so much of it. Part of being clever is knowing what to keep beyond your own time - accumulated wealth and strengthened families.

Quist held the file at arm's length and leaned to catch light from the open doorway. He'd put on his reading glasses too, and was frowning slightly as he read.

The bokors entered by the other door at the far end of the room and moved unseen along the wall. The seldom used room was musty and the bokors' passing disturbed dust mites that rolled in silent waves across the airless space. There was a scent of mineral like in a cave. The only sound was the gentle squeak of the chair as Quist rocked in absentminded concentration.

Had the bokors been more impatient perhaps the outcome might've been different, but all three, almost like the spirits they obeyed, glided to a stop along the wall and watched the Ambassador for a time. During those minutes he grew noticeably bored with his reading and finally rested his head on the chair back, the gentle rocking sent him off to sleep.

The bokors had not planned for this but the female crept forward with the poison pouch, and careful not to spill any on her hands, sprinkled its contents soundlessly near Quist's bare feet. He could not step in any direction without touching it. This was more in keeping with the usual arrangement for ending the life of an enemy or creating a zombie. The secret poison was spread on ground or floor and absorbed through the pores in the soles of bare feet. They'd prepared, if Quist was wearing shoes, to shake some poison in his face and eyes. Any means by which it entered the body achieved the same result. Nevertheless, the bokors were pleased with an opportunity to honor tradition, and took it as further evidence the spirits were in control of their actions.

One of the male bokors, wearing a dirty Angels baseball cap, leaned forward and blew a sharp blast of air into Adam Quist's right ear and stepped back unnoticed. Quist sprang from his chair, one foot in the powder. He glanced down, wiped it on his trouser leg and replaced his plastic slippers.

The Ambassador had no idea what had awakened him but he recovered the file and resumed his seat. Where did the powder come from? He'd dozed off more than once lately and guessed it was part of aging. Luckily, no one had discovered this new weakness. Much of his work was done at cocktail parties and strategy lunches anyway.

He set the file aside, meaning to place it on the nearby table but instead it slipped to the floor and spilled. Quist swore. He bent to pick up the papers and shove them back into the manila folder but his body wouldn't obey. His mouth had gone dry and his tongue had swollen. His lips were numb. The room appeared dark almost like dusk. The Haitian paintings and sculptures swam before him as objects in a fog. Nausea forced him to grip the arms of the rocker with both hands. Inside his thorax the various organs of his body were grinding to a halt. Lungs, heart, blood, breath itself ending in a quiet but rhythmic winding down. Something had thrown the power switch. Ambassador Adam Quist closed his eyes and accepted the dark.

The bokors came out of the shadows. The male with the damp paper towel dropped to his knees and wiped carefully at the powder. He made certain none of it touched his own skin, and when nothing was left on the floor he nudged the paper towel into a plastic bag he'd flipped from his pocket. They stood for awhile by the Ambassador, admiring their work. But it wasn't theirs of course, they were but obedient servants of the powers of darkness who demanded this life for reasons of their own. The bokors were instruments. Nothing more.

They left the room and finally exited the Residence by a rear door. No one had seen them come or go.

* * *

Peor was a witch. A bruja. She'd been resting along the wall behind the American Ambassador's Residence while her child squatted to relieve herself in the boulevard. Witches know things, of course, even before they see people like the three bokors slipping from the servant's gate in the Residence high wall. She didn't know they were bokors, but she knew they didn't belong there. The armed guards weren't easily avoided, though she had done it.

The two men and one woman turned away from her and crossed the street, rounded a corner and disappeared. She wondered about them. She wondered about everything and in fact it was her curiosity that kept her alive. She ate because she wondered. Who is that? Where are they going? Have I seen that one before? Does he live on this street? In a large house? Money in his pocket?

Peor loved money. She was very poor but poverty is no defense against greed. Her hunger for it drove her from street to street and zone to zone throughout the Capital. She was known by police of course, and by many others whom she'd approached for money or bewitched with fortune telling, a curse, persistent begging or larceny. Bruja wasn't a nickname it was her vocation. She had stolen the child who accompanied her. When she finished with it she would drown it like the others and get a younger one with a more appealing face. This one now was getting beyond the age where it could elicit enough emotion to pay well. Young and vulnerable was better. Cripples weren't popular though, she'd learned that. Too pathetic. Many people turned away.

That morning she decided to follow the bokors. She had nothing better to do. It was too early for the Malecón where her constant begging usually earned enough for supper and a pint of cheap rum. Those who knew her avoided her but they didn't understand that she knew them too, and could predict who would pay and who wouldn't, even where they might be at a particular time of day or night.

She didn't follow the bokors closely. The child was simple-minded and required constant prodding. "Venga Imbécil," she chided and they moved in the general direction of the bokors, sometimes on parallel streets or alleys. Peor knew the streets, the prize garbage drums and the profitable back doors of bountiful cafes. She also had a sixth sense about where people were going. They moved in patterns that were to her entirely predictable.

Her curiosity about them mounted as they dodged through narrow streets. These people were different, and didn't move like others, but walked in odd geometric patterns she hadn't seen before. Never crossed streets at oblique angles or rambled as others might, but followed a street to its corner before turning sharply left or right like robots. She realized they weren't familiar with the city, but yet knew exactly where they were going. Add to this the knowledge of where they'd come from, and she knew her curiosity and instinct had once again served her well. The new people, like many others, might bring her gain, even wealth.

They came to Avenida Maximo Gomez, a wide busy street, and before Peor could gather her wits, the three people she was following split and ran in three directions. One of the males sprinted directly across Maximo Gomez through honking traffic. A moment later it was as if they'd never been there at all. This behavior was unpredictable. Erratic. She'd never seen a thing like it before and it angered her to such an extent she knuckled the imbecile behind the ear.

Chapter One

Two pivotal events grieved me that autumn of 1972: the mysterious death of Adam Quist and my purchase of a television set for the maid. Both swung against the flow of my life, but the maid's TV troubled me from the first morning I switched it on.

Their uniforms crisp with sunshine, U.S. Marines slid Adam Quist's casket from the hearse, one soldier after the next shifting the load into his hands in the precise, formal manner of handling the honored dead. Adam Quist was the United States Ambassador to the Dominican Republic. I watched the screen, wondering if the Marines were guards from the U.S. Embassy. If so, this was more than formality. He was their boss. A guy who might've remembered them at Christmas, invited them to The Residence for a dinner or Fourth of July picnic.

On the airport tarmac, the television camera swung with the pallbearers as they stepped in solemn unison toward the dark, gaping cargo door of the C130. Ocean breezes ruffled the flag-draped coffin. A small group of North Americans overdressed in dark suits, waited alongside the cargo ramp, shifting their feet against the growing heat of the coal-tar.

Quist went up the ramp. There was a gap in the action until the pallbearers filed back down and the ramp door lifted slowly into place. The Marines formed up and marched away from the aircraft. The camera panned the crowd of Dominicans and third country nationals, surprisingly quiet and well-behaved for crowds anywhere in those days. The plane lifted off. A lot of airplane, I thought, for one small casket. Its Allison turboprops vibrated in the cheap television speakers and the Hercules disappeared into an empty sky. Everyone went home. I was about to switch off when Carmen, that's the maid, slipped up behind me and ran one of her hot, pudgy hands along the small of my back. "Señor," she said. "It's time for Esmeralda."

Esmeralda was a Dominican soap opera to which half the women in Santo Domingo were addicted. It's the reason I bought the new TV. Carmen considers it a love offering. She's lewd in a farmer's daughter sort of way, and adores me, as she adores taxi drivers, the pan de agua breadman and various street peddlers.

"TV's all yours," I said to her. "It stays in the hallway. You watch it after you get your work done. Otherwise I'll give the damn thing to one of my sisters or throw it in the street."

"No you won't," she said, cocking a hip, stretching the cotton fabric of her dress across a hard, protruding belly. She was short in stature and neglected her leg hair. Refused to lace her shoes.

"Yes, I will."

"No, you won't." Her hand came up to pat my cheek. She wasn't even a good maid, but I hadn't the heart to fire her and she knew it. I dislike change. She made great soup, washed laundry by hand, shopped for our food, cooked, cleaned, rose at five to wash both patios of my penthouse, had Sundays off, and was paid, besides room and board, $40RD (pesos) per month. About $32US. If I thought about it from a North American perspective, which I often did because my mother was from the USA, I'm a cheapskate. On the other hand, as a Dominican, I was an essential and dependable employer allowing an unskilled laborer to support her four children without the degradation of welfare, which we didn't have anyway. Carmen's problem was she had each child with a different father. She could name two.

There was the decadent penthouse, of course. The fourth, top floor, of an old concrete building in an old neighborhood. Rent, $225RD. No elevator and for half the day no electricity to run one. Great Caribbean view (why I paid the rent) but after you've done four flights of stairs a few thousand times it takes the shine off the azure sea.

"You have a telephone call," Carmen said.

"Why didn't you tell me before?"

She shrugged.

The telephone was downstairs in the ground floor apartment of the building owners, Felipe and Mercedes Villacampa. He's a dentist, she's a bitch. They didn't permit me to string a line up to my place because somebody told Mercedes two lines drained energy, leaving a weak signal so she wouldn't hear her sister, who she talked to daily, or make the Doctor's appointments. He was 76, she 79. He had few appointments, mostly people older than they were. The Villacampas disliked me but needed the rent money.

Since I'm from a good family, it obligated them to let me in the front door and speak politely. "Telephone is there on the glass bookcase," Mercedes said needlessly. "It is a woman." She slurred mujer to suggest whore, the type of woman I'd know.

I nodded. The living room was dark even in full daylight and crowded with heavy, dark furniture of a style not seen since 1920. Mercedes believed window screens inhibited the breezes, so small clouds of mosquitoes hovered under tables and around my ankles. "Hola," I said into the black mouthpiece.

"Sr. Espinosa-Jones?"

"Sí."

"This is Ethel Yancy. My father would like to see you this afternoon."

Ethel's voice had a creamy quality that matched her mellow nature but this summons was serious business. "What time?" I asked.

"At your convenience."

"I'll be there. Call me EJ like everyone else," I said. "I've known you since you were a kid."

Ethel giggled and hung up. A shy girl.

I wore shorts around the house, never in public. Mercedes stared at my bare legs as if she'd never seen anything more erotic, or shameless. "Thank you for the use of the telephone," I said.

"Your father is a tobacco farmer, isn't he?" she asked.

"Yes." She asked me this often enough to remind me of my country roots.

"I thought so," she said, satisfied.

I didn't bother to close the front door on my way out. The dentist's office was to the left and as I passed by I saw old Felipe hunched over a gapping mouth, peering inside the cavity, a flashing silver instrument not unlike a bent needle-nose pliers held at the ready in his trembling, arthritic hand.

* * *

Santo Domingo is an old city. So old you feel the humid weight of its years pressing against your skin as you walk along the worn streets. Before there was San Francisco or New York or Rio de Janeiro there was Santo Domingo. Not that anybody cared. I do because it's my home, when I'm not in the States, and I love the place.

In those days Santo Domingo was the Istanbul of the Caribbean. Fidel Castro's Communist Revolution was still at its height and CIA agents were as common at Capital cocktail parties as brassiere-less maidens. Cuban expats who'd escaped Castro with their cash or their work ethic, bought businesses or created them. Almost everyone I knew was involved in some sort of an intrigue, domestic or otherwise, and the lazy Latino economy had begun to boom. Even Francis Ford Coppola, two years later, saw Santo Domingo as the new Habana, and flew in to film Godfather II.

But that afternoon I saw Garrett Yancy, who is a travel agent, and much more. I thought Garrett a pretentious first name even for an Australian, but I've a high sounding name myself, Espinosa-Jones, Edgar Espinosa-Jones. Garrett Yancy called me Mr. Espinosa-Jones and I called him Mr. Yancy. Everyone else called me EJ.

"Please sit down Mr. Espinosa-Jones," he said musically.

Mr. Yancy's travel agency, Yancy Tours, S.A., was located in the upstairs of his pink and white concrete house in a solid neighborhood several blocks from the ocean. He had a sign on the street, a passport with feathered wings, but it was mostly hidden by the royal palms along the boulevard.

"Thank you Mr. Yancy," I said. "It's always a pleasure to sit here catching the sea breeze and admiring your fine view." At the time though, I was looking at Ethel, Mr. Yancy's daughter by his missing Dominican mistress. I thought again how she didn't look like any Ethel I'd ever seen.

Mr. Yancy smiled. He thought I was complimenting Ethel, in her mid-20s then and yet unmarried. I really had meant the garden view though, shimmering in the afternoon heat below the cool granite floor of his iron-railed balcony. Orange-peel waterfalls of bougainvillea poured over a high wall surrounding the property, descending onto a green field of grass edged with red hibiscus, creating a kind of privacy achieved only in art and solitary confinement. Outside, a disordered world seem to pass unnoticed.

Like his surroundings, Mr. Yancy exuded order and clarity. His speech contained no wasted words and his blue eyes captured your attention and held it in a manner I could only describe as imprisoning. And all who knew him, sought to know him better. Few did.

Ethel served us beer on a tray. When she served me, she smiled in a very pleasant way indeed. Mr. Yancy lit a cigarette and we got down to business. "Our usual arrangement again," he said.

Less than a month past I'd traveled to the Turks and Caicos Islands under the usual arrangement.

Surprised, I asked, "So soon?"

"Quite."

"Not another murder case?" I inquired softly, keeping an eye out for Ethel, never quite sure what she knew. Murders weren't my favorite investigation. I preferred a simple property recovery or solving a missing person puzzle. Murders are messy.

"Yes, and more," he said, fighting a tremor at the corner of his mouth. "This may be our last arrangement I'm afraid."

"Don't say that," I said. "Don't say that." He had emphysema pretty bad already then.

He crushed out his cigarette. "You're available?"

"Yes."

"Thank you."

"Please," I said. "Don't thank me yet, until I've heard the details."

Cut away the saggy skin weighting his lids, and Mr. Yancy's blue eyes held all the energy and recklessness of youth. "Murder," he said in a raspy voice. "Greed is worse, I think. Motivates the selfish to do evil."

"Yes. Wanting things gets us into lots of trouble." I grinned to mitigate what I said next. "Hope this greed talk isn't aimed at my exorbitant fees." I'd run up quite a bill in the Turks and Caicos. A nitrogen narcosis case that appeared straightforward until I learned the scuba diver involved was only diving in sixty feet of water. No accident. But I ran up quite a tab. Resort hotel, food, drinks, dive charter boat. Then doubled it as I tracked the victim's dive buddies to Chicago. Mr. Yancy, or his people, got stuck with thousands in expenses on top of my fee.

Yancy laughed and his blue eyes sparkled. "I broker many things besides our comfortable little arrangement. In any event, the money isn't mine, these arrangements are infrequent sometimes, and you make no great sum from your buzos. I hope you take no offense at that remark?"

"None," I said. By buzos of course he meant scuba diving. I owned the only dive shop in Santo Domingo in those days. Business was soft and heavily subsidized by my father. Dominicans, though island-dwellers, feared the water and especially sharks. The shop continued to struggle.

"This is a delicate matter," he said. "I can't leave it to anyone else. Your unique qualifications are exactly what's needed."

By "unique qualifications" Mr. Yancy didn't mean scuba but something I came by naturally - I'm mulatto. Half breed, Darryl Ferguson called me when he moved here from Florida in the fifth grade and took a dislike to me. It hadn't dawned on Darryl yet that the Dominican Republic was a mulatto country and we didn't see it as a disadvantage. Maria Fernandez gave him a bloody nose and later tattled on him as well. The teacher, mulatto herself, took a rather dim view of Darryl thereafter.

Being half Dominican and half American grieves me only in the States where they're so foolishly categorical - all those forms listing every manner of racial selection like Negroid, Hispanic, Oriental, Caucasian. I draw a line through them and write American. In the Dominican Republic nobody has such forms, if they did, I'd write Dominican. I'm at home in both countries and inside both skins, not divided by them.

From Mr. Yancy's point of view being a native of two cultures makes me a bilingual treasure, speaking good Caribbean Spanish and Midwestern English. "I assume you've been reading the papers?" he asked.

I chuckled. So far the 70s were turning the 60s into a preamble. "Col. Caamaño's revolutionaries in the mountains, blackouts, terrorists," I recited. "U.S. Ambassador drops dead of a heart attack right in the middle of it."

"The sudden death of Ambassador Adam J. Quist is a particular shock."

"TV had the honor guard loading his body onto the plane this morning. Shook hands with him once on Día de Duarte. Looked younger than 62."

Mr. Yancy rose from his chair and walked deliberately to the balcony that overlooked the garden and stared out at it unseeing. "Everyone in the world believes the Ambassador died of coronary thrombosis. His wife believes it, his staff, friends, both national governments, even his doctor."

I waited some time for Mr. Yancy to finish but he seemed to have forgotten me. "So," I said. "Everyone believes the Ambassador died of a heart attack but you. You think he was murdered."

Mr. Yancy shook his head. "I've no idea how he died." Suddenly he coughed so violently it forced him to spit down onto his perfect flowers. "I've arranged for you to meet someone in Port-au-Prince. In Haiti. Quist's youngest daughter. She thinks he was murdered."

"He had a history of heart trouble," I said. "What did the autopsy show?"

He shrugged, still facing away. "No autopsy. Family refused. His doctor confirmed the heart attack. Autopsy isn't required of diplomats."

"Then?"

He turned and grinned. "Listen to Olivia Quist's story. Appears the Ambassador's death was well-timed to fit the plans of every sinister son of a bitch both here and in the U.S. Olivia's like the rest of the Quists, silver spoon and so on, but she's very clever and not at all the socialite. Quiet, thoughtful girl not given to exaggerated stories."

"I don't recall seeing her or even a photograph."

"Avoids the limelight. No raving beauty like her older sister. Resembles the brother, at Harvard. Sort of genteel, though I suppose that's too old-fashioned a term for someone in blue jeans."

"I was just wondering what she might look like, so I'd know her."

"Oh, don't worry," he said. "She'll know you. I gave her a photograph."

"I didn't know you had one."

Mr. Yancy crossed back to his desk and perched on the edge. "I need to give you a warning now," he said, suddenly very serious. "Cigar? From your father."

"I recognize the box." My father, Gabriel Espinosa, was a tobacco farmer not a cigar maker, but rolled a few thousand every year to remind his customers he might go direct if raw tobacco prices dropped. It pleased Gabriel too, to give anyone a gift.

"I've known Gabriel and Rita for many years," Mr. Yancy reminded me. "Gabriel doesn't approve of your diving or chasing criminals."

"He loves water, but only to fish in," I answered. "And my investigaciónes, as he calls them, are barely tolerated. I'm an only son, you know. Four sisters at home. Papa's very traditional. Expects me to survive long enough to create offspring and carry on the name."

"You should've been married already," Mr. Yancy scolded.

I'd often wondered if Ethel wasn't in his mind as my match. "Someday," I said.

"Your parents Mr. Espinosa-Jones," Mr. Yancy wheezed. "I'm about to send their only son in harm's way. This matter must be handled discreetly. I remind you again that Caamaño is in the hills, our Presidente surrounded by political enemies, the nation remains suspicious of the U.S. and the energy crisis threatens our new economy." He caught his breath. "These are more than headlines. If it's even whispered that the United States Ambassador was murdered here in his own residence, we may endure 1965 all over again. You see why I'm concerned?"

I did. Lyndon Johnson sent American troops into the Dominican Republic in 1965, and though we Dominicans endured, as we did nearly 500 years of political upheaval, such adventures are always kindling for the world's crackpots. "I was born in the States," I said. "I stay away from politics there, and here too, but I keep up on things."

"The U.S. Embassy here is a nest of crocodiles," he cautioned. "I can't guarantee you that the daughter's suspicions are secret. Someone may be watching her, and if they are, they will soon be watching you. The dangers are real."

"What dangers specifically?"

"We don't know anything, you see. Olivia Quist may have it all wrong or only suspect the tip of the iceberg. She may even be someone's stooge. There's great danger in ignorance, Mr. Espinosa-Jones. Please don't underestimate our ignorance." He lit another cigarette and drew on it in a satisfying, fatal manner. "We do know a couple things. May I sketch them for you?"

"Please."

"Politics first. El Presidente's past involvement with Trujillo still gives rise to gossip and wishful thinking in certain quarters - civil and military, foreign and domestic. Quist wasn't popular with senior Embassy staff. Some there might see an opportunity to seize power now that he's gone. You'll need to know who benefits from Quist's death, and if the daughter hasn't the information, you will be forced to find out from other sources. Each one you tap exposes you more and more. The danger is that they will know you before you know them. You see that, of course?"

"Yes." I didn't think Yancy needed to lecture me on Dominican politics but held my tongue.

"And revolution," he said. "Caribbean politics ala Fidel. He's recruited Colonel Caamaño and hurled the poor sod onto a lonely, dark beach with some Russian machine guns and expects him to repeat the Cuban Communist Revolution. Foolishness. Dominicans have no desire for it - a growing middle class, bustling economy - hardly fertile soil for Communist mediocrity. So Caamaño's revolution will fail, and of course they will kill him. Nevertheless, this country's in an uproar, and Caamaño has friends. They might've struck a blow. Quist was a likely target but I'm convinced it would've come as a terrorist attack - a car bomb or assassination attempt - not a heart attack. They'd take credit for it, or what would be the point? You see what I'm getting at?"

"Yes," I said. "Too many suspects."

He nodded. "If it's even murder."

"The Quists themselves," I ventured. "There've been rumors about them."

"I've heard them. The girl can help you there, maybe."

"You say girl? You don't mean like, girl?"

"Young lady, I suppose."

"How young?"

"Well. She graduated last year."

"College?"

"High school."

"You can't mean we're undertaking all this based on adolescent suspicions?" I blurted.

"I'm leaving the girl to you," he said bluntly. "Make of her what you will. She's about 19, I suppose, if you're worried about age."

"All right," I said. "Tell me about Haiti."

He labored for another breath. "Emphysema is eating my lungs. Alveoli just puts enough oxygen in my blood to keep me alive." He grinned at this joke on himself. "Death enjoys its triumphs, I think, even against old men."

I squirmed a little, wanting to move on. "The trip to Haiti?"

"Oh, yes. Three reasons you must go Mr. Espinosa-Jones," he told me. "The first two are explained in this letter." He handed me a thick packet bound with clear packaging tape. "Explanations - one about voodoo generally, another about zombies."

Voodoo is always with us, but zombies? "And the third reason is the girl?"

"Yes. You must meet her secretly. Too many eyes in this country.

After you arrive she'll make contact."

Haitians and Dominicans were uneasy neighbors then, eyeing each other across the Cordilleras. Travel between Santo Domingo and Port-au-Prince was more snarled than between Jerusalem and Beirut. Relations had deteriorated into mutual distrust. The border was well-manned and closed, with a few exceptions. Smuggling persisted, but Baby Doc Duvalier wasn't a threat to anyone outside his own borders. Voodoo cropped up in the press too, from time to time. Voodoo murders, ceremonies, even supposed government cults. It made titillating headlines and every Dominican knew someone claiming to be a voodoo man or woman. But we're a Catholic country, with a very Catholic President in those days. Like the church, Joaquin Balaguer condemned all black magic and voodoo observances. Maybe I didn't take it as seriously then as I should have. It just didn't fit my idea of how the world worked.

"By the by," Yancy continued, "she comes with an armed bodyguard, a female companion, and a lifetime of diplomatic weariness."

"An entourage isn't the best way to achieve secrecy," I complained, listening to palms scratching along the house in the dry afternoon wind. Ripening garbage smells from the street leaked into the room. For weeks it had been too hot to rain.

I trusted Mr. Yancy but this girl bothered me, and voodoo. I'd no idea what pressures he might be under, besides his failing health. I'd never known who consulted him or how he brokered the things he did. I didn't want to know. Our culture is rife with intrigue. We love to plot. "I'm just confused," I said. "All hinges on this girl."

Mr. Yancy's blue eyes danced along the bookcases. "You'll be staying at the Splendid Hotel. When you arrive go to the pool bar and ask for Benwa. He's very trustworthy."

I stood to go.

"Gourdes for Haiti," he said, moving behind his desk. "I have some here." He produced a cash box from a bottom drawer and counted out thousands of the inflated gourdes.

"Muchas Gracias," I said, attempting to regain our earlier politeness.

"Pardon me if I don't get up," he said.

I turned, pretending to admire his garden but I was stalling, suddenly burdened that even after all these years I didn't really know him and feared to leave it at that. He looked sick. The late afternoon sun had crept across the speckled granite tile of the balcony, heating it like a griddle. "Tomorrow is Thanksgiving," I said.

"Yes," he agreed. "Indians and Pilgrims. Do you celebrate it?"

I nodded. "We celebrate all Dominican and American holidays. Last year we shot a wild turkey no bigger than a crow. Mother claimed it tasted like boiled owl, which even I didn't know they ate in Minnesota where she comes from."

"Come see me one morning next week, when you return."

"I look forward to it Mr. Yancy."

"It's cool up here in the morning, Mr. Espinosa-Jones."

Ethel saw me to the door. Following a step behind down the tiled staircase, her pumps made a determined echo between the open steel risers. We reached the lower level and I turned to say goodbye. "See you next week," I said.

Ethel nodded politely, like a mourner.

* * *

Arroyo Hondo is the suburbs. It doesn't look suburban in the poorer places, and while industrial cities usually grow systematically, Santo Domingo grew by happenstance. Happen onto a nice bit of land, build a house, or in the case of Cosme Ruiz, a barbershop. Unfortunately, Cosme had built his shop three feet below the edge of the road, and that day it began to rain quite hard.

I was in the barber chair, feet well off the floor when the flood came. Cosme stood calf deep in swirling brown water, a small river flowing in the north side door, out the south. I faced the open front door. Cosme finally shut it after a truck rattled by and sprayed water across my lap and legs. I cursed. Cosme apologized.

Cosme called his barbershop La Vida Nueva - a new life. I think he meant a new look. It was built mostly from flat sticks stood on end, painted robin egg blue outside and lavender inside. There was a cracked mirror about the size of my head, and a framed, faded photograph of John F. Kennedy. JFK was draped by a dusty plastic garland and the words "Gone But Not Forgotten," in English, headlined his portrait. I'd always been uneasy with the picture. Kennedy's wistful expression hinted that maybe he'd been photographed after death and the sun had been on it too, fading the paper. Cosme worshipped JFK.

There was a pig, too. When it wasn't raining the pig wandered in and out at will, bumping the footrest of the chair with its pudgy hind legs, scratching its bristly hide against the door frame.

I could've had my hair cut in a nicer shop but La Vida Nueva was a sanctuary. In the poverty-ridden gullies of Arroyo Hondo they knew me only as Edgar, a man from El Seibo. Cosme rambled about baseball, the taxi driver's strike, the price of peanut oil. "¡Ay! This Caamaño," Cosme groaned. "And the mother of this Caamaño. ¡Que madre!"

Caamaño, the revolutionary, was blessed with a loyal and vocal left-wing mom. She seldom shut up in fact, and her angry face appeared in most of the newspapers daily under headlines claiming the imminent ascension of her son to the presidency. "I'm tired of her too," I told Cosme.

"¡Cada día! Every day! I have even seen her on the television." He swung the scissors dangerously close to Kennedy's nose. "Doesn't she know they are making fun of her? Is she estúpida?"

"She's a mother," I said.

"Madre del lobo," he said. "A bad thing. All this talk that the soldiers can't catch him. Now they have to kill him."

"Yes. I suppose so."

"Muy malo," he said. "Very bad."

"Perhaps you heard of this Norte Americano who died? The Embajador de los Estados Unidos?"

"Sí," he said, tapping his chest. "Del corazón."

"What did you think of his dying so suddenly?"

"A fine man," Cosme said. He liked Americans and had a brother in New York. "I went to the airport with Margarita, the daughter who is in the English-speaking school, because she decided to write a report about it. A grand salida. The soldiers in white caps, khaki shirts, white belts, blue pants with red stripes. Not large men like so many North Americans, but lean and strong, carrying the coffin with honor to the avión. ¡Ay! And a new flag across the dark mahogany, red as blood. I wept. Margarita, too."

"Beside yourself," I said. "Do people you know take note of this?"

"¿Como no? He was the man for helping us," Cosme explained. "Los Estados Unidos is the bossy big brother Dominicans don't want. Unless," he grinned, "you find yourself outnumbered in a fight."

Here with Cosme it was like being in Minnesota on the farm. Simple people, simple solutions. But why care about this powerful foreigner he'd never met? Why did a poor barber weep for a rich man like Adam Quist? The answer, I guessed, was that he felt the loss. And I wondered, did Quist's own family feel it as greatly?

"Cosme. I am going to Haiti tomorrow."

"¡Ay! No! Por favor," he begged. "Don't do that. Haiti. Haiti. Why would you go there?"

"To meet a woman."

"There are plenty women here. Meet one of those. Nothing good comes of Haiti."'

"I'll be careful," I said. "But I wanted to ask you. What do you think of voodoo?"

"Evil. Pervérso."

"No. I mean is it real? Do you take such things seriously?"

He stopped cutting then and came round to face me. The childlike chubbiness of his face lent his words all the more gravity. "When I was in Nueva York to visit my brother we went to a famous church, I forget the name, at the front was a cross suspended by large chains. The cross was polished wood. The Savior was not on it," he said. "Jesu-cristo is on the cross here in Santo Domingo in my church, the church of my father. Here we have also the blood. We paint it red. This is because we have seen the blood and know it is on our hands. Do not go to Haiti, mi amigo. As the blood of Cristo is real, evil is real. Lo auténtico."

I reached around the drape and patted his arm. "Gracias. I appreciate your concern. Finish now. I'll be careful."

He went back to work. "You may be careful," he said. "El Libro says that Satan is the prince of the power of the air. How will you breathe?"

Directly across the street was a tienda. A small, poor kind of store we often call a colmado in Santo Domingo, where you buy a single cigarette, a can of tomatoes, cold beer, pigeon eggs or sweets. I recognized the bruja, Peor, a common sight in almost any quarter of the city. I didn't see her child. She knew my name as she knew many, but addressed me as Son of Gabriel. I'd always spoken politely to her but she responded with laughter. A deep-throated laughter from the stomach. She watched from across the street, smiling in a way that seemed anticipatory. Cosme's fear of evil had made me nervous.

Rain thundered on the tin roof of the barbershop and a new river of mud ran beneath my feet. The long dry spell had ended.

Chapter Two

The République d'Haïti isn't the place to go if you suffer a weak stomach. Barren, scarred hills rise behind miserable hovels on the flats near the airport. Juvenile trees creep cautiously up mountainsides as if the land is just now recovering from some dreadful war or natural disaster.

In the backseat of a 1956 Chevy I swept past fiber-limbed children watching with dead eyes from doorways and dirt yards, naked bellies swollen in the pregnancy of hunger. I stared. Their sunken eyes gave back nothing but disinterest.

Widespread poverty is tedious, and there's plenty of it at home. I stared at the back of the driver's head. What else could I do? Secretly, I wanted it to be their own fault somehow, like those long ago victims in Siloam. Haiti was giving me the creeps, and since I'd landed I couldn't shake the feeling someone was watching. On this, my first trip to Haiti, it didn't occur to me that I'd successfully ignored one-third of the island I called home. Ignored its people. It existed to me as something merely to mock, like some perpetual losing team. If anything, Haiti gave us reason to be haughty. We were richer, smarter, more Catholic.

Inside the city of Port-au-Prince, winding along dusty streets eroded by gullies of sun-drenched sewage, I decided the place reminded me of Nairobi as Hemingway might've experienced it. The main street was gravel and lined with ramshackle buildings, the larger ones had rusting tin roofs. Occasionally, grandiose government edifices rose up in the midst of the filth and slums. Trodden mud ran up tight to the marbled facade of a cathedral and out front, on steps and sidewalks, crowds of women in faded cotton dresses knelt praying in loud, wailing voices.

Traversing a hill, I ordered the taxi to pull over at a large sculpture - a black slave on one knee, arching his corded neck to the Caribbean sky, straining to blow a conch shell. The statue symbolized freedom for the black man, the driver told me.

Fifteen minutes later we rattled through the open gate of the Splendid Hotel and passed from gravel to grandeur. My eyes smarted from the blinding white of the high white-washed walls enclosing the property and fan-like front stairs ascending between gleaming columns to the mansion's open doorway. Thick stands of bamboo and green awnings softened the blazing white. In the time it took the taxi to arch along the cobblestone drive and roll to a stop at the immaculate stairs, I'd forgotten the oppressive heat, the wretched children, the open sewers. Escaped in a Chevy. Port-au-Prince was paradise.

I had forgotten too, why I'd come to Haiti. Instead of looking around to see if Ambassador Quist's recently bereaved teenaged daughter lingered in a wicker chair among the potted philodendron, I tipped the driver lavishly and followed the doorman inside along a soft green carpet.

The reservation clerk's white smile gleamed too, and he knew my name. Everything was prepared. Dinner at eight.

My spacious second floor room smelled of fresh paint and citrus flowers. Double doors led to a tiled bath and alongside it, raised three steps above the main room, an office banked by French doors open to a balcony overlooking the rooftops and a sparkling bay. Refreshed by a sea breeze, it was a setting to stir a young man's imagination, but inside me, where truth and fear live side by side, I felt an indescribable vagueness instead. Doubt deepening by the moment. Yancy's voodoo letters burning in my pocket.

I slid my sport coat over the chair and sat down at the desk, drawing out the thick sheets of paper on which he'd written about voodoo. As the words lifted from the pages they settled more in my heart than my head. They seemed alive with magic like double-headed snakes. The words were foreign to me - houngan, secte rouge, bizango, mambo. Only zombie I recognized.

Warm sunshine glowed yellow on the pages and across the backs of my hands but I was cold, fearing invisible secrets inside me, hidden evils, lying dormant until some future awakening. "The Prince of the Power of the Air," Cosme the barber had said. I shivered and closed my eyes.

There's a whorehouse back home at the outskirts of the Capital. A beautiful resort property with ponds and waterfalls, palms and lush green lawns. People ask about it on their first trip into the city, then they ignore it because they are offended that it's so beautiful and still a whorehouse. I've always done that with voodoo. All my life it's been there, but to me, nothing more than an unseen specter.

I opened my eyes and finished reading, but the words, and images provoked by them, hung in my eyes like lead weights and I couldn't keep awake. Siesta, I thought, and left voodoo on the desk, traded for crisp dry sheets and dreamless sleep.

Much later, I showered, dressed casually and went down for a drink before dinner.

Outside the dining room a small crowd had gathered for cocktails at a portable bar tended by a very black man in a starched white jacket.

There's no excuse. I should've seen her right off, but I was working from Mr. Yancy's description. He'd said she looked like her older brother, who I'd never seen, and that she was *no raving beauty*. I hadn't imagined a mustached teenager with a hump, but the fine-boned woman before me in a simple, sandy pink evening dress and heeled sandals, appeared to be in her mid twenties and spoke softly with a faint Eastern brogue. "Espinosa-Jones, I believe?"

"Mierda," (shit) I said. "You better not be the kid."

"Mierda," she said. "You better not be the detective."

We were making a fine start. "Actually, I'm not a detective. Most people call me EJ, and I'm a diver."

"Like a high diver or a pearl diver?"

"We're getting off on the wrong foot," I said, studying her clean, powderless face. "All I meant was I didn't expect you to be so mature."

"Braids, halter top, ragged bell-bottoms?"

"Something like that."

She slid her arm casually inside my elbow and guided me along the tiled veranda among a forest of potted greenery to a spot some distance from the cocktail drinkers. "Just for the record," she said. "Who sent you?"

"Garrett Yancy."

Her weight shifted and she seemed relieved. "I *am* Olivia Quist, and I'm nineteen, just barely. Thanks for the mature crack. I don't feel mature right now, just scared."

"We've got a lot of talking to do. When can we start?"

"Now," she said. "I don't plan to be more than ten feet away from you over the next three days."

"Man, do I love the 70s!"

"Don't get any ideas. Anyway, I'm alone."

"Bodyguard and personal maid. What happened to them?"

"They're with me in Miami, bereaving at my aunt and uncle's place. I flew there first to make it look good before coming here under an assumed name and diplomatic passport. I'm Irish, in case you're asked."

"Regular Mata Hari. How'd you arrange all that?"

"I have connections."

"Of course," I said. "Time for a drink. Be right back."

"They have a nice house Sauvignon Blanc here. French. I'll take that."

"You're not old enough."

"We're not going to start with that again, are we?"

I fetched the wine for her but what I really needed was a few minutes alone. I'd expected a teenager, found a woman. She wasn't gorgeous, neither was she anything near adolescent. Brown hair with streaks of lighter, random colors, inches beyond shoulder length, combed carelessly to the sides. A face not beautiful, nor plain either. I might've called it amiable, in a good-natured sense. Someone you wouldn't mind approaching even as a stranger.

The girl's eyes too, were startling. Brown with some hard mustard yellow in them, and nothing childlike in their frankness. Standing at the portable bar waiting for the drinks, I knew why Mr. Yancy had believed her story.

At the same time something was wrong. Just yesterday the Ambassador's body was flown to Washington, his wife in attendance, his older son and daughter meeting the plane. His youngest child in Miami? Why wasn't she on the plane? Why weren't we having this meeting later, after the funeral? I resolved not to turn my back on her.

When I returned she'd vanished. I stood there on the veranda, moonlight dusting the foliage with silver, drink in each hand, feeling as if I'd maybe imagined her. I strolled farther into the darkness, away from the dining room and the voices of the milling guests.

"Aquí," she said softly from the dark. "Here."

She'd reclined in the broad arms of a white rocker half hidden by potted palms and hanging pots. "Couldn't find you," I fumbled.

Her thin fingers touched mine as she reached up and slid the wine glass gently from my grasp. "Lo siento."

The apology was spoken perfectly. Apologies, like pledges of love, pierce the heart more deeply in native tongues. In love and music I preferred Spanish to English. I said nothing, stood clumsily there, facing her chair and inhaling scents of frangipani floating on the night wind.

"Did you know my father?" she asked from the darkness.

"Shook his hand once."

A truck or large bus made a rattling noise as it passed beyond the walls. It seemed far away. "The holiday is screwing up his funeral. The visitation isn't until Monday. Burial Tuesday at Arlington, then we all go to New York for a family memorial. We have an apartment there. I leave on the early plane Sunday to be in Washington in time to join my family. Will you take me to the airport?"

"Sure."

"Is that enough time for us to talk, or do what you need to do before you believe me?"

"You are just a kid, aren't you?" I said not unkindly.

"Sometimes," she said. "Sometimes I'm old."

"Well. That's how we all are, I guess."

I lit a cigarette, smoked it, flipped it onto the cobblestone courtyard and watched it burn itself out. She finished her wine and set the glass on a small table at her elbow and rose to her feet. When she stepped into the moonlight it sliced her face, illuminating a wedge of forehead, one eye, most of her nose and mouth. She said, "No one has given me a hug."

I took her in my arms and we were almost of equal height. Her hair smelled clean and tears ran quietly along her cheeks and onto my shoulder. Her arms, breasts and body were not warm but desperate. I held on. My sister Diana was like that, always in need of a hug. Or was this one born of coyness?

"Thank you," she said, pushing back. "I don't like being touched, but sometimes you need it. Let's go to dinner. I'm ready now."

The hotel's German proprietor, I learned, walled up the old mansion's formal dining room and made it a kitchen. Lacking a dining room then, he converted the grand ballroom. It occupied the northeast corner of the building, exposed to the outdoors by a series of high, broad arches. A fresh breeze flickered the table candles and the heavy afternoon heat had dissipated without the artificial coolness of most hotels. Below the long, eastern stretch of the room, an aquamarine swimming pool sparkled in the night, lit to a pale glow by its underwater lights.

"I think those are the real thing," Olivia was saying to the chandeliers.

"Glass."

"Crystal."

"Let's talk," I said, but the waiter appeared. Dinners and breakfasts were included in the $15 per night rate we paid. Two choices tonight; chicken with rice and eggplant, or broiled grouper with tomatoes and plantain.

"Order for me," she said.

I sent the waiter for the fish but he suggested a drink and fresh bread since the wait was at least an hour. Each dish was prepared from scratch by one chef and he was not to be trifled with.

"There are a dozen important questions in my head," I told her after the waiter disappeared. "Before I ask them, can you tell me what started all this? Why you suspect what you do, and why you called Yancy?"

"*Mr.* Yancy," she corrected. "And, I didn't call him. We spoke at play rehearsal. We both had parts in *Our Town*. My family is a Platinum Circle sponsor of the Santo Domingo Little Theatre and I enjoy amateur acting. He's quite good, Mr. Yancy."

"Why him?"

"Everybody knows about Mr. Yancy," she said matter-of-factly. "What he does. What he is."

Not everyone, I thought, but people with power and money knew. In the Dominican Republic official channels don't always function well. Business is done through the back door by someone you know, you pay, or is a member of your family. Mr. Yancy is one you pay. A broker who helps with anything from a new Mercedes stuck in customs to a business intrigue, even a murder. Mr. Yancy was the only immigrant I knew, who behind the cover of his travel agency, performed clandestine services. He took the difficult cases and rumor had it that he was a very, very powerful man.

"So," I continued. "Your father dies, you go to play practice?"

She inhaled deeply, sighing in an exaggerated, girlish way. "Okay," she said. "I'll tell you something. I wasn't sad."

"When?"

"When Daddy died."

"You mean like you didn't cry? You were in shock?"

"No. I mean I wasn't sad," she said. "My heart wasn't broken or anything. He just came to his end and if I felt anything, it was that the end was appropriate."

"So, I guess you weren't exactly Daddy's Girl then?"

"Don't be rude. A person is still dead."

"Why are you telling me this?"

She smiled and shook hair from her face. "Because, though there's plenty of evidence to the contrary, I'm going to say you aren't stupid. You can see I'm not sad about him, just scared and worried because it seems he was murdered by someone in my house. If I were you, I'd start thinking maybe this daughter, this person close to him, unmoved by his death, is a logical suspect. Isn't that the way you'd think?"

"It still may be the way I think."

"Me telling it doesn't earn any credit?"

"Maybe."

"I can't tell you why. Not important. We aren't a close family, however we may appear in public. We don't dislike each other, we're just sort of five different people who happen to live together. Like a school of fish." She snickered. "We swim together, feed together, but we don't love each other in the traditional family sense." She grinned at the chicness of a loveless family. "This is probably hard for a Latino to understand."

"I'm half American," I said. "Even that half has trouble."

"So don't believe," she said with a shrug.

The bread came, warm and wrapped in white linen. I sliced a chunk for each of us. "Go ahead. Tell me the rest."

"I like to sunbathe nude on the Residence roof," she began. "I was there then, and I guess they didn't know I was at home. My father died in a Kennedy rocker which had been a gift from President Balaguer. He never sat in that chair because he couldn't stand to rock. It made him dizzy, he said, and he did have a bad heart most of his life. Atrial fibrillation. An arrhythmia that's usually not life-threatening. Controlled by medications." She tapped her breast lightly. "When I came down from upstairs two of the new staff,

Alejandro and Dulce Baez, were standing over Daddy talking. I couldn't hear what they were saying exactly, but Dulce I think, said something about making Mr. Delbrick's day and then they laughed. It wasn't a mad laugh like *This really makes my day!* you know? Instead it was like it *did* make their day. Does that make sense?"

"More or less," I said. "Go on."

"When they saw me they jumped."

"Did you have your clothes on by then?"

"Naturally. I don't walk around in the nude."

"Just lie around on the roof. Go on. I only wanted to be sure why they jumped."

"I was wearing a one-piece swimsuit under a robe. I had on sandals and I was carrying a very large cream-colored towel. Does that set the scene? When the Baez's saw me Dulce began to cry, more like moaning, and Alejandro was clucking his tongue in the background and started mouthing Pobrecita, Pobrecita when he saw me. Funny, because he's not a warm man."

"And all this time your father, the United States Ambassador, is dead and draped over a rocking chair in the living room?"

"The Haitian Room, there's a great deal of Haitian art in there from the time he was posted here as DCM, and he wasn't draped. Sitting with his head to one side like he'd fallen asleep and kind of slumped down in the chair."

"This was the day before yesterday?"

"Yes."

"Nobody seems too torn up about it, then or now," I said, despite my longstanding rule to listen and not offer comment when witnesses tell their stories.

"I explained that, okay? Anyway, I got a feeling from them that they'd found him awhile before, but that's all it was, a feeling, and I asked if they'd called a doctor or anybody and they said Mr. Delbrick. I guess I was curious. I went over and took his pulse. You know, to be sure. There were no marks on him, or blood or anything."

"Let me get this straight," I said. "You find your father dead in a chair. You ask the servants if they called a doctor or anything. Then you take his pulse? Is that accurate?"

"Yes."

"Were you crying? Hysterical? In shock?"

"No."

"Why not?"

"I'm not an hysterical person."

I mulled this over and asked, "So you've lived here in Haiti too?"

"Junior high years. Until I was sixteen."

"Language?"

"French and Creole, yes."

"So you missed Papa Doc, the Tontons Macoute and all the rest."

"Baby Doc is hardly an improvement and the Tontons are still around, though not in the same way or having the same powers exactly." She gazed off toward the pool. "I'm comfortable here."

I bowed my head and closed my eyes. There was a piece missing. "Go back a minute to the pulse taking," I said. "Did he have a pulse. You didn't say."

"I thought so at first," she answered. "So faint and thready, like Rice Krispies. Guess I imagined it. Just wanted it, I suppose."

"Uh-huh. Wanted it. Why would you want it?"

"Why wouldn't I? He was my father. And there are lots of reasons to want people alive, aren't there?"

Perplexing response, I thought. Did life need a list of reasons to justify it?

Our meals arrived, well-presented and hot. We ate in silence, not the kind that weighs on you, a relaxing and quiet dinner. Old friends, dining well in anticipation of their evening together. Mierda, I thought. She's at ease here. Comfy, my mother's word. What's she up to?

She wasn't an hysterical person. During the meal she was attentive to me, the waiter, the food she cut and placed so efficiently into her mouth with such obvious pleasure. A skilled blackjack dealer, perfectly in control. She unnerved me.

Dessert was a gelled lemon delight with bits of rind in it and thickened cream with lime drizzle on a bed of something crunchy. Olivia finished hers and half of mine. I wished just then that outside this opulent refuge one of those malnourished children was pissing against the whitewashed wall.

"Isn't it ironic," she commented, reading my thoughts, "that in a country of such horrible poverty, the food is so good?"

"French influence, I suppose."

"Yes," she nodded. "Ironic just the same."

"Doesn't seem to have slowed you up much." I hadn't really meant this unkindly.

She smiled but with sorrowful eyes and spoke so quietly I barely caught the words. "Poor Mr. Espinosa-Jones. Have you believed anything I've told you? My appetite is good because I've eaten very little since Daddy died. My choice. Truth is, I just couldn't eat or cry or even pretend to." She sipped from her water glass. "Now you've made me comfortable and I got hungry. Sorry."

"I'm usually more polite." I remembered the softness of her hair against my cheek earlier.

"May I ask *you* a question?"

"Sure," I said.

"What are we doing here? In Haiti, I mean. Miami was easier for me and probably for you too. All this trouble, why?"

It would've been easy to lie, and more believable than the truth. "Mr. Yancy has some notions about voodoo, zombies, and the like," I said.

"Voodoo? Not as part of what happened to Daddy?"

"It relates in Mr. Yancy's mind. Gave me a letter about it."

"Can you tell me what it said?"

"In a minute. First, I've got some more serious questions. These people, Dulce and Alejandro, who are they? And Delbrick?"

"Duane Delbrick. He is, was, my father's DCM. Deputy Chief of Mission. Sort of officious and fastidious. You know the type, but he probably knows more about the Embassy than my father did. He hired Dulce and Alejandro a few months ago. They're Puerto Rican."

"Servants that do what?"

She hooked a thick strand of hair behind her right ear and puckered her lips. "Everything."

"Just servants."

"I don't like that word."

"Let's not get euphemistic," I said. "We'll just say servant when we mean servant and dead when we mean dead and not get all twisted around, okay? I need to know certain things without any sugarcoating. Think of me as your priest. These Puerto Ricans are your servants and Delbrick hired them?"

"Yes."

"Why are you suspicious of them?"

"We have a lot of ... servants. They're all Dominican." She began to wind strands of hair around her index finger. "They treat me ...

lovingly. The Baezs treat me professionally. They're not warm."

I nodded. This made sense to me. Dominicans are warm. Even in a city the size of Santo Domingo there are few crimes against women, children or old people. If Olivia Quist was kind, and so she seemed, the Dominican staff would soon warm to her. "How does Delbrick treat you?"

"Like a psychologist fascinated by the mind of a lunatic."

"Is he rude?"

"Never. He finds everything I say and do so gripping he can't hardly stand it. He once spent ten full minutes explaining to my father how I ate a mango, skin and all. Describing juice dripping from my elbows onto a polished floor, mess on my clothes and face. He did it all with high humor as if I were his favorite, misguided student and he was determined to make a lady of me. When we're alone things are different. If there was a safe way to murder my father, he's capable of it."

"Why would he want to?"

"To get his job."

"Is that a possibility? Aren't ambassadorships political?"

"Yes, but sometimes there are exceptions with experienced diplomats like Delbrick, and anyway he's a Democrat so Nixon is hardly going to appoint him, as if he didn't have bigger problems right now. Daddy said that if it wasn't for Kissinger the State Department would be in the same mess as everything else. I think now that Daddy's dead, Delbrick will be appointed acting Ambassador, and if he is, there's a good chance he can outlast a move to replace him in this backwater place - no offense - until a Democratic Administration takes office in Washington. Might simply be expedient to let him continue."

"You have quite a devious mind."

"I'm a diplomat's daughter."

I sipped from my water glass, crunching the last small bits of ice. "I don't think I've heard of any Ambassadors getting their jobs by knocking off the guy before them," I told her. "Sounds a little radical, even for a Democrat."

"Are you baiting me?"

"No. I've nothing against Republicans, I'm sure you're just as vicious, but it doesn't ring true. Most U.S. diplomats I've met speak to me in halting Spanish even after I tell them I'm bilingual because they're so afraid of offending one of the dark-skinned natives. Maybe they could kill someone, but I think it would have to be by proxy."

"I didn't say he did it, I said he's capable."

"Of course you did. I'm sorry." I slid my chair back. "Okay. If you had these suspicions why didn't you tell someone?"

"I did. Mr. Yancy."

"I mean your family."

She looked cornered. "We don't talk much," she said finally. "Anyway, it didn't come into my head like that. I started thinking how Daddy's death solved a lot of problems. He was supporting Balaguer against Caamaño. Standing in Delbrick's way. Promoting a dam project on the Ozama River to produce electricity and fighting some environmental groups. U.S. diplomats are targets anyway - extremists, terrorists, just plain crazy people."

Warm golden light from the dining room illuminated a high poinsettia bush in the garden, it's double yellow blooms reaching the eaves. I eased forward in my chair. "Given these suspicions, why didn't you demand an autopsy? Find out for certain what killed your father?"

She stared at me in amazement. "You don't know what it's like to be alone, do you? Big Latino familia. Two or three lovers I'm sure. Try and understand. I was scared. I *am* scared. Finally got up the nerve to tell Mr. Yancy because he's outside my circle. We both know what would happen if I called the police. You're not that naive are you?"

"No." Dominican police are corrupt beyond hope. Even good bribes weren't enough sometimes. "Avoiding the police was wise. But just so you know, there are a few I trust."

"I wouldn't know about that." Her face was flushed.

"We'll talk more later," I said. She wasn't stupid and knew on hindsight that she should've demanded an autopsy, but could I have done any better at her age? Probably not. "I want to ask more about your family. In private. I want you to hear Yancy's letter too, which I left in my room. Where are you?"

"Top floor," she said. "301. Nice veranda. Small refrigerator with cool drinks and a view."

I left her there and went off to retrieve Mr. Yancy's voodoo letter from where I'd hidden it carefully between the unused hotel envelopes on the writing desk in my room.

I've a sixth sense about danger. Before I crossed the room to the desk, I felt something. A kind of lingering presence in the empty space. Nothing visibly disturbed, but I felt uncomfortable all the same and studied the scant items on the desk to see if they'd been rearranged. The letter was exactly where I'd left it but a corner was showing. Someone had read and replaced it. Had I just interrupted them, I wondered? Did they wait nearby?

I searched the room. Electricity came to the Splendid as an afterthought and the lamps were old, low wattage. Candles sat strategically alongside ashtrays, matches on every table. The ceiling fan spun lazily. I threw open the French doors to the balcony. A warm night with a cooling mountain breeze. I gazed across the town to the sea beyond. There was nothing for anyone to find here, I thought, except the letter. I had that now. I changed into a short-sleeved guayabera, trotted upstairs and knocked on 301.

When I knocked a second time she spoke from the thick darkness behind me on the veranda. "Aquí," she said. "Come and sit down." She had changed into a light skirt and khaki blouse, dragged a large wooden chair to the railing where she sat with her bare feet up smoking a long cigar. Beside her on the table was a fresh glass of wine.

I dropped into the chair placed there for me, close to her, but not too close. "You're quite the rebel, I see. A cigar-smoking nudist."

She took this lightly and chuckled. "The cigar is one of your father's."

"They seem to be getting around lately for something not for sale."

"And I'm not a nudist. I just like to be tan all over. Evenly."

"Hard for me to understand."

"Well," she said smartly. "It's a Caucasian thing."

Time to talk voodoo. "I have the letter," I said, pulling it from my back pocket. "There's no light here to read."

She struck a match and lit the candle on the table. "There," she said. "The perfect setting for voodoo. Wouldn't it be fortuitous if the drums began to beat in the darkened hills surrounding the town."

I laughed because she used the word *fortuitous*, and because she said "darkened hills surrounding the town."

Then the drums began. One at first, soft as a night breeze tapping something against the building.

Then a second, closer and deeper. A primal beat, stirring, tingling hair on the back of my neck and forearms. I saw no surprise on her face, only satisfaction, and wondered irrationally if she commanded the drums, now joined by others in chorus. I scanned the hills, speckled with firelight flickering in the smoke. Charcoal fires, drums paralyzing the city sounds, a prelude to the ghosts of night and the repetitious beat calling them, drawing them from worlds I only imagined.

Voodoo is not a joke, a game of dolls and pins, I read from Mr. Yancy's letter. *It's a mixture of African black magic and Catholicism. It grips Haiti like a hand from the grave, rooted deep in the hearts of nearly every Haitian, so well planted as to crowd out the seeds of modern nonsense such as democracy, education or civic responsibility. Superstition rules hearts and heads in Haiti. Call that a condemnation if you like but truth is truth, valid on its own. My purposes here aren't judgmental but voodoo - Vodoun - is the most important dynamic in Haitian life, and even by our modern standards, not all of it is twaddle.*

You must know that I'm not given to snap judgements and greatly dislike generalizations about peoples or religions, but voodoo attacks the spirit in ways not imagined by most of us. Dominicans, and most Westerners, treat religion as if it were their favorite rocking chair, comfortably mobile without the complication of taking them anywhere. Voodoo isn't like that. It moves inside the believer, vibrating like a drumbeat. Eyes roll back. Bodies collapse to the ground. The dead walk again. These are their realities. Maybe we can't understand them because those of us who are traditional Christians or Jews have done so poorly with the most simple concepts of our own religion, like loving each other. We laugh at zombies, the dead walking, yet isn't Christianity about Christ, a dead man walking? Maybe the Haitians believe so strongly because they've seen it. Anyway, find out because it may be the key to Quist's death.

One more thing before I send you into the world of superstition. I'm as much a believer in the Devil as I am in God. Our culture denies evil in hopes it will evaporate, and so our prisons are full. Don't make the same mistake. There is a man in Port-au-Prince from Columbia University in New York, Dr. Charles Mercer M.D., and he has been researching zombies for years. Find him. He is a reputable scientist and while he has only issued some informal, preliminary reports, his findings are astonishing and may very well offer a reasonable and scientific explanation for the Ambassador's death.

I stopped reading and listened awhile to the drums. Now I knew for certain why we were here, but what did Mr. Yancy suspect exactly?

"Isn't there more?" she asked, smoke from the cigar clouded her face momentarily before drifting clear, gathering itself into a column and ascending above the old house.

"Yes," I said. "Is there any more of that wine?"

"I got beer for you. You like beer better, don't you? In the little fridge there to your left. I'm a poor hostess. Sorry."

I thought about saying I preferred the wine just to throw her off, but a beer sounded fine to me then and I opened the refrigerator door. Brown bottles of Union. German, of course. "Why would Mr. Yancy be speculating on your father's death in this way?"

"Because nobody dies of atrial fibrillation," she said. "It's very unlikely, anyway. A stroke might kill them because the heart beats funny, not of the atrial fib itself. Daddy used to say it's *atrial*, 'a trial' that won't kill you. He loved a play on words. It's the ventricle side of the heart that's deadly."

"You're so well informed about everything."

"I'm quite bright, actually."

"Why aren't you in college then?"

"I haven't decided on one yet. I've turned Harvard down. Yale, too. Maybe I'll go out West to school. Stanford of somewhere. But, of course, one always wonders about anything West. Berkeley and those, more into politics than education. David thinks Harvard's almost as bad."

"David?"

"My brother."

"Yes. I forgot."

"Are you going to read more of Mr. Yancy's letter?"

"Yes," and I began again. *I am not talking to you about superstition now. I have none. Dr. Mercer is a scientist and draws conclusions based on empirical evidence not politics or grant proposals. Listen to him. Ask whatever questions you wish. Benwa will give you his address. (Apparently telephone service there is undependable.)*

Finally, I want you to attend a voodoo ceremony. (Not those arranged for tourists, of course, but the real thing as it's practiced among the people.) Benwa will arrange this with your driver. The one who brought you in from the airport.

I stopped there and swore.

"Now what?" she asked.

"I hate it when he does that."

"Does what?"

"There were fifteen cabs waiting at the airport. How could he possibly know which one I'd take?"

"My," she said. "I thought you were supposed to be a detective."

"I told you, I'm a scuba diver. I just do this on the side."

"Oh, yes. A *buzo*. Did you take the first cab?"

"Maybe."

"Haven't you ever seen a spy movie? Never take the first cab. Mr. Yancy has a man at the airport - maybe this Benwa - he knows your flight time, sees you coming, calls to the proper cabby and he pulls up as you walk out the door. Simple."

"Humph," I said. "Lot of trouble just to impress me." Silently, I resolved never to speak to this Benwa.

She blew more cigar smoke into the drum-laden air. "Seems to have worked. Please read on."

I did. *The driver's name, by the by, is Johnson.* I stopped again. "He can't possibly be named Johnson. Who ever heard of a Haitian named Johnson?"

"Who ever heard of a Dominican named Espinosa-Jones? Please, read."

I began again. *He knows his way around and is very trustworthy. Do not, however, under any circumstances, take Miss Quist with you. Her safety is paramount.*

"Isn't he sweet," Olivia Quist said.

"Guess my safety isn't so paramount," I said. "Anyway, that's it except for ten pages of scientific material Dr. Mercer wrote about zombies, and Bizango, mambo stuff. That's for later. I'll contact this Johnson and do the voodoo thing tomorrow night. You'll be safe here at the hotel."

"Oh, don't worry. I'll be going with you."

"No you won't."

"Yes I will."

Smoke from the many fires thickened in the hills as darkness deepened and the drums seemed more urgent and sorrowful. Olivia was getting on my nerves so it seemed a good time to get serious. "I need your cooperation now," I said. At a detective seminar once the speaker said if you want someone's cooperation, ask for it. "Enough with the letter. I need the personal stuff. It's very important but might make you uncomfortable."

"I don't care. Ask me."

"Did either of your parents have lovers?"

"Really? That's the kind of thing you want to know? Dirty things?"

I took a long pull of the beer. "Look, it's not what you think. Murder is very often a family matter, if this *is* murder, since no autopsy was done and your father's doctor said he died of a heart attack, and should know his ventricles from his atriums. I have to look there first. Please try and answer the questions as honestly and fully as you can."

"Okay," she said, slipping the cigar to the side of her mouth. "I know my mother didn't. My father tried at almost every cocktail party on the island. He was notorious, in fact. For a diplomat he wasn't much of a drinker and after he had a couple he became amorous, even to the point of pinching. In Washington once he pinched the Russian Ambassador's daughter and she reached back, took his hand and kissed it. He had a reputation. If he ever got lucky I didn't know about it. There weren't any rumpled blondes stumbling down the residence staircase the morning after, or anything like that. At least I never saw any."

"How did your mother react?"

"Most days by four o'clock she's blind drunk."

The rumors about the Quists were true then, but hearing Olivia tell it, well, it just wasn't as juicy. The family seemed to live with lechery and alcoholism as others might with pimples and poor plumbing. "Your brother and sister. How did they take these things?"

"Are there no problems in your family?" she asked, suddenly turning to face me, cigar clenched between her teeth. "Does your father maybe have a son who can't take responsibility for his own life so he snoops into other people's?"

"Please," I begged. "I'm not trying to hurt you. We're all impaired in some way. Just looking for motivation, not playing peekaboo with your secrets, okay?"

It was the first time I detected any real emotion in her voice. "You have no idea what my life is."

"Tell me about your brother and sister."

"My sister is my soul mate," she said flatly. "My brother just got the hell out, as he says. It's made him bitter, I think. He was closer to my parents than I was and has a more needy personality, if you know what I mean. It's not like he can just forgive them. Their failures are weakness. It frightens him."

"Do you think he hates them?"

"Enough to kill, you mean? No. He's hurt not homicidal."

"Any other family or friends around?"

"Living with us?"

"Yes."

"We're gypsies, EJ." It was the first time she'd used my name. "All diplomats are gypsies. The rest of our family stayed in Maryland, Virginia, and New York mostly. I've been in four elementary schools and two high schools. We've never had a house. Our own house, I mean. Just the apartment in New York. In the back of my closet are two big old trunks I've never unpacked."

They weren't much of a family, the Quists, but it didn't seem like they had cause to begin killing each other either. "Thanks for the peek," I said. "Given the fact you aren't a close family, why did the rest of them refuse an autopsy? Let's face it, without examining your father's body no one can be sure what killed him."

"I suppose they just couldn't bear to think of him butchered like they do."

"But it's so important."

"No one else thought murder, I'm sure. Only me, later."

"Why only you? Besides the politics and all the rest. What specific thing made you think murder?"

"Do you believe in women's intuition?"

"Yes," I said, thinking of the feeling I'd had just an hour ago in my room. Even so, intuition isn't enough to create suspicions of murder when your father dies of a heart attack. I didn't like her reasoning very much. There wasn't a single fact in anything she'd told me, just suspicion and guessing. She seemed oblivious to my discomfort.

"Maybe you'll understand then. I've still got the creeps. Half the time I sit alone on the roof."

"Not in the nude, I hope." I said this to lighten things up.

It didn't work. Olivia Quist studied her cigar, which was less than an inch long, and using thumb and forefinger held it to her rich mouth for one last, lingering draw. Her lips parted, her nostrils flared and smoke flowed from her like thick steam from a power plant.

Chapter Three

Our second evening in Haiti, Johnson, the driver, flung open the back door of the Chevy hard enough to rip it from its rusty hinges. We were on our way to the non-tourist voodoo ceremony and he wanted to impress Olivia, as if he knew she was an ambassador's daughter. I was crabby. Johnson looked like a white guy in blackface to me. His lips were too pink, a radiant faky smile, whites of his eyes too white. He'd fooled me at the airport. I didn't like him, or this Benwa either, who I hadn't found yet.

"Oh, thank you Johnson!" Olivia cooed.

"His name's not Johnson," I told her.

"Of course it is," she said. "Why would he lie about his own name?"

"Every crook has an alias."

She had a way of crossing her legs high up that disturbed me. "Tell us about your name, Johnson," she said. "How did you come by it?" Leaning back against the dusty seat she could just as well have been at her ease in the official limo.

"My great-great-great grandfather was a black pirate from Africa," Johnson bragged.

"Of course," she said. "That explains it."

"¡Conchudo!" I swore. "That doesn't explain anything. Johnson is hardly an African name."

The aged car rocked out from the gate and onto the uneven road. "Pink Eye," Johnson said. "That was the only name my ancestor had aboard ship. The crew thought he had pink eyes the story goes. It was shortened to Pinky. The Johnson came later when a favorite captain died and he took his surname out of respect."

"Let me understand this," I said. "You want us to believe your great-great-great granddaddy was a bloodthirsty pirate named Pinky

Johnson?"

"I think he finally gets it," Olivia told him.

"Yes," I nodded. "I was a fool to question him."

Early twilight blanketed the dusty town in pink-brown fog. A few incandescent lights had come on, hung from weathered poles, reflecting weakly under rusty tin shades. I'd wasted much of the day searching for Dr. Mercer, who'd been swallowed by the place. Bloodthirsty Johnson made no attempt to turn on his headlights, saving his battery no doubt. We wound through the streets until I'd lost my way.

The streets were clogged with wandering crowds. Others came out from their modest dwellings to sit on wooden chairs or stand and watch the activity. Children darted everywhere. A sea of black arms, legs, faces. Bright scarves, faded dresses, bare feet, bright smiles, their bodies seemed trapped inside their garments. The city caught them in its energy, more likely they created it, and I marveled at what little effect the car had on the press of humanity. How it wound slowly among them, the hundreds walking, and how many touched the car, fondly, allowing their fingers to receive the remaining radiated warmth from its metal skin. It was integrated and so were we. The once overpowering poverty and hopelessness gave itself to the potency of the crowd's energy and it grew in me too, like desire.

I was glad now that the car moved slowly along the rutted streets, forced sometimes to stop until the road ahead cleared. I was drawn to the artless power of these people who barely noticed our passing. So intent were they, so charged, we must have existed to them only in shadow.

"Stop the car," I ordered. Almost without thinking I grasped Olivia by the hand and drew her from the backseat. She came willingly and I slid my arm around her waist, caressing the thin material of her sundress, suddenly aware of the bare, hot skin beneath. "Let's walk awhile."

The Haitians swallowed us and those who noticed our lighter skin smiled. Women sometimes reached out to stroke the white skin of Olivia's arms or hands. A tall teenaged girl caressed her hair and spoke in soft Creole as one might speak to an infant. The ground was littered with orange peel and banana, blackening with rot, all manner of other garbage, solid and liquid. Crude troughs, cut in the mud along the street, ran with a thin and persistent gray liquid that smelled of urine and something even more potent that made my eyes water.

Olivia flowed through the stream of bodies, a leaf among the rocks, twisting and drifting, obedient to the energy. I followed in her wake and tasted salt on my lips and our movement among the bodies was like a dance.

She stopped in the center of the street and again took my hand, squeezing gently so I followed her gaze. Alongside the road a young, barefoot woman bathed her thighs, calves, and feet in the gray water. She held her dress high, bunched in one hand, pouring carefully from a rusting can that once contained cooking oil. One foot flat in the dirt and the other close to it, on its toes. The water fell along her leg, rinsing the light dust from her nutty, smooth skin, and in the failing light was converted from gray to fresh lavender.

"It's Saturday night," Olivia told me.

As we moved away I turned to marvel at the woman's beauty, a dark flower in a dump. "Shall we get back in the car?"

"In a little while," she said, and we walked on and she kept my hand until Johnson finally sounded his horn, tired of following in first gear.

A bond grew then between us. I know she felt it too. In the car she took my hand again and laid it gently in her lap and counted the fingers as her tender eyes sought out the faces that passed our window. She asked, "You like them too, don't you?"

"Yes," I said. "They have spirit."

"They make me feel like I've come home. Have you been here before?"

"No. I meant to."

"No one comes here, do they?"

"A few."

"Is it because they're black?"

I wasn't sure. At home, Dominicans weren't prejudiced in the traditional sense but the lighter the skin the larger the bank account usually. "Poverty is the worst sin of all," I said.

"How is it wrong to be poor?"

"It's not." I squeezed her hand. "Our guilt makes us turn away, then we're angry."

"I suppose." She was looking straight at me now. "You're funny. I never know what you're going to say. I can tell you what my father would say. He thought poor people had only themselves to blame."

"He might've been right," I said. "Doesn't matter. We can judge them after we feed them. I barely make a living, and live well. My father supports me when dive shop sales fall and I'm between cases, afterward he lectures and judges."

"Is he rich?"

"Well, he has a wife and four daughters to spend his money," I said. "Dotes on them all. Works hard and lives well. If it wasn't for me I think he'd have the perfect life. His farm is a balance between physical labor, which men crave, and intellectual stimulation. He wants to give me that and I won't take it. At 59 he's impatient for me to grow into him, but my mother says I'm just lackadaisical, which is a word I've never heard from anyone but her so it must be Minnesotan."

"It's not. *Are* you lackadaisical?"

"About age anyway. About money, maybe."

"About women?"

"Definitely about women." I took my hand back. "You've got to be able to care for yourself before you can care for others, especially a family."

"You're making *me* feel old," she said. "Even older than you." She grinned like a girl. "I don't believe any of it. I wouldn't feel safe with you if you couldn't care for anyone."

"You shouldn't feel safe. Remember Mr. Yancy's letter? 'Under no circumstances take Miss Quist with you,' I believe was his quote. What if voodoo is dangerous?"

"Don't worry," she said. "I lived here before, remember? Anyway, we have Johnson."

"Yes. We did get lucky there," I agreed. Johnson, meanwhile, kept his eyes on the road. "Let me ask you Johnson, do you believe in voodoo?"

"Oh, no," he said. "I don't go with the voodoo peoples. I'm a Methodist."

"Of course," I said. "Pinky the pirate was no doubt converted by a Methodist missionary just before he died."

"It may be so," he said, and brought the car to a sudden halt alongside a clapboard building at the end of a darkening alley. Several men gathered immediately and peered in the windows at us as if we were zoo animals. "This is voodoo," Johnson said.

I'd expected the ceremony to be held in some rural place. Some jungle. Voodoo dancers leaping out from the darkness to frolic in the firelight. Torches and painted faces. This looked more like bingo night at a small town VFW.

Inside the voodoo church, people stared openly at us. None spoke, except to make comment among themselves. I've no Creole French but the inflections were clear enough as we flowed with the crowd through the front portion of the building toward a packed mud courtyard which served as the sanctuary. Both hands pressed on Olivia's shoulders, I directed her to follow close behind Johnson.

The courtyard was surrounded by the neglected building on four sides. It had a tree of some stature. The largest and oldest tree I observed in Haiti, it grew slightly off center in the packed black dirt. In daylight I imagine it offered shade, though its leaves were sparse.

Someone had arranged a collection of patched chairs, boxes, benches and upended buckets as rectangular seating around the dirt and had left an aisle open to another part of the building. We were ushered by Johnson, joined by a large woman, to the better chairs and made to sit down though most everyone else was still standing. Johnson leaned over needlessly and said, "Shhh."

A drum started up, then another and people crowded around. Next to me sat a Haitian woman dressed in rich dark clothing. She was tall and kept her knees together.

"Do you speak English?" I inquired.

"Shhh," she said without turning. An instrument I couldn't identify joined the drums and the music took on a repetitive quality. Many in the crowd began to sway. This upset me. Should I remain stationary and appear stiff and uncooperative, or move with the others and have them think me presumptuous? So I wagged my head and tapped one foot. Olivia closed her eyes and swayed with the rest.

"I'm not from here," I said to the woman.

She looked me over then. Warm black eyes set in glistening pearl. She smiled. "Voodoo is the bridge between the living and the dead," she whispered in English heavily accented with Creole. "Here the dead walk and speak to us. Sometimes they act for us."

"How do they act?" I said, thinking of the dolls with pins in them.

"Some are zombies," she said.

It upset me that a well-dressed woman believed there were zombies but I nodded and tried to lift my shoulders to the beat of the drums.

"I saw a man near Mirebalais walk on the water like our Lord Jesus," she continued. "He walked across the Aribonite River."

"What an experience," I said.

Her eyes moistened and she murmured something I couldn't understand.

The drums grew louder and more insistent. Somewhere I heard sticks striking a hollow log but swaying bodies blocked my view of everything except the large tree and the black patch of dirt. The woman's body began gently to collide with mine until I moved with her. I smelled her sweat. She slipped from her shoes and dug her bare toes into the dirt.

I would've left then, but Johnson had disappeared and Olivia seemed to think she was at a teen hop.

Six barefoot maidens in poorly made cotton dresses, without brassieres, danced onto the dirt with their eyes closed. A male voice chanted, out of sight behind them, and their motions gradually grew in synchronized rhythm with the dance. Their heads were bowed, eyes closed, hands at their sides while feet, hips, and breasts swayed. Gradually they moved faster to the music and the rhythms, still smooth but more exaggerated. Their feet made dust, hips bumped and ground to the drums, breasts straining to be free and their heads came up. I smelled them too, and the dust they raised. A moaning noise seeped from parted lips and the dance grew spasmodic, the jerk of a seizure.

Their eyes flashed open and rolled back in their heads, bodies convulsed and the drums beat still louder and now the crowd moaned too, until the whole line of trembling women fell to the ground kicking and groaning with nothing but whites showing in their eye sockets. The well-dressed woman next to me slipped from her seat to kneel in the dirt and tear at her fine clothes. Her eyes were white holes. I shuddered and trembled, fearing I might cry out.

A hush came over them. The drums paused suddenly and their beat was replaced by a rattle noise, like a snake makes.

A thin muscular man entered the sanctuary clad only in a loincloth and ankle bracelets. He carried a gourd containing colored powder and used it to draw signs in the dirt. Inside the signs were numbers and other shapes that were neither letters or numbers. Later, I learned this was called ve-ve. The sight of these signs, these ve-ve, drew awe from many in the crowd, including the well-dressed lady who had regained her seat though her shirt no longer fully contained her. I searched the forest of faces for Johnson's.

The priest, if that's what he was, danced and chanted while one of the women who'd previously collapsed fed him liquid from a brown bottle. He danced awhile longer and then the women returned and surrounded him, their cheeks bulging. They spit on him, spraying and coating his naked body until it glistened. The sweet smell of wine hung in the air.

Suddenly he exhaled on two sticks he'd been handed and they ignited. The crowd caught its breath and I ran my eyes along his loincloth to detect a hiding place for matches. He exhaled again and flame shot from his mouth across first one stick then the other and back again to his lips. Before the crowd could react he swallowed the fire from both sticks and it was extinguished. A worthy performance.

As in church, no one applauded.

A new drumbeat, and we sang. I mouthed the words as closely as I could mimic them, always a beat behind, but clapping to the rattle. The well-dressed woman kept me moving on one side, Olivia on the other. The priest rested with bowed head and closed eyes. His face revealed the pain and torture of his connection to some other world. Gradually this pressure gave voice in the form of an almost feminine moaning that stilled the crowd.

His head came up, eyes frantic. He was savage. One of the women from before came back carrying a chicken by the neck. It was alive and wet, as if it may have been scalded to calm it down. She placed the chicken's head on a shabby wooden table, severed it with a butcher knife and handed the trembling carcass to the priest. He milked its neck, filling a crude bowl with steaming blood. I feared he might drink it but instead he handed the chicken back so the woman could cut off one of its feet. He dipped the foot, dancing again, dipping and shaking blood in the air like a mad priest with his aspergillum.

This was a crowd-pleaser. The dancing, noise, blood, the drums vibrating inside my sternum, I thought maybe I had vertigo and stared into the dirt. I wanted to focus on something solid.

I hadn't taken my eyes off the priest for long but I saw now that he held a machete. Without looking, he swung it above his head and down against the shabby table. The table quivered, then split apart. The steel blade sang in the air as he danced away.

During the next few minutes he danced with the long knife, twirling it in his hands and tossing it in the air, spinning it before him horizontally until both he and it seemed to defy gravity. I joined the crowd in their enthusiasm until he dropped the black handle in the dirt and placed the sharp steel point against the center of his chest.

Again, we fell silent.

The heavy knife pointed skyward, handle in the dirt, point guided by his own hand poised to pierce his flesh. We waited while he spoke. In a rush of fear my eyes seemed open to voodoo. It was human sacrifice. I was about to witness death. Maybe even some supposed resurrection of one of the well-dressed lady's zombies. Was this what she meant? Was this what they all expected? Death and resurrection?

Slowly the priest withdrew his right hand from the machete handle, then his left also, which had held the point against his skin. His arms stretched outward in the classic pose of crucifixion and he closed his eyes and lifted his chin. His face shown with a heavenly peacefulness as his body eased onto the steel tip. His legs left the earth. He balanced on the sharp point of the knife. Its steel bowed like a saw blade. The night wind made a slight sound in the branches of the tree and a fire crackled somewhere. The drums were silent and the crowd barely breathed.

* * *

Late that night I sat alone on the balcony outside my room drinking in the dark. Olivia had been quieted by the voodoo ceremony but not frightened, asleep now in her room. I was grateful. Before leaving she said something very queer about not wanting to be so close to me, at least not then. She was silent during our ride back to the hotel and we both listened to Johnson rattle on about his family, which he was now convinced interested us more than voodoo. Olivia barely spoke and her eyes held a kind of barmy gleam. Her skin slick with sweat.

My eyes were sore and red but I couldn't sleep. A man had balanced his body on the point of a machete and not suffered so much as a prick. No single drop of blood, no hole in the skin. A man who should've been disemboweled by sharp steel and left writhing in the dust of the yard, instead regained his feet and danced off into the night.

I replayed it in my head because I'm a practical man and because Mr. Yancy sent me here knowing I'd see such things. Why? Did voodoo kill the Ambassador, or was it something else? Did he merely want me to know things are seldom as they appear?

Beyond the scattered incandescent lights of the city I saw the lights of a ship anchored in the harbor and the black hole night had made of the surrounding sea. I stared at it. How did I know an invisible sea was there, aquamarine and clear and warm? Because I'd seen it in other light.

There was no blood because the man had built up a callous. The tip of the blade was positioned not in the soft tissue of his belly but at the end of his sternum, at the bone. I felt the spot with my fingers, the arch of bone giving way to flesh at the center of my torso. See it in other light. Or deny it with fabricated logic?

Behind the hotel there were still fires in the dark hills and some drums yet. Gaps of several minutes between rhythms and their answer. I smelled the smoke. What if there wasn't a callous?

When Moses and Aaron appeared before the Egyptian Pharaoh to plead for the Israelites, Aaron threw down his staff and it became a snake. Pharaoh's wizards did the same with their staffs and they became snakes too. Aaron's snake then swallowed all the others. A just ending, but I couldn't forget that Pharaoh's wizards had magic. It was a shock to me as a youngster to learn that evil had such power, and hadn't Mr. Yancy just showed it to me again? And Cosme the barber? I was missing something. Some evil or power of evil in Adam Quist's death.

In the hills, the drums stopped and I thought voodoo had lost its charm.

* * *

I was drifting, still conscious.

That notable last moment before sleep, the one in which the Bachs composed great music and Columbus saw a round world. For me it was mambos. I'd discovered them through Johnson. On the way back from the ceremony he'd explained about the dancing voodoo priest. He wasn't really a priest but a houngan. The drawings he made in the dirt, the ve-ve, were signs of lwa or spirits. Women houngans were called mambos, he said.

Lying there, it kept going through my mind. Better get the jargon down, I thought, especially if I ever found my contact, Dr. Mercer. But I figured Johnson probably knew more than some New York Ph.D. anyway, so I'd asked him.

"You know the Bizango societies?" he replied as he drove.

"Do I look like I'd know Bizango? Is it like bubble gum?"

"No. Bizango are secret voodoo societies where the houngans do petro, not the rada we saw tonight."

Even as fresh air ruffled my bedroom curtains, I smelled the dust again in the Chevy's backseat, and Olivia acting like she wasn't paying attention, but she was. "Tell me about it," I had told him.

"Black magic," he said. "Death curses, sex orgies, making zombies. From angry lwa. They call it Congo sometimes. Angry lwa."

"So what's rada then?"

"Happy lwa. Like family voodoo."

I loved Johnson. Guy made black magic into tapioca pudding. "You didn't happen to know this Mercer fellow, did you?" I'd asked. "You're awfully well informed, even for a Haitian."

"Everyone knew Dr. Mercer," Johnson had said. "He learned everything a white man can learn about voodoo. More than many Haitians. He knew zombies. He knew they are real, not superstition." Johnson shrugged. "A man must be careful with what he knows. I think maybe that is why he went home."

"He left?"

"To New York."

"And he believed in zombies? Scientifically?"

"I think yes."

I'd pondered this awhile. I should've asked Johnson earlier, and searched harder for Benwa instead of preoccupying myself with Olivia. Another thought came to me. "Johnson," I said with a cagey smile. "What's your real name?"

He sighed. "Johnson," he said. "Just Johnson."

So that night, as I drifted off to sleep, I decided to ask Mr. Yancy to send me to New York after Mercer. First, I had to get Olivia off my hands and onto a plane. Quist's bloodless death, his years in Haiti, a daughter both innocent and inscrutable, angry lwa. Voodoo, or someone wanted me to think voodoo. Yancy had been right, Dr. Mercer had the link. He'd discovered something that made Quist's death loom as a more sinister event. If he *was* dead.

* * *

I'm no coward, but vulnerable in bed. When I first heard the noise I convinced myself it was a rodent. The city was poor, the hotel old. Rats. Mice. Roaches. Sometimes roaches scamper, their hard shells clicking on a tile floor.

I heard breathing. Without opening my eyes I counted four, maybe three. Air moved as they passed the bed and silently swung open the bathroom doors. Before drifting off I'd been lying on my back thinking about getting up and turning on the ceiling fan but couldn't remember if the electricity had gone off again. I must've slipped away then. If the fan had been ticking maybe I wouldn't have heard them come in, or move around the room to their business.

The light sounds they made were purposeful. Nothing random. No one slipped or caught a toe on a chair leg. Well-planned movement, and I can't say why, but that was a comfort somehow. It's what kept me still, eyes shut, trying to breathe like a sleeper – noisy, without fake snoring, just a light rattle.

First I thought about getting killed. My mind flying in search of a weapon. I had none.

Flour doesn't have much of a smell but there's a dust. Don't ask me how I knew they were using flour, I just did. Probably because after Olivia and I were whisked away from the voodoo ceremony in Johnson's rattletrap and I'd asked about the drawings that he told me were ve-ve, he said they used flour quite often. So I listened to flour plopping to make ve-ve on the spare pillow next to my head. Some of the dust settled on my face and I feared a sneeze.

I don't think they were trying to scare me with the ve-ve, but protect themselves from evil spirits. They scared me pretty good though. A question came to me, one I wouldn't answer for a long time. Why did they need to protect themselves from me? I didn't think I was much of a threat.

In the end, I didn't do anything. Stayed quiet.

They left the same way they came in, by the door. It had been locked. I slipped from bed and tried the knob. It was still locked. I didn't like that.

I suppose they had a key and it didn't make even the slightest noise in the lock and though tropical humidity is murder on metal, the door hinges never squeaked. I suppose that's all true since it happened. Changing the story slightly wouldn't hurt if I ever had to talk about it - a gang of them held me at gun point while I struggled to get free and rip their arms from their sockets. They ran like the cowards they were. People who pay detectives have expectations, even if you're only part time.

After draining my bladder I looked to see what was taken. They'd stolen Mr. Yancy's voodoo letter. I swore, then thought of Olivia. They'd visit her next. She might awaken, scream, be hacked to death by machetes.

I sleep in my underwear and flew out of the room with nothing else on, taking the stairs up to the third floor two at a time.

When I rounded the corner onto her balcony I remembered too late that stealth might've served me better, since anyone hiding in the dark there could pick me up and toss me over the rail. They didn't, and I tried the knob on Olivia's door. It too, was locked. I pounded with both fists.

A full minute ticked by before she opened the door, blinked several times and asked, "Are you drunk?"

"We've been attacked," I said.

"Yes," she nodded. "They took your clothes."

I'm not a bad looking guy, and what's the difference between underwear and a bathing suit, besides the little mesh lining? The difference seemed humorous to her. She smiled now that she'd come fully awake.

"It's not funny," I said. "They broke into my room, held me at gunpoint and made voodoo signs all over. I knew we were being watched."

She pulled me into the room, turned on the light and examined my body carefully. "You don't seem to have put up much of a struggle."

"Who struggles against a gun?"

"Rockford."

The latest American TV detective played by James Garner. I'd never actually seen the show. As a real detective you like to think TV detectives are beneath you. "In real life," I remarked, "you think of your client first. Since you're okay I'm going back to bed."

"I'm not your client but thanks anyway." She ran her finger along the waistband of my underwear. "Don't you find briefs kind of clingy in the tropics?"

I went back downstairs. Darkness engulfed the second floor landing and I fumbled for the door knob. Inside, some light filtered in from the balcony but when I finally found my watch it read slightly after 3 o'clock. I was exhausted, fatigued. The room was dark and I switched on the bedside lamp. On the spare pillow, the ve-ve was gone.

Had enough time passed since my short visit with Olivia for someone to come in, clean up and leave? Then I heard a soft noise outside on the balcony.

A lamp is not a weapon, but I considered it. I had a long-handled shoe horn in my suitcase if I could get to it, but a shoe horn isn't a weapon. I snatched the pillow from the bed and rushed the balcony.

My bare feet slapped the tile as I flew up the short steps to the office and out the French doors.There I stopped. A dark man of medium height and build stepped into the light and held up his hand. "Wait," he said. "I am Benwa."

He was not menacing, only serious. His face seemed placid enough. "Benwa who?" I asked.

"Benwa is enough." He smiled. "I am not your first visitor this evening?" His English was Creole accented and formed softly by his full lips, rich tones catching the edge of each syllable to create an unhurried sound.

"You clean the mess?"

He nodded. "I was emptying a dustbin of flour into the night when I heard you come in. You should have come directly to me."

"I was busy with the girl," I said. "You're Yancy's man. How does everyone keep getting in my room?"

"It is a simple lock."

"You just happened to pick my lock at three in the morning so we could chat?"

"Actually, I used a key," he said, stepping inside and leaning the dustpan against the desk. He selected a comfortable chair in the office and eased himself into it. "Please close the doors and sit with me a moment, then I will be gone."

"Fine," I said. "Hope I can see you go."

He chuckled. "Voodoo touches even nonbelievers. You have not looked very hard for Dr. Mercer."

"I haven't had much time."

"Ah. The girl."

"Who are you, anyway?"

He steepled his long fingers and smiled quite pleasantly. "We have the same employer."

"Fine," I said, hoping he meant Mr. Yancy and not Satan.

He spread his hands, white palms upward in benediction and said, "Dr. Mercer left on the last flight to New York about the time you and the Quist girl entered the voodoo sanctuary. You will follow him?"

"Johnson told me," I shrugged. "Yes, I'll go after him."

"He has made important discoveries," Benwa claimed. "But Americans are always in such a hurry."

"Maybe Mayor Lindsay called him up to see if he could borrow a couple bucks."

"Do you know what he was researching?"

"Mr. Yancy said zombies but I only read part of the information he gave me because our friends with the flour borrowed it from the desk." I pointed to the brass crocodile mouth where the letter had been.

Benwa steepled his fingers again and closed his eyes. "They like their secrets. No matter. Dr. Mercer will explain it all to you." His eyes flashed open. "Are you familiar with the Bizango societies?"

"¡Ay Dios Mío!" I groaned. "More voodoo."

"This is Haiti. Bizango secret societies and their priests do the petro voodoo, not like the rada you saw."

"Petro, I know. Bad lwa. Johnson told me. Hard to believe this is the same island where I've lived my life."

"Monsieur Espinosa-Jones, are you so naive as to deny the prevalence of voodoo in your sacred Santo Domingo?" This thought seemed to amuse him. "You may want to remember that, when you go back home."

"We've sharks along the Malecón too. Doesn't mean I play with them." But I was too tired to argue. "So there's petro and rada. I've done Voodoo 101. What's left? Doesn't help me get any closer to who killed Adam Quist, if it even happened. Maybe it was just a heart attack."

"Dr. Mercer discovered something even most Haitians don't understand," Benwa maintained. "Unlike scientists who dismiss the idea of the walking dead, Dr. Mercer approached the problem from an assumption that if zombies did exist, then how could they be scientifically explained."

"So you had some white guy from New York running around here trying to prove there are zombies?"

"Yes."

"Maybe he became one. They've got everything else in New York."

"Your political humor is wasted on me."

"There's more Dominicans in New York than Santo Domingo, I'm sorry." It was late. "I appreciate your visit and the cleanup. I'll fly home tomorrow, check with Mr. Yancy and leave for New York soon as I can. If he says it's okay."

He nodded, then rose to depart.

Half way to the door I stopped him. "Have you been watching me since I arrived?"

"Both of you." He smiled. "A security measure."

"So how come you didn't see these guys come into my room?"

"I was relieving myself." He disappeared out the door.

* * *

The heat woke me again about 10:30. I'd closed and locked the balcony doors. The airless room had heated to equatorial temperatures. Someone was pounding on the door. "Who's there?" I shouted.

"It's me," Olivia said. "What's the matter with you? I've been waiting all morning."

I swung the door open.

"Fantastic," she said, striding past me. "Are you ever going to get dressed?"

"I just woke up."

"It's a hundred degrees in here." She flung open the balcony doors. "Smells like sweat and stale breath. Do you know what time it is? What kind of detective sleeps all morning? Do they pay you for this? I bet you don't even have a license."

"I need to go to the bathroom," I announced, and left her standing there tapping one foot like somebody's crabby granny. When I returned I sent her to the balcony while I dressed, but by then she wasn't speaking to me. "Now I need some coffee," I told her finally. "Join me?"

"I had breakfast hours ago."

"I'm sorry. Please come along."

"They won't have any coffee now."

"We'll go down to the pool bar," I said. "They have everything there."

She lagged behind as we negotiated the long staircase to the main floor and it wasn't until we'd been seated in the bar she finally spoke. "I was scared too, you know."

"You didn't seem like it." I sipped the strong coffee, absorbing its aroma. "That's a very nice dress," I said.

"Palm Beach," she said.

It was nice. A sun dress made of some light material, conservative but with spaghetti straps. She was barelegged and wore flat sandals with thin straps that barely contained her toes. I guess she didn't own any halter tops.

"Listen," I began. "I don't blame you for being sore. I wasn't kidding about the voodoo guys, you know, and when I got back to my room Benwa was there dumping the last of the ve-ve over the balcony. Mercer's gone and we might as well go too. So you're done with me. I'll take you to the airport and you can be in the States for cocktails."

She studied the tablecloth and let her hair hang. I drank the rest of my coffee. Our table was near a poolside railing from which hung a touristy bamboo matting to separate the bar from the pool deck. Olivia Quist swung catlike under the matting onto the deck and strolled away along the pool without a word.

I called the waiter from behind the bar for more coffee and noticed Benwa poking his head around the inside corner. I motioned him over.

"What are you doing here?" I asked when he arrived carrying my refill.

"I'm the bartender."

"Why haven't I seen you here before?"

"Because to my knowledge you've never been to this bar before."

"Oh," I said. Maybe he was right.

He stared after Olivia. "Not doing well with Miss Quist I take it."

"What makes you say that?"

"Usually, when ladies leave their gentlemen friends alone in a bar and walk away, things are not going well."

"I suppose bartenders would know things like that," I said, none too politely. "Anyway, I'm not her *gentleman friend*."

"Johnson says you are."

"Screw Johnson. Seeing as you and I have no further official business, I'd like two double gin tonics sent to the main floor veranda. We'll be in the rockers along there somewhere. Use Bombay gin if you have it and don't skimp on the fresh lime. I hate those little slivers of lime you get in bars sometimes. They grow on trees here, you know. No use to skimp."

"It's still morning. You just had your coffee."

"Are you the gin police? Bring the drinks. I'll get the girl."

Olivia didn't want to sit on the veranda and drink gin and tonic. She didn't like gin. I took her by the hand anyway and led her there.

There's no hotel in the world like the Splendid, and the ground floor veranda was its best feature. It wrapped the building from grand ballroom clear to the other side, richly furnished with comfortable rocking chairs, lounges, tables and foot stools. Built wide for

Victorian ladies in flowing gowns, it fronted west, avoiding the sun most of the day and opening itself to ocean sunsets at evening.

The surrounding hillside neighborhood complimented the hotel, making it a centerpiece. An array of grand old homes, some in disrepair, others still occupied by the wealthy, their metal roofs streaked with vintage rust. Below, the aquamarine Caribbean stirring in Golfe des Gonaives with Gonave Island at its heart, a deceptive green jewel. Across the mountains far to my right the Citadel, where mad King Christophe killed himself with a silver bullet, inspiring Eugene O'Neill to write *The Emperor Jones*.

All I wanted then was to recapture that moment of spiritual communion Olivia and I had experienced in the street the day before. I offered her a chair and sat on a hassock at her knees, she only gazed off across the rooftops toward the sea below and said nothing.

We sat like that some time and then I said, "Still mad because I overslept?"

"Don't be dumb," she said, still staring out to sea.

"Seeing me in my underwear then? The legs, right? Too hairless? Or the little beer belly? It's just a little one."

"Are you trying to drive me crazy?"

"Or get a smile."

"I want it to be like yesterday walking in the street holding hands." Her brown mustard eyes studied my face. "I thought you looked very nice in your underwear."

"Thank you."

"I'm going to let you teach me to scuba dive."

"Thank you. It will be my pleasure."

"Where is my cocktail?"

"I don't know. It turns out Benwa is the bartender, did I tell you?"

"No."

"Funny," I said. "I was thinking about yesterday too, there in the street." I stood and kicked the stool away. "I'm going to find that fool Benwa."

Benwa just hadn't gotten around to the drinks, he explained. I couldn't see anything else for him to do, since the bar was empty and all the glassware clean. Benwa was an odd duck. He finally located a bottle of Bombay and mixed the drinks. I carried them back to the veranda myself. Olivia Quist had gone away.

Chapter Four

I went home, and didn't see Olivia Quist for awhile.

Hidden behind the hibiscus hedge outside my apartment, I spotted the pan de agua man's tricycle and bread basket. Since no bread-of-water men live in our building, or deliver at 8:30 in the evening, I knew exactly what he was doing there. Carmen's lusts are her business, except she really doesn't need another mouth to feed. Her mother raises the four bastards she has already, and if she ends up pregnant again it'll surely cost me another ten pesos a month.

I struggled upstairs with my bags. The flight had been late, my ankles were swollen. There was Latino oompah drifting from the Villacampa's apartment. The Fernandez family on Two were fighting about who had the most cavities. By the time I made it to Three my legs were wobbly and the bags seemed weighted like flour sacks. Three was dark.

On Four I dropped the bags and pulled the keys out from under my shirt. Dominican homes are fortresses against cat burglars. Concrete buildings mostly, well-constructed, ugly and barred like prisons. Two concrete staircases led up from Three to my apartment - a main entrance and a servant's stairs that entered by way of a small kitchen balcony where Carmen did laundry, piled mops, pails, and other cleaning supplies. That entrance is locked by means of a barred door whenever she's not home. I use the main door. The penthouse occupies the entire fourth floor.

This entrance too, has an outer barred door, secured with a padlock half the size of my fist. Hardened steel. I bought it from a locksmith in New York - $85. This, and the inside wooden door, keep me safe. My windows are barred too.

When the door swung open William the Conqueror skidded to a

halt on the gray Italian marble and examined me with bloodshot eyes.
"Hi Bill," I said.

William was a forgetful black Labrador. He came with the apartment but Carmen usually relegated him to the back yard behind a dirty 12-foot wall that surrounded a vacant, unused space filled with trash, goats, chickens, and the odd pig. If I was absent more than a day or two Bill forgot me. But after prolonged sniffing, he barked a half hearted welcome. Neighbors disliked him. Encountering them on walks, they usually stepped aside and muttered, "Negro," *black* or sometimes *rotten* in Spanish.

Bill barked louder as I tossed baggage inside. This was followed by scrambling sounds, and Carmen's hushed voice at the rear of the apartment. The pan de agua man getting his walking papers. Within moments I heard his bare feet slapping down the back stairs.

Several minutes later Carmen lurched around the corner of the living room grinning and patting at a wad of the dyed red-brown hair sticking out in sheaves from the sides of her head. She wore a plain pink dress, faded to the color of boiled plantain, with large white buttons from neck to hem. The buttons were one hole off and her feet hadn't made it all the way inside her shoes. "You're early," she said, sweaty and out of breath.

"Didn't you hear me come in?"

"Ay, no," she said. "I was ironing and the radio was on."

"Claro," I said. I didn't disguise my hard stare at her belly. She always looked about six or seven months pregnant. A year and a half ago she miscarried in her toilet, invited me to view it, then asked for 50-cents to get a público to the hospital. My sisters, who periodically use my apartment as a shopping base, have adopted Carmen and spend hours lecturing her on everything from morals to birth control devices. They mean well, but Carmen's a country girl who understands one thing, and seems to have that down pretty well.

"You look tired," she said. "Let me help with the bags and find you a nice cold beer. Why don't you rest outside on the balcony? Not much breeze tonight but I'll open more windows and light the candles. Are you hungry? Maybe I should rub your neck."

"Yes to everything. Keep your hands off my neck."

She grinned seductively. "You don't know what you're missing," she said, lugging the bags off to the master bedroom. "Move your ass!" she ordered, swinging my briefcase in Bill's direction. She hated him because he sometimes had accidents she was forced to clean up. "¡Negro! ¡Diablo!" Bill bore this in silence since she also fed him his daily allowance of boiled rice, fat, and spoiled meat scraps, which he loved. She prepared it in the pressure cooker, adding water until it clotted - a pot of gray worms that smelled like sweaty feet. After it cooled she put it in the refrigerator. God help anyone who mistook it for leftovers.

I stepped out onto the balcony and breathed deeply. Up here the night air was balmy, the light mountain breezes fragrant, refreshing. My friends lived in modern homes west of Carol Morgan School or the new Loews Hotel, some along Mirador Park in chic apartments of sweeping glass and stunning vistas. But none had a balcony like mine. Steel reinforced concrete it held fifteen people comfortably in chairs and sofas, another twenty standing or dancing. Sliding doors opened onto it from both a large formal dining room and living room. The old penthouse was designed for entertaining.

Dominicans are gregarious. That's my word. North Americans say we're noisy. They're right, of course, but it's gregarious noise - music, laughter, shouts of greeting, songs of passion. Tonight was quiet. No one on the third floor. One car passed in the street below, and this a rarity. The building wasn't on or near a major thoroughfare. Traffic was light, mostly local.

I listened to the chatter of Carmen's shoes against the tile as she crossed the dining room with my beer.

"Gracias," I said, grasping the bottle. "Where's the glass?"

"You don't need a glass tonight." She set about lighting candles and brushing leaves from a nearby table. "Sit down. I have a message for you."

"A message?"

"It was delivered by hand yesterday afternoon."

"Well, let me see it."

"I will tell it to you."

"I'd rather read it for myself."

Carmen thought nothing of speaking her mind but never sat in my presence. She put her fist on one hip and cocked her leg. "I threw it away. It was from that rich bitch."

"Sonja Cadavid?"

"Yes. Sonja Cadavid. That man of hers came to the door. The very black man." Carmen said she liked a little cream in her coffee, 'café con leche.' If a man was too black she wouldn't date him. The only distinction I ever knew her to make.

"That's Hector. He's very nice. What's the message?"

"He drives a black car."

"That's Sonja's car. He's her chauffeur. What's the message?"

"Bodyguard. Corporal."

"The message!"

She shrugged. "Nothing important. She wants to see you. At lunch tomorrow you should go to her very important house on La Avenida Independencia, near to the place where El Jefe had his house and his horses and would torture us."

By El Jefe she meant former president for life Rafael Trujillo, gunned down in 1961 on a lovely stretch of the Malecón west of the Capital. His old compound was near Sonja's house. "You were never tortured by Trujillo," I reminded her. "Anyway, he's dead and Sonja was probably in elementary school at the time."

"Not in this country."

"So?"

"So, I don't trust her. She is not simpática."

"She is very simpática and you know it."

"Maybe," she said. "But it's an act. Cubans are not to be trusted."

"I thought it was Puerto Ricans?"

"Them too."

"Aren't we filled with prejudice today. Very black people, Cubans, black cars, Puerto Ricans. How about Americans? I'm half American."

"Oh," she brightened. "Americans can be trusted, as long as you keep one hand on their wallets and another on their cojones."

"Never mind."

"I will make you some tostónes."

I did not want tostónes, but they took time to prepare. It would occupy her. "Yes," I said. "Bring some fruits too. Maybe a small sandwich."

"What else would I be doing?" She clomped away.

Unfortunately, Carmen's dislike of Sonja Cadavid was shared by my family. But she *was* simpática. If anything, too simpática, too friendly. Her quick, easy smile, set in an almost cherubic face, lit her black eyes and pushed her chubby cheeks into the folds of her black curls. She was the first in any group to laugh aloud or state the obvious or be silly. I first heard her shrill laughter from this very spot when I gave a party for the new General Manager of the Loews Hotel. Because Sonja owned a small travel agency and planned to move her office into the hotel mezzanine, she made the guest list. I heard laughter coming from the street and leaned over the railing. She spotted me. “Hey! Is that Eddie?” she called to one of her friends in a loud voice. “Hi Eddie! Are you the host?” We’d never met.

She bounced toward the stairway - more jog than walk - and burst into the apartment moments later, embracing me in an unaffectionate and muscular hug that all but cracked my back. “I’m Sonja Cadavid,” she declared. “My, my they didn’t tell me you were so guapo. Are you a stud, Eddie? Come on, you can tell me.”

“Actually,” I said. “People call me EJ, not Eddie.”

“Well, I’m going to call you Eddie,” she said. “My little Eddie. So precious.”

“I’ll see to it you get something to drink.”

“Can I come with you?” She hooked her arm around mine like a vise and marched me toward the balcony bar. “I like this place. Bet you have a panorama of the ocean in the daylight. Maybe I’ll stay over!” Her eyelids flapped and she reached down suddenly and pinched me. “Oooo! Such a nice, firm butt.” This brought another fit of laughter, which allowed me to extract myself and leave her in the charge of the bartender.

Later, I asked one of my hotel friends about her.

“Cuban, I think. Lived in Miami like the rest. Sort of simple-minded but fun.”

After that night I saw her everywhere. She attended the important parties, usually in company with married couples, business people or large groups. I never saw her alone or with a particular man. She appeared on the social scene suddenly, for no reason, from no place in particular, and no one seemed to care. She quickly earned herself a nickname: tetonas bailando (dancing breasts). Her jogging gait set them adrift to convulse in sync with her legs instead of her torso. Even so, she wasn’t an unattractive woman, just odd, with scatterbrained prattle to match. People liked her but few took her seriously. I was among them. I would’ve dated one of my sisters before Sonja Cadavid.

Until the day of the accident.

My car, a two-year old Jeep Wagoneer I’d bought when the World

Bank rotated its fleet, was perpetually in the shop. Two years ago, on an extremely hot Friday afternoon, my Jeep in pieces, I borrowed a Vespa from my neighbor Alberto to run errands downtown. I should've taken a taxi because the Vespa and I parted company on Avenida Independencia when I swerved to miss an open manhole and an angry taxi driver clipped me, sending the Vespa into a very old flamboyant tree. I landed on the sidewalk, unconscious.

The spot where I landed was a stone's throw from Sonja Cadavid's front gate and her man Hector witnessed the accident. Two other manservants and Sonja herself carried me inside and placed me on an office couch where I awakened about five minutes before anyone caught on. I listened to Sonja's voice issuing terse orders in perfect Spanish, very crisp and formal, without the usual Spanglish and slang common to her speech in public. The men under her command answered señora or dueña, with utmost respect as you address an employer you take very seriously.

I chanced a peek now and then. Silly Sonja had disappeared. The foolish grinning mouth had given way to full, quiet lips, more expressive with less motion. Her hair, which I'd always seen teased to bounce from her head, seemed straighter, more luxurious. I began to think I'd taken a worse hit in the head than I first thought, until she walked across the room to order the maid out for warm, wet cloths. Her breasts moved with the rest of her body. The baile pechos were gone.

Moments later she caught me peeking. "You are awake," she said.

"Yes."

"Pain?"

"Back and head."

She nodded. With a flick of her fingers Hector and another man turned me gently on my right side. "Help him with his shirt," she ordered, and they striped it away. I felt Sonja's cool hands against my skin. "You have some abrasions on your shoulder and lower back. Unbuckle your pants please." She helped me. "The hip bone. I don't think anything is broken. We'll clean you up."

Sonja Cadavid then issued the necessary orders and disappeared. I didn't see her again that day. Hector took me home in the black car, a late model Lincoln with smoked glass and curtained rear window. La Señora was grateful for the opportunity to help, he'd said.

I suspected then that I'd discovered some secret about her and she'd turned me out to cover up. So I kept an eye on her, but I was wrong. Parties came and went, she appeared and disappeared. I thanked her once for the first aid. She made light of it. Her public behavior didn't change - she talked too loud, danced in exaggerated motions, her breasts hopped like popcorn. I began to wonder if I'd imagined the whole thing until one evening at the old Embajador Hotel when I was dancing with the second chef's wife, newly arrived from Paris, I found Sonja in my arms. The French woman, Billie Something, slipped from my grasp mid-step and Sonja had me.

"You've healed up well," she said, not in her party voice. "Why haven't you come to see me?"

Her split personality left me cold and suspicious. "Why should I?"

"How about tomorrow night? I'll cook something. Come early, around seven."

What can I say about Latin men without trapping myself? We are more handsome than other men, more aggressive, romantic, in possession of more machismo. It is stereotypical. It is true. Sometimes not. That night, both sides of my nature answered Sonja Cadavid's question. As a Latino I wished to pursue her. As an Americano I was flattered she was pursuing me. My answer to her invitation sounded indecisive, even weak. "I'll think about it," I said, and we danced.

The next night I went there, without flowers or even a bottle of wine. I dressed casually, a cream yellow guayabera and dark slacks, arrived in a taxi because my Jeep had failed again. I reconnoitered, first from the sidewalk, then the empty lot next door. Sonja Cadavid's house was as inscrutable as she. It looked almost like nothing if you zipped by on busy Independencia. The place was overgrown, giving an outward appearance of neglect. Trees in need of trimming, high wall around the property left unpainted, even the graffiti had faded. Through the iron gate which led inside, I saw no light. No evidence, in fact, that the house beyond was even occupied.

I waited patiently for a break in traffic and crossed the street away from the house. On the opposite side I selected a shadowed spot under a leafy branch and lit a cigarette. From here I could see inside the gate. I began then to notice other things about Sonja's property. The wall was higher than most and the profusion of branches from the forest of trees inside had been skillfully trimmed to keep them away from the top of the wall. A man could not stand on the wall and grab a branch. A man couldn't stand very well on the wall at all

- it was lined with treacherous broken bottles cemented into its lip. A thick wall - poured concrete, probably steel reinforced - unlike cinder block construction common in the city. At its base, where it widened, jagged edges of limestone rock were visible. It would take a tank or bomb to knock a hole in Sonja Cadavid's garden wall.

Nothing moved inside the gate, so I examined the gate itself. The ornate type common to older construction. At first it seemed old fashioned, then it was clear to me that it was held in place by significant steel posts embedded in the concrete. The hinges, six on a side, were protected by steel caps. The decorative design of the bars and beams bent and curled like most such ironwork except for two roses, one on either side. Three large bolts acted as locks - one at the top that sheaved into an iron cross beam, one at the center and another sunk into the concrete drive. How many men, I wondered, did it take to swing it open?

I found out sooner than I thought. Hector approached from the darkness inside and I stood very still in the deep shadow. I watched him pull the bolts and swing the right-hand portion with one hand and some pressure from his thick legs. Without a word, he motioned across the street for me to come in.

"Buenas noches," I said, after dodging across traffic. "I was just having a cigarette."

"Sí Señor," he answered politely.

I slipped through the opening he'd made in the tower of iron. "Quite a gate you have here," I said.

"Sí Señor."

"Isn't it sort of an inconvenience to open and close all the time?"

"No Señor." He closed and bolted it.

We walked side by side toward the house. It was much larger than I'd thought. My memory of the accident visit was sketchy. I'd been carried in and driven out. Except for a large foyer near the entrance, the only room I remembered was the one I woke up in, an office. Informal, comfortable. But now I realized the single level house was massive, yet nearly invisible from the street. One corner poked its bow from between thick palmetto, croton and hibiscus hedges, clumps of bamboo. Sonja's house, like the wall protecting it, was built to last. Concrete and iron barred windows. Its tan and blue paint peeling in patches like scales. A thousand rains pounding the red volcanic soil had formed a rusty skirt around its base and its window bars were flat black. Behind them, the louvered glass was frosted, translucent. Inside, I guessed, Sonja Cadavid waited.

The main door of the house, set deep into the concrete, swung open as we approached, held by another large man. He had a long-sleeved white shirt, black vest and black bow tie. I thought he was a waiter from Vesuvio's except I knew all the waiters at Vesuvio's and none of them were six foot, two. I chuckled. "For a moment I thought you were from Vesuvio's," I said to him.

"No señor," he answered, granting me a benevolent stare.

Behind me, Hector closed the door, soundlessly, like shutting a vault.

"Vesuvio's has the best pizza in the world," I said. "It's better than any pizza in New York even. That's why Italians fly here, all the way from Italy, to eat Vesuvio's pizza."

The doorman/waiter nodded indulgently and led me through the foyer, past a rectangular, closet-sized hanging garden that dropped from a hole in the roof and ended in a tiled pool. Water trickled down from somewhere. We cut left and the tile floor went from mud brown to white - a hallway, wide and salted with plants in black pots, some large as Datsuns.

"Someone has quite the green thumb," I told the waiter's back.

"Sí Señor," he said.

We turned again, this time to the right, and found ourselves facing a courtyard lit with candles, dancing torches, shaded lamps along stone sidewalks. Sonja Cadavid was leaning against a tall granite bar talking quietly with the bartender and another large man in a wine-colored guayabera. She kept talking but waved me over.

"Hi," I said. "I like your house."

She ignored the compliment. "This is Mejia. He's my business manager," she said. He nodded politely. He had a white scar extending from his left ear lobe to his collarbone. "He was just leaving," Sonja concluded. He left without a word. "So," she said. "You found my house. What can I get you to drink?"

"What are you having?"

"Wine," she said, retrieving a tall glass behind her on the bar.

"I'll take a double Cuba libre. Plenty of lime."

She spoke to the bartender, and like everyone else he nodded politely at me too. "Isn't this pleasant?" she said.

"It's a goddamn thrill," I said.

"Let me ask Luis to bring us some hors d'oeuvres."

"Which one's he? The Vesuvio's guy?"

"¿Perdón?"

"Luis."

"He brought you back here," she said. "He's the house boy. Wearing a bow tie, remember?" Then she giggled. "You thought he looked like a waiter at Vensuvio? Did you tell him that?"

"Yes."

"Sorry I missed it." I caught the rich, deep laughter, so unlike her party laugh which usually echoed room to room. She rang a small silver bell on the bar and Luis appeared from the hallway foliage, where he was undoubtedly lurking. "Some hors d'oeuvres now please, Luis."

He faded into the greenery and my drink arrived on the bar just then. The no-name bartender gestured to the tumbler, palm upward as if he were presenting a diamond pendant at Tiffany's. I drank off a third of it.

"Come and sit here," Sonja said, patting the chair next to hers. "Let's talk."

"About what? Our mad love affair?"

"Would you object to that?" She leaned toward me as I slid into the chair and I suddenly realized that Sonja Cadavid was the most desirable woman in Santo Domingo. The strapped black dress she wore heightened the white glow of her skin and melded the black of her eyes and glossy hair. Her feet were small and narrow inside plain black shoes but she didn't wear any stockings.

Luis appeared then with the hors d'oeuvres and placed them respectfully on a small iron table at Sonja's knees. "Please," she said. "Take one."

Luis disappeared. When I reached for an olive wrapped in bacon I saw that I was alone with Sonja Cadavid. Not a large man dressed in black anywhere to be seen. Breezes fanned the palms and torchlight flickered against a warm, starlit sky. I'm not stupid.

"Amazing," I said. "The bacon is still warm."

"You didn't answer my question," she persisted.

"Weren't you kidding?"

"Only a little."

"When do we eat?"

Sonja sipped her wine. "I'm cooking myself. Hope you don't mind.

An old recipe of my mother's, from home."

"Cuba?"

"Yes."

"There are many Cubans in Santo Domingo," I observed. "Must be strange though, living so close to home but unable to go there. I've two homes. Wouldn't want to lose either one."

"Nothing is ever lost," Sonja said in her private voice, and smiled. "The land was here before Columbus. It will be here after Castro."

"Yes," I said. "But it may be a long time."

"Life is full of surprises and sometimes shorter than we think. Fidel will not live forever." In her eyes I saw a spark of something hot and sharp. How did I ever believe Sonja Cadavid was a fool?

"I'd like another drink," I said. "Let's not kid around anymore about love affairs. I'm starting to like you."

Sonja swept the back of her fingers gently along the line of my jaw, picked up my glass and made for the bar. "I liked you the first time we met," she said, selecting ice cubes with a small pinchers. "You looked down at me from your balcony, remember?"

"Sure."

"You had a big American grin all over your lovely Latino face, and when I called you Eddie you were so hurt, so wounded. I laughed."

"Yes," I said. "Your party laugh."

"Ah," she said, wiping spilled water from the bar. "Shall we talk about it?"

"Is that allowed?"

"To a point," she said, bringing me the drink. "To a point."

I caught her hand. "How much money do you make?"

This surprised her and she snorted. "Eddie! So forward, so blunt."

"Sonja, you invited me here," I reminded her. "I've got eyes. Unless you have a chain of fifty travel agencies or someone left you a whole lot of money, you can't afford to live like this. Now that's blunt. But you asked for it."

She dabbed her lips with a napkin and slid onto my lap. "I guess I did. Shouldn't you kiss me about now?"

"Shouldn't you answer the question?"

"Kiss first."

It was a serious kiss, oddly familiar and I'm sure she felt me tremble. Afterward she rested her head on my shoulder and I could feel her body relax into mine. We'd relieved some tension between us that I hadn't known was there until it was gone. "You were right," I told her. "We did need to kiss first."

"May I lie here just a little while longer?"

"Where are the boys?"

"You won't see them again until morning."

"Is that an invitation?"

"If you like."

"Yes."

She pushed herself upright and placed a hand on each of my shoulders. "That was a very weak 'yes' Mr. Espinosa-Jones." Her dark hair dusted the base of her neck and she slowly shook her head. "Did you mean 'yes' you would like to spend the night but 'no' you won't?"

"Yes again," I said.

"Such a cautious fellow." She nestled into my neck again. "Do you think I could persuade you to change your mind?"

"Easily."

"Good. I'm satisfied with that. Ask your questions. Be a pain."

It was a warm night but her nose was cool against my skin and her hair smelled of citrus. "Why the act? The gay Miss Cadavid around town?"

"I'm going to tell you the truth about these things," she said. "I've meant to all along, knowing that my life is yours then. I live to free Cuba. Almost fifteen years since we lost our home but we haven't given up and we won't. The organizations that sponsor me have to work quietly, and so do I. When I was attracted to you it was a problem. I really am married to my job, and anything like normal relations between a man and woman must be approved. Understand?"

"So you got permission for me?"

"In a sense."

"How romantic."

She kissed my cheek and stood up beside me. "No, it's not. I hoped you wouldn't ask, but I knew better."

"So what exactly do you do?"

"I can't tell you that."

"But I can be like a diversion for you? The man in your life? I don't suppose marriage or family are options."

She picked up her wine. "You think I'm using you?"

"Aren't you?"

"We all use each other."

"Be honest then and tell me if you took the manhole cover off."

"Personally?" She chuckled. "You play too, Eddie. No one at your parties could guess what a clever little mind lurks behind that smile. Yes. I had Hector remove the manhole cover and the taxi driver who crowded you into the curb cost me fifty pesos."

"How did you know I'd be driving a Vespa past your house?"

"You told me yourself, casually, at a party the night before." She shrugged. "Someone watched your building. You came down. The plan was put into action. What can I say?" She shrugged again. "It's a living."

"Hell of a way to get a date. Knock some guy in the head."

"You were barely moving, and you look quite ridiculous on a scooter."

"I could've been killed. Mix me another drink."

"You fell harder than we thought. You must be a little clumsy. Done with questions?"

"Only a couple more," I said. "Are you CIA?"

She had moved back around the bar and I joined her. "Eddie. Please don't ask that. Whatever I answer will be a lie. Even if I say yes."

"Fair enough." I poured her wine and mixed my own drink. "Cuba libre. Free Cuba. You really mean it, huh?"

"Yes."

"You don't seem to have family. Is that part of it?"

"Yes. They're mostly dead, but that's a story for another day, okay?"

"Fair enough. Answer this then. Why me?"

"Because I knew you before. The little dive group at Klein Bonaire about three years ago. Remember?"

I stared hard at her face. "That damn crazy blonde who wanted to kiss underwater."

"So you see, it's our second kiss." She moved closer, popped the package of cigarettes from my pocket. "May I? You're a good kisser, Eddie. I never forgot it. Why did you?" She lit the cigarette with a match from the bar. After one drag she handed it to me. "I don't smoke much anymore."

"The hair fooled me, but just now our kiss was familar. I remembered."

"That first kiss was silly – for a photo – this one was serious. I want to know you."

"Not disappointed then? What if I'd been old and fat?"

"I wouldn't have cared."

I smoked in silence awhile. "Woman tried to pick me up on a plane once. Said she thought it would be interesting if we had sex. She was a little heavy-set but otherwise quite nice looking. I told her no. She was offended and stared out the window without speaking the rest of the trip."

Sonja stared at me and grinned. "You don't think I'm that silly?"

"No, I don't. But not everything tastes as good as it looks."

"I know," she said, grinning. "That's why I kissed you twice."

She had me after that. It was the first of many dinners she cooked for us at home. Hector, Luis, and the bartender, Jorge, who was really the equivalent of a butler, all learned to tolerate me. There were two maids as well, María and Sophie. And a cook whose name I never remembered. It was all a masquerade of course, but I played along.

We went out sometimes too, but I hated it. She acted like she always acted, slipping into character so smoothly I wondered if it wasn't the other half of her. She acted that way with my family when I finally introduced them and they formed an immediate and long lasting dislike. My father told me later she was an imbecile. My mother simply said, "Keep looking." Sonja blamed me. I should've known better than to introduce her to my parents and insist we try and lead a normal life together. After that I found off-beat restaurants where no one we knew was likely to show up and she could act sane for an evening, maybe even dance, talk like lovers instead of conspirators. My sisters finally hatched a plot to take her shopping and discover her secrets. At the end of the afternoon they had become as loud and obnoxious as Sonja.

Carmen was influenced by my mother, who questioned her regularly about Sonja and I. Was it serious? Did she sleep at my apartment? The usual probing. Through the reliable maid grapevine Carmen learned Sonja Cadavid had six servants. The only woman who possibly needed that many people caring for her was the Presidente's mistress, she informed me. Which meant I was fooling around with forbidden fruit. Pointing below my belt she said, "Kiss your cojones goodbye." So now, this night, home from Haiti, alone on the balcony, I knew quite well why Carmen was in no hurry to give me Sonja's message. Protecting my privates, I thought.

But I also felt that this night was too much the same as many others. Whatever Sonja wanted had been carefully planned, but I didn't want to play my part. The mysterious woman game had begun to erode my patience, since I'd rather solve a mystery than act in one. Intrigue was becoming tedium. To make matters worse, I knew what Sonja meant to me, but what did I mean to her?

I stood and walked to the rail. Across the road was undeveloped land. The Villacampas worried someone would build a high-rise there, blocking the ocean view. I stared across at the empty space and saw the orange glow of a cigarette. A breeze fanned the branches and I lost sight of it. There was no reason for anyone to be hidden there, and for the first time since I'd come home I felt uneasy. Was it my imagination or was someone watching? Had I brought something home with me? Something fearful?

I studied the darkness. On the dark bay beyond, the lights of a small freighter flickered as it swung at anchor a safe distance from shore. There it would rest in the soft night breezes until morning or until space opened at one of the piers. For the first time I had mixed emotions about Sonja, and home seemed less safe. Haiti had cast a spell, or was it Olivia Quist?

Chapter Five

The summons from Sonja Cadavid was intriguing but I had other things to do first that next morning. I wanted some straight talk from Garrett Yancy. No hints. No more letters or machete dancers. Later, I needed to talk to Mickey Alba, my oldest friend and police lieutenant in the Policía Nacional, because he knew the island in ways only a cop can, and if a huge sinister voodoo culture existed here too, he'd know it.

It was mid morning by the time I reached the travel agency. Ethel let me in. Mr. Yancy was not in his office but at the rear of the house lying on a chaise lounge. An oxygen mask covered his mouth and nose. He apologized. "Twice a day now," he said. "Enriches my blood."

I told him to rest while I drew up a chair and spun for him my Haitian adventure. His eyes widened when I told about the drums. He was a good listener, even when I shared my growing concern about his reticence to give me the full voodoo story.

"Why do you think I sent you after Dr. Mercer?" he asked, voice muffled by the plastic mask.

"So I'd understand your voodoo letter?"

"No," he said. "To find the truth."

"About voodoo, zombies and the like?"

He nodded. "That, and the danger of not knowing. You are exposed." He struggled to roll slightly onto his side. "I can't tell you where I get my information. You know that. My sources say Quist's death is a voodoo thing. I understand your confusion, but please, pursue it nonetheless."

"Well, Mercer's in New York."

"Go there at once." He struggled to sit up, grimacing noticeably. "There's something else."

"What?"

Mr. Yancy's face had turned to paste and his translucent skin was slick and yellowing in the morning light. Blue veins crisscrossed his forehead and nose. The old man cleared his throat. "I think they may try to kill you now."

"Kill me?" I should've been a tobacco farmer like my dad. "Who?"

"Those who came for Quist are coming for you." He hooked the mask on his chin. "There are drums here, too. I have sources in the voodoo community. They first told me of a voodoo connection to the Ambassador, now they say you are known to the bokors. You threaten them. We must act fast. You know what bokors are?"

"Yeah, like priest guys." He was giving me the creeps.

"Bokors act by spiritual direction, from spiritual force. Understand?"

"Yes. I get that."

"The spirits now directing them are evil. I was told they mean to kill you."

"Like right away? Don't they want to talk to me first? Threaten me or something?"

"Didn't sound that way."

"Just kill me outright?"

"Yes."

"It's a little sudden. Couldn't they escalate a bit first?" I stared at him but there was no hint of a smile. "So how soon can you get me a ticket to New York?"

"Tomorrow morning. First flight out."

"Fantastic. I just got here."

"Now I have something more gratifying to tell you." Mr. Yancy was pleased with himself. "You're one of the few guests invited to attend Ambassador Adam Quist's burial in Washington at Arlington National Cemetery. Quite an honor. Stop on your way to New York, just don't forget what's important. Find Dr. Mercer. I know part of the voodoo story but he has the science. Be careful now."

"I can take care of myself." These bokors were making me angry but I wondered if maybe Mr. Yancy's illness wasn't making him overprotective. Exaggerating the whole thing. I didn't know anything worth killing me for. "Where did this funeral invitation come from?" It dawned on me. "Olivia."

"Yes. She called not a half hour ago. Arrangements made by some uncle or other important personage. You're to take official charge of an investigation into Quist's death as well. Very, very unusual. I can't imagine what power Miss Quist must wield to pull something like this off. She's been on the phone to some influential people in Washington and you're to be given full cooperation."

Was this my exposure? Was I dangerous to them now? "Better than we hoped," I said.

"Yes," Mr. Yancy answered. "Miss Quist also asked that I pass a personal message to you - 'boxers not briefs,' she said. Do you understand what that means?"

"Yes," I admitted. "Nothing important. Kid's stuff." Mr. Yancy's brows knit. "Sorry," I mumbled.

"Well, you best get a move on. Ethel will send your tickets over this afternoon - New York via Washington. The burial's at two tomorrow. We'll have you on the ground before noon."

"Doesn't give me much time for all I've got left to do here," I complained.

"Best you get about it then," he said, but he was grinning.

* * *

The world is flipped sometimes in the Caribbean, especially in the Dominican Republic. Most cops in the United States are honest and only a few take a bribe or break the law. In Santo Domingo it's the other way round. Police Lieutenant Miguel Alba was a homicide detective, my friend since childhood, and the most crooked cop in Santo Domingo.

Mickey Alba and I came a long way together and I didn't feel any need to make apologies for him. There's no better cop, and he's very businesslike in taking his bribes. If you lived here you'd admire that.

People often think their morality is universal. Pot heads squeal when they land in jail here for doing what merely cost them a fine at home. Likewise, when a foreigner's house is robbed they're shocked when police respond by asking for a bribe, then claim it can be solved quickly.

It wasn't my mission to defend the system, but I know a police lieutenant is paid $150 pesos per month, about $110US. A cop can't live on that any better than anybody else so why not take a little extra from each victim? Grease the wheels of justice.

An American friend of mine complained that first he was robbed by burglars, then the police. His television, electric typewriter, jewelry, stereo, most of his cash, were all gone in a night. In the morning, the police asked for the rest. What could be more frustrating he wondered? The answer, of course, is not having any of those things in the first place. You just can't expect poor people to sympathize when rich people lose their toys.

That doesn't make it right. I know that. Mickey did too, I suppose, but he had a wife and five kids to support. He did what he had to, and that meant no bribe, no investigation. He shared with his men, after all. I paid him too, though he often refused. He wouldn't have taken anything except he believed I was rich. Sometimes when he sat on the balcony of my penthouse overlooking the city and the sea, he got teary-eyed and thanked me for being his friend. But he loved to sit there and smoke those awful little black cigarettes that smelled like a tire fire. If it wasn't for Mickey Alba I wouldn't be any kind of detective.

About criminals, Mickey was fond of saying, "It's an island, Idiot. Where they gonna go?" He knew the fences, the informers, the money changers, the dopers and the rest. Every policeman at one time or other worked robbery, even homicide detectives, because robbery here is common. The highest robbery rate of any nation on earth. If you live here, you will be robbed. The good news is you'll probably get most of your stuff back - if the cop is good and the bribe is sufficient. "It's an island, Idiot."

And it is a system of *justice*. The poor steal from the rich, the cops steal from the rich, the poor give the stuff back, keeping some for themselves, everyone sacrifices a little and the rich stay in power. And the system works, but I feared for any burglar who climbed Sonja Cadavid's wall late at night. Somebody would shoot him sure as hell.

That morning I met Mickey at Karin's, a German sidewalk cafe about half way down on the Malecón. A modest place. Great view across traffic to the ocean crashing against low limestone cliffs. Karin, a large-boned German married to a Dominican, waited on us herself. We ordered a basket of garlic bread and cold beer. The cafe was nearly empty this early. I didn't care what time of morning it was, I wanted a drink. Mickey could drink anytime.

"¿Qué pasa, 'Mano?" Mickey liked to get down to business.

"Yancy's got me back to work."

"So soon?"

"Quist."

"¿Verdad?" Really.

"Got the rest of today and tonight to ask questions, then I'm off to New York via Washington, D.C. for the funeral, and to track down some voodoo guy."

"Hey, man slow down." He held up his hands. "Funerals? Voodoo? Are you smoking something?"

"It's a long story. I need your help on a couple things. Always a few dolars with Mr. Yancy's schemes, no?"

Mickey leaned back in his chair. It was a fresh morning. He'd tossed his gray police cap on the table, wearing the gray uniform instead of plain clothes permitted lieutenants and higher grades. "I've got court," he said, seeing my eyes on his outfit. "I mean, voodoo? Why you? This isn't another one of those deals like the UFO people?"

"Hell no," I promised. He meant ISEI, the International Society for Extraterrestrial Intercourse. An early case. They hired me - partly because I'm a certified scuba instructor and partly because I was then a novice detective - to participate in their worldwide attempt to communicate with alien life forms. They needed divers to man a communications device that sent and received underwater, in case aliens were water folk and couldn't talk through air like us. Even as a novice, I knew these people were nuts but Mickey persuaded me to tell them I was an expert underwater communicator and take the assignment for 600 bucks.

They agreed. We submerged that day with their communications gear, which we didn't set up because it looked like they made it with Legos and aluminum foil. We shot three nice grouper instead. Their check, however, must've been drawn on a bank in another solar system since it didn't clear at the Bank of America on El Conde street. Mickey never let me forget it.

"Can I remind you," I said, "that I wanted to stay home on that one? You wanted to go diving and clip those guys for 600 bucks."

"They came looking for you," he said. "How did they know which sucker to look for?"

"I had an ad out."

"So now you're going to do voodoo?"

"No," I said. "I'm going to do what Mr. Yancy pays me to do. Voodoo or whatever. His checks don't bounce. Are you going to help me or not?"

He chewed awhile at the tough bread, washing it down with cold Presidente. "Doing what?"

"Go to the American Embassy and Ambassador's Residence to interview some of these characters."

"What characters?"

I told him the whole story of my trip to Haiti with Olivia Quist and her suspicions.

"So you've been to Haiti with this carina?"

"She's not a babe. Just a girl."

"Really? Then why were you alone with her for days in some swank hotel lying around the pool drinking rum punches? I bet she had her top off."

"She did not have her top off and it wasn't a swank hotel, it was an old house, and if you'd ever been to Port-au-Prince you wouldn't be envious and let your imagination get the best of you."

He shook his head and sighed. "Your father is rich and married a rich American. You're a rich business owner. You have a rich benefactor who pays you for my expertise. You live in a penthouse, and me? I'm a simple, honest cop with barely a centavo. What have I done, do you think, to have offended God in this way?"

"Quit whining. Are you going to help me or not?"

"All right," he said. "I want $200 American."

"Are you loco? I don't have that kind of money and if I put it on my expense account what do you think Yancy will say? 'I hired you not Alba.'"

"Solve your own case then. I don't like this voodoo. Do you read *Última Hora*?"

"I read it. I just don't believe it."

"Well, mi amigo, you can believe the last two voodoo stories. The details are wrong of course but the crimes are real. Voodoo has its very dark side. So much so lately my skin crawls when I see voodoo trinkets in the tourist shops. Yancy can pay me to solve it."

"I'm not asking you to solve anything, just go with me to the Embassy and the Residence," I pleaded. "Tell them you have no official status, just tagging along, whatever. You're in uniform. Send them a message. They know how we work here and I'll get my questions answered."

"So it should be worth two hundred."

"I can hire some beat cop in uniform for five pesos."

"Maybe," he said. "But will he look as smart and tough as me?"

The haze-gray uniform of the Policía Nacional, starched and

pressed with black shined shoes as Mickey wore it, was impressive. More impressive was "the look." Mickey had it. Some of the other cops too. It was more than tough. Hard. Mean. Merciless. When Mickey had the look on, you thought you were staring death in the face. You were too, I suppose. The Policía had a reputation for ruthlessness they did little to discourage. Prisoners in their care were not treated kindly. Traffic violators were not treated kindly. Police stations were constructed to look like fortresses and painted an ugly shade of green. Even when I visited Mickey at his office I was never comfortable until I made it past the gate guards and the eyes of his colleagues to the safety of his office.

I had an American friend, Jeff, whose eldest daughter was abducted by a lunatic rapist who escaped from the Veintiocho (28), the notorious insane asylum at mile marker 28. The family was picnicking on an isolated beach. The girl went for a walk alone and the lunatic tied her to a palm with his belt and sliced her awhile before the rape. Somehow she escaped and the man was apprehended the following day. A week later Jeff was invited to a rural police station where the colonel in charge explained that rape wasn't tolerated. He led Jeff to a back room where the lunatic hung by his wrists from the ceiling. He was naked. One eye had been gouged out with a spoon and left on a nearby table. Blood seeped from sores and open wounds, dripping from his toes onto the dirty concrete. He could've stood it, Jeff said, even participated when the offer came, had it not been for the rapist's scrotum. The size of a pineapple, swollen until the blood vessels burst and burst again, leaving it black. Jeff thought the man was dead, but as he stood before this lunatic who had attempted to rape his daughter, a Policía took a pencil from his pocket and tapped lightly on the swollen scrotum. The corpse awoke and screamed a high, pitiful wail.

The colonel handed the pencil to Jeff.

Stories like that get around. The gray uniform made people nervous, and guys like Mickey Alba used that to their advantage. When he had the look on, you feared he'd do what those country policía did. You feared it, and you believed it too. Even I believed it sometimes.

So, Mickey was right. I couldn't hire that for five pesos.

"Okay," I said. "I'll give you a hundred."

"One fifty."

"Deal."

"See how easy that was?"

"It won't be so easy when Mr. Yancy sees it on my expense account," I complained. "Drink up. We'll do the Residence first then the Embassy."

"What am I supposed to say?"

"Nothing. Two people, Dulce and Alejandro Baez, found the Ambassador's body. I'll question them first. All you do is stand there and look at whichever one of them I'm not talking to. Make 'em squirm if you can. They're Puerto Ricans."

"I've no trouble making Puerto Ricans squirm."

"Good. I'll meet you there right after lunch. I've got an errand first. No siesta today."

* * *

I had to see Sonja Cadavid. I thought of asking her about Quist's death, but didn't dare. She might actually know something. Didn't make sense she'd be involved, unless Caamaño, our Cuban-trained revolutionary, was implicated somehow and crossed one of Sonja's underground organizations.

Even if she wasn't involved, she'd know things. Things that might help explain what happened to Quist, but our lives had never wrapped together in this way. Her work was hers and mine was mine. So I decided to keep the visit on a personal level.

I arrived early - 11:45. She'd be in the courtyard away from city noise. Jorge led me back. Even when she expected me, Sonja never opened a door or stood by a window.

Her back was to me and Luis leaned over her as they discussed some culinary matter, I assumed. Two place settings were laid out on the glass-topped table. Luis bowed slightly as I approached and said, "Buenos días, Señor." More to warn Sonja I was behind her than as a greeting.

"Good morning, Luis," I said. "I missed you." He inclined his head to let me know he'd heard, and that I was funny. "Morning, Sonja. I missed you too."

"Hi," she said. "Luis will have lunch out in a minute." He and Jorge departed. "Sit. Tell me about Haiti."

Had I told her I was going? "Is that why you sent Hector to summon me?" I dropped into the iron chair across from her. "Carmen doesn't like me being ordered around."

"It wasn't a summons." She made her it's-all-so-confusing face, pouring espresso from a silver urn and passing me the raw sugar. "I'm glad you're back."

I sipped, smiled, raised an eyebrow. It was good to be home. Her courtyard was cool in late morning and the giant banyan tree at its center filtered white sunlight through the leaves, dappling the grass and stone walks. One of the staff had washed the patio earlier and it gleamed aquamarine and golden beneath the remaining wet places. The sun climbed in the sky and baked it.

"Come on, tell me about Haiti."

"Not much to tell. No trees. Very poor. Their beggars are starving, ours are only hungry."

"That's not what I meant."

"What did you mean?"

She sighed. "Edgar." She called me that sometimes. "Obviously, I want to know about the girl."

"The girl?" I said, puzzled, staring up into the branches of the banyan tree. "The girl...."

Sonja Cadavid wouldn't break a sweat if you tied her to a post and promised to bayonet her guts into a pile at her feet. "I don't mean to pry," she said. "Wasn't suggesting anything.... unsavory."

We're incriminated more by thoughts than actions, I mused. "Why am I being interrogated by the CIA? How do you even know I met Olivia Quist in Haiti? No one is supposed to know. For that matter, where do *you* go half the time when you come back and tell me it's none of my business?" I tossed my remaining cold coffee out onto the grass and poured more. "I don't like this double standard crap."

Sonja smiled and passed the sugar back to me. "I'm sorry," she said. "There is a double standard and you're right, I shouldn't know about Miss Quist. I know too much about too many things I really wish I knew nothing at all about. Somebody thinks I have a need to know when I don't. I wasn't spying." She shrugged. "On you, anyway."

I loaded my cup with sugar. "Two years is a long time to wonder."

"Aren't we happy the rest of the time? Am I deficient somehow?" She glanced down at the silk blouse, hugging her body.

"No," I said. "What if I wanted to marry you?"

"Do you?"

"Can't we just discuss it hypothetically?"

"Would you want a mother for your children who disappears for long periods, can't be reached, and one day simply not return? Is that a family?"

"Of course, you could never give up your hopeless crusade to save the motherland!"

"Please, Eddie. We've been over this ground time and again. I will never give up. Never."

"Patriotism is kind of out of fashion these days." A low blow and I knew it.

"I wish it were patriotism. That makes sense. Maybe it's revenge, or sorrow. Compulsion anyway." She reached for my arm. "It's me. I promised long ago I'd tell you. Do you want to hear it? Is that what it will take?"

"I don't know."

"My darling Eddie. Mi amor. You are funny man. How many men wouldn't die for what you have, a woman who wants to love you without any commitment? Who does not complicate your life with pregnancies, requests for money, demands on your time. A woman who even disappears occasionally and leaves you alone. Aha," she said. "Here comes lunch. I even feed you."

Luis served us in his usual deft and silent manner. Green plantain fried in peanut oil, grilled ham and cheese, green tomatoes, salad, papaya juice with milk, and a fruit medley he always called a fruit *melee*. On the tray he also carried a large conch disgorging an array of pink and white orchids, which he placed at the center of our table. "Bon Appétit," he said as he departed.

"Is he studying French?" I asked.

"Maybe you are studying French. A little Creole perhaps?"

"Sonja. You're jealous." I reached across and picked up the small silver bell, ringing it above my head until Luis appeared. "If you wouldn't mind, more hot coffee, Luis."

Luis retrieved the bell from me and placed it close to Sonja. "Only la Señorita Cadavid rings the bell," he told me. "This is not your house."

She ordered the coffee. Luis departed without glancing at me. "They're just protective," she said. "We're like family and with you," she smiled, "they are cautious. In time." She noticed my frown. "Luis is quite a singer. I'll have you ask him to sing sometime and maybe he will thaw a little."

"He can freeze up and shatter for all I give a shit."

"My Eddie, my little Dominicano/Americano, are you going to tell me about Haiti?"

"Yes," I said. "First, you tell me why you want to know."

"We were asked by our people if Quist's death was political. Castro's man Caamaño is here. Is it related?"

"I can't be sure, but I think not."

"Is it okay if I ask then, why meet Quist's daughter in Haiti? Outside the country?"

"To keep our meeting secret, which doesn't seem to have worked, and because there may be some sort of voodoo angle."

"Voodoo?"

"Don't ask."

"And what did you learn?"

"Olivia thinks her father was murdered, probably by someone inside the Embassy. They didn't allow an autopsy so the whole thing's pretty thin."

"What will you do next?"

"Go to New York tomorrow and track down some voodoo expert, just in case."

Luis returned with our coffee. Sonja poured. "If it's not political we aren't interested," she said flatly. "I don't know anything about voodoo or Embassy intrigues."

"Have you heard anything about Quist's death?"

"No."

"So who wanted you to talk to me?"

"I can't say."

"You're in the CIA, right?"

"Why is everybody so crazy about the CIA? I told you, I can't say. Leave it there. Anyway, I'm not interested, *we're* not interested. Investigate to your heart's content. Just be careful with this Olivia Quist. It has been told me that she speaks Spanish quite well, is intelligent and not unattractive. You have probably already kissed her. I am a jealous woman and not without my resources. Do you understand me?"

"Sonja, you have such a suspicious nature. Olivia is nothing but a kid. Nineteen years old. While we were in Haiti I spent half my time wiping her nose."

"What an awful liar you are." She had a very nasty grin sometimes, Sonja did.

Chapter Six

Entering the American Ambassador's Residence that afternoon, we passed through a gate guarded by Policía Nacional. US Marines guard the Embassy but local cops guard the Ambassador at home. No wonder he's dead, I thought. We rolled to a stop at the guard shack in Mickey Alba's shiny unmarked car.

"Bueno Día," Mickey greeted the bored guard. "I am Lieutenant Alba. We are here on official business."

"Sí, Señor," the guard said, and the gate swung open.

"Five pesos," I told Mickey. "Get us in just as quick."

"Don't be so sure. These guys may look bored but they have toes."

By that Mickey meant they hadn't shot them off. Low ranking policía sometimes lacked shoes and were often country recruits who took the job to get a square meal. Riding from place to place in the back of trucks or standing a boring watch somewhere, they'd absently slide their little toes into their rifle barrels. Many policía were missing a little toe. Some were missing two.

"See Peor outside the gate?" I asked.

"I saw her."

"Gives me the creeps. She was watching me when I got my hair cut."

"So what? She watches everybody."

"She smiled at me."

"'Papá, she's looking at me!' You sound like my kids."

"Why don't you arrest her?" I asked him.

"What for? Anyway, I've arrested her on more than one occasion. She smells like dried piss, and you can't pin anything on her. I've got enough trouble without arresting stinking brujas. Get ready now for your big investigation, Kojak."

We swung wide to our right on the circular drive and momentarily lost sight of the mansion as we passed a clump of royal palms surrounded with bushy croton and well-tended flower beds. The drive came around under a gothic portico. Mickey pulled to the side and we sat a moment admiring the entrance.

"Like the White House," Mickey said.

"How do you know?"

"Like pictures, I mean. Funny, I've lived in the city all my life and never been here."

"It's a house," I said. "Let's go harass the help."

The door opened to a radio voice singing "Feliz Navidad y Próspero Año y felicidad." Rushing the season again, I thought. Thanksgiving barely over, but then here we had no Thanksgiving. "I want to wish you a Merry Christmas" the song went on in English.

The woman who answered our knock was on the short side of medium, and stocky. She had no neck to speak of and small, piercing eyes like Cosme's pig.

"My name is Espinosa-Jones," I told her. "I've come about the Ambassador's death. Someone in the Quist family has maybe called about me."

"No," she asserted, happy to disagree. "The Embassy called about you."

"Fine," I said. "May we come in?"

"Who's he?" She tossed her head in Mickey's direction.

"Just an advisor. He's not here in an official capacity."

"This is American soil," she said, continuing to block the door. "Just like the Embassy."

"I understand. May we come in please?"

The door swung barely wide enough for us to file inside. "He can't ask any questions here," she said.

"He won't. Can I get your name please?"

"Dulce Baez."

"Isn't that sweet," I joked.

"I've heard that one before," she said. "It's not funny."

We followed her from the foyer to a formal reception hall. Our footsteps echoed. "You can conduct your business here," she said. "Who do you want to talk to?"

"Who's here?"

"My husband and I, one cook, one maid, one driver. Everyone else was given time off because of the Ambassador's death."

The room held a grand piano, a dozen straight-backed chairs, two ugly antique couches and a forest of poorly-watered potted greenery. The walls were adorned with large paintings of soft looking people on picnics or alighting from carriages. They were in gilded frames with little brass lights bent over them. "I was hoping more of the staff would be here," I said.

"I told you who was here."

This conversation was entirely in English, a language Mickey found impossible to learn. He had wandered to the piano. Dulce was keeping a pig eye on him. I spoke to her in English because I wanted to establish myself more as American than Dominican, here on American soil. "I'll begin with you then," I said. "The Lieutenant may not be here in an official capacity, but I am. My investigation is authorized by the Quist family and the United States. Do you understand?"

"You don't look American," she said.

"I was born in Miami."

Dulce was not a woman easily put off. She volunteered nothing, waiting for me to make the first move. "You found Ambassador Quist's body," I said.

"My husband and I."

"Where?"

"In a chair."

"Would you show me please?"

"That chair is gone."

"Gone?"

"Destroyed."

"Why?"

"It is bad luck to keep a chair in which someone has died."

"It is?"

"Ask anyone."

"Can I see the room then where he was found?"

"That room is closed." There was an arrogance about her that proved Olivia correct. This was no servant.

"Open it." I issued this order more to see how far I could get than to see the room, which was most likely of little or no help.

Dulce didn't answer but led us to the room. I remembered what Olivia had said, that Daddy died in the Haitian Room. It was very Haitian. On the wall, a young woman with unrealistically round breasts sat with a homemade drum between her legs. Similar bright paintings hung on all the walls, together with wood carved masks, machetes and the twisted figures of old men. Sculptured mahogany people, flower pots, fruit baskets and giant heads were crowded onto tables, even the floor. Above a fireplace, a photograph of The Citadel fortress loomed, obese, its stone bow like a giant slave ship sailed from the canvas and seemed to hang in the air. It was a good place to die.

"Show me where the unlucky chair was before it was removed," I said to Dulce.

"Here," she answered, pointing to a spot of floor space near the door. The kind of place you'd put a chair no one ever intended to use. A fill-in.

"Really?" I said. "And the stairs to the second floor?"

She jerked a thick thumb to another doorway behind the former chair's space. I nodded and took a look. The stairway was outside across the hall. This then was the route Olivia had taken down from her nude sun bath, into the Haitian Room through this doorway where she found her dead father and the Baez couple giggling.

"Where exactly were you standing when Miss Olivia Quist entered this room and discovered her father's body?" I asked.

Before Dulce answered, her husband, Alejandro, entered by the third door and bore down on us at a trot. "This room is closed," he announced. "It is in bereavement."

"Rooms don't bereave," I chuckled.

"Ambassador Quist is buried tomorrow. Until then the room is closed. You come with me to the kitchen."

I could see Mickey picking up on the Baez's attitude though he didn't understand the conversation. One thing about Mickey, he had a short fuse when it came to attitude. He liked everything formal and polite.

The kitchen was large, functional. A simple table for the staff set to one side. We were ushered there. Dulce promised us coffee.

"Is there a problem?" Mickey inquired in Spanish, a clear edge to his voice.

"No, no," Alejandro said. "It is more comfortable here."

"Diplomats have diplomatic immunity," Mickey said. "People working in diplomat's homes don't have shit. Understand?"

"Of course." He didn't seem afraid.

"Good," Mickey said, swinging his holstered .45 forward

slightly to be more comfortable as he sat down. "This house is an island on an island. One step from this property puts you under my jurisdiction. It would be more advantageous for you to answer Mr. Espinosa-Jones's questions here than my questions later at police headquarters."

"We understand," Alejandro assured him. I noticed a poorly disguised sinister glint in his gaze. Had they been expecting us?

"Good," Mickey repeated. "I take my coffee black."

Mickey had the look. Dulce and Alejandro appeared unconcerned. We waited in silence for the coffee. We'd see how Dulce fared when I asked her why they were laughing after they discovered the Ambassador's body. No mystery why Olivia had been suspicious of them. They were suspicious serving you a cup of coffee.

Once again, I didn't get to ask my question. After two sips I burned my mouth. Dulce, suddenly solicitous, fetched water and apologized. We talked awhile about burning the roofs of our mouths and what it's like to have little skin tags come loose.

"Okay," I said in a more official tone. "The two of you are under suspicion. Let's see if we can't clear that up."

Dulce smiled at me in the same way Peor had. I felt confused and when I looked across the table at Mickey his mouth was slack and his eyes seemed glassy.

"Your best course of action," I continued, "is full disclosure. Tell me the whole truth. We'll begin at the beginning." I sipped more coffee. The room spun around. I focused on the table until it slid back into place and the cup centered in my vision. The coffee wasn't hot any longer. I caught my breath, my vision cleared but there was a great black hole growing in my stomach.

Dulce said, "You look kind of sick. Are you sick? Do you see Alejandro there?"

Obediently, I searched for Alejandro but my eyes moved as if they were floating. Alejandro was leaning back against the refrigerator, arms crossed, smiling. "What's so funny?" I said, or thought I said.

Dulce hovered near me. A demon. An overweight, eager angel of death. "Look at your friend," she said.

Mickey was sitting very tall in the chair. He seemed to be stretching his neck to make himself even taller. Blank-faced, his glassy eyes remained unfocused. I was shivering with cold and my lungs took long minutes to inflate.

Dulce's face was close now. She had black hair from the roots but the rest of it was dyed a deep red like dried blood and teased out to make her head larger. I studied the hair because something was moving inside it. Something with legs. A tarantula. "You have a spider in your hair," I told her. I was pleased to find this irregularity in her appearance.

She only smiled. "That's Jaime. He has his nest there."

"I don't believe you."

"You are a stupid man," Dulce told me. "Come here to frighten us? No. No. Tonto. Imbécil. You are a dead man. Don't you feel sick? Focus. Look at me. See how I watch you stupid man? See how I watch you die? After you are dead I'm going to eat you. Jaime is going to suck on you."

Dulce laughed. She had even teeth. Her laughter rang in my ears, amplified to a sound that struck me in the chest, then faded. The room went silent and even the air in it was ugly and frozen with cold.

I sipped more coffee and fell to the floor. I remember falling, nothing after that.

I awoke choking, someone had snaked a hose down my throat. I heard a sucking sound and tasted bile. A bright light hurt my eyes and several people above me were talking at once. "He's awake," someone said. "See if you can get a little more." A woman's voice told me I'd feel some discomfort. My head began to clear and I reached up to grab the hand holding the hose inside me. "It's coming out." A male voice. "Relax. Just a few more seconds." The hose slipped out between my lips and I coughed.

"How do you feel?" The man asked.

"I'm going to puke."

The man moved inside my range of vision and held an emesis basin while I vomited, then removed a surgical mask. "I'm Dr. Perez. Do you speak English?"

"Yes."

"Good," he said smiling. "Then you've heard of a Mickey Finn. Somebody gave you a very strong one. We pumped your stomach. Just in time. Looked like a heavy dose. Seen more than a few when I did my residency at Cook County in Chicago. Does someone have it in for you? Your friend seemed to think so."

"My friend?" I still wasn't myself.

"The police lieutenant. The guy who was poisoned with you."

"Mickey," I said. "I mean Miguel not Mickey Finn. Where is he? Is he okay?"

"Next room. Fine. I'm going to put you both in a room down the hall in a couple minutes and watch you a few hours. Then if everything looks okay we'll let you go home."

The nausea was fading. The headache I still had. "I was poisoned, Doctor?"

"Yes."

"What's in a Mickey Finn anyway?"

"Barbiturates of some type. Seconal is a common one these days."

"What's that? Seconal?"

"Sleeping pills."

"So somebody gave me a sleeping pill."

He chuckled. "Somebody gave you lots of sleeping pills."

"How would they do that?"

"Open some capsules and pour out the Seconal, mix it with your beer, fifteen minutes later, or less, you drop."

"That simple." I remembered Dulce and Alejandro then. The coffee burning my mouth. "Could it be in coffee?"

"Sure. Alcohol is most common and cooperates with the Seconal, but coffee would work fine."

"How much would it take to kill me?"

"A couple grams should do it. One gram is serious. Two, usually fatal."

"So somebody just tried to kill me."

"Both of you. Lie back now and we'll get you cleaned up."

"Thank you, Doctor." He was a young man with a bald head. "It's not much of a way to die. Always thought I'd go out in a blaze of glory. Pretty mundane being poisoned."

"I suppose," he said, smiling. "But if it's any consolation, you end up just as dead."

The nurse who bent over me said, "You banged your head and earned a couple stitches. I'm going to wash the blood out of your hair. Slip out of your shirt for me."

She helped and I suddenly felt good lying on the cold table with strangers, knowing I was alive. Warm cloth brushed my forehead and I heard the clink of a water basin being set down behind me, felt warm water against my scalp. The nurse's hands were gentle and her black face seemed smooth as sea-washed stone. I reached up and touched her cheek. "You feel good," I said and closed my eyes.

Later, I awoke in a large hospital room. There was another bed several feet away but it was empty. Overhead a ceiling fan hummed, spinning down a flood of humid air. The room was windowless. I swung my legs over to stand and a voice from the doorway said "Wait. I'll help you." It was Mickey.

"Glad to see you," I said. "Aren't you supposed to be in bad shape too?"

"She must've given me less," he said. "Or I drank less. I drove us here. Crashed into the building at about twenty. Smashed hell out of my squad. Sorry about your head. They dragged us in here just in time."

"Dulce did this?"

"Obviously."

"What hospital are we in?"

"It's a clinic. Didn't have time for a hospital."

"Is she crazy? Trying to kill us in the Ambassador's Residence? Guards saw us in. Half the U.S. State Department knew we were there. The Policía. She's nuts. And her husband."

"Maybe not so nuts."

"Why?"

"Can't find either of them."

Mickey allowed me to rest an arm around his shoulders and walked me carefully around the room. "I'm feeling better," I said, standing unsupported. "What did they have to gain from poisoning us? It's senseless. Estúpido."

"Can you get dressed?" Mickey had his clothes on. "I have to show you something."

"What?"

"Evidence. Back at the Residence."

"What time is it?"

"Past four."

"Day's shot and I've got an early flight tomorrow. You went back there? What evidence?"

"You'll see. I didn't go back. I sent somebody."

I put the temperature near 90 when we stepped out into the parking lot. The concrete burned through the soles of my shoes. "Warm enough for the beach," I told Mickey.

"It's winter," he said.

Dominicans avoid beaches in the winter. Many wear jackets. Tourists swim now. "Some people like to swim in the winter," I told Mickey.

He stared at me a moment, grinned, and said, "Sometimes I forget you're half gringo."

"Get in the car," I told him. "Take the Malecón. I want to feel the sun and smell the sea. My head's full of sand and somebody's shoveling in there. Do you know how lucky we are?"

"Have you seen my car?" He halted near the front bumper, which he'd obviously been working on while I slept. It was fastened to the grill with wire. One headlight was broken. "Do you know what parts cost? They'll make me pay. It's a Chevrolet. Two years old only. It's the first time I've had a car. The only lieutenant. How long do you think I can keep it now?"

I hugged his neck. "Will it help if I go to the colonel? Tell him you saved my life and made yourself invaluable to the United States of America and may soon bring great reward to the Policía Nacional when you help me solve the case of who murdered the U.S. Ambassador? He'd listen to me."

He ducked under my arm. "The colonel thinks you're a bobo."

"Fine," I said. "Then let's drive down the Malecón and get some sun. I'll help you fix the damn car and to hell with colonels of the Policía, but I think he likes me. Anyway, I have a Norteamericano mechanic who is a genius."

"What's he doing here?"

"Tax problems," I said.

"Another idiot. You know more idiots than anybody on earth. Almost everyone you know is an idiot."

"Especially policemen."

"Get in."

A nice breeze blew off the water and there were noisy gulls swooping for garbage that flowed from the mouth of the Ozama. A faint smell of rot and feces. The water along the Malecón was often brown, especially when it rained in the mountains and the river swelled, carrying to the sea whatever debris lined its banks. A half mile from the mouth surfers bobbed on their boards, though one recently lost a leg from sharks feeding in the turbid flow where the cool, garbage-laden fresh water met the warm salt sea. It wasn't like us to post signs warning people off. After all, everyone knew there were sharks and if you surfed there anyway, well, you took your chances.

From inside we couldn't see the damage to the car, but damaged cars were common, especially police cars since most cops were poor drivers and issued licenses only because of their jobs. Mickey found some good merengue on the radio and we felt like a couple guys who'd just cheated death, which we were.

"How'd you get me to the car?" I asked. "At the Residence, I mean." My memory was completely blank.

"Dragged you on a small rug," he said. "All that smooth marble. You could shave off a couple pounds, you know?"

"What were Dulce and Alejandro doing then?"

"Talking. Encouraging me to get you to a doctor, I think. Commenting on your pallor and telling me I didn't look so good either, and to hurry."

"Why didn't they finish us off? I mean they planned to poison us. Kill us. Why let us walk away? You were in no shape to fight them off."

Mickey lit one of his black cigarettes. The smoke, even in an open car, made my eyes water. "Not often corpses remove themselves from a crime scene. Why stop us? We were dead anyway, they figured. Walking dead. Let us drive off, let the guards see us go, then later our bodies discovered along some city street, stinking in the sun. Perfect." He gripped the foul little cigarette between his teeth. "Aren't you supposed to be a detective?"

"Didn't think of that," I admitted. "But what if we hadn't driven away?"

"I'm sure they had another plan for us."

"But why? We didn't know anything. All we came to do was ask questions."

Mickey sucked the heavy smoke into his lungs and it coated each word as he spoke. "Panic maybe, or just plain meanness. That Dulce is one mean mujer. I don't know. They had the poison ready, probably from when the Embassy called to say we were paying them a visit, so they had *some* reason. You don't kill on a whim. Not here. This isn't New York. We solve our homicides."

"It's that risk I was thinking of. Killing a detective assigned by the U.S. Embassy and an officer in the Policía Nacional." I watched the thin parade of tourists along the sidewalks, sweating in the late afternoon sun. Locals wouldn't come out now until evening. "Every day this business gets more complicated. Makes less sense."

"Well, when you see what I found at the Residence you'll really be confused."

"What?"

"Patience my little mestizo, we'll be there in a few minutes."

"Did I ever tell you what happened to Darryl Ferguson when he called me that in fifth grade?"

"He got his butt kicked by some fat chick. I've heard it a hundred times."

"She wasn't fat."

"Like your little novia down on Independencia isn't in the CIA." He flipped the cigarette toward the ocean. "Hah! Women are always taking care of you."

"Sonja doesn't take care of me."

"More than you know, Amigo. I checked on her once. Do you know she comes and goes from this country without question? No customs. No immigration. Who do you pay for that privilege? Not lieutenants. Not colonels either. Maybe generals, maybe higher. She is dangerous too, because while I was asking, and very discreetly, I was told that if I asked another question about Sonja Cadavid I'd be picking pineapple in Bonao. Your little novia has the bite of a scorpion. Be careful she doesn't poison you, too."

I laughed at this. "Spoken just like a married man," I said.

"If I wanted a woman I could have one," he said lightly. "More beautiful than some Cuban who hides from the world. Not every Dominican man is monogamous, but it is what I choose for myself. It's not envy. I'm telling you Sonja Cadavid is dangerous. Any woman with that much money and influence is dangerous to the man she's in love with, namely you, a scuba man who plays at the detective business, which should be left to professionals."

"Are we there yet?"

The wide Chevy swung north onto Avenida Abraham Lincoln and we were silent until Mickey turned right again, this time onto Avenida 27 de Febrero. "Are you in love with her?"

"I suppose," I said. "For the very reasons you're suspicious of her. She's an enigma. A fantasy."

Mickey nodded. "So, you really are a man who likes mystery. Don't forget, Amigo, mystery just about got you killed today."

"I know. Can I ask you something?"

"What?"

"Was there a spider?"

"What?"

"Did Dulce have a spider in her hair?"

"Amigo. I like you, you know? I even respect you. But sometimes. I don't know. Sometimes I think you need to take a little rum in the morning."

"Fine. Forget it. The drug. Forget it."

After several more turns we arrived at the east gate of the Residence. A guard with toes passed us through. Mickey left the car beneath the portico. A plain clothes officer stood guard, nodded to Mickey and allowed us inside.

"Which way?" I asked.

"The Haitian room." He moved ahead of me to the door and swung it open carefully. "On the floor." He pointed to a ve-ve the size of an extra large pizza.

I went over and knelt down by it, wet my finger and tasted it. More like cornmeal than flour. "How in hell did this get here? It wasn't here before."

"Well, it's here now. They found it an hour ago when I sent them for Dulce and Alejandro," he said. "Voodoo, huh? Drawn to scare us?"

"It's voodoo, but not necessarily Dulce and Alejandro. Need to know what it means before we know who, I think. Damn! Wish I had a camera. Must be saying something about a spirit, probably an evil spirit."

Mickey seemed skeptical but squared himself off with the ve-ve and studied it carefully. At its center were straight lines, curves and half circles that resembled a clam. One vertical and one horizontal line intersected the clam. Two U-shaped lines intersected from the sides and another from the bottom. All these lines ended in a cross with two overlapping U's behind it. The whole thing had a snaky appearance and my first instinct was to destroy it.

"We can come back with a camera," he said. "But I can draw this just as well." He slipped a small notebook from his shirt pocket and very quickly duplicated the ve-ve twice on two different pages and tore one out for me. "Here."

"Thanks. I'll be in the States tomorrow. There's a guy in New York who's supposed to know about all this stuff. I'll show it to him."

"I've never been to New York," Mickey said, still staring down at the ve-ve. "Maybe you should bring me a little present."

"Like what?"

"Whiskey."

"Johnny Walker, no doubt."

"¿Como no?" Why not? "Two bottles. Black Label."

"Two!"

"One for the colonel so I can keep the car."

"You're a leech," I said. "Get me out of here."

"I suppose you will have another liaison with Olivia Quist in the States," he said, turning to go.

"Where did you hear about that?"

"Your mother."

"What's she know?"

"Probably more than you think," he said. "She's not happy with you. How long has it been since you called her? Didn't she just celebrate a holiday and you were with this baby girl in Haiti? Is that a way to treat your mother? Go tonight and see her before you fly to the States."

"Is that an order, Lieutenant?"

"A man does not need an order to visit his mother."

Mickey bore an irrational love of family. Not just his immediate family but cousins, second cousins, their spouses, others even further removed. He bailed the troublesome ones out of jams, loaned them money they never repaid, found them jobs even if he had to show up in uniform and lean on an employer. Mickey Alba was the most nepotistic man I ever knew, but he had local sources even Sonja couldn't match.

"Okay," I said. "I'll visit my mother." Couldn't do any more in the city now anyway.

We walked outside together and already the afternoon sun cast long shadows. Two and a half hours to my parents farm, if all went well. Roads in the country were poor and thirty miles per hour often seemed like flying, but the food would be good and my father loved to sit outside on the porch and smoke a cigar with me. He might even know something about voodoo.

"Drop me at the mechanics," I told Mickey. "I'm not taking some chicken bus all the way to El Seibo."

Mickey the family man smiled.

Chapter Seven

My childhood home in El Seibo had no beaches, no spectacular mountain peaks, no rain forests or large cities - no tourist marvels. A place of valleys and small farms, fields among low rounded green mountains etched against blue sky. Flocks of white egrets roosting in trees and on the backs of long-horned cattle. A place of dark volcanic soil, sugar cane fields and leafy rows of rich tobacco.

Our finca dominated a fertile plain barely sixty miles from Santo Domingo, but torturous roads turned a quick trip into a journey of three hard hours driving. Narrow roads wound through a mostly mountainous and hilly landscape where traffic was often delayed by crossing herds of cattle or goats. Undependable bridges, severely damaged or washed out, regularly forced vehicles into water and wooded ravines. I endured an hour behind a grinding old Mercedes truck, crawling along in low gear, blowing black smoke from two straight pipes under the bed. The road had only a few places wide or straight enough to pass.

I cursed the bad roads and gave thanks for the peace and isolation they preserved. The brief tropical twilight had faded before I saw the house, ablaze with yellow light in the dark. It was concrete, beamed with dark mahogany - a large, golden two-story the color of beach sand, set on high ground because my father feared floods that never came. Thatched tobacco sheds dominated much of the landscape on the road in, unlighted and invisible in the night. I knew a cart trail paralleled the road at the edge of the fields.

Gabriel Espinosa, my father, owned more than a thousand acres and nearly one hundred people lived on his land. He was soft-spoken and known throughout the valley as a soft touch. His workers lived rent free. My mother, on the other hand, would just as soon pick you up by the ears as look at you. She despised laziness, suspected all children of malicious mischief, could frighten any malingerer man or boy, and might've been thoroughly disliked were it not for an explosive sense of humor and an unselfish nature. I always thought it ironic that she, a pale-skinned Minnesotan with gray eyes and light hair, should be the hot-blooded Latina, while my swarthy father was a pussy cat.

There were my four sisters - Claudine, Diana, Alexis, and Ed, that's Edwina, the baby at seventeen. I'm the oldest, which didn't save me from them, but gave me just enough running room.

My headlights swung across the porch and Ed was there, sitting in the swing an arm's length from Felipe Guzman - my father's idea of a date. Felipe liked me because I conspired with him and they both smiled and ran to the Jeep.

"My poor old brother," Ed said. "What are you doing out here so late?"

"I missed you."

"Hola," said Felipe. He was shy.

"If you missed me so much," Ed teased, "why weren't you here for Thanksgiving? Nobody, I mean nobody, goes to Haiti! Imagine, grossly offending your entire family, even your distant relatives, to vacation in Haiti. That's what we had to say when people asked, *Oh, well, he's in Haiti*. My God! How embarrassing! I bet it's because of a woman. You're not *diving* in Haiti?"

"Edwina," Felipe said, and she was silenced. His ability to do this was one of the main reasons I liked him, though I'd no idea how he did it. No one else has ever been able to get Ed to shut up.

"Mr. Yancy sent me there," I said. "Where is everyone?"

"Inside," Ed said. "Drinking. We've all become hopeless alcoholics since you've abandoned us. Daddy's the worst, drinking straight from the bottle like one of those winos you see living in dumpsters in the alleys of New York." Ed had dark brown hair cut short to the tops of her ears with little spit curls at her temples and bangs hanging almost to her eyebrows. She wanted to look European. Her eyes though, were dark Dominican and her smile crooked and sassy. We spoiled her. I don't think she weighed more than ninety-five or a hundred pounds.

"I'm glad to hear about the drinking," I told her. "I could use one after choking on diesel smoke half way here. Let's go in."

"Sit on the porch," Felipe offered. "I'll go tell them you're here and get you something. Rum?"

"Yes. No ice."

Ed threw herself in my arms then, kissing me repeatedly on both cheeks before taking my hands and kissing them too. "I really *did* miss you. It's no fun here when you're gone all the time." She led me up the short flight of stairs to a chair and pushed me into it. "Claudie and Alexis are shopping, going to the movies, shopping, eating at hotels, shopping, going to parties with the same people over and over. And you know Diana. She drives to Miches and sits on the beach all alone for hours almost every day. Thinking, she says. One of these days she'll be sitting up there and get raped and murdered and nobody will ever know. Her disgusting, withered old corpse will wash up on some lonely beach, the eyeballs eaten by ravenous reef fish. We won't even be able to identify the body. All because you weren't here to protect us."

"Mom and Dad are here."

"What help are they? Daddy's in the fields or the sheds or the office. Mother, well, you know Mother! Last week she delivered somebody's baby. I'm not kidding. Out in some bohío. What did she do before that? I can't remember. Something with water or hepatitis or liver flukes. And she baby-sits and tries to teach people English, like anybody around here needs to speak a foreign language! Church. What about church? We're the only Protestants in this whole valley and she hired two missionaries or something to come here from North Dakota or someplace dumb like that to talk birth control. Wait until the Pope finds out! I'm not kidding, EJ. Either I need to move to the Capital with you or you need to come home."

"Too late," I said. "I'm off to New York first thing in the morning."

"You mean you can only stay one night?"

"Part of a night. I'll probably be up by three or three-thirty."

Edwina dropped into my lap and hugged my neck. "I miss you," she said. "I really do."

"You have Felipe."

"I know, but except for Daddy, you're the only man who doesn't require a carabina." Chaperone.

"It can't be as desperate as all that," I chuckled. "There must be an old beggar somewhere or a missionary pastor maybe that you can talk to."

"Go ahead and laugh," she said. "You won't think it's so funny when I marry some perfect dope, some gigolo, just so I can talk to a man or get a kiss maybe without some old carabina breathing down my neck with her sour old carabina breath. You don't know what it's like. Men can do anything they want in this country and that's why all the women my age are moving to New York or Miami so we can wear pants if we want to and kiss somebody."

"Here comes Felipe with my drink. Get up now. Your bony little butt hurts my leg."

She hopped onto her feet. "Take me to New York with you. Please?"

"It's business," I said, accepting the tall glass from Felipe. "No gigilo-kissing, pants-clad girls allowed."

"You're just like the rest," she said, marching off indoors.

"What are you going to do with her?" I asked Felipe.

"Marry her. Make cigars. Fill her with babies."

I was slow to answer because I liked Felipe. He was a kind man. "I wish you luck in that," I said finally.

"It is the Dominican way," he answered. And, of course, it was. "The rest of your family are in the oficina. Diana is speaking to them about advertising, I think. They often have meetings here at night now. The girls have new ideas."

"Gabriel must love that."

"Your father is a fine man."

"I wasn't criticizing him."

"They wanted me to tell you they would be right out." He followed Edwina inside.

I thought maybe I'd offended him. He admired my father, all the more because his own died young. His property, less than forty acres, adjoined ours. Felipe learned the art of rolling cigars from another grower in the valley who had his own brand and wanted now to establish himself as a cigar maker. It was an ambitious dream for a poor young man from El Seibo, and I knew my father, and perhaps Edwina too, encouraged him.

When the front door finally swung open it was my father's thick, middle-aged frame that filled the doorway. "Edgar," he said, embracing me. "The others are inside preparing hors d'oeuvres. They'll be out in a moment. I asked for a little time alone first, since we see so little of you, even at the holidays."

"I'm sorry. I was in Haiti. The ambassador's death."

"Yes," he said. "Garrett Yancy was kind enough to telephone us and accept responsibility. Will you walk with me to Número Uno?" Tobacco Shed Number One, closest to the house and the first shed he built as a young man just starting out.

"It'll feel good to stretch my legs after the long ride," I said, leaving my drink and following him down the steps.

The path, northeast from the house, was unlighted but well-worn and easily followed through a grove of mature plantain plants until it opened finally into a large field of cultivated land. Starlight lit our way and soon we arrived at the small door that led inside the end of the building where my father kept a field office. He flipped on a light. A simple room with a desk, straight-backed chairs, cheaply framed awards for select tobaccos, two gray filing cabinets and a rusted water stand that held a fresh five gallon glass bottle.

"Sit," he said.

"Thank you."

"It's never easy to talk seriously with those we love," my father began. "When Carlos, the field foreman, sits here with me I can tell him a thing simply. He asks a question or two and then he's off. We understand each other and there is no emotion." He smiled and leaned against his old desk. "With you, it's different. What I say sometimes sounds like a lecture and what you hear can make you defensive. This happens not because we can't understand each other but for a more tragic reason, because we are a father and son and love each other. I want to steer you away from my mistakes and you want me to let you make your own, I suppose. We collide when we don't mean to. Am I making sense?"

"Yes," I said. "Why are you telling me this?"

"I'm coming to that," he said. "I'm coming to that." He moved closer, drawing up a chair to face me. "I am not an old man yet, but soon. These fields are my life's work. Whoever I give them to must begin to learn about them now, while I'm still young enough to teach all it took me a lifetime to learn. You, of course, are the logical successor, but whenever we've talked before you avoided the responsibility. You've never said to me 'no' or 'yes.' Simply postponed. I will be sixty next spring. We can't wait any longer."

My father had planned his speech carefully, ready with it though he had no idea I'd be there that night. It came at a poor time, I thought, when I was torn with thoughts of Olivia Quist and her dead father, voodoo, Sonja. I felt the old resentment rising and fought to control my tongue. Why tonight? Couldn't this wait until things quieted down and I had time to sort it all out? "Early in the morning I leave for Washington and New York, Papá. Can't it wait just a little longer?"

"We have waited too long." He had a square face, craggy in the low light. "Felipe is the logical choice for the farm. He loves the land. He loves your sister. He works like a fool."

"Felipe," I said. "Is that fair?" I was hurt much more deeply than I had any right to be.

"Have you worked this land, Edgar? Dried the leaves? Fought the weather? Eaten the dirt? Sweat away the years here and fallen into bed too tired to sleep? You've lived in the city since college, but the land feeds you. How can you inherit without sweat?"

"Papá. I don't hate the place. I grew up here. When I get back we can talk."

"No. We are talking now. I've made other provisions for you. A trust. A share of the profits until I'm retired or dead."

"I don't understand the urgency," I snapped. "It doesn't have to be decided tonight."

"It will be decided this moment," he said, standing. "¡Mañana, mañana, mañana! The favorite word in this country. No more. Let's not be angry now with each other. You cannot make this decision, Edgar. It's a dilemma for you. On the one hand you love this place, your memories are here, but on the other hand, my son, you are not a farmer."

"I do love this land," I protested.

"Yes. I believe that, but you don't love to work it. Land must produce, like a woman." He smiled then and rested a hand on my shoulder. "Even there you have some trouble, no?"

It struck me then that I felt lighter. Most of my inheritance was suddenly being swept away and I felt more relief then despair. This decision which had hung over me since high school was in a moment being lifted. What had always clouded my mind became clear. I wasn't a farmer. My father knew it and planned for it. The plan was fair. "Felipe can't afford this place," I said almost to myself.

"I've drawn up a paper. He will pay some money each month, give a small percentage of the crop when times are good, allow us to live here until we die and then the house and some small acreage will pass to you," my father said. "In the end, he will pay what I paid. I seek no profit from land that has given us life for a generation. Now let it feed my grandchildren, should I ever be so blessed."

I stood up and put my arm around my father's neck. "Not every day I lose a valley." He smiled. "What's so funny?"

"Life," my father said.

When we approached the house everyone was waiting. We walked out of the plantains and I said to him, "I think you're a good father."

He paused there in the dark a moment. I could make his face out clearly in the lights from the porch but his eyes were shadows. "You are my son," he said. "You aren't required to live my life. Like what I like. Come. I have some good rum left from before the war. You can tell us about the Ambassador's death and Haiti and about when you will find sunken treasure."

"Sí, Papá."

"Keep quiet about our talk for awhile. Felipe knows nothing yet. I don't want this to sway his affection for Edwina. I want him to have the land whether he marries her or not." He grinned and shrugged his shoulders like a boy. "I don't know a damn thing about love. If I did, I wouldn't have married a gringa who can't stand to see me sit down for even ten minutes. Do you hear me, my encantadora?" he shouted. "I am a lazy old man!"

"You're a hunyack," she said from the porch. "And your son too. Come up here out of the yard and mix the Cuba libres."

"What's a hunyack?" my father asked. "Did you learn that when you lived in the States?"

"I never heard it except from Mom."

"Well," he said. "Sounds bad. I never wanted to ask her."

So we passed an evening on the porch - laughing, teasing, telling those old family stories no one wants to hear again but does just the same. I felt I was included in a new way and yet detached like when someone dies. I had passed from one place to another and the passing was bittersweet.

At bedtime I went to my old room and it felt like the final night I would spend there. Not once during the evening did I mention Olivia Quist or Haiti or the Ambassador's death. I deflected their questions or made light of them until we forgot outside things and were just a family like when I was young.

* * *

A horn blew in the distance. Sound came in blasts, then a pause, more blasts. Sharp bursts of noise, persisting until I opened my eyes to the wall. The soft paint was alight, dancing yellow and white from the window. Something outside was burning. The house. My head cleared. Concrete didn't burn. I sat up.

Outside the world was in flames. Through the window I saw my father, hair matted, naked except for white boxers, pounding the horn of my Jeep still parked in the drive. "Agua! Agua!" he shouted. "Manguera, por favor! Una manguera."

Número Uno was ablaze. No amount of water, no hoses could save it. The building was engulfed, flames gushing into the night outshining the stars, yet oddly, the building stood almost untouched at the center of all that heat like the Biblical burning bush. I felt the heat even inside and when I ran to my father there were tears streaking his face, his voice hoarse from shouting. I pried his fingers from the horn. "It's gone, Papá," I told him.

"There was no water," he said.

"We don't need it now."

Men were arriving from their modest houses along the fields. Some carried shovels and rakes. The front of our house and the drive was aglow and we saw each other's faces in the firelight and no one wanted to speak. My mother and sisters stood stubbornly on the porch, except for Ed, hunched in a chair, crying and rocking on the balls of her bare feet.

"What happened?" I asked.

"There has never been a fire here," my father said.

The sheds were two and a half stories high with peaked roofs of deep thatch. The long sides were wood slats nailed to upright poles. A Caribbean pole barn, except for Número Uno which had a concrete floor at one end to accommodate my father's office and some storage. I watched the thatch burn, sparking up and dripping down onto the curled tobacco leaves that hung curing in the shed. Thousands up in smoke. The shed could be rebuilt in weeks, the tobacco would take another season.

Finally the sides began to collapse. Still I could see some of the giant leaves hanging. Maybe they were only ash, I thought. The white ash of a hundred thousand cigars never rolled, never held gently between two thin feminine fingers on a balcony while voodoo drums sang in the hills. Sparks drifted away on the breeze.

The fire died slowly and darkness returned except for a cherry mound of coals and some poles left standing. The heat was still intense but my father moved toward the shed and I followed.

"I had some nice wrapper leaf in there," my father said. He was calm now. "Best I'd seen in years. A fine maduro. Smell it?"

I did. The air was rich with it.

We walked around toward the far end where his office had been but the heat was still too intense and we doubled back along the cart trail. I grabbed his arm. "Stop," I said.

He stared at me a moment, then back at the trail. "What is that?"

"Ve-ve," I said. "A voodoo sign. Drawing of a lwa - spirit. This is an evil lwa I suppose. It's not a warning to us but a communication with them."

"What kind of crazy talk is that?"

"Voodoo," I said.

"Voodoo? Here?"

"It followed me. I brought it to you."

"Edgar. What have you gotten yourself into?"

I stooped down, wet my finger with my tongue and touched the ve-ve. "Cornmeal," I said. "Did you know that sometimes the lwa mount you. A taxi driver told me that. When he said it I laughed and thought instantly of *The Tingler*. 50s horror film. Tingler looked like an iron bootjack with feelers and lobster feet. Mounted his victims, crawled up their spines or necks and killed them. Doesn't pay to laugh, though. Really doesn't."

Gabriel was not laughing. The look on his face was like that of a man whose loyal wife suddenly said she had a lover. More bewildered than shocked, sad than angry. He turned and walked away from me along the cart track, away from the glowing tobacco shed, toward his home.

I followed him. The fire was no accident. It struck at me directly, at my family. The evil of voodoo, or someone wanting me to think so, it didn't matter. I was being watched, followed, threatened. Such things happen for a reason and aren't accomplished by ghosts. I needed to learn everything I could about the evil side of voodoo, and quickly.

My mother called the ve-ve hogwash, told Papá to wash up, and told me to get packed and on the road or I'd miss my plane. It was already three o'clock in the morning. She sent the girls back to bed and when we were alone on the porch she asked, "What is all this voodoo business?"

Trapped, I gave her a brief report, ending with Mr. Yancy's conviction that voodoo played an important role in the Ambassador's death. Everyone in my family respected Mr. Yancy. "After I talk with this doctor in New York I'll have a better idea," I concluded.

She glanced toward the smoldering remains of the shed, nodded her head slightly and closed her eyes. "Lutherans have a tough time with things like voodoo," she said. "Be careful in New York. I was there last Christmas and the place has gone down."

Chapter Eight

Pelted by rain, Pan Am 847 dropped out of the clouds and streaked toward the flashing runway lights of Washington's National Airport. There was a bump as the landing gear lowered and the aircraft picked up the drag. The flight was late but from National it was a short cab ride to Arlington. Wouldn't do, I decided, to be late for my first diplomatic burial.

The Washington Monument slid by in the gray mist. From the air it seemed almost as insignificant as the replica at home on Avenida George Washington. There was an important difference, of course, this structure was clean and fresh. Americans took obvious pride in their obelisk. Dominicans used theirs to post sales posters and political placards - all of which helped cover the graffiti.

I'd visited Arlington National Cemetery before, to see Kennedy's grave, the Tomb of the Unknown Soldier, and to bury a close friend. It's larger than some small cities and its roads wind aimlessly among hills, tombs, and trees. Ambassador Adam Quist's interment was set for two-thirty, among the last of the day. I arrived at the Memorial Drive entrance before two and continued on with the taxi to Audie Murphy's grave near the amphitheater. The war hero and actor had died in a plane crash since my previous visit and I wanted to see where they laid him. In life and on the screen he represented to me the perfect American - young and laughably underestimated, capable of spectacular feats and sorrowful tragedy.

The driver waited while I took the short walk to the end of a row of white government issue tombstones where Murphy, the most decorated hero in U.S. Army history, was buried in the same simple splendor as a common soldier. Most of his medals weren't even listed. Mother would approve of this, I thought. In rural Minnesota, moon landings are described as *pretty good.*

I'd worn my black suit and topcoat but forgot an umbrella or hat. Rain clung to my hair, though it was a light rain and the wind came only in gusts. A passenger had informed me before landing that we could expect snow by evening. With luck, I'd be in New York by then. I turned and walked back to the cab.

Arlington conducts fifteen or twenty burials every day and they are good at it. The information office had given the driver precise directions and I arrived at Quist's burial just in time. "Pull up here," I told him. There was a hearse and a small motorcade. "I'll walk over."

A Marine Corps honor guard similar to the one that carried Quist onto the plane in Santo Domingo, now slid him from the hearse and after a few quiet commands, bore him away toward the grave tent. The bold red stripes of their trousers and the gleaming white hats protected by plastic dish covers seemed almost inappropriately festive for the occasion. I followed at a distance, blending with the stragglers. A small crowd. Less than thirty.

I spotted Olivia walking with her mother, sister, and brother. A large man with gray hair and protruding stomach accompanied them. I assumed he was the uncle, her father's brother. Olivia appeared more curious than sad. She did not wear black like most of the others, but a plain gray dress ending six inches above her knees. Over that, a short nylon jacket like those sold in ski shops. She carried a small purse on a long string and was protected by a large umbrella with a mortuary logo. This was held for her by a young woman in somber dress - a mortuary employee I assumed.

They all followed the minister who followed the coffin. A picture perfect funeral. An Army bugler waited a dozen yards to the left under a large elm. He too had an assistant holding an umbrella.

We gathered beneath the tent and the minister said what ministers always say and the bugler played well and several people wiped their eyes. An absolutely perfect ending to a public life and the rain kept right on falling like it was scripted. I failed to catch Olivia's eye but somehow knew that she knew I was there. When I finally wandered back to the taxi and climbed into the rear seat, she was right behind me. "Hi."

"Hi."

"I didn't get any lunch," she complained.

"I've got a flight to New York in a couple hours."

"There's a little deli not far. Okay?"

"Fine."

She gave instructions to the driver and we pulled around the hearse and two black Cadillac limos. Adam Quist waited patiently off to the left until the living departed. Later, he would be unceremoniously cranked down into his grave by a couple guys in gray coveralls who did it all day long.

The deli was so small there were only three tables. One by the window, where we sat. "Why aren't you with the family?" I asked.

"Later," she said. "Anyway, I'm familied out. We haven't spent this much time together in years, all crammed into a suite at the Four Seasons. Nice of you to come. I didn't expect it, really."

"When are you heading to New York?"

"Tonight or tomorrow," she said. "Mother wants us to take the train. Not appropriate to fly so soon after laying Daddy to rest, she says. I think she needs a couple hours in the bar car. Then we have to spend two more days together at the New York apartment discussing 'the future' she has in mind for us. There's a will too, but almost everything is left to her so that shouldn't take long. Daddy was big on advice though, so maybe we'll have to sit through a reading of that, since his life was going so well I'm sure he wanted all of us to benefit from it. Maybe I'll sneak out. You can take me dancing or something."

"I've got to track down Dr. Mercer. He's at Columbia."

"They're still on Thanksgiving break," she said. "Stay awhile and I'll show you New York."

I laughed at this. "I've spent a good deal more time there than you, I'm afraid. Most of my family live there."

"I didn't mean Washington Heights," she said.

Washington Heights is a heavily Dominican neighborhood near West Harlem - images of poverty, empty buildings, rampant crime. I saw the regret on her face the moment the words came out but decided not to let her off the hook and said, "It's got a whole different flavor than the Four Seasons, of course. The old campfire in a fifty-five gallon drum down an alley off Amsterdam Avenue, roasting a few wienies, planning our next gang rape when the white chicks get off work."

She stared out the window. A man and his wife were trying to squeeze a Chevy Impala into a parking space barely large enough for a Volkswagen. "I'm not a prig and I'm not prejudiced."

"Sure you are," I said. "We're all prejudiced. The whole human race enjoys making fun of each other. Exercise a little self-restraint and we'll make it okay. Calling me a half-breed or a spick irritates me but I've heard it enough to shrug it off."

"Very broad minded of you."

"Focus on the big picture. Life's too short. You'll figure that out when you get older."

"I'm not that young."

"Yes," I said. "You really are."

"Now you're making fun of me, just when I was starting to think you're cute."

"Olivia," I said firmly. "We're not sweethearts, we're cooperating in a murder investigation. Because I happen to like you is beside the point. Don't be so girlish."

"Girlish? I'd say that evens us up. Buy me a pastrami on wheat and I'll try and eat it without drooling over you, you big Latino hunk."

I ordered the sandwiches from a little man in a white apron and thought about telling her what happened at the farm and to Mickey and me in her former residence. After I shelled out a few bucks and grabbed a couple bottles of Coke, I thought maybe I better skip the fire story and just do the one at her place. She ate while she listened and didn't ask any questions.

"Anyway," I finished. "Mickey's pretty pissed. You don't happen to know anything more about this Dulce and Alejandro, beyond what you've told me?"

She shook her head. "No. I was suspicious of them, like I said before."

"Mickey figures they took the risk of trying to kill us because they had some fool-proof plan to escape the country or some hiding place so good we'd never find them. Or maybe they're just dumb."

"At the risk of making you all crabby again," she said, "why would they want to kill you anyway? You don't know anything."

"I made that same point myself," I told her. "Maybe the answer is so obvious we missed it, or they *are* just dumb."

"Well," she said. "Maybe Daddy *did* have a heart attack."

"Dulce and Alejandro didn't think so. You don't try and kill a member of the Policía Nacional unless you're crazy or desperate. I'm afraid your father's death may be just the tip of the iceberg. Somewhere I'm missing a connection. I don't suppose anyone in your family relented at the last moment and asked for an autopsy?"

"No."

"Oh, well," I said and finished my sandwich.

Olivia ate as she had that night at the Splendid, systematically and with obvious pleasure. The kid in her, I thought. When she finished she said, "It's only been a couple days."

"Since Haiti?" She seemed to be getting inside my head again.

"Yes. Seems like a million years."

"Different surroundings."

"Different feelings."

"Well," I said. "It isn't often you meet someone new and immediately drag them off to a voodoo ceremony."

"Don't forget Johnson. It was Johnson who took us."

"His name wasn't Johnson."

She reached across then and took my hand. "I could use another hug," she said. "I'll settle for a hand. Maybe a kind word, if you have one."

"Would you settle for an observation instead?"

She dropped my hand. "God help we should have any kind of a tender moment!"

"Sorry," I said. "It's just Arlington. Your dress. It didn't seem like you were dressed quite as respectfully black as everyone else."

"That's your observation? That I wore a gray dress? You didn't by any chance happen to notice my legs? It's a short dress. Plenty of leg. Did you notice my legs?" She swung them out and slapped one up onto the table. "What do you think? Pretty nice? Thick ankles? Knock-kneed? What?"

"I didn't mean to get you all upset."

"The legs. Did you notice the legs?"

"Yes."

"Fine. That's why I wore the dress, stupid!"

"Oh." Was I supposed to be flattered? "Like I said, we're not sweethearts."

"Is everything they say about Latin men wrong or is your blood watered down or what? For your information, American men notice my legs. My 66-year-old uncle notices my legs. I wear a dress no bigger than an apron and you notice that my short, sexy outfit isn't as somber as it should be." She put her leg away. "I'm going to buy you a trashy novel and read you the love scenes. You're pathetic." Her manufactured laughter faded and she reached for my hand again.

"I've met so many men who've liked my legs. So few I've respected. I'm sorry. Guess I did kind of lose my cool today. He was my dad after all. I couldn't cry. I couldn't. Later. I'll do it later."

"Okay. I'm sorry too." I patted her hand and returned it. "Was Delbrick there?"

"Yes."

"Where?"

"The man supporting my mother, if you noticed."

"I thought that was your brother."

"He wasn't there."

"You said before that he's not bitter."

"No. I told you he wasn't homicidal."

"Seems rather an overreaction, not attending his own father's funeral." I feared she was hiding something. Olivia wasn't the kind to volunteer things.

"Did I look like *I* wanted to be there?" she asked.

"Doesn't matter. You *were* there."

"Well, my brother wasn't. I've no problem with that. Sorry you do. Anyway, thought you wanted to ask about Delbrick."

"Just wondered if he was there. Haven't talked to him yet, since I got poisoned in your house before I could go over to the Embassy and look him up. Was he sad?"

Olivia drank the remainder of her Coca Cola and blew a short, tuneless blast across the empty bottle. I felt the spray from her lips. "He was appropriately sad, just like me."

"Where did they all go now? Your family, I mean."

"Back to the hotel for a reception. Lasts until dinner so people that couldn't make the funeral and burial - people from State and Republicans on the Hill - can pay their respects after work."

"Delbrick?

"Of course. Important people will be there. He must look appropriately sad for them."

"Like the rest of you?" I asked.

"Yes. Like all of us. I might even cry."

She could say things like that without sarcasm or rancor. Olivia was, by some magic, emotionally severed from her parents. Their survival on earth seemed of little concern. Love dies, of course, if it isn't tended. "Have you ever been to Mr. Yancy's office?" I asked her.

"No."

"On his desk is a photo of his daughter Ethel as a small child - three or so - and she's terribly cute with a little straw hat on her head and a flowered sundress that seemed homemade to me. I asked once why he kept it, Ethel being grown now. Why not a more recent photo. 'I like to think of her this way,' he said. Comforting I suppose, to think of people as children. Preserves their innocence, generates sympathy."

"So we don't hate them, you mean?"

"Yes. So we don't hate them."

"I told you before. I didn't hate my father. Why do you keep going back to this?"

"I'm not really. There are accidental deaths, old age deaths, illness deaths, but there are no hateless murders - not many anyway. People don't go around killing each other for conveniences of the plot, like in movies. They kill for money and sex, revenge and out of insanity or anger. I'm trying to find any of those things here but I can't." I really wanted her to understand. "I need to talk to Delbrick. Maybe he could kill for power. Something is terribly wrong about your father's death." I tossed some greenbacks on the table. "Servants don't try and kill the police when they come to ask a few simple questions. I'm confused. Maybe it *is* voodoo."

"So you're going to come back to the hotel with me? Have you got time before your flight?"

"Just enough."

"Delbrick may confuse you all the more."

* * *

Duane Delbrick didn't confuse me, he made me laugh. Why hadn't she mentioned his head? He had a little bitty head and the fine, blonde hair of a toddler. I hadn't noticed it at the funeral because he was wearing a black hat and I was trying to believe he looked like Olivia because I thought he was her brother. As I stared at him after our introduction, I thought maybe he'd been a forceps baby, uncorked from the womb and dragged out by force. Through the years, his body grew and his head remained as it was; flat-backed, bubble-foreheaded, wide above the ears. Right in front of him, Olivia whispered his nickname in my ear - pinhead. I couldn't help it, I laughed aloud.

He was trying to shake my hand at the time, not enthusiastically, since he knew the purpose of the introduction. "It's great to meet you," he said, dishonestly.

"Likewise," I lied.

A cocktail party mood had dispelled any lingering funereal depression among the dark-clothed former mourners. "I see you already have a drink," Pinhead said. Did he think he was the host?

"Yes," I complained. "Couldn't find any good Dominican rum."

"Washington is a tough town," he said.

"Santo Domingo is a tough town. Your employees there tried to kill me."

"The Baez couple."

"Yes."

"I got the call." He sighed. "What could they have been thinking?"

"I was hoping you'd help with that."

He managed to appear offended and wounded at the same time. "How should I know? They weren't *my employees*. I didn't hire them. I'm a diplomat not a butler. What goes on at the Residence isn't my concern."

"I understood the Baez's employment application came through you or your office."

"May have," he said. "I get stacks. Anyone bilingual - it's very hard to find bilingual staff - is referred wherever they are needed. The process is ongoing. It's also confidential like all employment matters. We do background checks as best we can in an open society without trampling on people's individual rights. Once in awhile a black sheep slips in, I suppose."

I noticed that he wasn't the least bit intimidated by me. Questions didn't bother him and I remembered what Olivia said in Haiti, that he made her feel like a child. His voice and manner were superior and he talked down to me with such effortlessness it seemed almost unintentional. Good eye contact too, I thought, except the left eye slanted away slightly and the eyebrow above was squished down onto its lid and it made me grin because I thought maybe that's where the forceps had slipped. "Euphemisms like *black sheep* aren't appropriate to those who attempt murder," I pointed out, stepping to within inches of him.

Instinctively he backed up. "Maybe you and your friend got some bad chivo," he said, recovering.

"Barbiturates," I explained.

"Drugs," he said indifferently. "The plague of modern times."

I stared at his droopy eye. "We'll find out about the drugs," I said.

"The Baez people, if that's who they are, won't get far and may be encouraged to name their associates."

"Wouldn't count on it," he said. "Do you have other questions? I really need to circulate."

"Where were you when the Ambassador's body was discovered?"

"Working."

"At the Embassy?"

"Yes."

"At the Penson and Navarro address?"

"That's where it is."

"I just want to be certain you were in that building. And that's where you were called?"

"Yes."

"By whom?"

"Alejandro Baez."

"Isn't that cute. Back to our homicidal friends with the drugs."

"You do know, don't you Mr. Espinosa-Jones, that Adam Quist died of a heart attack?" He shook his head and glanced at his watch. "Ah, you and your little cop buddy. Your drug-induced episode, however conceived, has no bearing on Adam's death. You only have my cooperation in this abecedarian investigation as a favor to his family. Not to put too fine a point on it, but take your parlor game suspicions and shove them cleanly up your ass."

Olivia giggled as Duane Delbrick strolled away smiling and confident. "You're quite a success," she said. "I haven't seen Pinhead that happy since he got introduced to Bob Woodward at the *Post*."

I shrugged. "Want to know something?"

"What?"

"He's right about the abecedarian part. This is pretty elementary." I accepted another glass of red wine from a passing waiter. "No evidence. No real suspects. No motives that make sense. Voodoo."

"And the Ambassador's daughter," she said. "The one who got you into all this. It's all my fault isn't it?"

"I suppose." I fed her a sip of my wine. "Mr. Yancy believed you, though. I do to, even if it makes me look like a fool."

"Thanks," she said, for believing her or for the wine I didn't know.

"I better get to the airport. Maybe I'll see you in New York?"

She uncovered the flap on her little string purse and scribbled a phone number and address on the back of an envelope. "Call me.

Please. There's a little place in Midtown if it's still there - the Whaler - and they have great seafood. Iced blue points and cold beer. A nice thermidor. It's not fancy and no one I know has ever been there."

"It's a date," I said.

* * *

Who was it that said "Just because you're paranoid, doesn't mean you aren't being followed?" The moment I paid off the cabby and dragged my bag onto the sidewalk in front of the Eastern Airlines departure entrance, I had a knot at the back of my neck, butterflies and the shivers. Someone was following me.

I headed toward the main Eastern counter at a run. Half way there I slid to a stop and spun around. Except for the guy who had to jump around me, no one stopped or swerved or did anything suspicious, but the hunted feeling didn't go away.

After I picked up my boarding pass I still had a few minutes and found a bookstore, mostly to see if there were any steamy love titles that might educate me to the needs of budding womanhood in the new "me" generation. I moved toward the counter to ask the clerk when I spotted Dulce Baez. She had on a yellow sweatshirt, NYU lettered boldly across the front, and the cloth stretched dangerously over her bulbous breasts so the letters appeared Chinese, and her chubby little butt was encased in tight, bell-bottomed jeans. She wore high-top sneakers. She was smiling at me.

I thought I might be imagining things, but could two people on earth have the posture of a squatting frog? Little rubbery fingers dangled from arms which at first appeared useless, but when flexed were strong and longer than they seemed. Her fingernails were painted blood red and so were her lips, in ripe contrast to the bright yellow shirt.

Something hard jammed into my ribs and somebody hissed "Shut up!" I wasn't saying anything. When I turned it was Alejandro. He said he had a gun in the coat pressing against my back and he didn't have much to lose by shooting me. Then Dulce flew over and hugged me and kissed my cheek and said to "start walking" so they didn't have to blow my guts out all over the picture postcards. Their timing was bad since my next planned stop was the men's room.

I was hugged and hustled to a row of plastic chairs near a large beige garbage bin and pushed down. Dulce was all smiles, babbling away in Spanish about what she hoped I'd buy her for Christmas, drawing understanding glances from passersby. Alejandro whispered, "In my hand is a suppressed 9mm automatic. Big hole. Small noise. Sit still."

"You're in big trouble," I told them. "Mickey Alba's after you."

"Mickey Alba. Another Dominican wog who can't find his ass with both hands," Dulce said in English.

"Wog?" I asked. "What's that? That stupid ball of fat between your ears? Do you know where you are? National Airport, where half the officials in Washington catch their planes. I stand up and scream there'll be ten cops here in two seconds."

"Just in time to find your body," Alejandro said. He was dressed in soiled bellbottoms, a tie-died shirt and leather jacket. A knotted string of beads hung around his neck.

"What are you?" I asked. "Some kind of Latino hippie?"

The suppressed barrel of the alleged pistol gouged my ribs. "Why are you following us?" Alejandro wanted to know.

"I thought *you* were following me," I said, reasonably. "Must be some kind of communications error. Glad that's cleared up, I've got a flight to catch." It was early in our relationship then and I was inclined to take them less seriously than I would later. An unfortunate mistake that nearly cost me my life.

Dulce inclined her head and said something to Alejandro about *baggage area* and he jerked me to my feet. She was obviously the brains.

"This is ridiculous," I rambled on. "Don't you people think you have an irrational desire to kill me? I mean, the first time we met you poisoned me." My memory of that was still somewhat hazy. "Didn't you have a spider in your hair?" I asked Dulce.

She smiled. "Jaime" We began to walk. They had me sandwiched between them.

"Is he still in there?"

"I'll be feeding him in a few minutes." The grin was back.

She imagined herself as some sort of demoniac I think, but tarantulas aren't quite the menace they're cracked up to be. They bite if provoked, like any wild thing, but aren't very deadly. A bee sting to most people. Dulce had an overactive imagination. Liked to frighten people. It was the 9mm that had my attention, not Jaime.

"Usually when we kill someone they stay dead," Alejandro said. "I'd like to take more time with you than we have now."

"You people are pissing me off," I said, trying hard to take them more seriously.

"Shut up," he said. "Walk."

We crowded into an unoccupied elevator headed for the ground level baggage claim. When the doors closed Dulce kneed me expertly in the groin. I doubled, she drew back and smashed both my ears with the heels of her hands. Pain jarred my head, leaving me deaf and weak. Alejandro ground the gun barrel into one ear and spit on my hair. I was more troubled by their senseless hatred than the pain. And I still couldn't shake the notion there was something comic about them.

"Stupid man," Dulce told me. "You dare to offend the spirits?"

"I regret it won't take you long to die," Alejandro repeated.

"We all have our regrets," I managed, the sound of my own voice pounding my skull.

"Offal," Dulce said in Spanish.

"What have I done to you?" I asked.

Alejandro traced my chin with the gun sight. "Not for you to know," he said. "Only the Reine Voltige can tell you. She will not."

I thought then that maybe he meant Dulce, but I had no way of knowing about flying queens or werewolves then. Wouldn't have believed it anyway. Secret Bizango societies were the furthest thing from my mind. I was desperate to escape before the elevator reached the baggage level.

It stopped and the doors opened.

I heard the carousels beeping, a loudspeaker, cacophony of voices and I knew this was my last stop. Do something now or it would be too late. Might be already. The confusion here could cover anything. Certainly a silenced pistol. A shot to head or heart I was sure. The Baez couple didn't leave a job half done.

We stepped from the elevator and Dulce moved in to hug me up against her again for the walk, I managed a kind of quick dos-a-dos that left her between me and Alejandro, then ran like hell.

I didn't glance back until I'd sprinted twenty yards or so, reaching a stairway back up to the ticketing level. They'd decided to give chase instead of blast away at me with the pistol. I dashed up the steps two at a time betting they'd hold their fire until they'd closed the distance or caught me. I had a ticket and boarding pass. A cop might see us running.

None did.

I thought about screaming like a maniac but they'd only think I was one. My best hope was the gate. Airplane hijackings were gaining popularity, gate officials might see a fat woman and a Latino hippie chasing a well-dressed Dominican as out of the ordinary.

They didn't.

No one even looked up as I ran toward the check-in counter. There was a long line and more people dressed like Dulce and Alejandro than like me. I veered right along a row of seats, hurdling bags and outstretched legs. At the end of the row I zigged left and headed toward the jetway door to the plane, now open and guarded by a large black woman who I hoped was in no mood for nonsense.

I swept past her. She shouted. Dulce, who was outrunning Alejandro by a furlong, tried to push past the gate attendant as I had. The black woman laid a solid block to her chest and Dulce finished up on the backside of her stretch denims. "And just what do you people think is goin' on here?" my savior inquired.

"That is a wanted man," Dulce announced, scrambling to her feet and pointing at me. I peeked around from the jetway doorframe.

"You got police ID?" No response. "You got a ticket?" the agent asked Dulce.

"I'm not on this flight," she admitted.

"Then you got no business at this gate," she said. "Unless you saying goodbye." Still blocking the way she motioned me forward. "You got a ticket?"

"Boarding pass, too." I produced them.

"Go on in and sit then," she said, turning to Alejandro, who had only just joined us with a gun bulge under his shirt. "You two skedaddle or I call a cop. On second thought, maybe you best wait here a minute." She drew a radio from her belt.

Dulce and Alejandro skedaddled. I boarded the plane.

The timing was perfect. I buckled in, smoked barely three drags and the plane was pushed quietly back from the gate. I'd been watching the door. Dulce and Alejandro were not aboard.

Rain streaked the window. The little baggage tractors snaked among planes, pickups and idle equipment. Men stood with ear protectors on their heads or around their necks. The activity was reassuring. Normal.

We glided backward and I glanced up at the receding terminal. There, in the smoked glass, a bright yellow sweatshirt.

Chapter Nine

New York City began its collapse in the mid-sixties and was an urban shithole by 1972. There were still people with raised eyebrows who thought it was some kind of a phase and there were still decent sections of Manhattan, but the Bronx, and the city itself, was tired and broke. For awhile, even the federal government washed its hands.

But to Dominicans, Nueva York *is* América, and honestly, it is to me too. I love New York. Parts of it anyway.

Then there's baseball. And baseball, well, baseball is more important to Dominicans than cows are to cheese. Major league players, sometimes entire teams, travel to play in Santo Domingo during the off season. My mother struck up a conversation with the wife of a Minnesota Twins player at a waterfront cafe once and a week later eleven major league players and their families came to the finca for dinner. Even weeks after, the campesinos removed their straw hats in reverence as my father walked or rode through his fields. Major league players dined at his table. This was a thing men truly revered.

In the Capital, displaying local team colors like red or blue, can create a brawl that might involve an entire bar, stadium, or street. Baseball is serious business, and no matter what anyone thinks of New York, New York is the home of the New York Yankees. If they ever leave town like the Dodgers did, there won't be enough planes to carry all the Dominicans back home.

This love of baseball is instilled in us from childhood and most Dominican 8-year-olds could play well on half the high school varsity teams in America. I was no different, and like so many Dominican boys, dreamed of a life at the plate. In fact, I was a gifted hitter but couldn't run fast enough. Hit doubles and ran for singles. Too many others could do it all.

This left me disappointed for awhile but I had other interests and it didn't crush me as it did my father. Gabriel was once a pitcher and threw his arm out in high school. He pushed me, hoping the running deficiency was something I'd outgrow. I only got slower. Even now I'm not fast and would never have outrun Dulce and Alejandro if I hadn't been so scared, and lucky.

I was met at La Guardia by my cousin Angel. He drives a livery cab and owns New York. Angel Espinosa. A man who can only be described as cool. Angel glides through the city in his black car, smells tourists three blocks away, makes more money in a week than I do in a month, and lives like a Park Avenue hooker - every nickel to clothes and image. He's always broke.

"¿Que pasa, hombre?" he shouts. "Get in, man. You lookin' sad, man. Where'd you get that suit? Minnesota?"

"I need this?" I climbed in next to him. "They have cabs around here, you know?"

"You're too cheap," he replied. "Where we are going? ¿Tía's?"

"Sí." His mother, my aunt. No one in the family comes to New York without paying their respects to Tía María. She does indeed live in Washington Heights and puts you up there, feeds you Dominican food and forces you to date the daughters of her friends. All nice Dominican girls barely out of high school.

"She been sick," Angel said. We merged into the departing traffic.

"Serious?"

He shrugged. "Her leg. She fall from the steps where she work. You know, that building on East 34th."

Tía María, like many Dominicans, had little education and no technical skills. What she did have was an ambition to make a life for her family in New York, and negotiated a contract to clean a small apartment building. For the most part she did this single-handed, with help as needed from other Dominican woman she hired. Uncle Bono, her common law husband and my father's half brother, worked at a small Dominican grocery as assistant manager. Between them they were more solvent than the city itself. Handled their money better too.

"Has she seen a doctor?" I wanted to know.

"How do you say bruised bone?"

"That's how you say it. Bruised bone."

"She has it."

"Nothing broken?"

"Naw."

"So who's cleaning the place?"

"Some women." Beside being cool, Angel could sweat machismo. Ironically, women adored him, especially American women. "Open the cooler," he said, pointing beside my feet.

Inside were six iced Presidente's. "¡Que bien!" I said. "Three apiece."

"¿Cómo no?"

We drank while we drove. Angel handled the wheel with one hand, a beer with the other, and the horn with his elbow. The Lincoln glided through traffic like a fine yacht. "How busy are you the next few days?" I asked.

"¿Qúe pasa?"

"I've got to see some people. Think I can get around on my own for most of it, but I don't really know what I'm getting into. There's other people who have a bad habit of turning up when I least expect, trying to do me harm. I wouldn't mind someone watching my back once in awhile."

"Groovy, mi primo. I've got some pistolas."

"Never mind that," I told him flatly. "Just a ride sometimes. Watch my back at night, maybe. I'll be gone in a couple days."

"Who's after you?"

"Some Puerto Rican woman and her husband."

"You are joking me?"

"No."

"You are running away from Puerto Rican women now? Loco, man. They got plenty women here, man. Why you want Puerto Rican women?"

"I don't. They want to kill me, not kiss."

"A Puerto Rican woman wants to kill you?"

"Yes. A woman named Dulce. She and her husband chased me with a pistol an hour ago at the airport in DC. At home she poisoned me and Mickey Alba both, right in the American Ambassador's Residence. We had our stomachs pumped. All part of a deal I'm working on with Mr. Yancy."

"¿Verdad?"

"Really."

"Mickey Alba," he said, wheeling around a taxi and flipping the bird as he drank and elbowed the horn. "Difícil."

"For all I know they could be on their way to New York by now. And that's not all." I took a long pull on my own bottle. "I've got to find a guy and talk to him about some voodoo."

Ignoring traffic, Angel stared at me. "Voodoo?"

"Tied in with the murder of the U.S. Ambassador back home. I've got to see a guy at Columbia."

"Voodoo. Government. Puerto Ricans. What's happened to you, man? Muy duro. Why don't you let me get you a black car, man? Make a few bucks. Relax. Friday nights, Saturday nights, man, you get some nice piece of ass and you feel good, you know? No hassle. We don't have no voodoo here, hombre. This is New York! Civilization, man."

The sun shafted a pale yellow as it faded behind the urban canyons to our left and lights winked in the dark monuments of civilization. Darkness promised a reprieve from the piles of garbage and graffiti. Did Olivia make a flight or was she in a railroad bar car somewhere watching her mother get drunk?

I rested a hand on my cousin's shoulder. "Angel. Can I count on you?"

"What are you talking about?" He grinned like a boy. "This Puerto Rican. She was hot, eh?"

"She is built like a barrel of crude oil. Don't worry. I've no lack of women. You will meet one of them tomorrow if you drive us to dinner." I felt no guilt using Olivia this way. She was the one showing me leg, let her take the consequences.

"Bien," he said, chuckling. "You're pretty funny. Voodoo!"

The sun continued its decline and I settled back in the leather seat, sipping the remainder of my beer. I felt safe finally, escaping to a more familiar world. Outside, the day was cooling, the city awakening to the night. A city so much larger than Santo Domingo but sharing the beat, the quickening. Not exactly a Latin beat, but the same potency and somehow uniquely American. That's a comfort, I don't know why.

We Dominicans make great New Yorkers but we aren't loved here, like New Yorkers aren't loved in most of America. We arrive impatient, demanding, short-tempered, and we hate waiting in line. Few of us could make it in a place like Minnesota, where they're quiet, wait their turn, don't honk even if someone waits through a green light. "What do you think, Angel?" I said aloud. "Do they love us in New York?"

"¡Conchudo! You are in here ten minutes. Have one beer and talking some social shit! Relax. This is New York. Nobody likes anybody."

"Sorry," I said.

"If you want to preocuparse, you can worry about why that white van is following us. Maybe your Puerto Rican woman is not done kissing you. Don't look around! Sit still and put the seat belt on. I know these streets."

"Wait! How do you know they're following us?"

"I am no paranoidic. This van changes lanes, fighting traffic, always the same distance back. No easy thing. I've done it. They are following."

"Listen, Angel. I left them in DC. Really. Dulce, the woman, was standing at the window when my plane took off. She couldn't possibly be here in some van already. Let's not get killed because some guy is changing lanes while he's listening to disco."

"Que manojo! I take good care of you. I know a place near here. When I stop the car follow me and run like hell, man."

Maybe he just wanted to get in the spirit of the thing, I thought. The Lincoln accelerated, overtaking a transit bus on the right and narrowly missing a line of parked cars, then swung left nearly clipping the bus's nose and drawing a horn blast, left again, slower this time until the car was hidden behind the bus. There was still plenty of traffic in the farthest left lane but Angel jumped in and turned left onto a cross street, accelerated madly, then left at the first intersection and again at the next.

The car screeched to a halt near a photo shop. "Come on!" he shouted, and I followed him inside at a dead run.

"Problemas," he reported blandly to the old proprietor as we dashed through a curtained doorway to the back. "Here," he said to me, opening a wooden door on our right. We passed through. He locked the door and opened another that led to a kitchen. This door he also locked. "See?" he said, pointing to a small one-way mirror that looked out into the shop. "They use it when they eat to keep watch. See now if your woman comes."

When the shop door opened it wasn't Dulce who entered but two black men. One I'd never seen before, the other was Johnson, our Haitian taxi man.

"¡Mierda!" I swore.

"The husband?" Angel asked.

I shook my head. "No. Voodoo."

Angel was beginning to believe me I think, and led me outside into a narrow alley, dodging dumpsters until we found ourselves on the other side of the block. I was lost. Angel hailed a cab.

"Now what?" I asked him.

"Tía María," he said.

"What about the car?"

"Remember Manny? Manny García?"

"Little Manny, sure."

"Not so little now. He drives for me on my days off. He can pick up the car in a few hours and take my nightshift. They won't keep following him all night. I have a safe garage for the car. There are black cars all over the city. No one can follow them all." He studied my face. "You are in much trouble."

"Maybe more than I thought."

"What will you do now?"

"Lay low at your place until tomorrow when I have to look for Mercer."

* * *

In the morning I took the train. Easier to watch your back. Got off at 116th Street and walked east to Amsterdam Avenue, then north to 118th Street, stopping occasionally to check behind me, twice crossing the street and jogging back the way I'd come. Nothing. Or nothing I saw.

Foot traffic was light. Dr. Mercer, who I'd reached by phone earlier, told me he was temporarily housed in the International Affairs building facing West 118th Street. The basement.

His office, which had a door like a dentist's, was identified by a hand lettered cardboard sign swinging on a string from the doorknob and read simply Dr. C. Mercer, MD, Ph.D. - ENTER.

It occurred to me as I pushed open the door that I'd been looking for this man half my life but it had really only been a few days. "Dr. Mercer?" I inquired.

"You must be the fellow from Santo Domingo," he said, rather sternly I thought, and strolled out from behind a neatly arranged desk to offer a limp handshake. "Sit over here." He indicated a tattered love seat and overstuffed wingback that constituted a small lounge area in a corner of the room surrounded by bookcases and stacked boxes.

"Thanks for seeing me on such short notice." I sat on the loveseat. "I'll only take a few minutes of your time."

"I'm not worried about my time," he said. "I'm worried about your intent. You don't look like a detective to me." The doctor was tall, well over six feet, and not young.

"It's a part time job," I began. "Garrett Yancy gave me your name. Do you know him?"

"Never heard of him."

"It's about voodoo, you see."

"Stop right there. You said tropical medicine on the phone."

"Well, I didn't want to spring that on you unless we were face to face." I grinned.

"Why not?"

"Oh. I don't know...."

"Let me tell you something. If you're from some tabloid newspaper you can leave right now. I've got nothing to say, understand? I'm a scientist. This is science not sensationalism. I think you better leave." He'd remained standing all this time and now pointed toward the door. I guessed his age as close to seventy, skinny with sacks beneath his eyes and a veiny nose.

"Please," I said. "I am *not* from a newspaper. I *am* investigating Ambassador Adam Quist's death on behalf of his family, and there are definitely medical questions I need to ask you. I'm sorry about the voodoo stuff. I was told you were in Haiti doing research on zombies and things. I'm sorry. I know how dumb that sounds, but I went to Haiti looking for you. Please don't throw me out now that I've finally found you."

He took a step closer, studied my face a moment and pursed his lips. "Let me see some ID," he said. His breath smelled of coffee and his teeth were stained yellow-brown, gums nearly eaten by pyorrhea.

I pulled out my Dominican driver's license, my Florida driver's license, my Minnesota driver's license, my American Express card and a note from Mickey Alba written on the back of his official police business card asking people to cooperate with me. "Here," I said, forcing them all into his hand.

Dr. Mercer's saggy eyes examined each carefully. "They seem authentic," he said. "Now convince me that you are."

"How?"

"Tell me, from the beginning, how you got involved with this business and why you think voodoo is part of it."

I decided to give him the long version, including the trip to Haiti, the voodoo ceremony, Johnson, all of it. Half way through he dropped into the chair and swung one leg over the arm as a much younger man might do, but he listened without comment and most of the time kept his eyes on the rug. When I finished he sat silent for some time. "Well," I said finally, and for the second time, "that's pretty much it."

He nodded, then got up quietly and came to sit on the arm of my loveseat. "Do you know what happens when science and religion butt heads?" he asked.

"Debate?" I ventured.

"Anger," he said.

"Yes."

"I went to Haiti as a scientist to examine claims by a religion that there are zombies." He shrugged. "I also went to understand the religion. Voodoo. Vodoun, the academics say now, but that's a misnomer. Do you know what my colleagues think about that, Mr. Espinosa-Jones?"

"No."

"They think I'm nuts. They think even acknowledging the idea of zombies is nuts. And now that I've investigated it, or part of it, they think my science is nuts too." He went back to his chair. "Do you know what that makes me?"

"No."

"Nuts." He laughed. It came out Ha!

"I wish I could offer a second opinion," I said gently, "but the truth is I've got no idea what voodoo has to do with Quist's death. Don't know anything about zombies. Always thought, you know, zombies. Mr. Yancy, who I guess you don't know, knows you or knows of you. Why'd he send me to you?"

"Easy answer," he said. "I'm the only scientist in years to publish an article supporting the existence of zombies. He has no doubt come across it somewhere or been told about me. You can imagine how this is being received by the scientific community. One reviewer of my paper actually called it 'tabloid science.'"

"What is it really?"

"Nothing more than a beginning. We don't understand voodoo. V-o-d-o-u-n is the academic spelling, but to Haitian peasants, the real practitioners, it's voodoo. To them, Vodoun is a dance when spirits mount and possess a believer. We don't understand. We think a zombie is a cocktail in a hotel bar. I've been there for the past year and I know better, whether it's science or I'm nuts or what." He got up and went to an old fashioned coffee percolator plugged in behind his desk. "Let's talk," he said. "We'll have coffee."

The coffee was strong, the way I liked it. We talked a long time and the talk was frightening. Dr. Mercer had a way of trolling an idea through my mind that left me hungry. He started with Columbus, moved forward in time to the French plantation owners and their African slave imports, and later, the twelve year struggle of these slaves to win their independence. Voodoo, he said, had its roots in African black magic but flowered in the unique culture that is Haiti.

At some point in his history of black magic in Africa, I called a halt. "Doctor, please give me a moment," I said, rubbing my face with both hands. "You are piling up hundreds of years of spiritual thought in a heap. I'm losing the point. Can I just ask you some questions?"

For a second I thought the interview was over again but he finally smiled. "That's the trouble with scientists," he said. "We tend to tell everyone too much. Just because you know it doesn't mean you should say it."

"Same is true of some scuba diving I've done. Just because you *can* go that deep, doesn't mean you *should*."

"Okay. Ask away."

"First, no offense to history, I don't need it. I need a way, a means by which someone could use voodoo to kill a man and make it look like a heart attack. But if that's not possible, then I need some other logical, scientific answer. It's that simple."

Mercer paced a while. At last he asked, "Are you Christian?"

"Yes."

"So you believe a Jewish rabbi named Jesus is the Messiah?"

"Yes."

"Do you also believe in his resurrection from the dead?"

"Yes."

"And you're Catholic?"

"No. My father is. My mother is Lutheran. I've sort of sided with her."

"I see," he said nodding. "The differences are more political anyway. What I'm getting at, is you believe in a dead man walking around after his death. You believe that?"

"Yes."

"You see, that's a zombie in voodoo. A resurrection of sorts, but with a more sinister purpose. That's what I went to Haiti to investigate."

"I don't think Jesus was a zombie," I said.

"Nor I. The point I'm making is one of faith not science. You believe in the resurrection, you and millions more, by faith. Practitioners of Voodoo believe in zombies by faith." He chuckled. "Now add this. People claim to have seen them. I have seen them, too. I also know how they are made. What do you think of that?"

I shrugged. "Maybe it's not such a mystery why people think you're nuts."

"An honest answer," he said laughing. "I'm beginning to like you Mr. Espinosa-Jones. I'm really beginning to like you."

"You might not like this," I said. "Zombies don't help me much. My guy's dead, not walking around. I watched him buried yesterday afternoon."

"I went to Jean-Claude LaRouch's funeral in Petonville, Haiti last year," he said. "I shook hands with him about a month ago. He remembered my name."

Our new found friendship wasn't going to last, I thought. Not if he expected me to believe that. "I'm sorry," I said to explain my gapping mouth. "How is that possible?"

"Faith and drugs," Dr. Mercer said. "Notably, a chemical tetrodotoxin from the puffer fish. A sort of anesthetic powder that when mixed with other drugs, creates for the believer, a death-like trance. A zombie. Sometimes zombies live and walk. Other times it's a death sentence."

"So a U.S. Ambassador could be made into a zombie, running around Washington to cocktail parties? Might explain the Supreme Court."

"See how easy it is?" He dropped back into the chair and swung his leg up again. "So easy to mock."

"I'm sorry," I said. "Wasn't making fun of you. Tempting, you know? Anyway, who makes these zombies?"

"The Bizango," he said. "Secret societies in Haiti since the slave days. Black magic left over from Africa adapted to the New World. Zombification is their death sentence to their enemies. Not so different from our own methods, really. Hanging has never been much fun, or electrocution either."

"You're serious?"

"Completely."

"And no one believes you."

"A few. More will understand after I complete my research and publish something substantial." He sighed heavily. "I rushed into print to protect my grant money, you see, and that's always foolish. Anyway, there are zombies and there are men who can make them. They are on the same island as your ambassador. Whether the two came together, well, that's your problem."

"My problem is that the guy was pronounced dead by a doctor and buried yesterday in Arlington National Cemetery. That's my problem."

"I pronounced Jean-Claude LeRouche dead," Dr. Mercer said flatly. "He had no pulse. His pupils were fixed and dilated. I could detect no breathing. I stood and watched them lower him into the ground. He was dead. Then he was alive."

"How?"

"Faith and drugs. I explained that."

"Convincing enough to fool even his own doctor?"

"We're not that infallible and often see what we expect to see. Had I suspected something, like a drug-induced trance, I might've discovered his secret grip on life. I didn't. Maybe your ambassador's doctor didn't either."

"So how did this Jean-Claude guy come back to life?"

"He was never dead. Enough air inside his coffin for a few hours. After we were all gone they dug him up."

"Well, my guy's in Arlington. Nobody's going to be digging there."

"Are you certain?"

"That he's there?"

"Yes."

"Saw him yesterday," I asserted.

"Him or a coffin?"

"Don't kid around."

"I'm not suggesting anything to you," he said. "I'm talking to you still about faith and science. Science is empirical. If you did not in fact observe this man placed in his coffin and lowered into his grave, and if you are not certain he remained there, you don't know he's really dead, do you?"

"Everyone else saw him."

"Was an autopsy performed?"

"No," I admitted.

"So you have the witness of his physician and some weeping family members?"

"Yes."

"Dig him up."

"Hold it a minute." The guy was making me dizzy. "Can I smoke?"

"Cigarettes?"

"Yes."

"No." He shook his head. "I don't like cigarettes."

"Fine. Just let me get this straight. Adam Quist could be alive in his casket, dead, or a resurrected zombie - those are my choices?"

"He's probably not alive in his casket if he was buried yesterday, unless someone lined the bottom of it with oxygen tanks. Otherwise, you're on the money."

"And you want me to dig him up?"

"It's the only way to be certain. Exhume the body and see."

I laughed out loud. I really wanted a cigarette. "'Mrs. Quist,"' I said, quoting myself. "'I'd like to dig your husband up because I think he might be a zombie.' Is that your advice?"

He slapped both his knees and smiling said, "Now you know a little of what it's like to be me! This has been a most enjoyable morning. It's so seldom I really get to share." He laughed even harder and slapped his legs again. Tears formed in his eyes from the mirth. I never saw a man so eager to share his misery. "God," he said. "It's priceless."

Another thought occurred to me while he regained control. "Suppose," I said, "that someone - maybe even someone in his own family - decided to use these drugs to kill him or make him a zombie or whatever, and botched it? That's possible, isn't it?"

"Unlikely," he said. "The formulas for the poisons and zombie powders are all African holdovers, too. Hundreds, maybe thousands, of years ago. There's no recipe book. It's all passed down through the ages in secret. If I told you some of the things I had to do, places I had to go to get my information, well, you'd really think I'm nuts."

"So it couldn't be a straight-out poison crime gone bad?"

"It could be anything. I'm saying it's unlikely."

"Damn."

"Mr. Espinosa-Jones. I told you in the beginning this is about faith and drugs. Not the two separately but the two together. Do you understand? Your ambassador should believe or maybe it would go wrong, you see? He might then just be drugged, and while that *could* result in Zombification, it's more likely to result in death. Whether he was dead at the time he was discovered in that rocking chair you told me about or not, well, that's neither here nor there. We'll never know. He may have had a faith no one knew anything about. Faith has power. Tremendous power. I tried life as an agnostic and didn't like it. Science explains many things. Faith explains it all."

"Adam Quist wasn't the type. Not according to his daughter, anyway."

"Who knows what's in a man's heart? A great many clergy today cloak themselves in holy robes and are little more than religious bureaucrats who believe some, or none, of what they offer their parishioners. Commandments to them are a behavioral menu from which they select only what is palatable. Everything else is provided by a Sugar Daddy god who forgives all things, loves all things, tolerates all things. As mainstream religion in America loses it's appeal, watch and see how quickly the bishops, priests and preachers of the world slough their principles. That's what I learned in Haiti. We might argue that they have faith in evil, but we can't argue that they don't have faith, or that it doesn't produce results, combined with a good dose of zombie powder. How do you like them apples?"

Dr. Charles Mercer was one very odd duck, I thought.

"If you have time," he continued. "I'm going to outline the actual steps a bokor takes in creating a zombie - the poison, its administration, possible results, case studies I've made on my various field trips to Haiti. Will you listen to that?"

"Of course."

He proceeded to outline "zombification" as he called it, in intimate and outrageous detail. I knew, somehow, he'd uncovered the truth, whether anyone believed him or not.

"One more thing," I said a half hour later, reaching inside my breast pocket for Mickey's drawing of the Residence verve. "Can you interpret this?"

Mercer spread the paper out on his desk and smoothed its wrinkles. "Where did you get it?"

"On the floor of the Ambassador's residence."

Dr. Mercer studied the paper. "Remember the bokor?" he asked.

"Like a priest."

"More like a sorcerer. Haitians live under constant threat from the spirit world. They need a sorcerer for charms, spells, and other sorcery." He glanced back at the drawing. "This may be part of a l'envoi morts, a sending of the dead, a critical aspect in creating a zombie." He smiled. "I'm not an expert on what every verve means, nor do I pretend to understand all the sorcery of every bokor. It's said that some can even transform themselves into werewolves. My guess is that this is one more reason to confirm your Ambassador's death."

My first thought was of Dulce. Dulce the werewolf. "How am I going to explain this? Who's going to take me seriously enough to grant an exhumation order for one of the highest profile cemeteries on earth?"

"Nobody," Dr. Mercer said, smiling. "Mad scientists are sent to the basement." He extending his hands palm up to feature his surroundings. "God knows what they do to mad detectives. I think you'll need to become very resourceful."

"Well," I smiled. "Maybe I'll create some voodoo of my own."

"Yes," he nodded. "Be careful. Voodoo is only a joke to nonbelievers."

* * *

"Angel, what do you think about helping me dig up a body?" I asked later that afternoon.

Angel did not have angel eyes. If anything, I suppose they were bedroom eyes, or what he thought were bedroom eyes. This once I delighted in seeing them wide, white, fearful. "Like in a cemetery?" he inquired.

"Thankfully," I said, "I don't know where any other bodies are buried."

"I think I'm going to be busy that day."

We stood side by side in the semi-darkness of the garage where he kept his black car. One low-wattage bulb lit the cramped space from overhead. We rested from rubbing the car down with clean towels, which Manny had already done after the nightshift but Angel insisted on doing it again just in case there were hidden scratches, dents or abrasions. Even in the anemic light the ebony surface gleamed like oil.

Earlier, I'd lunched with Angel, Tía María, and assorted cousins, then telephoned Olivia at the Quist apartment and was told by her mother that she would meet me at The Whaler on East 43rd Street at 7:30 that evening. Her mother hoped we would have a nice dinner. She didn't sound drunk to me. I planned to ask Olivia for a meeting with the family to see if I could persuade them to exhume the ambassador's body. My problem, of course, was how to ask this without mention of voodoo or the notion that I was beginning to suspect a United States Ambassador was now a zombie.

"Where is Olivia now?" I'd asked Mrs. Quist.

"She left awhile ago to meet a friend who flew up from DC," she'd said. "Duane Delbrick. Maybe you know him?"

"We've met." I tried to keep the worry out of my voice. "Any idea where they are?"

"Not a clue," she said. "They're such good friends. He's been like a second father to her."

"Isn't that sweet," I said.

After hanging up I'd sat thinking awhile and then gone with Angel to the garage. Once again I'd been overcome by unfocused suspicions. What was wrong with the picture? Why did the colors bleed and blur?

"Angel," I said. "Why does a girl, a woman, go out with a man she detests?"

"To cut off his balls."

"I can always depend on you to get to the heart of the matter." I stretched across the hood of the Lincoln and buffed along the chrome center line. "But you see this girl didn't mention her meeting with this man or that he was in town or that any relationship existed between them other than an adversarial one. How about that?"

"She's screwing him."

I pushed back off the car and stared at him. "No. She's nineteen." Something was seriously wrong. "I still need to know why she's with him."

"How can you find her?"

"I have a hunch," I told him. "She was at the Four Seasons in Washington. We're such creatures of habit. You have one here?"

"On 57th Street off Madison. Nice hotel. Almost new."

"Let's go see."

Twenty minutes later in light traffic we pulled up to the front door. "The doorman is Roberto Martinez from Santiago," Angel said. "He knows me."

Roberto allowed Angel to wait and I trotted into the lobby to check if Delbrick was registered. The more I thought about it, the more it seemed a diplomat's hotel. I got lucky when I glanced into the bar first and spotted him sitting alone in a booth. It wasn't worth the risk to go inside where he might spot me so I strolled back to the lobby and found a chair with an easy view of the bar's entrance. Delbrick was out of sight but I could observe anyone entering or leaving.

If Olivia was around I wanted to catch them together. If she'd already gone I was too late. I waited half an hour. The place was beginning to fill up now in late afternoon. I saw a bartender in a white shirt placing fresh baskets of some kind of hors d'oeuvres along the bar. Most of the patrons seemed to be guests, arriving without coats. Four young women arrived together but Olivia wasn't among them. I slid my chair further behind a heavily flocked Christmas tree, which seemed more concealing than a newspaper or hat over my eyes.

I was beginning to feel better. The bar was almost full now. Delbrick hadn't come out and Olivia hadn't gone in. I began to wonder who had. Or was he just sitting there alone drinking and wondering if he shouldn't be getting back to DC?

I waited another couple minutes then decided I'd tell Angel to get ready for a quick departure. One more peek at Delbrick. Maybe he'd met with some new suspect. As I stood up, Olivia came almost at a run and I turned into the tree, knocking it crooked in its stand. She flew into the bar. I followed as far as the door. I had to know. She was already seated with Delbrick, clutching his hand. Both seemed to be talking at once.

"Take me somewhere near the water," I told Angel outside.

He'd seen the look on my face and for once kept his mouth shut.

A short time later he parked in lower Manhattan not far from the ferry terminal and cut the engine. I apologized. "You just want to trust people," I told him after a while. "More and more as you get older, I think."

"Primo," he said. "You are not a bad man.

Chapter Ten

Golden beams of light from The Whaler's recessed windows caught the drifting snowflakes and reflected on the sidewalk and wet street beyond. Radio reported riots and looting in the Bronx. Another large fire there out of control. Here the streets were relatively quiet. The snowflakes, large and awkward, tumbled from a dark sky, clinging to porch railings, melting on the pyretic floor of the city. I waited for Olivia in a shadowed doorway across East 43rd Street, determined to see if she arrived alone.

The logical possibilities had poisoned my mind. Olivia killed her father and Delbrick was blackmailing her. Delbrick had killed her father and Olivia was blackmailing him. They were in it together. I was the stooge. Dulce and Alejandro were blackmailing both of them and trying to kill me so I wouldn't spoil their gig. He wasn't dead, he was a zombie living in Canada. Dr. Mercer masterminded it as an elaborate hoax to promote a new book he was writing on Vodoun in Haiti. I did it, and simply forgot.

Olivia arrived in a taxi, unaccompanied. She paid her fare and went inside.

I followed a few minutes later.

The table I'd reserved was by the window. This had seemed a good idea at the time. Now I felt exposed. Worse, I felt alone, deserted since spying Olivia with Delbrick. It was immature to trust anyone really, when you thought about it. Immature.

I persuaded the maitre d' with a twenty and we were moved from the window seat to a booth where I could watch Olivia and the door. She didn't seem to mind, chatting about her family.

"Where are you staying?" I asked after the drink order was taken.

"The apartment. I told you."

"Not the Four Seasons?"

"That was Washington, silly. We've got our own place here."

"I could've sworn I saw you there this afternoon when I pulled over to buy a cigar. Wasn't that you?"

"No. I was across town having my hair done. Like it?"

Her hair was combed, maybe it did seem thicker. Why was she lying when it was so easy for me to catch her? Why not pretend she was in the Four Seasons getting her hair done? Even claim Delbrick asked her for a drink. She wasn't stupid. She knew I'd talked to her mother. Why was she lying?

"The tropical humidity makes a mess of it really," she went on. "They put giant rollers in and straightened it out the way I like it. Don't you prefer straighter hair? I do. Not that your curls aren't cute, but on a woman I mean. Don't you think?"

"Your hair is great," I said. "I don't think I've ever seen such pretty hair. In fact, it's the best damned hair in New York."

"Shhh! Okay. I'm glad you like it."

"Bien. Fine. Let's eat then. I'm starved. I'm really hungry. I could eat a horse. What's good here? This is your place isn't it? What do you recommend?"

"For you I'd recommend a double Scotch."

"I hate Scotch. I don't know how people can drink Scotch. It tastes like jet fuel. They just do it to be cool. Half this country is populated by idiots who do things just to be cool."

"So, a Scotch is out then?"

"We ordered drinks already, remember? Are you losing your memory? Maybe you can't remember that we already ordered drinks because you've got so many conflicting things to remember, like when you last got your hair done, or where you were this afternoon, or who you might've had drinks with, or what you're doing in New York really, or what you've done with your father's body. Does any of this make sense to you?"

"EJ."

"Yes? Got something to say? Say it."

The waiter, who I now noticed looked a whole lot like Paul Simon, brought drinks and passed them out. Mine was a martini and hers gin and tonic. No Scotch. "Hey!" I said to him. "Where's Garfunkle? Have you heard that one before? I bet you have. I want another martini and a glass of ice water. Make it a pitcher. Got any water that didn't pass through New York? You know, in underground pipes? I want bottled water."

The waiter nodded his Simonlike head and disappeared. "Hope he understood about the water," I continued. "No way of knowing, you know. None whatsoever. I mean, what's to stop them from backing a big water truck up to a hydrant somewhere and filling it? We'd never know the difference and just pay for some disease-ridden water that's probably worse than what comes out of the taps. So many things in life are like that. You just trust and trust and trust because you simply don't have any choice. Like in this murder thing with your father - if it was murder - you begin wondering why so many people are involved, lying to each other and following and chasing and even trying to kill one another. Then pretty soon don't you start wondering if you should trust anybody? I mean, what if the whole thing's a big lie, nothing but some hydrant discharge. What if?"

She started to cry. I couldn't bring myself to care. Not really. Let her cry, I thought. She's a dirty liar. Probably lied from the beginning. Yancy just got sucked in because they went to *rehearsal* together and he was a sick old man attracted to a vulnerable rich girl able to make herself appear innocent, even pretty, though in fact she was plain as milk. I felt like telling her how plain she was, but I didn't. I didn't want to say a single thing. Just let her cry. Let *her* say something.

"Go ahead," I said. "Say something."

She hung her head so her hair, richly textured in the low light like maybe it *had* been done, swung forward and hid all of her face but her mouth, nose, and one eye. "I know you think I'm a liar," she said. "I don't blame you."

"Oh," I said. "It's big of you not to blame me. Other people have sometimes blamed me when they've lied. Thank you. It really is big of you."

"I understand why you're sarcastic."

"Screw understanding. Tell me why you were in the Four Seasons bar with Delbrick."

"Can't you figure it out for yourself?" she asked, staring at the table. Her eye, the one I could see, didn't once lift to a level beyond the linen tablecloth directly below her chin. "Didn't you notice I wasn't wearing a coat?"

That, at least, was the truth. She hadn't been wearing a coat. I'd noticed, just hadn't thought much of it. "Oh," I said. "So now you're telling me you *were* staying there."

"No."

Tears were dripping again. One trembled on the tip of her nose. "Oh shit," I said. "You were in bed with him?"

She sobbed.

"Answer me!"

She nodded.

"He's old enough to be your father." It was the only thing I could think of to say.

"I know you think I'm a whore."

"Quit telling me what I think!" Most of all, I wanted to slap her. It was none of my business. Why should I care? We barely knew each other. I shouldn't even be thinking about it. "Yes," I told Olivia. "You're a puta. Happy?"

"Do I look happy? Can I tell you about it?"

"Why do I want to know?"

"I know you don't care," she said to the table. "I know. But you cared in Haiti. Don't tell me you didn't."

"Okay," I said. "Tell me."

"I know I've ruined it," she sobbed, wiping her eyes, pulling hair from her face. "I've ruined everything. That's what's so funny. I was trying to fix it."

"Fix what, exactly?"

"Us."

"Us?"

"I was only there to tell him I couldn't see him anymore."

"Because of me?"

"Who else?"

"God knows."

"Don't make fun of my love for you. Say what you want. Call me a puta all you want. But I love you. I should've told you before, after we walked in the street in Port au Prince and saw the pretty lady washing her feet I knew then I loved you."

"Tell me about Delbrick."

"What about him?"

"All about him. How old is he?"

"43."

"19 and 43. Does that make sense to you?"

"It wasn't about sense."

"Obviously."

"I deserve whatever you say to me. Do you want me to tell you about him or not?"

"Yes."

"Everybody might want to date the Ambassador's daughter, but guess what, they don't dare ask. I sit home mostly. Daddy's working. Mother's drunk. My sister lives in her own world and my brother's gone. I've got servants." She drank off a third of her gin. "Duane stopped by a lot. He checked on things and arranged the few things I did, like take rides or go on a day sailing trip or make some kind of formal visit to somebody. Sometimes I went to cocktail parties with the family. He was just always there and he has a sense of humor, kind of. Makes a joke of his stuffiness. He's very caustic about Republicans too, and that appealed to me sometimes when I was feeling rebellious, even though I guess I'm one myself, though I don't do anything about it. I hate politics. Even though I've got a good mind for it, Duane says."

"All right. All right. How do you get from there to bed?"

"He was teaching me to putt. At the Santo Domingo Country Club."

"You're kidding? He's like 'Let me show you how to hold a putter' and then gets behind you and snuggles?"

"Pretty much."

"Sickening."

"We just started kissing and then he took me into the trees. We left the cart by the green. After that we just did it when we had time."

"Like a quick snack."

"Don't make light of it." She dried her eyes with her napkin. "Do you think I'm proud of it? He's married. I baby-sit for them."

"How convenient."

"I only do it on the maid's day off. Their son Gary is six. I need to get out of the house. I'd do almost anything to get out of there sometimes."

"Obviously."

"You can be as cruel as you like, I don't care. I know I deserve it."

"Please shut up. The self-depreciation is worse than the slatternliness. Has it even occurred to you that you just gave your lover *Duane* the best motive in the world for killing your father?"

"How?"

"If your father found out, don't you think he'd take some action? Like maybe finish Delbrick's career for him somehow? And if he confronted Delbrick, threatened him say, then Delbrick might retaliate. The best way would be to shut his mouth forever and make it look like an accident - or maybe just a nice little everyday heart attack."

"Don't you think I'd know?"

"Sure. Delbrick's probably just as stupid as you are. 'Say honey. I just murdered your daddy. How about a quickie?' I met him. He isn't quite *that* dumb." I polished off my martini and drank water. "There's another possibility, of course. The two of you worked it together."

The lines around her mouth hardened. "I don't think I *did* deserve that one."

"Not a good idea to get me started on what you deserve. Anyway, it's really none of my business. You're free to be with anybody you wish. So am I. Where's Paul Simon with my other martini?"

"You don't have to believe a single thing I say," she said. "In Haiti - I can't explain it - I've never been like 'in love' the way people talk about it. With Duane.....we hid from his wife and talked about logistics and it was a kind of conspiracy, almost a game. It was exciting. I don't have any excitement in my life. And men are so easy to seduce. Like it wasn't hard to get Duane to show me how to putt. But with you, I was alive in the street that day for the first time ever. I felt my skin tingle and those people were my people and we belonged to them, and to the place, and I wanted to cry and it was like joy. I told Duane before the funeral I had to talk to him but he refused, and then when he met you I think he figured it out, maybe by the way I look at you or something. Finally we met this afternoon and I told him and he said Latin men were creeps. I'd be sorry. You had a woman in Santo Domingo and were just using me. Is that true?"

"Using you? How? Have I showed you how to putt yet? Where's the singing waiter?" I snapped my fingers over my head, at no one in particular, and drew some stares.

"He ordered me to stay away from you. He said the lady's name is Sonja Cadavid."

Paul was directed to me by another waiter. When he saw me, he put a finger to his head and pulled the trigger on his forgetfulness, then scurried off toward the bar. I stared at Olivia for the full ten minutes it took him to reappear with the martini. I was thinking about what to say, if anything, about Sonja. I was also thinking how nicely this whole thing had got turned around and now I was on the defensive. Amazing, since she was confessing her love for me, her infidelity, her dishonesty, and all I'd done was try and figure out who murdered her dad. I don't remember once saying I loved her.

Why then, did I feel jealous?

"Won't you even talk to me?" she asked finally.

"Let me tell you something about future love affairs," I said. "Don't tell your supposed new boyfriend about your old boyfriend on the same day you tell the new boyfriend you love him. Puts you in a bad light. Pisses him off, too."

"You aren't perfect either. Anyway, you asked." Her eyes were cold and treacherous.

"If you're referring to Sonja, that's not a topic for discussion. Period."

"What's the difference between me and Duane and you and her?"

"Age."

For some reason she couldn't find an answer for this and again we sat for some time without speaking. "I don't suppose you want to have dinner with me now," she said.

"Please! Don't start that again. Just answer one question. Did you have anything to do with your father's death? Anything at all? I mean even knowledge of it before or after? Answer truthfully."

"No," she said without hesitation. "No." The self-deprecation had gone from her voice.

I had no reason to, but I believed her. "Okay," I said. "Forget Haiti. Forget Delbrick. How come you made up that story about calling him Pinhead?"

"I didn't. That's what they call him."

"Your lover?"

"I just slept with him. It didn't mean anything."

"You really are a kid, and you couldn't be more wrong. It always means something. You lost a part of yourself you can't ever get back. Sex isn't a game, and neither is murder. So let's eat and see where we go from here."

"And Haiti?"

"Maybe we had a moment in Haiti, but it's not going anywhere. Even if things were different and I didn't have Sonja, who I'm not going to discuss, and I was fifteen years younger, you don't treat it like some romantic toy and hop into bed so it gets all confused. How do we know then if it's real? Love and sex should sleep apart awhile."

"Thanks teacher." She sneaked a smile at me. "I guess it's hopeless then. Will you order for me like you did at the Splendid?"

"I want steak."

"It's a seafood place."

"Seafood places have the best steak."

The Whaler was done up so you felt like you were dining at the captain's table of a sailing vessel. Lot's of beams, portholes, pointless coils of rope, but it was intimate - low lighting, mix of tables and booths. An ample array of gray heads in the room, always a good sign.

Paul Simon dropped by to take our order and replenish our drinks. I added wine to the liquor bill, a New York red I drank whenever I was in town. Olivia said she hated champagne and we talked about that for awhile, then I told her about Dr. Mercer in painstaking detail and she was more attentive than I'd ever seen her. I did my best to quit thinking about Pinhead but I kept seeing his lips on her, his crummy little head between her naked breasts. My concentration wandered and so did my soliloquy about Mercer, so much so, I feared I was repeating myself.

Olivia sat quietly through all of this. Maybe she knew what was really on my mind. At one point she said, "I underestimated you. I was wrong to tease you about being a poor detective. You're very persistent. Plodding. I mean that in a good sense. You won't give up, will you? Until you know the answer, I mean?"

"Try not to, but at this point I'm more confused than I was in the beginning."

"I don't know what else I can do to help you."

"What I really need - what we all really need - is an autopsy. This is all nonsense unless we establish a scientific cause of death. You have to understand that."

"Daddy's in the ground."

"We have to dig him up."

"What?" She wrinkled her nose. "Are you crazy? Mother will never permit it"

"Then you have to persuade her."

"How can I explain this to you? Look." She puffed her cheeks and sighed. "Suppose you had some insurmountable difficulty in your life like cancer or a million dollar debt or you were in prison for life, then suddenly fate stepped in and swept it away. What would it take to convince you to go back? What would it take?" She shook her head slowly. "I'm telling you, mother will never allow it. That heart attack - the belief in it - saved her. I don't think she hated my father, but there was no love between them. When he died she got the cure. She won't go back. Never."

"Then I'm wasting Mr. Yancy's money, or somebody's money, and I might as well go home."

The food arrived and we didn't talk much while we ate. Olivia picked at hers. Her usual relish for eating had turned to stirring, cutting, and sorting. I felt good about that. At least she'd lost her appetite and I took credit for it.

My mind wandered. This dinner was a mistake. The reason I became a detective, an investigator, was because I liked the detachment of solving a puzzle without caring about the outcome. The solution remained outside me. I didn't care who did it or what became of them, or really, what motivated them except as motivation might relate to motive. They were actors in some private drama of my own. I had feelings now for Olivia, when it was perfectly clear she manipulated her sexual relationship with Delbrick and was probably doing the same to me for some reason.

After dinner we had port and coffee. "Are you really going home?" she asked.

"Yes, I'd better."

"I'd get you the permission if I could."

"Thank you."

"Is there any other way?"

"Only grave-robbing, I'm afraid. I suggested that to my cousin. Shook him up."

"You were joking, of course."

"Mostly."

"Mostly?"

"Well, I mean, it's not impossible. If the body was taken to a qualified medical examiner and quietly returned we'd have the answers and nobody would be hurt."

"He's buried in Arlington," she needlessly explained.

"I know."

"It's run by the Army. I think they probably shoot grave robbers."

"If they catch them."

"You're not serious?" Her eyes sparkled for the first time that night.

"Maybe I could go to the press or the DC police or even the State Department, but I doubt anyone would listen. They're all going to accept the doctor's death certificate and I probably would too in their shoes. It's just that nobody looked for a scientific cause of death and you can still do that now with an autopsy. Traces of some drugs stay around awhile in human tissue, and of course heart attacks leave evidence."

"Oh!" she said and shuddered. "I touched his hand before the funeral. It was so hard. How do they do that? Find drugs inside him, I mean?"

"Skip it. They do it."

"We're all such ghouls, aren't we?"

"I suppose we are." The idea was growing more magnificent as I toyed with it. "If it's the only way, would you help me?"

"Dig up Daddy?"

"Yes."

"How?"

"You're a member of the family. My cousin has connections. Forge some papers, make some calls. It's worth a try. Naturally, I'd have to set up the examination in advance. Find a location close by in DC. Have him moved out and back again quickly before there's talk about it."

"Oh," she said, and smiled slightly for the first time that evening. "I was thinking it would be different."

"Like at night? Lanterns? Dark of the moon? Moaning wind? Shovels?"

"Yes."

"No," I said. "Backhoe. Broad daylight. Mortuary truck and a hearse. Nothing to hide."

"Unless you can't get permission, even by using me."

I chuckled. "If we can't fool 'em I think we'll just give up."

"Why haven't you done that already? Given up, I mean."

"Dulce and Alejandro. Nobody comes after you the way they did unless you're very close to something. Wouldn't surprise me if they're sitting across the street watching us right now. Talk about persistence."

"Are you scared?"

"Scared enough to have someone coming to pick us up in a few minutes."

"Are you scared for me too?"

"Doesn't appear they're after you, but never hurts to be careful. You might want to curtail your *rendezvous* for awhile." It hurt her, that remark, and there was a stiffening around the eyes.

She spoiled it by saying, "I know I deserve that."

"Okay. I'm sorry. So you'll help in the grave robbery?"

"Sure."

"I'll call Mr. Yancy tonight about the cost. Won't be cheap. Goes a little beyond what he usually pays."

"You don't need his permission," she said flatly. "You've got mine."

I started to laugh but held back. "Yours?"

"Yes, mine."

"Since when are you paying?"

"Since the beginning." I noticed a new clarity to her voice and a hardening around the eyes.

"I know you told him about your father but now you're telling me *you* hired him? You're funding all this?" If she was lying she was doing it well. "Do you have any idea what it costs?"

"I have the money."

"I didn't mean family money."

"Neither did I."

"Did you win the lottery?" I asked, making light of it to manage the sinking feeling she was telling the truth.

"No," she said. "Made wise investments. Technology stocks, some utilities, and housing starts. Started buying in high school. Junior high, actually."

"Invested your allowance no doubt."

"Yes," she said. "I did. My portfolio should break a hundred thousand this year."

"Dollars?"

"EJ. Being nineteen doesn't automatically make you a fool."

"So this whole thing is your doing? Why didn't you tell me?"

"Mr. Yancy told me to keep my mouth shut and my eyes and ears open. His exact words. Not that he doesn't trust you, he just likes everyone tending to their own business, I think. Anyway, money's yours for an exhumation, but I won't go against my mother. She isn't perfect but she deserves the truth afterward. Whatever we find at the autopsy."

"Okay," I said. "We'll have to come back here again and talk to her. You arrange it?"

"Of course."

"Fine," I said. "What about Pinhead?"

"He's heading back to Santo Domingo. He's in charge there now."

The more I thought about it the more it made sense. Mr. Yancy would never break her confidence and she had nothing to lose by hiring him. He could take action where she couldn't, and who else would care? Not Delbrick, or the family. It was the smart play. But that night it felt wrong to me, and more people would die before I understood why.

Angel pulled up to the curb right on time. The meal was $47. I left three twenties so Paul Simon could rent some studio time and we bolted out the door and into the car in case Dulce and Alejandro were lurking about. Angel stepped on it for a couple blocks then glanced back over his shoulder at Olivia and addressed me in Spanish, "What a firm little piece of ass you found there."

"Thank you," Olivia answered in the same language. "But it might be more beneficial for us if you kept your eyes on the road."

"Una problem in Nueva York," Angel said. "The damn gringas speaking the Spanish."

"Be polite," I told Angel. "We're going to be working for her the next few days."

"Bueno," Angel chuckled. "Maybe I teach her some new words."

"Maybe I teach you some manners," she answered.

I could see it was going to be a fine trip back to D.C. Apparently there's no honor among grave robbers either.

Chapter Eleven

Grave robbery is better left to dark and foggy nights. There's something about cruising up Arlington's Memorial Drive on a sunny winter afternoon in a rented Ford, followed by a borrowed hearse and a flat-bed truck groaning under the weight of a yellow backhoe that's shamefully unromantic, lacking the proper gothic gloom of grave digging. Even worse, everyone seemed in high spirits. Olivia particularly. One last chance to see Daddy, perhaps.

I was terrified. We'd made it through the gate with our phony exhumation order. Olivia had signed the necessary paperwork as a family representative but it only took one insightful question, one curious mind, and we were finished, undone by the foolhardy overconfidence that always precedes disaster. People forget that Noah was the only guy in the whole world who built a boat. Nobody else believed it was going to rain.

"You're looking a little peaked," Olivia said. We were in the back seat of the rental. Angel was driving.

"This is Arlington National Cemetery," I said. "The most hallowed ground in America. What we're doing needs doing. For your family, national security even, but I served two tours in Vietnam you know, and I just can't feel good about sneaking in, even if it's through the front door."

"What was a Dominican doing in Vietnam?"

"Keeping his head down."

"Seriously, it wasn't your war."

"Technically, I'm a U.S. Citizen. Born in Miami."

"So you got drafted?"

"Volunteered."

"Men are hard to understand sometimes."

"Point is, this is hallowed ground to me too, and it's making me very nervous."

"Hey Primo, calm the hell down, man. Hombre, this is nothing. I thought you were going to make us do it at night," Angel said. "The Haitians, man, they got this guy Baron Samedi, you hearda him? Wears tall black hat, black clothes, one of those capes, carries a cane and walks the graveyards at night to find some fresh meat. Tall, thin, black guy."

"Angel."

"Don't Angel me, man. I had this Haitian chick, I mean like we were in bed this one night, afterwards you know, she's telling me about this Baron Samedi who hangs in cemeteries at night, connects you with the spirit world, you know. Dead voodoo spirit guy. But maybe he's hungry and eats your head, man. But this chick is telling me about how one time she seen this Samedi. They stop to rest by a cemetery on the way to some town, Porta Pox I think she said, and this is the middle of the afternoon. Hot. They got some beer getting warm and the cheese is melting in their sandwiches, she says, or they never would've stopped by a cemetery. You know those voodoo peoples is pretty suspicious. So this chica says they don't want to go inside the gate, you know, but it has a big tree with shade so they do it anyhow. Half way through lunch this Baron Samedi comes strolling through the graveyard all in black, smoking a big cigar and wearing wrap-around sunglasses. Throws his head back and laughs 'Ha, Ha, Ha.' Man, they're gone. She swore to God, man, she wasn't makin' it up."

"Angel," I said. "First, it's not Porta Pox, it's Port-de-Paix. Second, Baron Samedi has never dined on anyone's head that I know of, since he doesn't exist. He's like sasquatch."

"I don't know this sasquatch but the worse thing ever happened to you man, is you went up there to that Minnesota and got all messed up with those Lutherans at that college you were at." Angel slapped the steering wheel. "Where is this Porter Drive? No kidding, Primo. Too much education, reading from books, what does that teach you about life, man? One night with this Haitian chick, I know more about Haiti than all those Swedes up there teaching you some kind of mashed potatoes stuff from books, man."

"I agree with Angel," Olivia said suddenly.

"Who asked you?" I said. "First of all, last night you couldn't stand him, and second, shouldn't you be the one person here showing a little decorum?"

"'First of all, second of all,'" Angel mimicked. "Calm down professor. You see Porter Drive? I have to turn left, then right. Or the other way around or somesing. Watch for it. This place is too big, man."

Olivia and I had just been here for Quist's funeral but it all seemed different today. "Pull over," I said. "We'll let the grave digger lead."

Nacon Brown owned one of several excavating firms that contracted with the Army to prepare gravesites. They alone were authorized to dig and we had been forced to hire one of them if we wanted the work done. Nacon was the only black contractor and had held the job for less than a year. This was his first exhumation but he knew the cemetery well and up to now had said little about the task at hand.

Angel stopped and I went back to his truck. "Mr. Brown," I said. "Do you know the way? We seem to be confused."

"Tole that boy you got drivin' I should lead. Couldn't find his ass with both hands. New York! Ain't never been up there. Don't want to. First we put 'em down under, now we diggin' 'em up. Lotta unnecessary disturbance of the dead, you want my opinion."

"I agree," I said. "No choice this time. We appreciate you coming out on such short notice. Really. It's a service to your country, helping discover what caused the Ambassador's death. Important to the family too."

He'd seen Olivia. Today she wore black. He seemed to like her and called her *missy*. "I reckon," he said. "We got to cover everything real nice while you got the gentlemen off to the doctor there like I tole you, then put it all back like it was when y'all is back again. They done this sometimes before, but the administration, they want it all according to the book, you know? We got funerals goin' on here pretty much all the time and horses and caissons too. This ain't no potters field you got here. This is the Arlington National Cemetery. Everything by the rules. That's why we're here late. Funerals is done for the day."

"Yes Sir," I said.

"Y'all follow me then. Tell that fella in the hearse too." He cranked the window back up.

I walked to the hearse and told the driver, a pasty-faced boy of about twenty, to stick with Nacon, who had already swung around our little motorcade to take the lead.

We arrived at the gravesite within minutes.

Some sort of artificial sod was laid across Adam Quist's grave and the sight of it caused Olivia to weep. She hadn't shed a tear at the funeral. Now she broke down and we stood alongside Nacon Brown's yellow backhoe, staring at our feet. The sobbing unnerved us and Nacon hesitated to start the machine's loud engine and begin the digging. This truly is hallowed ground, I thought, even the second time around it yields its dead only with sorrow. If it was genuine. I never knew with Olivia.

The fresh Vietnam dead were scattered around us. I'd been here six years earlier to watch a close friend tucked into this same ground. I avoided his grave the way I'd avoided nearly any thought of him over the years. Those were times to snub honor, vilify war, and warriors too. How could I come to grips with his death while the country he served despaired of itself? First in war then in Watergate. There were times when I thought Norteamericanos the most foolish people who ever gathered to form a nation.

I lifted my head and gazed across the field. Olivia's sobs were fading to sniffles. There was no end to the tombstones. It was a noble foolishness then, I suppose. Who knows, in the end maybe it's only those people willing to die in large numbers who can be great. I'd been willing and it was only half my country. It seemed split now and me along with it.

"I am sorry," Olivia said, regaining control. "Go ahead. Bring him up." I looked closely at her then. Her face was mottled and contorted but her eyes were dry and clear. I turned away to hide my astonishment.

Angel and I removed the sod rug and Nacon started his machine. I saw from the beginning he was the right man for the job. The narrow bucket moved in sweeping fluid motions, entering the earth straight, removing no more dirt than necessary before returning. He built a neat pile to the right. His hole was long and narrow. By the time I'd finished folding the sod rug he cut the engine.

"Mr. EJ," he said. "Give me a hand." Nacon, not a small man, stepped down gingerly into the bucket which he'd left suspended in the hole. "The broom there."

I handed it to him and he dropped into the bottom and began

sweeping. "Doesn't look all that deep," I commented.

"This here's the crypt. Your cement vault. Casket's inside. We'll get her nice and clean on top so no dirt gets in when I lift the lid."

We lined the grave rim as he worked. An industrious man, the broom moved quickly in even strokes until the concrete lid was visible, then clean. It was a new vault without chips or any telltale marks on it.

"Heavy," I said, wondering how he planned to lift the concrete cover.

"See the wire cables there on the ground? Drop them down to me."

He quickly attached them to the lid through steel eyes set two on a side near the ends, then looped the cables over the bucket and climbed from the hole. We stepped back. "Where will you put it?" I asked.

"To the left. Then we strap the coffin and bring it out and set it on the lid. We're the pallbearers. All to be done proper."

The lid came out easily once Nacon lifted the bucket. He repeated the process more slowly after strapping slings under the casket. When the machine was silent again I moved over to the casket and asked Olivia if she wanted to wait in the car while we looked inside.

Nacon placed a large hand on my shoulder. "We don't be openin' no lid here," he said. "That ain't proper. I got a flag for the top and then the coffin goes in the hearse. You take it where you got to, but we ain't goin' to be opening no coffin out here in the weather like that. No sir."

"I'm sorry," I said.

Nacon lined us up, two on a side - Olivia and I, Angel and the hearse driver - spread the flag over the coffin and nodded, picking up the end. We marched solemnly to the back of the hearse and slid Ambassador Adam Quist inside. It struck me then that I'd seen him moved twice before and now was doing it myself a third time, after digging him up. I suddenly felt ashamed.

Nacon went back to his machinery and I hopped inside alongside the coffin to begin working on the lid. I had no intention of waiting.

Opening the lid of a coffin isn't quite the Hollywood "push" and "click." In fact, it was locked tight and sealed. There was a button about half way back and alongside it a hex fitting. I tried a screw driver from the tool box on that. No luck. I called Angel and he tried to pick it. We worked quickly and in whispers to keep Nacon from becoming suspicious. Olivia had gone back to the car.

"I can't open this!" Angel cried in frustration. "Why do they make it like this? What do they think, persons want to steal the dead?"

"Angel. Think about it. What are we doing?"

"Okay, okay. Know what I'm thinking? We got to get this thing someplace where we gots tools, man."

"I'm thinking the longer this takes the more likely Nacon sees us. Find a tire iron. Something strong I can pry the lid with."

The coffin was highly polished walnut. Had it been metal I'm not sure even the tire iron would've worked. As it was, we made a mess, splintering the wood around the lock and leaving deep gouges along the seal. Olivia showed up at the back door of the hearse just as I popped the lid.

"My God!" she said. "What are you doing?"

"No key," I explained.

"Why couldn't you wait until we got to the pathologist?"

I swung the lid up and peered inside. "We're not going to the pathologist."

Olivia scrambled inside on all fours, shoving Angel against the curtained window to see for herself. "I don't believe it," she said, crawling now onto the top of the lower lid, skirt hiked up almost to the tops of her thighs.

"Just what in hell we got goin' on here?" Nacon shouted through the back door. "Missy! Get on down off that coffin there. What's the matter with you people? Some kind of freaks? Goin' after dead folks?"

"Nothing like that," I told him, almost laughing.

"What you think? I'm some kind of fool? I heard about body snatchers. Damn hippies! You there girl, this really your daddy?"

"Yes," she said. "Please come inside and look."

"No thank you!"

I slid out to stand beside him. "Better do as she says. It's important."

Nacon looked like he wished he was the one holding the tire iron, but climbed in and crawled slowly forward. I watched as he cautiously lifted his head high enough to see inside the casket. "Shit," he said.

"Frightening, isn't it?" I said.

Nacon gripped the lower portion of the coffin lid and pulled it up. Beneath were four sandbags laid carefully in a row. The sand, wet when it was shoveled into the bags, had seeped onto the fine silk bedding like tan blood. "This ain't legal," Nacon announced.

"Take a good look," I told him. "Remember what you see. Later, there's a good chance someone will ask you about it under oath."

Nacon nodded, then patted the material around the sand bags to be sure the body wasn't hidden beneath. "I don't like this crazy business," he complained. "Don't want no more exhumations. No sir. Once they're put down, don't pay to disturb 'em. What you want me to do now with this here empty coffin?"

"Bury it," I said.

Nacon approved this idea and we lugged the coffin back to the crypt lid. No flag this time and we handled it more carelessly. No longer deserving of our respect. Poor Quist, I thought. Was he dead? Alive somewhere? Cremated maybe?

Nacon slid the straps beneath the box, climbed back onto the backhoe and swung Quist's coffin back into the crypt. I attached the cables for the cement lid and that too was replaced. Twenty minutes later the hole was filled, the backhoe loaded onto the truck. I watched Olivia Quist and Angel Espinosa spreading fake sod across a mound of black dirt hiding the unoccupied grave of a missing United States Ambassador who was once thought to have died of a heart attack.

I walked over to Olivia. "Give us a minute, Angel. Please."

He moved away.

"Olivia," I took her hands. "Did you have a private viewing, before the wake or funeral?"

"Yes. Didn't I tell you? I touched Daddy and he was hard, like wax."

"You never saw him again?"

"No."

"The casket was closed at the funeral itself?"

"Yes."

"But you saw him, touched him, here in DC only hours before he was buried?"

"Yes."

Her answers so pat, so perfect, so preposterous. "I can't understand it," I said, simply. "Somebody has to know how he's in a coffin one minute and gone the next, and I don't." Worse, I didn't even think it was possible. Not without a great deal of planning and bribe money. "Can you drive back to New York with Angel? I'm going to call Mr. Yancy and see what comes next."

"Okay. When will I see you?"

"Tomorrow. I'll call the apartment from here or New York. I need some time to think."

A small flock of sparrows scattered overhead. Somewhere in the distance I heard a flag pole chain clinking in the breeze. Nacon Brown stood beside his large dark truck staring absently at the impressions his backhoe tires had left in the rich Arlington grass. I walked over to join him. "I've got your name, phone and everything," I said. "Maybe I shouldn't mention this. Don't mean to scare you. There's been some trouble since I've started looking into this. So far it's just against me, but keep your eyes open, okay? Don't wander down any dark alleys for a few days. Nobody but those present here today know what you saw. Somebody might not want you to remember."

For the first time I saw Nacon Brown smile. "You may not be trying to scare me but you're doin' a fine job of it," he said. "Seen this was a funny business from the start. Figure you to be all right though, Mr. EJ. Truth is, I'll be awful glad when you get back to that island you come from. Awful glad. Don't worry about me. Once you're gone, Old Nacon Brown be just fine."

"If I have my way you'll be right back here digging him up again," I said.

"Well," Nacon responded. "If he climbs back in there meanwhile, I'll be sure and let you know." He chuckled and stuck out a large, callused hand.

"Thanks," I said. "Next time I'll buy you a beer."

"Don't drink beer," he said. "Like coffee though. You like coffee?"

"Stronger the better."

Nacon climbed aboard the truck and rolled the window down. "Find your way out?"

"No problem."

The diesel coughed black smoke and the heavy equipment was soon lost among the hills, crosses, and bare branches. "Let's get out of here," I said. Now I did know something that could get me killed.

* * *

Garrett Yancy was sympathetic on the telephone. I called him from the airport, his voice was clear and he sounded stronger. Dominican telephone service is excellent. All the operators speak English and the equipment is new, owned by Canadians. "Mind boggling Mr. Espinosa-Jones. Absolutely mind boggling."

"Yes," I said. "Now what?"

"Keep your mouth shut," he advised.

"You're kidding? The coffin's empty. Anyone can see that. All I need now is the proper authority to take a look and we can get official help."

"Really?" he said. "So you had proper, official documents for your exhumation, is that correct? What will law enforcement say to the truth? Not to mention the Army? That's federal ground. You're a US citizen. Have you visited Kansas? Little facility there near Leavenworth? No. Say nothing to the authorities. They're likely to think you and your little band of grave robbers took the Ambassador."

"What should I do then?"

"Two things. Gather the Quists and speak to them. Forcefully! Then come home while you still can. The answer is here."

"The Quists?"

"They deserve the truth. Tell it. See what seeds it plants. Let them order a legitimate exhumation if they wish." The intake of Mr. Yancy's breath was clearly audible. "And if one of them is involved, your visit may force some response."

"Like a .45 caliber round to the forehead."

"Please," he said. "Be careful." This started a coughing jag. "Wrap things up there quickly. I'll have you on the night shuttle to New York in a couple hours. Talk to the Quists tomorrow and be home here by six. I'll make the arrangements."

"It's your money." My hide, I wanted to say. Dulce and Alejandro might still be lurking somewhere nearby.

"Will you go back to Washington Heights?"

"No. I've involved my family enough. I'll go to the Soldiers, Sailors, Marines and Airman's Club on Lexington Avenue. Midtown. I'm going to disappear. Club's safe and I'll be anonymous. Stayed there often in the 60s when I was at the naval base in Bainbridge, Maryland."

"Suit yourself," he said. "Doesn't sound particularly comfortable. I'm more than willing to authorize a hotel."

"Bunk beds and communal baths," I said. "Couple bucks a night, but I'll sleep better there than at the best hotel."

"Our client will appreciate the savings, I'm sure," Mr. Yancy said.

"Olivia, you mean. Don't worry. She told me. She paid cash for the grave digging operation."

"Pardon me?"

"No reason to pretend," I said rather crossly. "She confessed that she's your client. Should've been obvious I suppose. I just didn't think of it. Her age, no doubt."

"I have no idea what you're talking about. Olivia Quist is most certainly *not* our client."

"But she told me."

"I don't care what she told you. She spoke to me about the case as I said. Her involvement goes no farther. Are you telling me she paid to have her father exhumed?"

"Sí, Mr. Yancy. Sí. And it wasn't cheap. Is the identity of our client secret then?"

There was a long pause before he answered. "Yes. The client is not to be identified. We've worked that way before. Is it a problem for you?"

"Yes. It's a problem. It leaves a mountain of unanswered questions."

Again the pause. "I promise you," he said. "This client's identity could not possibly relate to your investigation in any manner."

"Why can't you tell me then?"

"Perhaps one day I will. Is there anything else?"

"Just one thing, and I'm not sure how to ask you but, how did Olivia tell you this suspicion of hers to begin with? I mean, I know she found her father dead there, but why didn't she just believe the doctor like everybody else? Why was she so suspicious of foul play? There was no evidence of it."

Mr. Yancy wheezed and said, "I don't know. It never came up."

I hate talking about anything important on the telephone. I need all my senses and at that moment I wanted to see my old travel agent. "Help me a little here. Please Mr. Yancy."

"Truly," he said. "That's all I know."

What could I say? "Angel is right," I told him. "I should get a black car, make some money, and get some piece of ass."

"Excuse me?"

"Never mind. When can I get back to New York?"

"Where are you?"

"National Airport."

"Have yourself a nice dinner. Put it on the bill. Drop by the American Express office in an hour or so. A ticket will be waiting."

"Fine," I said, anxious to get off somewhere and think.

"EJ."

"Yes."

"Maybe it's as dangerous for you there as here. Watch yourself."

"Yeah."

"Good day." He hung up.

How can an airport give you the creeps? I flagged a cab and drove into one of the black neighborhoods near the Capital. Even with the unrest there, the anger and bitterness, I felt safe among darker faces and dingier cafes. It turned out the food was better too.

Why, I wondered over my catfish, did Olivia pay for the exhumation when she was not Yancy's client? I saw only two possibilites. She knew what we would find or she didn't. If she didn't, it made sense. If she did, it made a very different kind of sense. Either way, by the time I got to New York I thought she better have some answers. And a very good reason why she lied to me.

* * *

The Soldiers, Sailors, Marines and Airman's Club in Manhattan is three steps down from Lexington Avenue and the front door is forged steel and thick, glazed glass behind more steel bars. I love it. Between wars they had space available without a reservation and even gave me a private room on the third floor. It overlooked Lexington and the bathroom was close by.

The Club's been around since 1919, a refuge for servicemen in Manhattan ever since. An aging, 19th Century brownstone with a ballroom on the second floor, live combos on Friday and Saturday nights, dancing, nice girls invited in from Queens and nervous young men far from home. A library with pool table on the ground floor. Lamps with fringed shades. Heavy drapes. Fireplaces. A little tacky like your grandmother's parlor and just as reassuring. The last place anyone would look for me.

The window ledge in my room was large enough for two people but I sat alone with a cigarette and disturbing thoughts of Olivia. Why had she lied? Why had she paid? What other lies had yet to be uncovered? Delbrick? Could that be a lie? The whole thing - her discovery of the body, her feeling for me, blasé attitude toward family and her father in particular. All lies?

The radiator said something and dripped rusty water into an old coffee can but kept the room warm and cozy. I rested my head back against the window frame and glanced out at the traffic three stories below. Yellow cabs and boxy cars. The comforting flow of Nueva York. Except for Dulce Baez standing across the street staring up at the building. She was dressed in fur, probably muskrat or some other rodent, and my first thought was to wonder where on earth she found a coat that short and wide. Could I be hallucinating? Losing my mind?

A limousine waited at the curb. I assumed she'd just gotten out of it. The door opened again and Delbrick slid to the sidewalk and stood beside her. Alejandro was probably driving, I thought, toying with his .45.

The Club had a phone booth on the second floor. No phones in the rooms. I'd told no one but Mr. Yancy I was coming here, not even Olivia. When I'd called her earlier to arrange a family meeting, I'd explained it was better if she didn't know where I was, just in case. I took the train in from the airport so even Angel didn't know. Nobody knew, except the people trying to kill me. They knew. So if I got to the phone, who would I call? Not the police. Angel wouldn't have time to get here and what could he do if he did? I was on my own.

In a crisis, our first instinct is to get help. That's often our undoing. I thought again of Audie Murphy and what made him a hero. The cold day in January 1945 when he faced six German tanks and 250 infantrymen. Murphy ordered his men to fall back but he stayed to call in artillery, then climbed onto a burning vehicle and using its machine gun, did battle alone with the advancing army. They attacked him on three sides. He killed fifty of them before they hesitated and with his men he counter attacked. The Germans were driven from France. They gave him the Medal of Honor. He became a movie star and made more than forty films. A crazy American story. But that wasn't the point. When the war ended Audie Murphy was twenty years old and understood what it took to succeed - action.

I packed my few belongings, slung the bag across my shoulder and started down the stairs. Where were Johnson and his friend? Waiting out back? Three out front and two out back. Poor odds if you're in retreat, I thought.

At the front desk I handed my key to the same thin man who'd checked me in. "Goodbye," I said. "Change in plans."

I hauled back on the door and jogged up to street level. Dulce's eyes were bugging out and I saw her poke Delbrick, who stepped behind the car to hide himself.

Traffic swept north. I dashed across the street when it broke and arrived directly behind the limo. Dulce stood transfixed. I closed the distance and with my fist balled tight, I threw all my weight into a punch that caught her square in the nose. I felt it collapse and heard the crunching sound of breaking cartilage. The force sent her sprawling onto her large behind and I turned my attention to Delbrick who'd swung to face me. "You're nothing but a pinhead," I shouted in his face and hurried off up 37th Street.

I don't suppose Audie Murphy would've been impressed by this pathetic attempt at heroism, but I felt pretty good. Except for my knuckles. They were skinned. The pain seemed minor compared to the satisfaction I felt at the collapse of Dulce's nose and the shocked expression on Pinhead's face. I'm sure no one dared talk to him in that manner.

I slipped into the city library and read for three hours until my appointment with the Quists at a small diner named Solaz. Olivia had arranged the meeting and told me by phone earlier that her mother was now anxious to see me.

Solaz (French for Solace) seemed more utilitarian than chic. Not the kind of place you'd expect to find rich people. Maybe that's why they went there. A long, narrow cafe with a lunch counter to the right and small tables on the opposite wall. The grill and a tiny kitchen behind the counter, main dining area in back.

I stood just inside the door searching for the Quists - Olivia, her mother, brother and sister. To my right, the man behind the counter was Latino. I addressed him in Spanish. "A group of three women and one man. You've seen them?"

"Sí," he said. "You are Espinosa-Jones?"

"Sí."

"The private room. All the way back, around the bathrooms."

"Gracias," I said, starting back, then paused. "You're Puerto Rican?"

"Sí," he admitted. "You?"

"North American." I said in English.

He stared a second and smiled. "Sí, Señor. I'm at your service." There are almost as many Puerto Ricans in New York as Dominicans.

The Quists were sitting in a circle at a table near the center of the private room. They stopped talking and looked up as I entered. No one greeted me until I was almost on top of them, then Olivia said, "We saved you a chair."

About the size of a single car garage, the room was empty except for us and the tables, chairs up on their front legs, leaning. "Got the whole place to yourself," I said, sitting.

"Yes," Olivia's mother answered. "We're rather well-known here you might say." I don't know what I expected of her close up. Maybe some sort of decayed drunkard with baggy eyes and spider veins. She was about my mother's age and actually quite attractive; collar-length auburn hair, green eyes above high cheeks, broad shoulders. Her voice was sugary and she spoke as if we'd known each other some time. I found her charming and wondered why her daughter seemed unable to get past anything but her alcoholism, if that hadn't been exaggerated. They were drinking coffee except for Olivia who had Coke in a bottle.

"My name is EJ," I said.

"Margaret," she said. "Olivia you know. This is David and Sarah." She pointed them out. They nodded politely. "Olivia has filled us in on much of what's happened and Mr. Yancy's concern about foul play in Adam's death. I've called the mortuary in Washington that prepared his body and they've assured me he was in the coffin when they locked it just prior to the funeral. They admitted Adam was left unattended for a period of time, maybe half an hour or so, when we were in the private chapel with the minister." She spoke directly to me and smiled slightly when she paused. "He was alone there before being taken into the sanctuary. I can only assume that was when he was...abducted, taken, whatever you call that."

"The lock was no easy matter," I told her.

"So we heard." She seemed very matter-of-fact and unemotional, as Olivia had been until the exhumation. "Do you think a half hour is enough time?"

"Not for me," I said. "Maybe they had some sort of skeleton key. Sorry I damaged the coffin."

She nodded. "It's we who owe you a debt, EJ. Thank you for your persistence. Our only problem is what to do now."

"Report everything to the police," I said. "Won't do me much good and I'm going to ask you to wait until I'm out of the country tomorrow, but it's the only sensible thing to do. I'm not one bit closer to discovering who killed your husband today than I was the first day. I'm sorry. There was no autopsy. No physical evidence he's even dead, except the doctor who pronounced him, your testimony and the undertakers who embalmed him, I suppose."

They were glancing back and forth.

"He wasn't embalmed, I'm afraid," Margaret said.

"You just told me....what did you just tell me?"

"The Mortuary received the body from the military and the paperwork carried from Santo Domingo said he was embalmed there and fully prepared for burial." She shrugged. "There was a great deal of....what should I call them?....logistical difficulties in making all the funeral arrangements with Arlington, a private mortuary, the clergy, the military, State Department, family, planes and hearses. It just got lost in the shuffle. I found out by accident. They sent a stack of things to be signed and I saw the transportation paperwork and knew it wasn't right because I hadn't authorized anything in Santo Domingo. No autopsy. No embalming. Everything to be done here."

So there it was, staring me in the face. How convenient that this so-called body was examined by the family doctor who saw what he expected to see. How advantageous there was no autopsy to confirm the cause of death or even verify a death occurred. And now. Now, the body hadn't even been embalmed. But, of course, there was no body anyway, was there? And if it had been embalmed it wouldn't have done us any good to dig it up.

While these thoughts flashed through my mind the Quists waited patiently, discussing their intention to order toasted bagels.

"I think your husband is a zombie," I told Mrs. Quist.

It was a conversation stopper. The room became quiet as if a wind had stopped. Olivia focused on a small napkin and began ripping it into tiny strips. I listened to the grill hood motor beyond the wall. It caused a minor vibration inside the room.

"We've only just met," Margaret Quist addressed me. "I'm sure you aren't making statements like that lightly, or to be insolent."

My hand was swollen and began to throb.

Olivia's brother and sister eyed each other covertly and the brother raised his brows and did the finger tap to the temple. I ignored it and spoke again to Mrs. Quist. "I know how crazy it sounds coming from me, but if you heard it from someone like Dr. Charles Mercer from Harvard, now at Columbia, it might not sound so outrageous. Want to hear it from him, you can. I'll give you his number. Walk down there. It isn't far. He's going to write a book about zombies."

"I don't think he's from the Harvard that's in Massachusetts." This was David Quist's first verbal contribution to the discussion. He had a high, thin voice. "I'm quite certain I've never heard of the great zombie research project there. I attend Harvard."

"Well," I said, "hopefully you'll attend it long enough to get an open mind."

"Boys," cautioned Margaret Quist.

"Sorry," I said. "I'm not on a crusade to prove there are zombies and I didn't come to the conclusion easily. I did the research. There is a Haitian component to this. Zombification is one possibility."

"Well, that's somewhat better stated," she said. "We won't rule it out then. However, since to my knowledge, it would also be the first time in recorded human history to have happened, we shall not embrace it either. Do you find that fair, EJ?"

She had a quick mind for a drunk. "Fine," I said.

"Please understand, this is quite a mess for us now," she explained. "I will do as you ask and call the police. I will report it to the State Department and to Arlington. I will insist that Adam's body....his coffin....be exhumed. But you see, without any evidence that he's dead his death certificate may be invalid. We may be locked into a kind of international limbo for years trying to sort out his insurance, bank accounts, the will, and all of that. Right now I have one child, closed minded as he is, in college. I have to pay the tuition bills. I have another daughter about ready to start if she ever picks the one she wants. Sarah is about to marry and I've various bits of real estate, an apartment here in New York, automobiles, credit cards.... Get the picture? If this mystery of Adam's death or whereabouts isn't solved quickly, our family will be greatly affected."

"I understand," I said.

"We started with a naturally dead man and legitimate death certificate just a few days ago," she went on. "Now you come with stories about missing bodies and zombies. You see?"

"Why don't you order those toasted bagels," I said. "You need to listen to me for a couple minutes. I've done you a lot more good than you know. Go ahead, order. I'll have one too."

Margaret nodded to David and he headed reluctantly for the door. She swung my direction again and smiled. "Olivia speaks very highly of you," she said. "She's young but I've always known her to be a good judge of character. Makes quite a study of people sometimes. You're some kind of a diver too, I understand. Deep sea, I think she said?"

"Scuba."

"This detective work is a natural for you then. Zombies and all. I'm sure you're quite adventuresome."

"I know what you're thinking, Mrs. Quist. But let me tell you, if my adventures included zombies....well, it's simply too fantastic to believe. I wasn't kidding when I said I didn't come to these conclusions easily."

"You believe there are zombies?"

"Dr. Mercer does. Believes he's proved it."

She drummed her well-manicured fingers on the Formica and studied them. Finally she said, "Very well."

Several moments later David returned and said the bagels would be out soon. He resumed his seat and slouched.

"I didn't ask you to meet me so we could argue. I'm really on your side." I smiled at Olivia. "This isn't a game to me. Zombies aside, we need to examine the facts. Your husband, Mrs. Quist, is not buried at Arlington National Cemetery. No one knows what he died from - not for certain. No one knows if he's dead at all. Dr. Mercer has the death certificates of Haitians who died and are not dead. Doctors pronounced them dead. They were actually buried and later seen alive by hundreds of people. Maybe that happened to the Ambassador, maybe not. The point is, we don't know."

"So, what are you suggesting?" Margaret asked.

"Did you know that the DCM in Santo Domingo, Duane Delbrick, is associating with two of your servants from The Residence who attempted to poison me and a lieutenant from the Policía Nacional?" I made no mention of Pinhead's other family association. "That they followed me to Washington and tried to shoot me at the airport? Did you know that a cab driver Olivia and I used in Port-au-Prince is here in New York where he chased my cousin and I?" I slid my damaged right hand toward the center of the table. "This is the result of a fight with Dulce Baez and Delbrick not three hours ago on Lexington

Avenue. You're right to see me as a thorn in your side, but I haven't done myself much good either."

All four of them stared at my hand, which had previously been under the table. Olivia reached across and gently stroked the swollen fingers. "I'm sorry," she said.

"How can we help?" Margaret asked.

"Push for a full investigation. Pressure the State Department to deal with Delbrick. Swear out a complaint against the Baez couple. I need them off my back. You don't have to say you believe in zombies but if you don't legitimize this investigation, it's going to end without a resolution. You may be in limbo, as you put it, not for years, but forever."

"That simply won't do," she said. "I'll do my best. Duane will be next to impossible. We'll see."

The bagels arrived then, with coffee, carried by two grinning waiters. They acted as if they were serving royalty. "Come here often?" I asked.

"One of the loose ends we'll need to tie up," she said. "Adam bought this place eleven years ago. I don't know why. A whim I think."

"Hard to picture him as a businessman," I said.

"Not as hard as it is for me to think of him as a zombie," answered his wife. "Now, EJ. Who do you think is doing this and why?"

I spread butter onto my bagel and watched it soaking into the brown texture of the bread. There was also cream cheese - plain and strawberry - grape jelly and mango chutney. "If I were the police, I'd probably suspect one of you," I said, taking a large bite.

Margaret was beginning to find me slightly amusing, I think. She nodded. David was beginning to hate me. He glared. It was Sarah who spoke. "Do *you* think it's one of us?"

Sarah had her mother's voice and intimate way of speaking. She must be effective at a diplomatic cocktail party, I thought. She was prettier than Olivia, and taller. More controlled. I guessed she was marrying a diplomat.

"When is the wedding?"

"In the spring."

"June?"

"Yes."

"A diplomat?"

"He's in Iran now."

I nodded. "It could be one of you. It could be political. It could be terrorists. It might even be something so bizarre none of you could conceive of it, like your father was somehow mixed up with voodoo and was made a zombie. It could be some or all of those things together. Or maybe it's something completely different."

"A heart attack?"

"I don't rule that out."

"EJ," Margaret said. "How will you turn all this speculation into a solution? Quickly."

"Whatever happened," I said, "happened in Santo Domingo. I'm leaving this afternoon. When will you be back?"

"David and Sarah remain here," Margaret said. "I'll be back on the island to supervise the packing and so forth in a few days. If it's finished by Christmas I'll spend it in New York. If not, then I guess I'll still spend it in New York and go back again and finish up. Won't be easy now without Dulce and Alejandro. Olivia will come with me."

"I'll call on you in a week or so. Have you heard anything about a new ambassador?"

"No. Delbrick is familiar with things. They'll keep him on awhile I'm certain."

"Isn't he a Democrat?"

"Democrats are popular again now since Watergate," she said. "Adam was a Nixon appointee, you know. He had money. Or has it, if he's a zombie. Have you considered the money angle EJ? There's quite a chunk involved."

"Quite a chunk?"

"Ten or twelve million dollars I should think," she said. "Plus the real estate. I'm going to inherit all that, plus I have a few million of my own you see. I'm not a detective, but I've known money to be quite a motive - it influences marriages, careers, politics, sex. Maybe it makes zombies too."

"You didn't kill him, did you?"

"No," she smiled. "I didn't like him much but I didn't kill him. If I was going to do that, I'd have done it years ago when I still had my looks to go along with my money."

"I must disagree with you there," I said. "The years have been kind. You're lithe as a palm and the passing years have done little more than warm your skin and stir your hair."

"Please!" David said.

Margaret grinned at Olivia. "You were right. He's more Latino than American."

We all smiled at each other, sort of. Olivia's face had gone slack and her eyes had the glazed look of the voodoo dancer. Then she smiled too. I shivered. There was a draft along the floor when the door opened up front. Time to go home, I thought, where there was sunshine, warmth, music, and the safety of familiarity.

Chapter Twelve

Dominicana Airlines suffered from an ambiguous safety record and high expectations as a source of Dominican pride in the air, representing the nation as its flag carrier. Passengers applauded successful take-offs and landings, but the food was good, service even better, and drinks were free. When the recycled 727 banked on its final approach to Aeropuerto Las Americas, we tried not to care that everyone onboard believed we had about the same odds of landing on the runway as the water.

Half the passengers were drunk, as usual. Wheels screeched on the asphalt, the nose settled, engines roared and a cheer went up. From the window seat I'd been watching the city as we circled out over the Caribbean to land thirty-five kilometers east. It's a bright city at night and forms a jeweled crescent, hugging the black sea.

I cleared customs and grabbed a cab for home. Away from the airport lights, the sea was an invisible dark presence. In daylight, the drive into Santo Domingo was perhaps one of the most lovely in the Caribbean. Mile after mile of park on President Balaguer's new concrete four-lane highway, winding along the coastline and offering vistas of the sea that were usually seen only in travel brochures. No condos, hotels or McDonalds, just a small army of gardeners working to maintain the stone walkways, benches, and flower beds. In the heat of the day you'd spot one high in a coco dropping fruit to a fellow worker. A setting in deep contrast to the poverty and dirt encountered the moment you crossed the Ozama and entered the city. A contrast most North Americans found appalling.

This arrogance irked me. The Dominican poor weren't starving as in Haiti, nor are measures of wealth universal. Not everyone wants shag carpeting. If I learned anything during my years in the

States it was that Americans had forgotten or perverted their own dream, substituting financial gain for liberty and defining wealth as freedom. How could they forget that their men at Valley Forge were as barefoot and ragged as any Dominican campesino? They struggled for generations to achieve wealth, then pitied the rest of the world, boasting they were the greatest nation on earth. I always felt such conceit could only lead to shame.

It's the smell mostly that makes Santo Domingo home. Not the fresh smell of a Minnesota pine forest or crisp winter night. Not a pleasant smell even, but the smell of people; their food cooking, their garbage and waste. Rotten and ripe. Inhaling it from a taxi window renewed my appetite for living. For the first time in days, I felt comfortably tired, the salty ocean air tangible on my skin.

We were almost to Luperon when I told the driver, "Pull up here a second." I jumped out and bought four pieces of pan de agua and two cold Presidente for us.

When I climbed back into the cab he asked, "How long have you been away?"

"Few days."

He didn't laugh. "Sí," he said. "Coming home is always the same."

The cerveza was packaged in those brown paper sacks common to alcoholic beverages, a necessity in the tropics. I swung one leg up on the seat and wedged my back into the corner by the door. I've always liked to drink and drive. I lit a cigarette and watched Christmas stars and angels glittering in the night, attached to the simple homes and tenements of the urban poor.

Johnny "El Caballo" Ventura was on the radio singing his new politically motivated merengue *El Tabaco Es Fuerte Pero Hay Que Fumarlo* (The Tobacco Is Strong But You Have To Smoke It) and the spicy smells of pollo chicharrones drifted up from the smoking cafe grills along the Malecón. When I got home, I decided, I'd have Carmen mix me a martini and I'd sit on the balcony awhile, let the balmy night air ease the tension of the past few days, along with the still persistent pain in my swollen right hand, then a snack and off to bed. Carmen always had something in the fridge, even if she didn't know when to expect me.

"How's the weather in Nueva York?" asked the cabby.

"Cold," I said. I hadn't told him I was in New York, but if you were gone from Santo Domingo, you were in New York.

"Sí," he agreed. "My brother lives there. Too hot in summer, too cold in winter."

When we finally pulled around the corner and onto my street, Calle Cabral, dreams of martinis and bed evaporated. Calle Cabral is the oddest street in town. It's four lanes wide, with a large grass median, and it's a dead end two blocks long. I'd always guessed some general or politician lived there once, maybe even in my penthouse, and had the street specially built. Good thing too, because now it was clogged with parked cars, all from the people attending the party in my apartment.

"Oh," the driver said. "Someone is having a fiesta."

"En casa."

"Your family, welcoming you home."

"I live alone."

"Well," he said. "Perhaps it's not your liquor."

"It's my liquor, my food, and it will go on until dawn. It's my sisters. They've done this before."

"These things happen."

"They're from the country," I explained, but didn't understand, since hadn't we just survived a serious fire and potential threat to the family?

"You don't need to explain to me," he said. "I have nine sisters."

"I have four. It seems like nine." They got by with this because Carmen was scared of them. Individually, she held her own, but when all four came together, Carmen simply did whatever they told her to do. A decision I often made myself.

I paid the driver and started up the stairs. Mercedes Villacampa reached out of the darkness and clutched my arm. "You are having a party," she told me.

"Just got home." I showed her my bag.

"Young people nowadays have too many parties. They don't know what it is to be serious." She had over-powdered her face and wore a hair net.

I pried her strong old fingers from my arm. "I just got home. I didn't know there was a party."

"If there is trouble," she said, "I will be forced to disturb the Doctor." This threat she delivered with an evil grin.

"Frightening," I said. "I'll make sure there's no trouble."

"Good," she said. "Very good." She slipped back into the darkness.

On the third floor landing two young people were necking like hungry animals. "Excuse me," I said. They continued unabated and

I had to swing my bag out over the railing to squeeze around them. The dance music above stopped for a second, then began again. It's live, I thought. They have a band in my apartment.

I went up the back stairs, entering by the kitchen. There were two uniformed maids and a large sweating cook scurrying about. I'd never seen any of them before. "Where is Carmen?" I asked.

"Who are you?" the cook wanted to know. She had a big bust and wet hands.

"Edgar Espinosa-Jones."

"Hallelujah," she said. "We're saved."

"This is my apartment."

"If it is," she took a closer look at me, "then you're late for your own party."

"Where's Carmen?"

"I don't know," she said. "Find her yourself. I've got to get another tray of shrimp out."

Naturally, none of my sisters would go near a kitchen, so I thought maybe I'd find Carmen and get the story from her before confronting them. From the back balcony I walked along to one of the guest bedrooms and through it to the hallway which led to my room, all without entering the main part of the apartment.

A drunken woman was passed out on the bed in the guest room. Her mouth open. She was white, wearing a long cocktail dress with bold flowers. No one had bothered to take off her sandals or provide a pillow. She looked dead. I bent over to listen for breathing and was rewarded with a sputtering, wet noise from her throat. I jumped back in case she was sick. She gurgled, drooling a small stream of clear liquid down the side of her face onto the new vicuna bed spread, a gift from Sonja.

Unnoticed, I slipped down the hall to my room and started to undress. I didn't want to confront an overcrowded room full of strangers in a rumpled suit and tie. When I got down to my pants, Carmen came through the door. "I've been looking for you," I said. "Should've known all I had to do was take my clothes off."

"Your sisters are having a party."

"No kidding? There's a drunk woman in the room down the hall."

"There are more drunks in the room next to it. All white women who can't hold their liquor."

"Great," I said. "What are you doing in that outfit? Looks like one of those uniforms French maids wear in films."

"Your sisters made me."

"Why? You've never worn a uniform in your life."

"There are important people here, they said."

"What important people? All I've seen so far are over-sexed kids and passed out drunks."

"Have you been in the living room? The veranda? They have a band where the dining room was. Have you looked in the street? Some Mercedes, two Cadillacs, and plenty of Ford LTDs. Generals, politicians, diplomats, and rich people. One schoolteacher."

"Who is working in the kitchen?"

"People your sisters hired."

"I hope they paid them."

"Your sister Claudine said you have very good credit, but now that you are here, I'm sure they will want to be paid cash. The band too. The food and liquor is on your bill at the Supermercado Nacional."

I dropped onto the bed.

Carmen moved closer and ran a hand across my bare shoulder. "You are tense." She spotted the swollen hand. "What happened? I will rub you."

"No. You will not rub me. I bumped my hand. It'll be fine." I glanced up and noticed for the first time that two of the gaps in her mouth were filled. She also had an odd odor. "What happened with your teeth?"

"Your sisters sent me to a dentist. They are false teeth. You have rented them for two days."

"Aren't they yours?"

"This dentist is a woman and has an office on Duarte. She rents teeth."

"Okay," I said. "What's that smell?"

"A new hair product."

"My sisters."

"No. Found it myself when I went to the dentist to rent the teeth. It straightens the hair of black people."

"Smells like urine. Take the scarf off your head at least. Give it some air."

"Thank you," she said. "The scarf is to hide the rollers but I will remove it since you ask so nicely. Will you be coming out to the party when you're done showing off your naked chest?"

"Find one of my sisters and send her back here."

"Which one?"

"Either Diana or Edwina. The other two are hopeless. I can't believe Ed is here, is she?"

"She is dancing with her new boyfriend."

"What new boyfriend?" I jumped from the bed. "Where's Felipe?"

"She can't spend the rest of her life tied to a timid campesino."

"Why do they tell you these things?" I yanked a light blue shirt from my closet. "Wait until my mother finds out!"

"She's on the veranda. Do you want me to send her in too?"

I sat back down on the bed. "By all means," I said. "Send the whole damn pack of them in here."

Carmen grinned unabashed, her rental teeth catching the light, much whiter than her real teeth. I spotted the retaining wires but didn't ask why she'd only rented two teeth, when three were missing. The uniform was tight over her behind, which she wiggled invitingly as she strolled out my bedroom door.

Five minutes later my mother entered with Diana and Ed. All were dressed in floor-length evening gowns. Mother and Edwina both had their hair up, obviously a professional job. Mother's dress was coral pink, Ed's gold with black flecks, and Diana's nearly as green as her eyes. Mother was showing a little cleavage.

"Hi," I said. "All three of you didn't have to come in here."

Mother and Ed kissed me. Diana held off.

"How was New York?" Mother asked.

"Cold."

"We're having a party," she said. "Naturally, we would've asked you if we'd planned it a little more in advance or knew you'd be coming home so soon."

"It would be nice to be asked," I said, working on being polite.

"I explained that."

"I hate flying, you know. I'm tired. My ankles are swollen, I hurt my hand, and what I really wanted was to come home and have a nice quiet drink on the veranda, a light snack, and go to bed." I was trying very hard not to sound peevish - the wounded householder returning unexpectedly to the chaos of his servants and family run amok.

"Oh well," she said. "You'll survive. Your hand does look a little swollen. Come out now and join the party. We'll all weep rivers of tears as you play the reluctant host."

"Mother." I said. "There's hardly cause for sarcasm, since you're the ones barging in here and taking over the place without permission."

"Without permission? I need permission? Do you know how many times I've had to write out a rent check for this place when you were 'a little short' that month? Consider this a landlady's privilege."

It's no good to argue with your mother, and Ed wore a particularly smug look on her face. Only a few days ago she couldn't live without seeing me every day. Diana stood composed as always, probably not even aware we were having a rather tense family moment. "Fine," I said. "I'll be out in a minute. Why did you decide to have a party now anyway, after all that's happened? You do remember the fire?"

"Don't be silly. Anyway, Edwina needs to meet some new people."

"All of a sudden?"

"She broke up with Felipe," Mother explained. "She was feeling a little down, and I was too, after the fire and everything."

"I like Felipe."

"I like him, too," she said. "But it's Edwina who has to like him, not us."

"Well, I don't think we should encourage her to flit from one man to the next like some sort of country butterfly," I asserted. "Felipe has deep feeling for her."

"Be sure and change that shirt before you come out," my mother ordered. "Blue always makes you look anemic and washed out. Try a warmer color. We invited your *friend*, Sonja. In case you're interested."

"Is she here?"

"Not yet. Or else she has laryngitis."

Ed giggled.

"I don't think that's funny," I told her.

She stuck her tongue out and left with Mother. "Very mature," I told her back.

Diana remained. "I like Sonja," she said. "If you get her alone, she's very articulate and sensitive. I think she really feels for people. All that laughing she does, maybe it's from nervousness or the discomfort of being around large groups of people. I'm like that."

Edwina always described Diana as a mystic. She wasn't. Just quiet. I suppose I liked her best, or if not liked her best, was more devoted to her because we shared so many opinions, feelings, even the same sense of beauty. Oddly enough we didn't look related. I favored my father and the Dominican side and she appeared so completely North

American, even her skin was pale.

When Diana was about two or three she fell into a swimming pool at the Country Club and when they fished her out she was wailing - a new party dress ruined, wet hair. Everyone tried to comfort her but she came to me and crawled uninvited onto my lap, where she sat with a towel around her the remainder of the afternoon. I was about twelve then and holding her all that time created a bond between us that lasted, though I don't think we've ever mentioned it.

"I'm glad someone in the family likes Sonja," I said.

"Everyone likes her okay. You know how they are. Looking out for you, I mean."

"I know."

"Did you go to the Ambassador's funeral?"

"Burial."

"Was it very sad?"

"Not really."

"In Arlington?"

"Uh-huh."

"Don't you want to talk about it?"

"Later."

Diana kissed me then, a lingering kiss on the cheek. She moved to my closet and studied the shirts, finally selected a sandy colored guayabera and handed it to me over her shoulder. "This will make Mother happy," she said. "I think you look fine in blue."

"Maybe I'll dance with you later," I said.

"We're all staying here the night you know."

"Guessed as much."

"Everyone's shopping in the morning."

"Surprise, surprise."

"We stayed here last night too. Carmen made us arroz con pollo. It was very spicy. I like the way she cooks but I think she's sort of promiscuous. Men came up and down the back stairs twice that I know of."

"Must've been a slow night," I said.

She hung up the blue shirt. "Take my arm. We'll make our entrance together. You'll know quite a few of the people. The rest, who cares? After you make the rounds you can go out on the veranda just like you planned and I'll bring you a martini myself."

We started for the door. "Is this change in Ed serious?" I asked.

"Carmen says she has a new boyfriend already."

"That medical student from St. Paul, remember? Mother sort of adopted him because he's from there. Minnesota. He's come out to dinner a couple times, practicing his Spanish and getting something to eat besides rice and beans, which I think is all he can afford. Ed's been sort of taken with him. I don't think it's anything. She's just trying her wings, but it's scaring poor Felipe to death."

A five piece band on the veranda played a slow merengue and we wound our way through the crowd holding hands. I wasn't recognized by anyone. Not that there weren't some familiar faces, mostly from news reels and the papers. Carmen was right. I spotted the British Consul. The frugal British had their embassy on Independencia above the Ford tractor garage. I counted four generals. Superintendent Rosco V. Crowell of the exclusive Carol Morgan School was there - he never missed a party. Two 3M executives, the head of ARCO Caribbean, the U.S. Information Officer, minor diplomats, the Dominican who headed U.S. Steel interests, some people from the World Bank, and the Datsun dealer, who was no doubt the wealthiest man in the room.

Reading my mind, Diana said, "Alexis and Claudie made up the guest list. Of course, it was Mother who pulled it off. I think if she invited Balaguer he'd be here. She has such a way with people, don't you think?"

"She's a pain in the ass."

"EJ!"

An overweight British woman with dyed blonde hair holding a cigarette above her head with one hand and a drink with the other, pressed by me and said, "I'm so sorry handsome, but as you can see I just wasn't built for these affairs." She winked. "All this rubbing together is quite nice though, don't you think?"

"Just got here," I said.

She took a long drag from the cigarette, blew it from her nose and moved on. "I'm sure she's terribly important," I told Diana.

"Look," she said. "There's a free chair by the railing, across from the band."

"I want to be on the other side, away from the band."

"Such a baby. Come on then. I'll get the chair."

"I can stand."

She brought it, a rental. Quite a lot of my furniture was missing.

"There," she said, placing it near the railing. "Now sit, enjoy the view and relax just like you planned. There's music and dancing. Cheer up, can't you?"

"I'm sorry."

"I'll get your martini."

"No. Find Carmen."

Before she could turn around, Carmen shuffled toward us through the crowded living room carrying a tray of little sandwiches that had olives stuck to them with cellophane-tipped toothpicks. Carmen had removed the scarf from her head. People moved aside to let her pass, some were horrified, others giggled.

"Can you believe she has rollers in her hair?" Diana said.

I stared.

Carmen did not have rollers.

"You're mistaken," I told Diana as Carmen moved closer. "Those aren't rollers, they're the cardboard things left over after you insert a Tampax."

"My God!" She stared. "Oh no! They're dirty. She must've got them from a wastebasket."

Carmen stopped to give us a sandwich and smiled warmly.

"I'll take two," I said. "Could you make me a martini while you're up?"

"First I have to give out all these little sandwiches."

"No hurry," I said.

Carmen turned, smiled again at Diana, and moved off through the crowd. Diana's knees gave out and she sank into my lap. "Socially, we're finished in this town," she said.

"Not immediately. For the next few years we're going to be characters in an extraordinarily funny story."

"Everyone has seen her," Diana moaned, and covered her face with both hands.

"Tell Mother, she'll fix it."

"I'd rather just sit here."

"Run along," I said. She rolled her eyes and did what she was told.

I was still chuckling when I heard Sonja Cadavid's horsy party laugh above the babble and the band. Despite her private allure, Sonja's public behavior set my teeth on edge, forcing me to glance around in case some sly person might be looking my way and thinking, *Your lover is a buffoon.*

These thoughts evaporated as she walked up casually and winked, after she was certain no one was in line of sight. A good wink too, straight-faced and slow enough to be seductive. Her public persona had it's private compensations. "When I got the invitation I didn't know you'd be here," Sonja said.

"Nobody did, and I was hoping for a quiet evening and an early night."

"Did you know that your maid is serving food to your guests with used tampon cartons in her hair?"

"Yes," I said. "It's the 70s."

"There are quite a few important people here."

"Maybe they'll go home."

"Poor Eddie," she said, moving gracefully to rest the small of her back against a baluster, one delicate hand on the railing. "Well. It's your house."

"I'm only a tenant."

"Fine," she said, quietly. "Now look directly over my left shoulder, in among those trees."

I glanced up and saw nothing at first. The four lane street, the abandoned acreage so often used as a dump site. Years ago, a family of squatters put up a fence for their goats and chickens there. I remembered those mornings, waking at dawn to the cockadoodledos. Lately, it had become overgrown with a coiled vine that lay thick among the tall grasses and brushy trees. At night it was a dark tangle of twisting branches with dangling pods, dead leaves, discarded plastic bottles and old fencing.

Tonight, at the very precipice, before the limestone tableland dropped almost vertically a quarter mile to the next level of ancient seabed, a torch burned. I stared senselessly at its light and the two figures on either side of it - Dulce and Alejandro Baez.

I must've gasped audibly because Sonja asked, "What's going on?"

"What's she holding in her hand?"

"You tell me," Sonja said, eyeing the crowd instead of the scene behind her.

"Looks like a beheaded chicken," I said.

"Then that's probably what it is, since very little else looks like a beheaded chicken."

For another minute I stared almost unbelieving, "I can't make out if that woman has a broken nose," I told Sonja. Then I waved to them.

Chapter Thirteen

The next day I felt jet-lagged, hung-over. And thanks to Dulce and Alejandro I had the creeps in my own home. My bravado the night before, when I waved to them, couldn't hide the fact that they'd returned to the island so easily, were able to stand boldly outside my apartment with a lighted torch, and it didn't take a voodoo expert to grasp that showing me a beheaded chicken wasn't a dinner invitation. They meant to kill me, and my guess was they meant to do it soon.

My response was sensible, I thought. I drove to meet Lt. Mickey Alba for coffee before my scheduled morning meeting with Mr. Yancy. Mickey didn't like Dulce and Alejandro any more than I did, and had the power to deal with them once and for all.

I turned left onto the Malecón, headed to Karin's. To my right the sea was quiet, almost flaccid, sloshing against the dark limestone cliffs. I thought about Mickey. He'd take the Baezes to the Ozama Prison if he caught them.

It's nothing to be proud of, I suppose, a place like that. You wouldn't find it in a *civilized* country. The walls were nearly 500 years old, inside prisoners were kept like farm animals. Straw on the floor, a drain in the corner of each cell served as a toilet, little if any food. I'd only known one North American imprisoned there. He lost sixty pounds. His complexion went from golden tan to oatmeal, his teeth began to loosen before his girlfriend started bribing the guards to smuggle decent food to him. He was held for what Americans sometimes mistake as a minor offense, drug possession. In this case, one marijuana cigarette and a book on how to grow more.

Dominicans took a dim view of drug use, like most Americans. Unlike Americans, Dominicans took a firm hand in solving the problem and jailed the users. Whether heroin or pot, cocaine or red devils, it was all the same. Go to jail and stay there, usually for years, unless you died or escaped. Dying was the escape of choice for many. There weren't any appeals. Generally, you were arrested, convicted, and sent to the Ozama Prison until you rotted.

I told Mickey once I thought this a little harsh. Why not target the dealers and suppliers, the heavy hitters? Mickey laughed, "You know why," he said. "They have the money to pay us off. So, we take their bribes and lock up their customers." It was an ideal system, I suppose. The market stayed small and the cost of doing business high. Word on the street was, even the Mafia thought the Dominican Republic wasn't worth the bother. We weren't drug-free, but the rest of the Caribbean was overrun with illegal narcotics; corrupted by it and forever soiled. The United States itself was devastated, destroying entire generations of its youth and making a mockery of racial equality.

Mickey said Americans lacked the political will to make drug use so frightening it was unthinkable, and lost the war on drugs before it began. If he got his hands on them, Dulce and Alejandro would hear the sure sweet sound of a heavy bolt rasping home, and face desolation.

He was sitting in Karin's under the gigantic almond tree. I preferred a table farther away as the fruit often fell from a great height and cracked you soundly on the head. I sat across from him and glanced up. "The place is nearly empty and you sit here," I said.

"Shut up. What's this about these gilipuertas (fartheads) getting back into the country? I told Immigration to put a hold on them, coming or going! Are you sure it was them?"

"Positive."

"¡Coño!"

"Don't you want to ask me how my trip was?"

"Screw your trip. This is my country and these people move in and out like they own the place."

"If it makes you feel any better," I said, "they do it there too. They tried to shoot me in DC, followed me to New York and back. I did get in one punch. I broke Dulce's nose."

"You got close enough to break her nose and all you did was break her nose?" He ordered us two coffees. "What did you do, hit her and run?"

"Of course not," I lied. "She's a woman. Should I go around

beating women now?"

"She's not a woman, she's an obesidad. A murdering puta!"

"What'd you have for breakfast? So worked up. I don't know if she's Quist's killer. She's unpleasant but...."

"I don't know if she's Quist's killer either," he said, picking an almond from the patio and flipping it sidearm at a beat cop walking past on the sidewalk. It struck his leg. Mickey waved him over. "I do know she's *my* killer and *your* killer and the only reason we're sitting here discussing it is because we got our stomachs pumped. A few days ago, Genius, have you forgotten?" Mickey turned to address the gray uniformed policía now standing at attention beside our table. "This individual is without a mind," he informed the officer.

"Would you like me to arrest him, Lieutenant?"

"No. There's no law against idiots, but there should be. Instead, I'm going to give you a note to take to the official in charge of Aeropuerto Immigration. It will ask him why he has allowed two fugitives who attempted to kill a policeman to enter this country unchallenged. Tell him to make a written response to me. You will wait for it. Do you understand that?"

"Sí, Señor. I have no transportation to the Aeropuerto."

"I will give you money for the público."

"Gracias. I have no permission to leave my post."

"I will write you another note for your sergeant."

"Gracias. I will be away during lunch."

"Fine. I will give you enough money."

"Gracias. Where will I find you?"

"Bring the response to my house this evening. I will write down the address."

"I cannot read."

"I will draw you a map."

"Good. I will walk there."

"There will be plenty of money to take públicos."

"Gracias, Señor. I will walk and save the money for cigarettes. You are a very thoughtful man."

"Yes," Mickey said. "That's why I'm always broke." After several minutes of scribbling and repeating the instructions, he sent the patrolman on his way. "It's a wonder anything ever gets accomplished in this country," he told me.

"Not much does," I said. "I was thinking all morning maybe it's not such a bad thing Dulce and Alejandro are back. She was pretty surprised when I approached her in Manhattan, but they got right back to the old game of taking the offensive. So I got this idea."

"What idea?"

"Now, just calm down and listen a minute," I said. "It's really genius."

Mickey slumped in his chair. "I won't be able to stand this, I know it."

"Just listen. Listen. How about instead of dodging them, I let them follow me?" I grinned. "Then you follow them."

"I don't want to follow them," he said laughing. "I want to find them. When I do, they won't be following anybody again, or standing in the weeds watching your apartment or beheading some poor squatter's chicken."

"No," I said. "And I won't be solving my case either." I slapped my hand on the table and he sat up. "There's Delbrick too, you know. He was with them. What does that mean? Guys like Delbrick have a lot to lose and he wouldn't risk being implicated in this mess unless it was absolutely necessary. I think it was even his car in New York. I have to talk to these people Mickey. Makes sense of it. Fulfill my contract with Yancy."

"That's all of it," he said grinning. "Money. Yancy's money. If you were a good honest cop now, you could take your coima and forget it. Anyway, what does that mean 'follow you?'"

"I don't think they did it, that's why. We've got to question them." I sipped my coffee. "They're on someone's payroll or obeying orders, but they didn't plan Quist's murder. They botched a simple poisoning."

"Not by much. We got lucky. What if you're wrong and in this *following*, they kill you?"

"Then they kill me."

"Easy for you to say." He sat a moment fussing with his napkin. "Easy enough to get them to follow you for awhile I suppose, then lose them and turn the tables."

"Exactly." I was breaking him down.

"Then after we find out where they're going I'll drag them down to the Ozama and beat the snot out of them, throw them in a cell without food or water for a few weeks, and then see what they confess to."

Mickey had a youthful, innocent smile. "You're not doing any such thing," I told him.

"EJ. You're a dope."

"Shut up. Will you help me or not?"

"Okay," he said. "But consider what happens if I lose them while they're following you, and *they* catch you."

"Don't lose me."

"I can put twenty men on you," he said. "I've got manpower. Unfortunately, you just saw me talk to one of them. If they don't have cab fare you might get your throat slit before they *walk* to your rescue. ¿Comprende?"

"Sí. Comprendo."

Mickey Alba had a very fine black mustache. He combed it carefully with his forefinger to brush away any coffee foam or raw sugar crystals. "I'm your friend," he said simply. "You are half of a gringo - sometimes I think more than half - but you are my friend." His fingers interlaced, I noticed again how nearly feminine they were, nails professionally trimmed and lacquered. "When my little Margarita was born with her spine bent you had a soft heart for her. Your money, your family's money made her well. You asked for nothing and came with us to the Mayo Clinic in Minnesota. I cannot repay you and I don't try. I know you did it from your heart and ask nothing, but sometimes mi amigo, that same great heart of yours is foolish. This isn't a game with these people. There are men in this town who can be bought for a few pesos to kill you. I don't want you to play with them."

"It's no game Mickey," I said. "You're right - I'm half a gringo, or more, I don't know myself. Honestly, I can't be like you. I try and solve these puzzles because it's one way of finding some truth, and I don't know Mickey, guess I like it."

He was quiet awhile, then slouched back in his chair again and stared out to sea. "So," he said. I followed his gaze. A large patch of garbage, disgorged into the sea by Rio Ozama, drifted west with the ocean currents. Underneath there would be sharks. "You look for more in this crime than who killed Adam Quist?"

"Yes," I said.

"It answers a deeper question?"

"Partly."

He nodded. "It is a job to me."

"I know."

"I don't have many friends," he said. "We are very different, you and I. You are calculating, logical, persistent. I admire the whole race of white people who are like that, because they are efficient, but their intersections are electrically controlled. I like a man standing alone in the intersection directing each car. It's personal. Not rats in a maze." He smiled. "This is talk we should be having when we are drunk." He paused to sigh. "Look now what's here."

Peor stood staring barely ten feet away.

"Better not let Karin catch you in here," Mickey warned. "What do you want?"

"Twenty seven pesos."

"Loca. Where is your child?"

"The church has taken her."

"Good."

"They will give her back. I know that priest. She will shit on his floor and he will give her back. It has happened before. Give me twenty seven pesos."

Mickey moved his chair to face her. "No. Get out. Now."

"I will cast a curse on you," she threatened.

Before Mickey could speak or shoot her, I said, "You don't cast a curse, you cast a spell. Like if you wanted Mickey to fall in love with you, you might cast a spell that he would suddenly find you beautiful, irresistable. Not only would he give you twenty seven pesos, but all that he owns." Peor continued to stare and Mickey's face darkened. "Anyway, what do you want with twenty seven pesos?"

"I want to buy a cow."

"You can't buy a cow for twenty seven pesos," I told her.

"I can buy a cow for forty pesos," she said. "I have thirteen pesos now."

Mickey's chair toppled back as he snapped to his feet. "Disappear you crazy bruja!"

As she backed away I said to no one in particular, "She can't buy a cow for forty pesos either."

"I can buy a cow for forty pesos from Oscar Tomas. He killed two with his taxi on the Bonao road and I will buy one. Not by the money of you or this policía! A curse on you both!"

"She's eating roadkill," I told Mickey.

He laughed. "Go eat your roadkill," he shouted after her.

But when she reached the street she called back above the traffic, "I curse you policía. You die today. I curse you Espinosa. Go to your dark place forever." She scampered, not unlike a hyena, through four lanes of honking traffic and disappreared.

Mickey sat back down. "She'll never get run over, you know. I've seen her do that a hundred times. You or I might do it once and die."

"I guess she really is a witch," I said. "I didn't know she knew me."

"No one pays any attention to her," he said. "I don't either."

"But it's a heavy burden."

"What is?"

"That someone wants you to die. To be in a dark place."

"Let's get to work. I have some ideas." So we hashed out the details of our trap to turn the tables on Dulce and Alejandro, which we planned to put into effect right after lunch if they began following me again. Meanwhile, I had to make some kind of report to Mr. Yancy.

"One more thing," Mickey said. "This Delbrick. I had him followed. He has been three times to The Residence. I don't know why. He doesn't live there. I don't trust him."

"The Quists may have sent him there for things. They'll be back to start packing pretty soon."

He shrugged. "Okay. Be careful around him."

"I've got several reasons to be careful of him," I said. "Where should I meet you for lunch?"

"Llaves del Mar," he said.

"Twelve-fifteen at Llaves?"

"There you go! Twelve-fifteen. What kind of a time is that? Twelve-fifteen? Lunch, I said. Lunch! I will see you there for *lunch* not at twelve-fifteen or twelve-sixteen. Just go there at lunch, Amigo. And wait."

I could tell he was exasperated. Our talk, and Peor, made him nervous. "Fine," I said, grinning. "Lunch. Of course, I'll be there at twelve-fifteen."

He swore and left the cafe, head down as he walked to his obvious, but unmarked, police car.

* * *

The similarities between the Dominican Republic and Minnesota are sometimes oddly profound, but architecture isn't one of them. In

Minnesota, ugly steel buildings grip the ground as if they might be suddenly uprooted and blown across the prairie, but here Spanish Caribbean architecture and its aesthetic manipulation of useless space, is soothing. Mr. Yancy's house especially. His office wasted more space for more effect than any room I've known. It's balcony was large enough to entertain a busload, and it *was* lovely there in the morning. The air seemed yellow, the light breeze cool, the café con leche rich, whipped by Ethel's own strong but delicate hand. I reclined in a Kennedy rocker with my feet on the railing and waited.

Mr. Yancy came in behind me, making quite a clatter with his small oxygen tank in a wire stand. "Excuse my rattling and clanking about, won't you Mr. Espinosa-Jones?" he said. "I frighten the little street urchins when I go down for the mail. All this paraphernalia."

"Don't apologize," I told him. "Glad you find some relief, at least."

"Well," he said, "I see Ethel has brought you coffee. I'm anxious for your report. Tell me it all from the beginning."

I did as he asked, careful to leave nothing out. From start to finish he didn't say a word but listened intently. I wrapped up with the torch scene and the beheaded chicken. His face had darkened and I knew he felt as Mickey did, that the Baez couple were homicidal.

Mr. Yancy drew in several torturous breaths before he spoke. "I have some bad news for you," he said. "Which I'll get to in a minute. First, let me say you've done a fine job. A fine job. Great initiative in Washington. I'm impressed. Quist not in his casket!" He was caught up in a coughing fit of smiles. "Wish I'd seen that lot. You've stirred the pot, and good too."

"The bad news?"

"Well, well," he said. "You've stirred a might hard perhaps. I've been on the phone to Olivia, you see. The family took your advice, filed a formal request for an investigation. Another exhumation. A letter to the State Department. Everyone wants them to shut up, Olivia told me. Government's in enough turmoil with this Watergate mess going away so slowly, if at all. They don't need more scandal. Works in our favor in the long run but for now they've focused on you, I'm afraid."

"On me? The United States, you mean?"

"I'm afraid so. The Embassy here has sworn out a formal complaint against you - meddling in diplomatic affairs and the like.

I'm sorry, but it was pouched to Washington and I think for the time being you may be the scapegoat. Official position is that you've stirred up this mess, a sort of unofficial, amateur detective slash scuba beachbum seeking cheap publicity. The official investigation, which they now claim has been ongoing, will likely turn up something quite different. Apparently, from what Olivia said, they've referred to you as a neurotic Caribbean playboy dabbling in voodoo. There was even a line she said, in which you were reported to have claimed Ambassador Adam Quist was a zombie. She added that you can expect a call from someone at the Embassy very soon. If you continue to investigate Quist's death, they will release this zombie business to the press and you will be discredited. Bad news, you see."

"Who do they think they can discredit me *with*? The papers would think it's a great story, probably run it with some voodoo photos on the front page."

"Yes," he nodded. "But be careful. These people deal in power. Remember how much aid the U.S. pours into this country every year. Millions. A sizable chunk of it goes into the various pockets of key politicians and military men. To protect their golden goose, killing you would be a minor detail."

"I have friends too."

"You're going to need them," he said softly. "I'm afraid I've gotten you into something far more dangerous than one man can handle. You may quit, if you like. I'll drop the matter. Let the official investigation, however long it takes, wind to its final conclusion. Your chances for success are slim now at any rate. And I'm no longer pleased with Olivia's role in this affair. Shall we retire from the field and return to fight another day?"

"No," I said instantly. "No, no, no."

"So sure?"

"I don't think Adam Quist is dead," I told him. "He may even *be* a zombie, but whatever or wherever, I want to find out and I'm not waiting for a government report. Delbrick is behind this hostility from the U.S. He hates me and there's something going on between him and Olivia. Loose ends everywhere. Your own man Johnson, or whatever his name is, chased me half way across Manhattan."

The sparkle rekindled in Mr. Yancy's eyes a moment. "He wasn't chasing you. He was your support. Said you dusted him off in a photo shop."

"Sorry." Again I felt the fool.

"You had no way of knowing. Hadn't gotten around to telling you with everything moving so fast. My fault too." He collected his thoughts. "Where do we go from here, then?"

"On the offensive," I said, and explained what Mickey and I had planned for the afternoon.

Mr. Yancy stared absently at the floor and I noticed he'd not worn his usual polished black oxfords, but leather sandals with thick wool socks, bright blue. I must've been smiling. "The extremities," he said. "First to lose oxygen. Seems odd to keep them heated in the tropics, don't you agree?"

"I didn't mean to stare, Mr. Yancy. I'm sorry."

"I couldn't find anything but bright blue this morning. Ethel will scold me soon enough. Don't be sorry. We have to laugh. You know that. We have to laugh."

"I don't."

"Well, thank you," he said, moving to stand beside me. "Thank you for that."

"Maybe you'd just as soon I didn't pursue this any further. Aren't you in danger too?"

Mr. Yancy reached over and ran his hand along my shoulder, down my arm to my hand, as old people do sometimes almost absently just to be touching warm flesh, to make human contact. His hand was large and large veined. "I am never in danger my friend." His eyes were blue and steady. "I'm untouchable, and not because of my disease. An old man, especially an old man without a son, likes to tell about himself. I would tell you if I told anyone, but I cannot. Some mysteries, I'm afraid, must follow me to the grave." He brightened. "How morbid! No. I am in no danger. Not from this, or anything like it. Believe that."

I did believe it. When I was a boy my father told me about Garrett Yancy, who came here shortly after World War II. Those were the Trujillo days and men walked softly. But Yancy prospered. When Trujillo was assasinated in 1961, he continued to prosper. His daughter had been born around 1947, but he never married and no woman was connected to him. Now, under Balaguer, Yancy was highly regarded. Balaguer was a devout Catholic and Yancy shared his faith. I'd seen a black limo at the curb beside Yancy's house more than once, and I know the Secret Service detail when I see them. It didn't pay to ask questions, but Garrett Yancy had nothing to fear. I should've known that.

* * *

Later, inside Llaves del Mar with its shabby floors and dim walls, I told Mickey I thought Mr. Yancy was acting strange. Mickey wasn't listening. "Did you hear what I said?"

"No," he said. "Did you hear what *I* said?"

"No," I admitted.

"I *said*, push this button to talk. Release it to listen." He held the radio so close to my face it was only a blur. "You're not very mechanical and if you can't operate these things none of this is going to work, though it probably won't work anyway."

"First, I'm very mechanical. Who fixed your regulator the last time we dove La Caleta? Second, why won't it work?"

"It's just not one of the things we do well. If they've got all these reports on you like Mr. Yancy said, somebody else might be following you, like the Marines. Did you really say the Ambassador was a zombie?"

"Do you want to shut up? Just shut up!"

"One thing for sure, you need a radio." He placed it on the table in front of me. "Pick it up. Which button to talk? Which to listen?"

I gave him the finger.

Llaves del Mar, Keys of the Sea, was the best seafood restaurant in Santo Domingo. It had the worst atmosphere. Dead sharks, puffer fish, star fish, rays, sea horses, even a collection of trumpetfish, all hung on greasy string from the ceiling. Some were taxidermied into lights with colored bulbs for guts, crispy brown with age and cigarette smoke. So much of it, so many fish and parts of fish, it succeeded beautifully where a tasteful decor might've failed. Unlike the lighting, the lobster on your plate was so fresh I'd actually seen the headwaiter send a boy with snorkeling gear across the road and into the surf when they were a tail short.

Tourists found the place occasionally, but it was too near the river and the end of the Malecón for crowds. "Do you know what time it is?" I asked Mickey.

He had a Rolex. A *gift*. "About twelve thirty."

"What time did you get here?"

"I don't know!"

"About fifteen minutes ago," I said. "Twelve-fifteen!"

"You're an idiot."

"It's the power of suggestion. I'm going to keep giving you exact times for things until your subconscious creates an automatic clock inside your brain. Eventually, you'll be on time and never know why."

"Gringo."

We ate sandwiches thick with mayonnaise and moist chunks of cold lobster on fresh homemade bread. Washed it down with squeezed lime juice in ice water. "Our main problem," I said, "is getting them to follow me in the first place so we can turn the tables on them."

"As it turns out," Mickey answered, "that's not a problem. See the thin guy across there fishing with the long pole?"

I squinted. "There's a dozen guys fishing there."

"The guy who's looking over here instead of at the water," he instructed. "Whatever made you want to be a detective?"

"I see him. So what?"

"He's watching us. He'll signal the Baezes when you walk out."

"How do you know?"

"Mira hombre. Why do you think I came here *after* you? I have eight guys around this cafe. The fisherman is a Baez lookout. Dulce and Alejandro are two streets over, near where you parked your car. They've been following you all day. A beggar with a box full of dirty pictures is watching them for me." Mickey dabbed his mouth with a napkin. "Now, our main problem is you. Let me take them right now. I'll have them inside the Ozama in ten minutes. Ten more minutes and they will be talking so fast you won't be able to write it all down. They will tell me everything they know, but even if they don't, I promise, they won't follow you or poison you again. Dulce and Alejandro Baez will simply disappear and no one will know anything. Ever. Unless, some night you get me drunk and I tell you."

"No," I said. "Stick to the original plan. Let them follow me. I lose them and you tell me where to pick them up again. I want to find out what's going on, not seek some kind of revenge. If they report to whoever is controlling them, then you get them all."

"A little revenge can feel good."

"They say the same about heroin, but it's addictive."

"Está bien, Profesor," he said. I could see he was disappointed but resigned. "Listen to me then. I want you to walk first to your car, drive up the street to Conde and park, then walk into Parque Colón (Columbus Park) and get a shoe shine. Gives me time to get everything in place, make sure they're going to follow you themselves and not delegate. Read the paper awhile, when you're ready, look at your watch to signal you have an appointment. They've been waiting now awhile for us to eat lunch. They wait for you to have a shine and read. They're impatient, anxious to follow. Maybe careless looking over their shoulders. I don't know. At least it gives us time to see if there are others, besides the fisherman."

"See, you are good at this," I told him.

"Keep the radio hidden in your car, under the seat or someplace. Don't talk on it, just listen. ¿Comprende?"

"Sí, mi general."

"When you leave the parque and get back in your car everyone with them will have to move to follow you. Then we will know. You will hear it on the radio. Don't answer, just drive west to the Hotel Embajador - I picked that on purpose," he smiled at this ingenious joke. "Park in the lot, leave the radio so they won't see it, walk through the main door and into the bar. You know the bar, you've been there enough. A new bartender will be working. He will show you through the kitchen and outside to a white Nissan pickup. The bartender will give you the keys. Another radio will be on the seat. Wait until I tell you where they are, then you follow them. Simple."

"What if they see me go off with the bartender?" I asked.

"They won't. Move fast. They can't follow that close."

"Where will you be after that?"

"Doing our best to cover your ass."

"Sounds very affectionate."

"There will be a hardhat on the seat. Put it on, it's your disguise. And please EJ, don't talk on the radio when you are in direct line of sight with their vehicle."

"What is their vehicle?"

"A blue Datsun 210. It looks like every público in town so don't take your eyes off it." He chewed the remainder of his ice. "It's still not too late for me to grab them."

"No. I want whoever is behind this."

Mickey Alba was filled with nervous energy but seemed rooted in his chair. He watched the fisherman awhile then picked up the radio and pressed a button. There was a small screech. "Okay," he said. "So we begin."

I stood.

"EJ," Mickey said. "Por favor, be careful. I have a bad feeling about this."

"Aren't you ready?"

"I have my best men." He shrugged. "They are armed. I myself carry two pistols and there's a shotgun in the car. Maybe it's the witch. I don't know. My palms are sweaty. Just be careful."

"Tonight we'll be drinking cold Presidente and smoking Hemingways on my veranda."

"Tonight I will be listening to Paulo's fourth grade teacher tell me he needs to keep his mouth shut in class. Maybe after that I will drop by. I'll need a beer by then. Anyway, get out of here."

I walked out the door grinning, confident. We were on the march.

Chapter Fourteen

It was siesta. The park deserted except for a few old men and the two who played dominos sitting at their usual table. I slid onto a bench in the shade of a 600-year-old banyan tree, my back to the Catedral de Santa María la Menor, its first stone laid in 1514 by Columbus's son Diego. Scaffolding covered it to the roof, thanks to the Ford Foundation. The restoration would take several years. Strange. Not a shoeshine boy in sight. We'd have to skip that part of the plan.

Across the street at the Supercolmado El Conde two laborers sat in the shade drinking refrescos. Traffic was light on El Conde and around the park plaza. An old lady with a scarf on her head went inside the church and on the sidewalk directly behind her an emaciated dog was attempting a strained bowel movement. All the people who were supposed to be following each other were invisible. This worried me since I thought I should see at least some of them.

I did find two folded scraps of the *Listín Diario* and read a feature story about a woman who'd seen a vision of the Madonna in Higuey. Bored, I read it a second time. Still nothing moved. No tourists crossed the terra cotta. The usual army of beggars must've been somewhere in the shade. The witch Peor bathed her feet in a small fountain, gripping the hand of the slack-eyed child. I read another story. Col. Caamaño's mother now claimed her son had defeated the Army's elite regiments almost single-handed and was poised to fall upon the Capital with hoards of gun-toting peasants.

I worried about Peor, and the missing shoeshine boys. The best laid plans, I thought. It wasn't exactly pivotal, but as a lover of detail, it bothered me. Sometimes when things start going wrong they just keep going wrong until everything falls apart. I stood and strolled back to the car. Mickey and his guys must be anxious for the chase to begin by now. Enough time had elapsed for everyone to get into position. I opened the door and got behind the wheel.

The quickest way out of the Zona Colonial was east to the Puerta and around Parque Independencia but there were so many one way streets, all narrow and easily blocked. I decided to go south back to the Malecón, four lanes wide, then head west toward the Hotel Embajador. In the light siesta traffic, tailing me should be a breeze.

Traffic flowed easily and I made the trip in less than fifteen minutes. I arrived at the hotel without spotting even one of the supposed pursuers. The lobby of the Embajador - cavernous, ornate and extremely green - was deserted. One clerk behind the reservation desk ignored me as I walked briskly behind a large portable partition separating the bar from the lobby.

The bartender motioned to me, thrust keys into my palm, and I was out the back door within seconds. Everything like clockwork, I thought.

Minutes later I was behind the wheel of the pickup, wearing my hardhat disguise. I pressed the button on the radio. "Mickey?"

"What?"

"I'm in the truck."

"They're still in the parking lot watching your car. Talking." There was static. "They're going in. Move north. Park near Sarasota. Then it's up to you."

"Where were all you guys downtown? I didn't see anybody."

"Stay off the radio."

I drove to a side street without trees and parked behind an old Chevy. Time dragged while Dulce and Alejandro searched the hotel, confused about how I'd ducked them. The small truck had no air conditioning and the seats were black. The radio tracked their progress from time to time and was finally silent. I waited.

This far west, Avenida Sarasota was all but empty. The hotel had a great deal of vacant, undeveloped property and new houses were going up sporadically along the boulevard. Visibility was good in both directions because most of the trees had been cut down.

The radio came back to life. "Moving your way. Blue Datsun 210. Pull onto Sarasota. Let them overtake you and pass. You'll seem less threatening. Good luck. We'll be close."

I released the clutch and swung onto Sarasota, feeling alone. Moments later Dulce and Alejandro sped past me. Dulce was driving.

Alejandro looked sullen. I allowed them to slip ahead and then kept pace, attempting to block their view with at least one other vehicle. I prided myself in my tailing skills. At a surveillance seminar in Miami once, we broke up into small groups and followed each other around town. My opponents never saw me. I framed my Certificate of Achievement.

Mickey's voice on the radio. "Looks like we're headed back downtown. Don't fall asleep."

"I thought we weren't supposed to talk on the radio so much."

"What?"

"Never mind."

Públicos, public cars, traveled prescribed city routes and charged fifteen cents to cram as many passengers as possible into the little vehicles. Battered like demolition cars, they seldom had working turn signals or brake lights. Público drivers didn't communicate intentions such as braking or lane changing. Someone onboard said "Aquí" and the driver stopped dead. Alert motorists followed at a sensible distance. Others you read about in the daily papers.

Sometimes a detective, intent on his quarry, might make the same mistake.

I didn't call it a crash since I only lost one headlight and crumpled the público's trunk. Some of the red duct tape he'd been using as a taillight was scraped off, but other than that, it was little more than a bump. I could've quickly backed up and been right on the Baez's tail again if all the people inside the taxi hadn't jumped out and started milling around in the street. "Mickey!" I shouted into the radio. "Get up here quick."

He arrived and sorted it all out, but by then we'd lost them.

"Now what?" I asked, waiting on the endgate. He could see how foolish I felt.

"They were headed downtown. I've got eyes there. Let's start that way. Somebody will pick them up and if they turn toward the airport there's only one bridge. They have to cross it. I've got guys on each end. It's an island. Let's go."

I swept through the light traffic without regard for Mickey or his troops. I didn't care if they kept up or not. How many times had Dulce and Alejandro slipped through my fingers? If I got downtown in time, maybe I'd get lucky.

Streets originally built for foot and horse traffic aren't suitable for large motorized vehicles. One solution was lots of one way streets. Heading east, there were only about a dozen key downtown streets. Watching those, you could find just about anybody. Dulce and Alejandro were spotted ten minutes after I left the accident scene.

They were headed north on Duarte. I wasn't more than a few minutes behind them. "What now?" I asked Mickey on the radio.

"I'll let you know."

I sped north to parallel them and cut onto Mella or one of the other east-west streets to intercept them. The little pickup bounced along over the potholed streets, swirling garbage and litter in its wake. City dwellers habitually stepped into the street without looking and I hunched over the wheel, tense and watchful.

Five minutes more and I heard nothing on the radio. Should I continue north? Turn east?

"Where are you?" Mickey's voice rose through the static.

"Almost to Mella."

"Turn east. I've got them blocked with some traffic for a few minutes. Let me know when you cross 19 De Marzo."

"Okay."

A few minutes later I called him back. "I'm there."

"Pull up near Duarte and wait."

It was happening fast now. I braked at the curb alongside a push cart loaded with household goods and clothing.

"Hey!" the vendor said. "Don't park here."

I nodded.

He came around to my window. A shallow-chested man dressed in poorer clothing than what he was peddling. "If you aren't buying, shove off. I have to make a living."

"I'm just waiting for somebody."

"Wait somewhere else, Asshole!"

There's something in people to make them street hostile, even worse than when they're drunk. "Calm down," I told him, "or I'll come and beat the shit out of you."

"¡Mierda!" he screamed. "¡Mierda! This man is full of mierda! Look at him. Mierda Man!" He threw his arms above his head and ran up and down on the sidewalk.

I pulled away just as the Baezes roared past. I fell in behind them again, closer than before. "Okay," I told Mickey. "I've got them. Some idiot just called me Shitman."

I expected a caustic response but the radio was silent.

The blue Datsun made no evasive moves and headed straight for the bridge which led across the Ozama and east to the airport. Once past the Tres Ojos, there was the ocean on their right and little to the left except scrub, squatters, Haitians selling voodoo trinkets, and a few poor cafes. No major highways until Boca Chica.

Tres Ojos National Park flashed by, three major caves leading straight into the earth. The Baez Datsun sped on toward the airport. Something was wrong. I worried that I might've been spotted. They couldn't be leaving the country again.

City traffic thinned as we made our way along the ocean. I settled down and stayed far enough behind to keep them in sight and blend with other traffic. Avenida Las Américas was the most well-patrolled stretch of road in the country. Highway Patrol officers in their green and white cars were difficult to bribe and took their sweet time with every traffic stop. I needed no tickets today.

Behind me, I hoped Mickey and his men were in place, watching my back.

The winter sun was hot on my neck as we approached La Caleta, the new ocean park and favored dive site near the airport peninsula. Mickey and I dove the reefs there often. The bay was empty that day and I followed Dulce and Alejandro past La Caleta, past the airport road, and finally even past Boca Chica. I was getting worried.

After the airport, the road narrowed to two lanes, split a couple times, then came back to the ocean again, winding along high black cliffs and rough water. It was here I noticed the Datsun slowing and worried I might overtake them. I eased my foot from the gas and coasted, considering the options.

The Datsun slowed too, almost stopped, then sped up. Dulce found what she was looking for and turned left, away from the ocean onto a dirt trail that wound back into the sea grape and stunted palms. I hesitated before following them. Mickey was nowhere in sight. Was there a labyrinth of trails ahead perfect for losing me or was I driving into a trap? No time to weigh the options. I turned and followed.

Already they were lost somewhere ahead. The Datsun left a dust trail and I managed to turn three or four times onto other trails without losing it. The air was hot and still. I tried the radio. "Mickey. I turned left about nine or ten miles past Boca Chica. Small trail. There's a broken palm just before that. I'm a half mile back in. Turned left twice again, I think, then one to the right. Can you hear me?"

I glanced at the radio and saw it had somehow been turned off. I clicked it on and repeated my message. There was static now. No one answered. I tried again. No answer.

The brush was thinning. I slowed down in time to see the Datsun parked some distance ahead near a limestone cliff hung with vines. I pulled into the sea grape and hid the truck. Dulce and Alejandro had vanished.

When ancient volcanoes flung the island of Hispañola from the sea, limestone tableland was left along the coast as the land mass grew and the water receded. Coastal land became a series of steps or plateaus. My apartment sat on one such plateau. The limestone rock, beaten by the sea for generations, was porous. Large and complicated caves like Tres Ojos were formed, then hidden by proliferous foliage. The Baezes had found such a cave and disappeared. A footpath led inside, through tangled green vines.

Again, I hesitated. Mickey was late. The caves were undoubtedly frequented by locals because the old ocean blow holes, cracks, and small canyons let in light. The limestone opened to lighted rooms probably used for family picnics or the odd tryst. I'd been careful. Mickey however, was lost. Eventually, he'd find the pickup. I checked to be sure the radio was tucked safely in my belt and parted the leafy green curtain.

Inside, it was twilight. A small entrance led immediately to a room the size of a gymnasium, lit from above by old blow holes and from one side by a second entrance, much larger and veiled with foliage. Yellow-green and golden light softened the rock walls and I stood a moment in awe, inhaling cool air in mid-afternoon.

Dulce and Alejandro had vanished. I strode quickly to the large entrance but it was only a courtyard with still more cliffs and foliage rising several stories. I turned to follow a worn stone slope toward the dark interior of the cave.

There I heard footsteps and voices ahead. Walls narrowed and the ceiling dropped to within twelve or fifteen feet but the stone underfoot was still well-worn. Here and there cigarette butts, scraps of paper and plastic cups - a comforting layer of litter.

I carried no weapon or flashlight, pressed the radio switch to be sure it worked, then turned down the volume.

A muffled sound like laughter or crying came from somewhere

ahead. I stumbled in the dying light. The yellow glow had faded, replaced by a humid grayness. Dark holes pocked the stone. The walls were sweating. The air was thick with salt, stale and undisturbed. My breath came easier if I inhaled by mouth.

The sounds drifted from the left, beyond a fork in the passage. I lurched forward into even darker, narrower space. I should've brought a stick at least, something to probe the blackness. Guided by sound, I blundered on as light diminished to a glimmer, forcing me to bend at the waist and go forward at a squat to avoid cracking my head. The walls closed tighter and I thought about turning back, though Dulce and Alejandro were probably just ahead and Mickey not far behind. But the fearless detective was alone in the middle, trapped if things went wrong.

Mickey and I had a rule when we were diving - if you get into trouble; stop, quit swimming, kneel on the bottom and think it through. I sat down on the floor of the cave. Should I risk a radio call? If I heard them, they could hear me.

I listened.

Ahead, the sounds were clear. Voices. A man and a woman. Dulce and Alejandro. Behind me I heard nothing. No tramping of policeman's feet. If anyone was coming they were being very quiet. I feared I was alone. Mickey could be miles down the coast. He might've driven past the dirt road and kept right on going. If so, what were the odds he'd ever find it? The smart move was to get out, get on the radio, or back on the highway, though the Baezes seemed confident and gave no indication they knew I was following them. Now finally, I had the upper hand. People didn't crawl into caves without good reason. Maybe they'd hidden something or come to meet Delbrick or whoever controlled them, even rebels from the mountains. I weighed the risk.

The voices faded again. I had to decide.

Gripping the damp wall, I edged ahead in a crouch. There wasn't enough room for them to jump out and overpower me. They needed light to shoot me. Creeping ahead, stopping, listening, seemed to make sense. More sense than giving up.

So I followed their voices for what seemed a long time. Sometimes I heard nothing but refused to hurry. I moved a few steps, stopped to listen awhile, moved again, stopped, waited.

My hand came to rest on a fair-sized rock. Limestone is light, jagged and sharp. I kept the piece, some measure of security. Dulce already had a broken nose, she wouldn't want this against her jawbone. I grinned at the darkness.

Sound inside a cave is similar to sound underwater - directionless. The voices, which I was certain now belonged to Dulce and Alejandro, came and went in echoes - distant random noise, then sudden clarity, like a radio signal from far away.

Minutes later I stopped again. I felt the cave widening, becoming much larger and bathed in a kind of reflected gray light, its source ahead and below. No sooner had I lost my claustrophobia then I felt exposed without close walls and a low ceiling. Was it safer to edge toward the light or find a nice damp wall to put my back against?

I couldn't be sure, but the voices sounded like they were to my right. I slipped left and made for the light. If there was another entrance below, it wouldn't hurt to be near it.

The voices stilled. Had I made noise? I dropped to one knee and waited, straining to see into the gloom where I thought the voices originated. I saw and heard nothing.

Somewhere water dripped and trickled. I stood slowly and peered at the dark. There was another faint noise near the gray light. I moved carefully toward it.

Behind me I heard a sound like a .45 slide makes when it's cocked. The muzzle jammed into my spine just above the belt. "Be still," Alejandro ordered. "Drop the rock."

I disobeyed, gripping it tighter. "The cops are coming," I said.

Dulce came across then from the right and smiled up at me. Even in the dim gray light I saw she had white surgical tape over the bridge of her swollen nose, and two black eyes. "You hit me," she said. "You hit me."

"You started it," I complained.

"We're going to kill you." She slapped my face, and stepped back for a good swing and slapped it again. Then again and again. She switched hands and slapped more. I tasted blood. My nose ran freely. Dulce had big hands. "First we need you to bleed," she went on calmly. "Bring him over."

Alejandro shoved me ahead toward the gray light. We stopped at the lip of a deep hole. "Do you know what's at the bottom?" Alejandro asked.

"Snakes?" I said. It was the worse thing I could think of. The

Dominican Republic doesn't have poisonous snakes.

"Rocks, black water and crabs. Flesh-eating crabs."

"Maybe you should just shoot me," I said.

Alejandro ground the pistol into my back. "It's an option."

"Why are you people so hostile?"

"You're bleeding very nicely," Dulce said. "We don't owe you an explanation."

"Sure you do," I said, wiping my nose on my forearm. "You can't throw people down holes to be eaten alive without an explanation. Who are you working for?"

"He's 007," Alejandro told Dulce. "We'll give him some big clue now just before he dies, then he pulls out his shoephone and calls Moneypenny or makes his jock strap into a grappling hook."

They both laughed. "I don't think he has anything to fill a jock strap," Dulce said with renewed mirth.

"Why don't you check?" Alejandro dared her. "Use my knife."

"Go to hell," I said, and jumped into the black hole, hoping the shaft was straight and smooth clear to the bottom.

Air whistled past my ears. No other sound but its rushing. I crossed my feet at the ankles and folded my arms across my chest, then I hit the water. My body entered at an angle. I spread my arms and legs to slow my underwater descent but this proved unnecessary. My left hip collided with rock and pain shot down my leg and up through my buttocks and back. I lost half the lung-full of air I'd grabbed on the way down and fought for the surface, arms flailing.

The water wasn't deep. I would've been better off if it had been. I broke the surface with as much silence as I could manage so Dulce and Alejandro didn't start shooting down the hole. They'd heard the splash, now they had to think I was dead or dying.

Cautiously, I swam until my hand touched stone. The pain in my hip radiated throughout my body and made me dizzy. My elbow caught something and I ran my hand over it. A rock ledge just above the surface of the water. Even in the dark I could tell the bottom of the hole was much larger, hollowed by centuries of sloshing. The water was also salty. The ocean.

After a painful amount of silent struggle, I managed to crawl onto the ledge, which was the size of a bathtub and worn smooth by the sea. I lay down and listened. No sound from above. I was shivering and dizzy. Alive.

Chapter Fifteen

There are stories about crabs, how they've eaten the eyes from the corpses of sailors. This crab seemed large and curious, nibbling gently at the wrinkled skin across my stomach, preparing, I thought, to take a serious bite. It didn't know how angry I was, how cold and hungry after two days in a hole. Or how patient I'd become as it moved sideways along my belly, keeping its claws pointed up in defiance.

I'd had several crab incidents since Dulce and Alejandro thought they'd killed me. One aggressive crustacean had nipped a nickel-sized chunk of flesh from my left ankle. I kicked it. Another I smashed with my rock but it sank before I snatched it. Hard to hit them square in the dark. I still had my rock. Had it the whole time.

Springtime drew female crabs ashore to lay their eggs along the coastline. Thousands swarmed across Avenida Las Américas. Their crushed bodies, blood, and mangled entrails turned the four-lane highway into a slick, stinking mass of carnage worse to navigate than any ice-covered road in Minnesota. The ripe crunching of crab shells under your tires, the smell of it, the road crawling before your eyes at night, was a sight you never forgot, like a battlefield.

This migration came in June, but there were crabs now too. Plenty. Nobody ate them for awhile after the migration because we remembered the clicking of their hard bodies as they crossed the road. This crab eyed me and shifted his weight. I wasn't dead yet. He slipped down onto the ledge.

I swung the rock and dealt him a fatal blow just behind the eyes. Raw meat, fresh and moist. I longed for a cool drink too, but the crab's bodily fluids filled the need. That first crab I ate in total darkness, but during daylight dining I was unable to eat the bloody entrails, veins or greasy cold blood that seeped and slipped among the mutilated meat and sticky yellow glands. A day later I realized my dehydration was more critical than my hunger and I ate everything but the shell. The fluids were too precious. I feared no one was coming to my rescue and sometimes I hated Mickey Alba more than Dulce or Alejandro.

I ate, picking broken bits of shell from the meat. Protein. But eating it in the dark didn't hurt. Two or three of these protein crabs a day and I'd have my strength back. Feel well again. I felt some better already. The throbbing in my hip had faded to a dull ache unless I moved suddenly or tried climbing the wall again. I'd been up and down twenty-eight times.

When I began diving I logged my dives, but the wall climbing numbers depressed me at first, then I took a morbid pride in them. I earned the twenty eight falls from the wall. Each time I slipped from its slick sides I counted, rejoicing a little because I knew eventually I'd succeed. You don't know the number of falls it takes to win so you count each. It may be the very next one, twenty nine, thirty. Failure is nothing to brag about, but endure enough of it and it hardens into faith, and faith is the parent of hope.

Time in the hole I measured by hours instead of days. I'd been down 48 hours over three days, going in around 4:00 or 4:30 in the afternoon the day before yesterday. The third day drew to a close and I knew one thing more than I'd known that morning - no one was coming. Hope placed on things outside yourself, like a smashed wet radio, is hope misplaced. Faith, that unquestioning belief you can succeed against all odds and common sense, that comes in handy in deep holes. Faith keeps count.

I went up the wall for twenty nine after I ate the crab. I tried it barefoot again since that had given me the most success before. It looked easy. The walls, though slick with humidity, were conveniently furnished with small holes, cracks, and jagged rocks that acted as steps. The first two body lengths of climb were childishly simple, then the wall became smooth for a distance. Over the hours and days I'd learned this smoothness extended around the entire hole and no crack or hand hold existed above it within my reach.

I tried leaping the smooth area at first, landing in the water. Later, I fashioned my pants and belt into a makeshift lasso, climbed and slung them up in hopes they'd catch and I could pull myself beyond the smooth area. This accounted for about nineteen through twenty seven. Twenty eight was my pants, belt, and shirt tied together. Twenty nine proved little more than exploratory.

Back on the ledge, I saw something I'd noticed before at this time of day. Green light in the water. It came for awhile in the late afternoon and disappeared after an hour or so. The color was not at the surface but far, far below.

Most likely, the sun was in a position at that time each day to reflect through various holes and passages until a small patch of color made its way into my dark hole. Had it not been so faint and so far away I thought maybe I could swim toward it and find a way out. I'd even tried lowering myself underwater and moving out some distance from the hole feeling for other passages that might contain air. I found none.

Climbing the wall was risky and I'd taken a number of dangerous spills. Swimming away from my only source of air, well, that seemed suicidal. I was able to hold my breath for a little over three minutes, which wasn't bad, but if I missed the way back or there was no new air space, I died on the first attempt. The wall allowed me twenty nine chances or a hundred and twenty nine. Swimming was all or nothing.

That night I went to sleep with fresh crab in my belly, feeling better than I had since I'd jumped. The next morning, on attempt thirty four, I fell backward onto the ledge and cracked my head so hard I lost consciousness. Most of that day passed in a fog of pain and cold. I was feverish and disoriented. Ate nothing. Crabs clicked and crawled across my naked legs and I did little more than brush them away.

I lost track of time. No longer meticulous about it, or consulting the luminous dial of my dive watch to compare my life in the hole to what I believed was happening outside it. I'd been connected, or thought so. Now I didn't care.

On the fifth day I realized I was in trouble. I killed one crab with the stone at about eleven o'clock in the morning and felt some better after I'd eaten, but I couldn't stay awake for long periods and slipped into a dream-laden stupor. Saw the farm in Minnesota and heard my grandmother's voice clearly. I answered, calling her by name, Mae. She was in the kitchen wearing a white apron over a print dress and talking about nothing important, just visiting about ordinary things. She smiled and talked, asked for a response but I couldn't speak. She told me about the ripe vegetables in her garden, how I liked them cooked. As she talked I smelled bread baking and started to cry. She couldn't hear me. I wanted to tell her I was there, still alive. She left the kitchen to go into the living room. I couldn't follow her there. I awakened to pain in my head. I was shivering.

That morning I'd become convinced that something was wrong with the flesh of my legs. I rubbed my hands along my thighs and feared the skin was sloughing like snake skin. In the darkness I sniffed my hands to see if I was rotting. The smell was sour and salty.

How long before my muscles atrophied? I wouldn't be able to climb anymore. Later I wouldn't be able to kill and eat crabs. They'd eat me for revenge. I rested.

The next day I awoke early and looked at my watch. My head had cleared and I decided it was my last day in the hole. I didn't control much of anything, but I could control where I died. Helplessness seemed worse than death to me that morning. Controlling where and how I died would be victory. I ate three crabs during the day and sucked every bit of juice and blood from their shells. Instead of climbing I exercised and stretched.

I've seen people dead from violence, old age, illness, accidents. The most peaceful death I've seen is drowning. It looks like sleeping, without pain or the slightest grimace on the faces of the dead. My choices were limited to hacking my veins open with the sharp rock, falling from a height not quite high enough to kill me, or drowning. If I swam toward the green light I would drown. The air squeezed from my lungs, head pounding for oxygen, I'd simply open my mouth and inhale water as fast as I could.

So that's what I was thinking that day as I waited for the late afternoon sun to send a far away green light for me to follow into the depths. It was possible too, that after awhile my bloated body might be caught in some underground current and carried out to sea where it could drift ashore and someone would find it and call the police. I wanted Mickey Alba to stand above my pale corpse and know that he should have found me, that he should have searched and searched until he'd peered down every hole on the island. I wanted him to tell my mother and see the hurt in her eyes when he admitted he'd given up though I was alive somewhere, waiting. Let him live with that. He wouldn't be able to get enough Rolexes during all of his life to block that out. So I waited for the green light. And it came at last.

When I saw it my heart sank. I seemed miles away. But it was real. It was the same light that came every afternoon and it appeared green and beckoning and it was the only light there. So I took a deep breath, then another and another. But I exhaled and dropped back on the ledge and curled up with fear. I was afraid to die.

What if the very next climb succeeded? What if I quit exactly one try short of making it? What if God would say to me in the end, after I drowned, "You idiot! You only needed to climb up once more. Just once." If I climbed, it would take the last of my strength. I couldn't climb and then swim. One or the other.

I sat up and folded my clothes. First my pants, then my shirt. I piled them neatly and put my shoes on top with the socks carefully rolled and stuck inside the right shoe. In the left, the smashed radio. This accomplished, I felt more content. If anyone found the clothes someday, I didn't want them to think I'd panicked and left a mess.

The water was warm as I slid from the ledge. Winter water temperature hovers around 82-degrees. Sounds warmer than it is. Normal body temperature is 98.6, after all, and anything less feels cool and will eventually chill the body since water takes heat away much faster than air. But it felt warm on my skin, almost like a bath. Anyway, I'd be dead in a few minutes. So many things, I thought, to be thankful for. I convinced myself that drowning was the way to go.

By controlled hyperventilation, I held my breath much longer than normal. Large breaths, taken in quick succession, holding the last, built up an oxygen reserve to delay the body's cry for fresh air. A great deal of success in breath holding is mental. Denying the brain's request for oxygen. Telling yourself again and again that you can go a little longer. There's risk, of course. Wait too long and you pass out, inhale involuntarily. No problem in open air. Underwater, an eternal drink.

That's the way I thought it would go. I'd deny my brain's request and pass out. Might never know anything beyond that. Like going to sleep or fainting. Not unpleasant, and you wake up in heaven. Unless you slosh around in the sea for a million years until God decides to call a halt to all this nonsense. Catholics endure purgatory, but Lutherans just sleep soundly until the resurrection. Such a sensible religion. It's nice to die as a Lutheran.

I decided to hyperventilate four times, slip underwater, open my eyes no matter how much they stung from the salt, face the green light, and swim steadily but not rapidly toward it. Before I passed out I'd head for the surface and feel around with my hands for an opening. Maybe I'd get lucky and steal a breath. That panicky time right then, when I needed the oxygen most, was frightening. I'd be crazy for a breath, pressed up against tons of rock above. That would be the time, the last few desperate seconds just before death, I'd be completely alone.

There seemed to be no time to waste. "This is it, God," I said aloud. "I'm coming."

I breathed in until my lungs ached, held it a second, then blew out steadily. Did it again and again, then held the fourth breath and pushed beneath the surface.

The green light was visible as a blur when I opened my eyes and began to swim. I started with a flutter kick but soon realized it tapped my strength too quickly and switched to a frog kick. The huge breath I'd taken created a great deal of buoyancy and I fought to stay down.

Concentration was the key, I thought. Focusing on a steady swimming stroke and thinking about distance and efficiency in the water, things that kept the mind from demanding air. The brain didn't need the oxygen it cried for. My lungs, after all, were saturated with oxygen. It took time for it to pass from the thin walls of the lung's air sacks into the tiny corpuscles that absorbed it into the bloodstream and sent it around to keep me alive. Mind over matter. Concentration. There were free divers who went down more than two hundred feet and held their breath for something like fifteen minutes. Surely, I could go three, maybe five.

The green light remained ahead, out of reach. I swam on and began to count my strokes. I decided I would surpass the number of times I'd tried to climb the wall. More strokes than climbs. That way the whole thing equaled out somehow.

My brain began to nag me about air. A quiet voice in the beginning. *A little longer*, it would say, *then you'll need to breath*. No, I thought. More than a little longer. I can ignore it quite awhile yet. If I don't, I'm going to die quicker and I've only counted to twenty six. I might go to fifty or a hundred and fifty. I often swam the length of an Olympic-sized swimming pool on a single breath. That's twenty-five meters, about seventy-five feet, or a little more. I did it to show off to my scuba students. Now I'd do it down and back - one hundred and fifty feet. Half the length of a football field on a single breath. Others have done it. I'd do it.

Strokes and feet. Add and multiply numbers. So many meters,

so many feet, so many strokes to swim the distance. Somebody somewhere, some swimming coach, knew all those numbers. I tried to compute them in my head.

It was my left leg that first started to cramp. I knew if I had trouble it would be there. The knot inside against the bone, where I'd struck the underwater rock when I first jumped, had loosened over time and become mushy. The swimming was knotting it up again.

I knew how to relieve a cramp. Rest. Rub. When you're swimming for your life there's no rest, so I talked to the cramp instead and told it not to tighten any more. To hurt, but not to tighten. I told God too, that I could bear the pain but if it tightened anymore I wouldn't be able to swim and then I would die from cramp-induced drowning, and that wasn't the plan. Straight drowning was the plan. It was my choice. It wasn't fair to have a really tight cramp that wouldn't let me swim.

The cramp didn't go away after I talked to it, but it didn't get any worse either. I counted out another two dozen strokes toward the green light.

The water must be clear, I thought. Even while I saw things as a blur of light and dark, the water was without impurities. No debris or particles struck me. The reason we can't see clearly underwater with the naked eye is because the eye can't focus in a liquid. It needs an air space to do that. Divers wear masks to give the eye this air space. This is a useful thing to know if you plan to live for some time. I thought that I knew quite a few more useful things. It wouldn't be good to waste all that. If God saw that, maybe He wouldn't allow it. He might think *What a waste!* and create an airspace above my head.

The brain's involuntary commands are demanding, hard to resist. I'd never resisted even the simplest demands to eat, sleep, and drink rum before. But these things were gentle urges, not like this. Not like the craving to breathe. My brain was screaming. My head overheating. My lung-full of air longed to push its way up my windpipe and explode. I wasn't yearning for a breath but an explosion. Expel the depleted, foul gas that had grown toxic inside.

There was pain. Chest, head, legs. I counted. *Forty-nine. Fifty.* Those were the wrong numbers. I knew that. I counted some more and thought that I'd limit the number so the count would be shorter and if the count was shorter then I could go up sooner and blow out the poison. Blow a little now? No. Wouldn't be able to stop. I'd blow it all out and suck water.

It was time. My head popped with black stars, the last thing you see before you pass out. I remembered I didn't want to do that yet. First I'd go up and see about the air space God had arranged for me. I reached up and swam to the surface.

My hand struck rock before it left the water. I bent my head to keep it from colliding but collided anyway, against my back instead of my head. The rock was sharp stalactites of limestone and ripped the skin, instantly sending spikes of pain throughout my torso. The pain awakened me enough to turn and push with my hands, to swim again until I scrapped my back a second time. More ripping. I was tearing my back to pieces. I swam again.

Disoriented, I wanted to go down and escape the pain but I turned and swam up instead. My head broke the surface. I exhaled. I breathed. I heard myself sobbing.

The place I had found was no larger than a small closet and the air was stale. I coughed after each breath and tears streamed from my eyes. I wanted to stay there for the rest of my life.

Beneath me and off to the left, the green light shone like emerald, spreading into the depths and reflecting on the low ceiling of the closet. When I looked back in the direction I'd come, I saw only darkness.

My head was clearing. Consciously, I slowed my breathing and took deep, even breaths. I was close to something big. How close I didn't know. My back was bleeding profusely, clouding the water. I hoped sharks didn't swim back into these caves.

Choices were limited. I had to swim again. The stale air wouldn't last and treading water was using up my reserves. The pain in my left thigh was sharp and insistent. I hyperventilated and sank below the surface.

This time I swam into light. Deep green gave way to pale green and blue and white. When I glanced up I saw the sun and swam to it. My head broke the surface of a land-locked lagoon open to the air. Too tired to cheer, I laughed and cried and flipped over onto my back and floated there with the hot afternoon sun warming my naked body. Somewhere against the ripping rocks I'd lost my shorts and that seemed hilarious. My laughter echoed, breaking out into an open blue sky.

After a rest, I began the search for a way out. The lagoon was ringed with limestone cliffs twenty or thirty feet high. Water had deeply undercut the cliffs several meters above the surface all around, with the exception of an area about the size of a small dock where rock extended into the lagoon a few feet high. From there, I saw enough ledge and loose rock to offer an exit. I swam to the low rock and climbed free of the water, marveling at the light and warmth of the air.

I hate an ingrate. "Thanks God," I said aloud, standing there naked and bleeding, feeling better than ever in my life.

From the rim of rock above I half expected to see Dulce's square head peeking down at me. A week was a long time to watch your kill I suppose, even for her. By now she would be pretty confident I was dead. I began the climb.

The surface of the limestone was rough and sharp, slicing my feet. I was leaving a blood trail. Better, I thought, than the swim back to get my shoes.

I reached the vertical wall where the rock was worn and the climbing easier. I thought of all the times I'd tried to climb the wall inside the hole. This steep cliff might've looked risky to anyone watching. To me it was child's play. I was on the rim in ten minutes, but still naked. It occurred to me that flagging a cab on Avenida Las Américas could pose some problems in the nude.

A footpath led from a spot near where I stood on the rim back into the sea grape and scrub land, undoubtedly connecting to some dirt road or even to the highway. People maybe came here to swim. I searched along the path until I found a piece of vine, ripped it loose, picked sea grape leaves and twisted their stems into the vine until I made an apron. Sea grape leaves are large and thick, covering me as long as I remained standing and avoided ocean breezes. I considered a couple leaves for my hair but my own giddiness at being alive might not be shared by the first people I met.

I followed the path to a small dirt road much like the one I'd taken to the cave so long ago. Standing there I realized it could very well be the same road. If it was, the pickup wasn't far along it. I could drive home. I hobbled as quickly as I could manage back into the sea grape trying to remember the turns I'd made when I drove in.

Fifteen minutes later I found the spot. The pickup was gone. The cave was still there. I turned and limped quickly back toward the highway. Of course the pickup was gone. Sold five times by now. Somebody had already installed mood lighting and a white fuzzy dashboard cover. I'd have to walk.

Things didn't go well when I reached the highway. Thankfully, traffic was light. Several públicos slowed almost to a stop and the drivers made rude comments, then sped away. A dump truck filled with cane cutters passed by at a speed not much faster than I was making, and the workers crammed in the bed reached a consensus that I had a very pretty ass and it would suit them just fine if I rode along with them a ways. I declined politely and after some discussion with the driver, they moved off. There were others too, who mostly drove by and honked their horns or shouted unintelligible encouragements. I soon realized that getting a ride wasn't only unlikely, it might be more dangerous than jumping in a hole.

There was a fine restaurant on that Boca Chica road. I'd eaten there several times but never remembered the name. I'd always called it "The Big Tree" because it had an immense tree out front which the owners wisely surrounded with tile and tables. It was a favorite eatery and watering hole along an otherwise empty stretch of highway. An idea came to me. I'd go there. Use their telephone and have someone pick me up. It couldn't be much more than a half mile walk. I felt stronger by the minute.

I reached the restaurant ten minutes later, adjusted my sea grape apron to best advantage and strolled to a table under the tree. Luckily, there were no other patrons this time of the afternoon.

Moments after I took my seat, a tall, middle-aged waiter arrived with a menu. His face showed no surprise at seeing a naked man, barefoot, his back covered in scabs, and a leaf apron partially covering his privates. "Buenas tardes, Señor," he said politely, laying the menu in front of me. "Can I get you anything to drink?"

I realized then how famished I was. The very thought of food and drink overpowered my senses, but I fought to maintain composure. "Yes," I said. "A cold Presidente would be nice. Do you have a telephone?"

"Sí Señor, we have a teléfono."

"Do you think I could make a call?"

"I am sorry Señor, but the teléfono does not function."

"Maybe the lines are down," I said.

"I wouldn't know about that, Señor. It has not functioned during the years I have worked here. Something about the payment, I believe. Would you like the beer now while you study the menu?"

"Yes," I said.

He was back shortly, the ice-coated bottle held on a round tray together with a frosted glass. "Your cerveza, Señor," he said, placing it on the table. "Would you like me to pour?"

"Why not," I said. "I've waited this long."

"I will be back for your order," he said, gliding away.

I stared for some time at the beer in the glass. Presidente is a premium beer, light in color with a fine white head. It sparkled in the sunshine. The slim glass, sweating as ice turned to water and ran in little rivers down its side, brought tears to my eyes. Could I disturb such a lovely sight? With both hands I drank deeply.

"What would you recommend?" I asked the waiter when he returned.

"The arroz con pollo is especially good this afternoon," he said. "The chef uses a particularly fine tomato sauce with just the right amount of spice to awaken your palate."

"I'll take it," I said. "Maybe a side order of tostones?"

"Why not?"

"Another beer, and some bread too."

"I am at your service," he said, reaching to clear my menu away. Moments later he returned with a cloth napkin, silverware, and a basket of pan de agua.

Half an hour after that he brought me food. If I've eaten a better meal, I don't know when it was. The two beers made me slightly drunk but the enormous quantities of food I consumed balanced things nicely. My only problem now was the bill.

The waiter must've realized that naked people rarely carry cash, but he'd made no mention of it. When he laid the check on the table before me, I said, "Please bring me a pen and some paper."

He nodded. "Sí, Señor."

Minutes later he returned with a small tablet and a lead pencil no longer than a cigarette. "Thank you," I said. He withdrew several steps and waited.

I wrote: *To Whom It May Concern: I, Edgar Espinosa-Jones, hereby declare I owe the proprietor(s) of this restaurant a sum equal to the cost of two cervezas Presidente and one dinner of chicken and rice with a side order of plantain. I inscribe my hand this 9th day of December, 1972.* I signed the document and handed it to the waiter. He looked it over and nodded gravely. "Muchas gracias," he said. "It has been a pleasure to serve you."

"Good afternoon," I said, standing with the napkin in my hand. Before I walked back out toward the highway, I draped it along the back of my outfit to add more protection. I wished it hadn't been lavender.

Less than thirty minutes later I came upon a colmado with a telephone wire running to it. The entire front of the store was open to the highway and a lady about my age stood behind the counter. I approached with the same panache I'd demonstrated at the restaurant. "Good afternoon," I said. "I've had a little accident. I need to use your telephone."

"Don't you come near to me," she said, wide-eyed. "Where your clothes went off to?"

"I told you. I've had a very unfortunate accident. I just want to talk on the telephone."

"I never heard of any kind of accident that makes you naked. You better get on out of here before I call the policía."

"Go ahead," I dared her. "Call the damn policía. They're the reason I'm out here naked in the first place. If you do call them they won't come for a week!"

"You get on out now."

"I'm willing to pay," I said. "I'm actually quite a wealthy man. My father is a tobacco grower and I'm a scuba diver."

"You're funny in the head."

"Please. Stand on the other side of the store where it's safe if you're afraid. I'll call my house. My maid will send someone in a car to bring me clothes and take me out of your life forever."

She was a heavy woman and she put her hands on her hips. "Well, don't suppose it's Christian to leave you out here all naked, but if you take one step toward me I'll pull that little leafy skirt off and tie it around your neck."

"It's a deal," I said, and climbed over the counter.

Señora Villacampa answered on the ninth ring. I explained to her three times that I was Mr. Espinosa-Jones not someone calling for him. Finally, this information registered in her elderly, sleepy mind.

"All I want you to do," I said, "is to go upstairs and get Carmen, my maid."

"People have been here looking for you," she informed me. "Some were crying. Some were angry. You should let people know when you are out of town."

"I was not out of town," I said. "I had an accident." I smiled at the colmado lady.

"You drive too fast," Mercedes said.

"It wasn't that kind of accident. Please! Get Carmen."

"You're expecting a lot," she said. "I haven't been up all those stairs in nearly twenty years."

"Send someone. It's a matter of life or death."

"I doubt that," she said. "I'll see if I can find Julio." She set the phone down.

Fifteen minutes later no one had picked it up. The line was still open.

"What are you waiting for?" the colmado lady asked.

"My maid to come to the phone," I said. "They have to go up to my penthouse to get her. It's on the top floor of an exclusive building in the Capital."

"Naturally," she said. "Be sure you don't touch anything."

"I won't."

Finally, Carmen came on the line. "Señor EJ?"

"Carmen! Thank God. I need some transportation."

"Where are you?"

"At a colmado near Boca Chica."

"Everyone has been looking for you. Your mother is crazy. The police. Sonja Cadavid. Other women. Your entire familia. What is the matter with you? Are you drunk?"

"Listen! I'm naked, all beat up, spent a week down a hole, someone tried to murder me, I'm half starved, feet ripped to shreds, swallowed half the ocean. Send someone!"

"Did you say you were naked?"

Chapter Sixteen

Carmen managed to persuade the Villacampas to send Julio. I recognized the spotless light green Datsun as it slowed on the highway and swung around to park in front of the colmado. A man wearing sea grape leaves and a lavender napkin isn't hard to spot. Without hesitation, Julio popped from the car and jogged toward me carrying a shirt and a pair of jeans.

"Señor, EJ," he said, sober-faced. "Carmen has sent some clothes." He nodded at the large woman behind the counter. "Put them on in there before we go."

"¡No Señor!" she said.

"I'll get dressed in the car," I told Julio. "Thank you for the use of your telephone," I said to the lady. "I'll send someone with money."

"No gracias," she said. "I've been paid well enough."

"Let's go," I said to the chauffeur and piled into the rear of the compact car.

I ditched the leaves and donned the jeans. They were loose. The shirt would be ruined by the seeping scabs on my back but I didn't care. I didn't care about the Villacampa's upholstery either.

"You are going to your apartment?" Julio confirmed.

"Yes." I'd thought of a quick stop at the nearest clinic to get my sores cleaned and bandaged but Carmen could do it. I wanted to find Mickey Alba. I planned to kill him.

The late afternoon sun dropped toward the surface of the broad bay and a jagged squall line waited on the horizon like a line of purple mountains. All during my time in the hole I'd wondered why Dulce and Alejandro were so intent on killing me. I'd discovered nothing about them. Failed in every aspect of an investigation that had created more questions than it answered. Why the persistent, repeated attempts on the life of someone who had nothing? Maybe, I thought, they were just stupid.

The coastal water was losing its aquamarine brilliance, fading to dark amber, like ale. If the Baezes weren't idiots, why spend time and money following me North if I didn't know anything? Or were they following someone else?

Julio was a small, compact man in his mid-thirties who loved the chauffeur life. The Villiacampas, both small themselves, used the car once or twice daily to shop or visit family. These trips were brief. The remaining hours of the work day, Julio spent washing, polishing and sweeping out the Datsun. Sometimes he ran an errand. Most of the time he visited with the various maids in the building, including mine.

"You keep the car very clean," I told him.

"Thank you. We import a special wax from los Estados Unidos. Turtle wax. I apply this at four o'clock every afternoon. A light coating is best. I use a soft cloth also, which I sometimes buy with my own money."

"Does it have air conditioning?"

"Yes. We don't use it. The strain on the engine will decrease gas mileage and cause piston failure."

"I see."

"La Doña believes air conditioning contains bacteria that infests the lungs and contributes to a variety of fatal illnesses. Cancer and emphysema especially."

"Ah," I said. "Seems like a pleasant evening and I'm getting a nice breeze back here."

"Carmen said you had an accident."

"I fell in a hole."

He glanced up at me in the mirror. "A deep hole?"

"Deep and dark. Had to swim out. Lost my clothes in the process. Lucky to be alive, I guess."

"¡Sí Señor! What an experience. What did you eat all those days?"

"Crab."

"Ah, well. Things weren't hopeless then."

"Not unless you prefer it cooked," I said.

I smiled. How roguish and indestructible I felt. A survivor, and much more. Master of my own fate. A lesser man might've died in that hole, his will destroyed by the seeming hopelessness of it, and that man's bones might be there for generations until some scuba diver popped his head up and came face to face with them. But not my bones. My bones were safe and sound beneath my skin.

Julio stopped at an intersection where a policía in gray uniform and white gloves directed cross traffic. He signaled us finally and we moved forward. As the oncoming traffic began to flow past my window I looked out at a Datsun 210 and into the face of Dulce Baez behind the wheel. It must've only been a moment but I saw her eyes widen and burn like jets of fire across the distance between us. A wave of nausea swept me. My pores responded and I was instantly bathed in sweat. Then she was gone. The light was poor. It was an impossible coincidence. Yes, of course, impossible. It had seemed so real.

I slid down in the seat and rode the rest of the way in silence, no longer indestructible. Julio asked permission to turn on the radio and listen to his favorite station. He promised to keep the volume low. Voices and music seemed odd to me after so long without human contact. I listened half-heartedly.

Julio didn't drop me in front when we got home, but pulled the car into its usual spot alongside the Villacampa's immaculate garden. "Thank you for the ride and the clothes," I told him. "I will come down and thank the Villacampas personally in the morning, after I've rested."

"Sí, Señor," he said, already walking around the tiny vehicle to inspect it. I'd once seen him picking small stones from the tire tread with one of the doctor's dental instruments.

Upstairs, Carmen stood in the front doorway smiling. She'd kept the rental teeth. "What's for dinner?" I asked.

"You are alive," she said and grabbed my hand. "You will be eating with Sonja Cadavid tonight but you don't look too good. Come to the bedroom."

"Carmen. I'm in no mood for jokes."

"I'm not talking about that kind of bed. You said you were injured. I want to see it. Maybe we need to call Dr. Villacampa up here."

"He's a dentist."

"It's all the same." She led me into my bedroom, took off my shirt and gasped. "¡Por Dios! This is bad."

"I swam into some sharp rocks," I said. "Wash your hands, with soap, and then wash the cuts if you insist on helping. Maybe you can clean the bits of rock out."

"It's going to hurt," she warned.

She returned with a basin of warm water and towels. I asked about Sonja. "Suppose she's been worried."

"I saw no tears," Carmen said, hiking her dress and climbing onto my rump. "Her jaw was set."

"I can't see her tonight," I said. "Before I do anything I'm going to find Mickey Alba."

She packed a large bath towel on each side of me. "Lift yourself so I can tuck this under," she said. "No one has told you, of course."

"What?"

"About Alba."

"Carmen!"

"He's been shot with a machine gun."

"What are you talking about?" I rolled onto my side to see her face.

"Downtown. The day you disappeared. No one knows what it's about."

"Is he alive?"

"In the hospital. Will he survive? I don't think so. Machine guns are a bad thing."

I moved to get up.

"Lie down," she ordered. "He's unconscious. Doña Cadavid told me this morning. Three bullets are in him. You should see La Doña, even before you see your family. I think she has important things to tell you."

"I'm going crazy," I said, resting back on my stomach.

She worked the better part of an hour cleaning the wounds, picking out bits of sand and larger pieces of limestone lodged under the skin. I bled enough to be worried about it but she said she'd seen worse in a knife fight once and explained that it was always very bad when the blood squirted or sprayed, this running and seeping was nothing to fear. After the cleaning, she found fresh bandages in a first aid kit I kept in my office. "Many of these holes in you are close together," she complained. "It would not be good to get tape over them and open the scabs when you peel it off."

I had to admit she had a gentle touch. "You've kept the teeth, I noticed."

"Only for two weeks," she said. "They gave me a discount."

"Sounds great."

"I'm not so sure. They itch."

Having smelled her breath often enough I said, "Maybe you should take them out and clean them."

"It's something to think about," she said.

When she'd finished I felt better and wanted a drink. "I really missed this place," I confessed. "All that time in the dark, dreaming of sitting on the balcony. Lights. Ship on the horizon. Balmy night air."

"Me?"

"Yes, you too, but not the way you'd like."

"Fine," she said. "Go sit on your precious balcony. Look at the lights. I'll bring you some medicine in a glass and you can drink all night." She left in a huff, a portion of which was real, the rest manufactured.

I didn't look at the lights but the place where Dulce and Alejandro had stood with the torch and a beheaded chicken. How long before they came again? She had seen me in the car. It wasn't a dream. It was real. Things that should be dreams had become real in my life and it took time to trust it as truth. Mickey, I said to myself. Mickey. They've done it to you too.

Carmen returned with my drink, peeved expression still in place. "Thank you," I said, taking her hand. "Thank you for everything you do."

Sincerity, especially from me, made her nervous. "De nada," she answered. "Should I go down and find Doña Cadavid on the teléfono?"

"I suppose," I said, dropping her hand and accepting the drink. "You'll be stuck cooking dinner for two later on."

She shrugged. "That's a woman who loves soup. I have some left over and I can make my squid and purple rice. You both like that."

"Fine," I said. "Make the call."

* * *

It wasn't the Sonja Cadavid I'd expected who arrived at my house. She didn't cling to me or cry or even take my hand, but marched stiffly from the front door to the balcony without a word.

After she was seated and ordered Carmen away for a glass of wine, she asked mechanically, "How are you?"

"Fine," I said. "Some crab bites and cuts. A bout with starvation. I'm fine."

"I thought you were dead."

"Maybe you'd like to kiss me then. Since I'm not, I mean."

"I'm more likely to kill you. Do you know what you're doing? What have you gotten yourself into? How many times does someone have to try and kill you before you start paying attention?"

"I can take care of myself," I said, defending my manhood.

She only raised an eyebrow. "Who did this to you?"

"The couple who had the beheaded chicken out here the other night."

"What are their names?"

"Dulce and Alejandro Baez. At least those are the names they used when they worked at the U.S. Ambassador's Residence."

"What do you know about them?"

"Not much."

"The same as you know about staying alive," she said bitterly. "I will deal with them."

This was the wrong thing for her to say and the wrong time to say it. "No," I said coldly. "You will not *deal* with them. You will mind your own business or you can go straight to hell." I had more to say but Carmen came with the wine.

I sat staring at Sonja. She stared at the wine glass. Finally, she said, "I love you. I've never been so scared in my life, not even when I escaped Castro. Where were you?"

"Where did you look?"

"Everywhere. I had everybody I know looking."

"I was down a hole inside a cave beyond Boca Chica."

She glanced up and flashed a quick grin. "Well, I didn't look there."

"Nobody else did either." I told her the whole story then and it softened her up. She cried when I explained my plan to drown myself.

"I knew about your friend Mickey," she said. "I've been to the hospital. He's heavily sedated and very seriously wounded. Another policía was killed. When I spoke your name he moaned and swore but I couldn't make anything of what he said. I saw him again yesterday. He was sleeping. The doctors say very little."

"I'll see him tomorrow."

"Can I kiss you now? I'm sorry for being so tough before."

"Be gentle," I said, standing.

She caught my head in both hands and it was anything but gentle. I felt better. "Come and sit on my lap," she begged after a second kiss. "Please. I want to feel your weight on me."

I lowered myself down carefully. She held me like a child. "Carmen is going to make us dinner," I said.

"Kiss me some more."

Later, I asked, "Am I heavy?"

"No, just sit still."

"I thought about you every day in that hole." Our position suddenly embarrassed me. I slid from her lap and stood by the railing. "It's funny. You take it all with you. Everything. Everybody. The physical world is spiritual too. I mean it's still there even if it's not. ¿Entiendes?" She pulled her feet up beneath her, eyes unblinking. "I talked to you. You talked back and said just the things I wanted you to say." I thought she might smile then but she didn't. "So we talked about your family, Castro, the home you lost. We decided some things. For example we decided I couldn't die and leave you. You'd be tormented too much by that."

"Tormented?" She rubbed her eyes.

"Sure. My death, just another reason the world's rotten. When you walked in tonight I saw it in your eyes. Like when you go to do your Cuba thing. Now this. More bitterness. Torment." I shrugged. "You want to avenge everything."

"Bitterness. Is that what you think it is? I'm like some jilted lover?" She stared down for a long while without looking up. Finally she said, "It's time. You can tell me if I have anything to avenge."

"Time for what?"

"To straighten you out my friend. You like stories. I'll tell you one."

"Oh?" I said. "Well, I'm not in the mood. I'm tired."

"Shut up and listen." She snapped. "Even though it's a good story it isn't a rare one. It's about a little girl, eleven years old, who lived with her father, who was a banker, and her mother, who loved the piano, and a sister who was thirteen. They lived in a thriving city 90 miles from Florida. Both girls were in school and the little girl studied mathematics, which she greatly loved, and spent her leisure time snorkeling in a quiet cove not far from their house.

"This little girl was not a politician. She did not understand politics or care about it. She cared about spotted eels, sea fans, sponges and parrot fish. Sometimes as she swam she would calculate sums in her head, multiplying and dividing greater and greater numbers until they made her laugh and she choked on the warm salt water.

"She came home one day carrying two nice conch in a mesh bag. She had very skinny legs, this girl. Her house was empty, even though it was almost 7:30 in the evening and she was late and due for a scolding. She wandered the empty rooms calling the names of her family. Mommy, she called. ¿Papá? ¿Papá? Letty? Aren't you home Letty? No one answered. Finally, crying now, she ran out back to the maid's quarters, and the maid, María, threw her arms around the little girl and comforted her. But it didn't last, because María told her how the people of the new "liberator" came and took her family. They were being held with others in the Church of the Altagracia, the church of her baptism. She was not to go there. María did not know what would become of the little girl's family but promised to go and seek answers, and meanwhile she must stay hidden. She mustn't be seen in the street.

"When María left, the little girl sat in her room for awhile among her things. All the things of her life. Typical things that little girls have - funny boxes with cigar rings and rare jewels, a plastic telephone, a chair too small to sit in, toys, stuffed animals, and dolls of course. After awhile these things were no comfort. Their shapes muted by the dark. She began to cry. Then she slept.

"It must've been almost midnight, or later, she awoke. María hadn't returned and there were noises in the house, just house noises but they frightened her so she ran outside into the garden. The night was clear and cool, a dome of stars she hadn't remembered as so bright. There were gunshots now in the night sometimes. It started the year before. Castro. She remembered that name. Where was María? Why hadn't she come back?

"She sat on the porch of the fine old house and waited and waited. She was as patient as any eleven-year-old girl can be."

Sonja crossed her arms hard against her breasts and said, "Then she went to the church.

"There things were different. Men with guns stood near the door smoking and drinking rum. They wore the odd green uniforms and bucket caps of the revolutionaries, like billboards and posters of Castro and Che Guevara. She asked them about her family. One of the soldiers spit on her face and told her she was a little capitalist bitch and pushed her inside with the others.

"The Church was crowded with women and children. Electricity was off and prisoners used altar candles for light. Hundreds packed the church, some sobbing, swearing, others calm and silent. The flickering candlelight was like a Christmas mass but no one sang or made a joyful noise to the Lord. She met two girls she knew and they directed her to a black recess behind an open side door, soldiers just outside, where she found her mother and sister. They were unharmed, sitting in the dark, huddled like survivors.

"Papá was taken. No one knew where. It was bad. Some of the women had been taken too. Mother didn't look like herself. Older, dark-eyed and tired. She wasn't crying but when she embraced the little girl her hands trembled. They whispered a great many things to each other there in the dark, things she can't remember today. It would be fine if she could remember them, just a few. She remembers the smell of her mother's sweat. The smell of fear.

"These guards by the door drank heavily and urinated often. Sometimes they went behind the low wall that supported the crucifix and took a girl along to entertain themselves. The girls didn't come back. Most were older than eleven. The night wore on, the men became more drunk. They took an old woman, joking about gray hair. They were very drunk.

"Mother saw that sometimes they were all gone at once, leaving the door unguarded. Small groups of women and children were regularly taken from the church, others were still being brought in. Soldiers milled around. Some civilians had brought food and drink and sat talking with the soldiers on the lawn. The mother of these two girls was very brave that night and she made the girls brave. Couldn't they swim to one of the small fishing boats left anchored in the harbor and start the engine or row along the coast to the house of their uncle, who was himself a fisherman? Tell him what happened. Ask for help.

"They must go alone because their mother knew they would be safer alone. Could plead ignorance. At worst, get a beating and be sent back. With an adult, they'd be shot or sent to entertain the drunkards. I won't tell you about the crying, or clinging, or the feeling in your stomach of being kicked. The girls waited until the communist soldiers were all urinating or screwing their classmates, then walked quietly away from the Church of the Altagracia, down to the harbor and stole someone's boat.

"Several days later they were in Miami. They never saw their mother or father again. That's the story. I didn't mean it to go so long," she said. "What do you think? How soon do I forget, marry a nice man like you, have my own children? How soon, Eddie? How soon?" She was crying. "Sí mi amor, I am tormented, but bitter, no. Sad, angry."

"You should've told me before," I said.

She shook her head and I passed across my handkerchief. I loved Sonja Cadavid.

"That was 1960," Sonja said. "Fourteen years ago. It's the fear. It feeds inside, eating until it hollows you out. Makes you empty. I remember everything pretty much still, but I don't have to remember the fear, I still feel it. Maybe when that's gone, when I've done whatever it is I must do to be rid of it, then I'll be a wife, even a mother. That's what I think."

"I'm sorry," I said. "Sorry for that little girl you were."

"I'm not sorry anymore. Not even for my parents. Parents die and we're kind of prepared for it all our lives. It's the violence against us, yes. But the disregard! Indiferencia en total. *Capitalists*, not people. I got drunk for the first time the night I heard Che Guevara died, and I'll live to see Castro in his grave. They call us the Jews of the Caribbean and we are like Jews. Butchered, but not destroyed. We are stronger now and it will not happen again. I'm a woman, but someday if I'm lucky, I'll get close to Castro and kill him. Not for my mother and father, or Cuba, but for the innocence he robbed from us, from all the children. In Cuba now an eleven year old girl sells herself along the Malecón. The church is destroyed. I think even God abandoned us."

In my own head was the media Fidel, a bearded, cigar-smoking revolutionary who seemed more romantic than vicious. His image roguish, his bloody hands hidden behind his back. Had Kennedy allowed him to keep his nukes, his name might be as foul as Hitler's.

"It's too late in the day," Sonja said, "for this kind of talk. And I know you're tired, and I'm still frightened for you, but I want to add something. Hector, Luis, Jorge, the maid, the cook, Mejia my business manager - all these are the children. They did not come with me but we met in Miami or somewhere along the way. I know you are uncomfortable around them. They too. It can't be helped. Veterans have their own reality that isn't shared. You should know that."

"What about your sister?"

"Miami. Married a banker like Papá. They have four children and she raises money for us and those like us." Humorously, Sonja placed a thin finger to her temple. "She forgets. I remember. It is better to forget. They are a happy family and my nieces and nephews are such American kids." She motioned me back onto her lap but I shook my head. "My work isn't relief from the past, it's healing, and you're what I think of in *my* hole. But Darling, one of us needs to find a job as an accountant."

I rested my rump against the wrought iron railing. Sonja Cadavid's hair was raven black and slick as wet stone.

After a long while Sonja straightened her legs and said, "Find me a cigarette. My legs are asleep."

I kept cigarettes in a small handcrafted wooden case on the coffee table. Montecarlo. Marlboro in the living room. I missed my lighter, which was still inside the right pocket of my trousers folded neatly at the bottom of a hole. Maybe I could fish them out somehow. I found a book of matches and lit her cigarette.

Sonja smoked like she did everything, with confidence. "Are you going to be mad again if I tell you some things I know?" she asked.

"What things?"

"Answer me."

"How do I know if I'm going to be mad before I hear what you have to say?"

"Because these are not things you want to hear."

"All right. I promise."

She inhaled hungrily and let the smoke snap on her pink lips as she spoke. "You are in much more trouble than you imagine. The rumor while you were gone was that you had fled the country because you are somehow implicated in Ambassador Quist's death. Some say as part of a cover-up. Others say you were hired by terrorists. The United States believes you are a meddling fool at best or maybe extorting money from Quist's grieving family. You've charmed the teenaged daughter, having slept with her at a secret Haitian rendezvous. You've robbed the Ambassador's grave in Arlington, lied to the family in New York, and molested U.S. citizens there in the streets, including the DCM, now U.S. charge' d'affaires to this country. Day before yesterday I know for a fact that high-ranking officials at the U.S. Embassy met with Dominican Secret Service to decide your fate. Mi Amor, you are in more danger than Castro and he has a dozen fake motorcades driving endlessly around Havana."

She grinned. "You fell off a scooter by my house."

"Delbrick," I said.

"Duane Delbrick?"

"I saw him with Dulce in New York. Slugged her. Cursed him. He's connected to them and he has the most to gain if Quist disappears." I looked at her for a moment. "He's sleeping with Olivia Quist."

"Well," she said. "That makes it unanimous then."

"You are now outside the bounds of my promise not to get mad."

"I know we've been over this before."

"I did not sleep with her. I'm not going to say it again."

"Sorry."

"Is that all?"

"No." She stood and carried her cigarette to the railing, dropping it carelessly into Mercedes Villacampa's immaculate garden. "There was a request to the CIA that you be terminated."

"How could you know that?"

"EJ."

"Okay. Why?"

"You don't ask *why*."

"Who?"

She shrugged. "Orders are orders. Those in charge don't expect questions from those who carry out the field work. More important is that such matters aren't easily accomplished or such orders easily issued. You've made powerful enemies. If such an order were issued against me I'd expect to live a year, no more, and then only as a mole somewhere. You might be dead now if you hadn't jumped into a hole."

Sonja was wearing a calf-length blue skirt and low-cut white blouse that ruffled across her breasts. Between them hung the amber tear-drop I'd given her last Christmas. "I've never known you to exaggerate," I said.

"I'm deathly afraid you won't take this seriously."

"One question. Can a single person instigate something like this?"

"Maybe, if they're powerful enough."

"I don't mean like the President. I mean like Delbrick or someone he might know."

"Hard to say. He couldn't order such a thing."

"Can you find out?"

"You want my help?"

"Yes."

She moved closer and draped her arms around my neck. "The order was rescinded yesterday. Do you want to know why?"

"Sonja! This isn't funny."

"Exactamente, my wooden-headed lover. I shock you so you accept the truth." She kissed me lightly. "Now, do you want to know why?"

"Thought you didn't know *whys*."

"I know this time," she said.

"So?"

"It was reported to the CIA that you gathered the Quist family in a New York restaurant and tried to convince them the Ambassador was a zombie," she said, looking closely into my eyes. "Is that true?"

"People are quoting me out of context," I complained. "Anyway, how would that save my life?"

"Even the CIA won't terminate a lunatic."

"You're kidding."

"No, I'm not. Keep in mind that Dominican Secret Service has no such scruples. Your only chance is to get your friend Lt. Alba to vouch for you and to raise hell about his dead officer and the attempt on his life. And he better make you the hero, if he can manage to stay alive himself."

A horrible thought came to me. "They'll go after him again."

"I've someone there around the clock," she said. "He's well protected without anyone knowing."

"So, we're on the same team."

"For awhile." She drew a breath. "Your Adam Quist is dead, Mi Amor. Whoever killed him is afraid of what you know."

"That's the trouble," I confessed. "I don't know a damn thing."

"Maybe you do." She kissed the end of my nose. "But until Alba can straighten this out or something else happens, we better stash you somewhere safe. Now you do look tired. Come to bed."

"Are you staying?"

"Someone has to guard you."

* * *

In the morning I left Sonja sleeping in my bed. My head throbbed and I was shaky. Night sweats and bad dreams left me jumpy and weary. Dulce's head had appeared behind glass in my dreams. I scrutinized the vacant lot across the street. Empty even of goats.

Ignoring the breakfast Carmen prepared, I caught a público to the hospital, stopping, changing cabs. Once I ducked out the back door of a magazine shop, crossed two alleys before catching another publico. No one followed.

Mickey was in a general hospital guarded by Sonja's man Luis, who seemed neither pleased nor surprised to see me. I made arrangements to have Mickey moved to a private clinic with iron gates and locked doors. The doctors there U.S. trained and expensive. Luis didn't ask questions and promised to stay on guard, relieved to be leaving the large hospital for a more secure one.

Only then did I go into Mickey's room. He was sitting up and his wife was spooning soup into his mouth. "I thought you were in a coma or something," I said.

"EJ! ¡Por Dios!" his wife María said. "You look worse than Mickey." After five kids and the hardships of a cops salary, María herself looked like a teenager. She had peanut butter skin and long black hair tied at the nape of her neck. A woman worth knowing, and almost like a sister to me. "Sonja's man told me you were okay. Come and kiss me. I've got to keep feeding him while he can eat. He's taken very little since the shooting. This place is miserable."

I kissed her on both ears. "He's being moved. Someplace safe, more professional. You ride with him in the ambulance. Luis too."

"Thank you darling."

"What about me?" Mickey croaked.

"I was hoping you weren't able to talk," I said. "Now I've got to endure the stories about how you were gunned down in the streets saving my life. I'll be an old man and still won't hear the end of it."

Mickey smiled. "Bastardo," he said. There were tears in his eyes.

His face held the pallor of illness and pain. His torso was swathed in bandages. "Who shot you?" I blurted.

"Alejandro. I saw the barrel come out the window when I was talking to you on the radio. Before I could drop it and pull my pistol up, he sprayed the car and the sidewalk. He knew we were following."

"Yes," I said. "They were waiting for me outside the city."

"What happened?"

I chuckled. "Followed them into a cave, they caught me, I escaped by jumping down a hole. Swam out finally and walked to the highway. Some scrapes on my back. Nothing like what's happened to you."

"They're like demons," he said. "I'm being moved because it's not safe, even now?"

"We know something, Mickey. They had the damn CIA involved. Don't think now. Get better. We need time. We're missing something. I'm missing something."

"EJ," María said. "I can't lose him. Stay with us?"

"Until you're both safe in the clinic." I caressed her arm and felt a shiver. "Then I'm going to find them. I'm tired of losing to these people." I turned to Mickey. "I need a pistol and a shotgun."

"At the house," Mickey said. "María can get them." He brushed the spoon away. "Amigo, listen to me. You can't hesitate. When you see them, kill them. Don't go back to your apartment. Change your habits. Disappear, understand? Then surprise them and kill them immediately. Without mercy, Amigo. ¡Sin compasión! Anyway," he said, resting back on the pillow, "you owe me money."

* * *

After that I did go back to my apartment, packed a bag and picked up my Jeep. Carmen was shopping and the apartment was empty. No one saw me. Sonja had gone too. The bed was even made. What she had said the night before comforted me now. For the first time since we'd met, I touched Sonja's vulnerability and it strengthened me. She was a closed book and if she opened and read a page to me it could only mean that she trusted me. I vowed then to reward it with action. First, find a small hotel or pension somewhere and check in under an assumed name for a few days until I could make a plan. I also needed to call people I knew would help me.

Cosme the barber had a phone and I needed a private place to make the calls. Hotel switchboards were not private and I refused to involve my family or lean on Sonja again. A little machismo in that, but what's the harm? My American half agreed with my Dominican half, so it had to be the right decision.

I couldn't get a phone in my penthouse but Cosme had one in his barbershop in the worst slum in Arroyo Hondo. He'd built along a major street with telephone lines leading to the homes of the wealthy, and I needed a haircut anyway and a manicure.

I didn't bother Cosme with my adventures. He'd been full of questions about Haiti. "Can I use your phone?" I asked finally.

"¿Cómo no?"

It was black, rotary dial, polished. I'd never heard it ring. "Looks new," I said.

"Sí. I don't give out the number."

"Why not?"

"The ringing bothers the pig."

"I didn't know that about pigs," I said.

"They have sensitive ears. It rang once two years ago and he pissed on the floor. Now, I don't give out the number."

"Very sensible," I said.

My calls were short. First to Mr. Yancy for a telephone number he was reluctant to give, then a Colonel in the Policía Nacional who owed me a very big favor, my father and mother to calm them down. Later, I'd call Sonja.

"There," I said to Cosme. "Thanks. I've been away and there are many details to arrange now that I'm back."

"You are done with Haiti?"

"I hope so." I eased back in the chair. My scabs were tender. "Anyway, I've got enough trouble right here at home."

"Voodoo?"

"Why did you say that?"

"Haiti is voodoo. The Haitians cut our cane and bring this with them. I've heard stories from the campo, even in the Capital." He ran his fingers through my hair, rubbing in the masculine-smelling, oil-based product used by barbers around the world. "Now you come from Haiti. Maybe you have brought it with you."

"I brought something with me," I said. "Time now to wash it off."

"Maybe I can help you," he said.

"I'm grateful for the offer," I told him. "Shouldn't be speaking of these things here. Please let me apologize."

"You are waiting for something bad? Someone?"

I took a closer look at Cosme. "Why do you say that?"

"Your eyes are restless."

"Yes. I'm waiting." I shifted in the chair. "Don't worry. I was careful coming here."

"How long have I cut your hair?"

"Long time."

"Then I can help you."

"Cosme," I said firmly. "This is not your business. I'm sorry I mentioned it. I'm sorry my eyes are restless, too. Everything is fine. I just need to disappear for a few days."

For awhile Cosme worked in silence. I heard his chickens clucking and pecking in the mud behind the shop. Traffic moved on the road and the voices of children carried intermittently through the two glassless windows. "Señor Espinosa-Jones," Cosme said formally. "I can disappear you."

"Disappear me?"

"Sometimes a man likes to be invisible. Times when not even one person knows where you are. Have you never felt that?"

"When I was a kid," I said. "It's more difficult for adults."

"I can arrange it."

"Oh?"

"I have a place."

I grinned at him. "But then I wouldn't really have disappeared because you'd know where I was."

He returned my smile. "No matter. I'm only a barber."

"You're serious. Where is this place?"

"Near here. It's used sometimes by men who are having trouble with their wives, understand? A simple place but comfortable. It has a floor."

"Could I put my car there?"

"Maybe, but we can walk."

"From here?"

"Yes."

"Now?"

"¿Cómo no? I take you," the barber said. "You will vanish and at night nothing will disturb your rest."

Chapter Seventeen

Behind the barbershop the city died out. A short walk through packed mud, a scattering of tall plantains, along a rusted barbed wire fence to a broken wooden gate, and I not only vanished but exchanged metropolitan for rural. Chickens replaced públicos and wood replaced concrete. Buildings were homemade, people everywhere, most of them poor.

My first thought was that I'd just made a huge mistake. Everyone was staring. "Maybe this isn't such a good idea," I told Cosme as I followed him along a winding path between the simple homes and garden plots.

"I will tell them about you," he said.

"Tell them what?" I asked.

"You're having trouble with your wife," he said, turning on the path.

"I'm not married."

"I know," Cosme grinned. "You're safe here. No one knows your name. A man doing what men do in secret."

"Okay," I said. The sudden opportunity to disappear got a grip on me.

"A young woman, not old and ugly like your wife," the barber chuckled, "will come to take care of you. My daughter, Vivian. She's eighteen."

"Your daughter? Isn't that carrying friendship a little too far?"

He patted my arm and smiled. "I have many daughters. This one has a bad reputation, but what people believe is not always the truth. She will bring you food and stay with you until morning. She is a virgin."

"Cosme...."

"Follow me," he said, turning back along the path.

I followed, determined to see the place, then find a hotel. I'd really had enough teenaged girls. This is what happens when you peek into the private life of your barber.

We passed through an arch of bougainvillea into a sandy yard surrounded by a solid cactus fence of impenetrable needles. At its center was a frame house - pink walls, blue windows, white trim, and a green porch, set on concrete blocks and topped with a rusty tin roof. Under the porch there was a gaunt dog, chickens, and a large iguana tied with a rope around its neck.

"Alberto," Cosme explained.

"The dog or the lizard?"

"The dog is worthless. The lizard we keep tied. Let him loose when you go to bed. He stays in the yard and eats what he can find. He is very quiet."

"I really hate reptiles," I admitted.

Cosme whistled. The lizard, at least five feet long, stirred and crawled out from beneath the porch. "Come Alberto. Here. Come to me!" Alberto came running, forked tongue flicking the air. He ran out of rope at Cosme's knees and from his pocket the barber tossed him a treat of some kind. The lizard swallowed it whole. "He comes when you call him," Cosme went on. "I'll show you the inside." He started for the steps, Alberto at his heels.

"Can't I see from here?"

Cosme stopped at the steps. "Just walk normally. Speak to him. Not loudly."

In the west, near Lake Enriquillo, we have crocodiles that give you that same lustful look. I dashed up the steps.

Inside, the place was a real sugar shack decorated in blood red and black. An over-sized bed waited under a red and black paisley spread. I gazed at the scattering of plain tables and chairs; tables sporting candles stuck in wine bottles, windows covered with roll-up bamboo shades. A floor of swept boards. There was a small kitchen too, but the main cooking area was out back next to a laundry sink.

"Cozy," I said.

"Sí," he responded with pride.

"Gracias," I said. "I'll think it over."

"Wait." Cosme strode across the room to the bed and pointed down at an old telephone on the bedside table. "You can work here."

"This place has a phone?"

"¿Cómo no?"

Cosme led me to the window and showed me the line, propped on homemade poles leading across the dirt yard and into the trees. I walked back, sat on the bed and lifted the receiver. Strong dial tone. "Well, maybe," I told him, thinking about what Mickey had said and of days ahead ducking into alleys, watching my back. "Okay, I'll take you up on it but I'll need some things and a place for my Jeep."

"No problema." He smiled. "We will drink rum tonight and kill some chickens for a feast."

Within an hour the entire community of squatters had cleared for action - my Jeep hidden, shotgun and pistol by my side, people dropping by to introduce themselves, pay their respects to Edgar the Virgin's new lover, and the lizard was taking a shine to me.

By mid-morning I was sitting comfortably on a sexy black and red bedspread talking patiently with Mercedes Villacampa. "You have to speak louder," she was saying. "The signal is weak today."

"Put the receiver by your ear," I suggested. "This is Edgar Espinosa-Jones. I live upstairs. I want to talk to my maid, Carmen."

There was a long pause while she took all this in. "Are you lost again?"

"No. I just need to talk to her."

"This is not a public telephone," she complained and dropped the receiver.

I took this to mean she'd given in and was gone to call Carmen.

"¿Señor EJ?" Carmen's distant voice finally questioned the receiver.

"Listen. I'm going to Miami for a few days and do some Christmas shopping," I lied. "I'll be back by the fifteenth. Sixteenth for sure."

"Aren't you coming home to pack?"

"No," I said. "I've got enough and can buy whatever else I need there."

"How is your back?" Carmen inquired.

"Better. Nice hard scabs." I checked Carmen's name off my list on the pad by the phone. "Take a few days off, why don't you? Go to Bonao and see your mother. Spend time with your kids. If there's any money left in the cookie jar buy presents for them from me." This was always a popular suggestion. She told the children the presents came from her, of course, then confessed to me about it later, sometimes with tears. On such occasions I allowed her a drink.

"Will you miss me in Miami?"

"No."

"Who will tend your back and change the bandages?"

"Don't worry about me. I'll be fine. Lock up when you leave and make sure the steel doors are locked too."

"Sí Señor. Maybe you can bring me a radio from Miami?"

"Goodbye Carmen." I hung up.

My next call was to the clinic to check on Mickey. He was fine and Sonja's men were taking turns standing guard, though the police colonel I'd called earlier from the barbershop had already sent a dozen armed officers to surround the place. Truthfully, I had more faith in Sonja's few, but machinegun-totting men in uniform are such a pleasant deterrent. And you never know, they might shoot somebody.

Then I dialed Sonja and told her what I planned to do. Her voice had an edge. "This is not clever. This hiding," she warned. "Stay where we can protect you."

"Tried that, remember?"

"Not with me," she said. "I'm not the policía."

"I know, Darling. You're tough as nails. Just please, please let me handle this."

"Eddie, listen to me," she begged. "I have a very bad feeling about this hiding of yours. Wherever you are, tell me so I can at least be with you."

"No. I'm only safe here if nobody knows. Take care of Mickey. I'll call in a couple days when I've figured this out, done what needs doing. Maybe we'll drive out to Punta Cana and ride horses. You like that. Hasta luego, mi amor." I hung up. Sonja would just have to sit this one out. I wasn't going to hide under her bed.

I called Mr. Yancy once again. Gave him my number at the Sugar Shack and he very carefully read me the number I needed. "Sure you want this number?" he'd asked. I'd anticipated the question and simply answered yes without explanation. "He won't cooperate with you unless I pressure him," he said. "You've thought carefully about this?"

"Yes," I assured him.

"Give me an hour," he said. "Then make the call." He wished me luck then, his voice frail and thready.

"You'll hear from me soon," I promised.

Then I made the most important call. Olivia. She was back on the island with her family closing The Residence and packing.

"Is it really you?" she asked when they called her to the phone.

"It's me."

"I've been crazy! I called that ridiculous Mercedes woman at your apartment. What is the matter with her?" She was breathless, running her words together. "Oh God, I thought you were dead."

"Everything's fine. Scratches and bruises, but I need to talk to you. It's very important. Can you meet me?"

"Anywhere!" she said. "Now?"

"Later this afternoon. I've got some things to clear up first."

"Where?"

"The Mirador in Naco."

"The high rise with the restaurant on top?"

"Yes, but in the bar. I'll even buy you a glass of wine."

"I'm more in the mood for bourbon," she said.

"Around four?"

"I can't wait to see you."

"One more thing, and I don't mean to be melodramatic, but please be sure you're not followed. Change cars. Go in and out the back doors of some places. Stuff like that."

"Sounds exhausting," she said. "Is all this really necessary?"

"When you get there I'll tell you what it's like to be down a dark hole for seven days."

"Sorry."

"My best friend's lying in a hospital with three bullet holes in him, an armed policeman surrounded by his own men. You're coming alone. Watch your back like I told you. We'll joke about it all later when the Baez couple are safe and cozy in a cell somewhere, okay?"

"I said I'm sorry."

"Just be careful. See you at four." I hung up.

Meeting Olivia was risky. I only wanted one thing. The answer to one question, but I needed to look her straight in the eye when I asked it. If she blinked, I'd know.

An hour later, already a hot day for December, I glanced down at the number Mr. Yancy had given me. Was I desperate enough to dial it? I stood and strolled to the window by the table. The yard had a few trees, palms and one young grapefruit. Here and there in the raked dirt a coconut had fallen undisturbed. If I dialed the number was I Espinosa-Jones, or Jones-Espinosa? Did I secretly think I was a Dominican who got to play American when it suited him?

An American who worked at the Embassy once told me that he never revealed his true nationality outside work. Whenever asked, he claimed to be Canadian. It was safer, he said, and avoided a lot of political problems. I didn't admire the guy, any more than the so-called Christians who pale at the mention of Christ. With such loyalty it's a wonder Christianity or Democracy succeeds at all. Now, I thought, it's my turn to be tested.

The number Mr. Yancy had given me was the home phone of Lieutenant Colonel Marcus Z. Blitzen, commander of our U.S. Military Assistance Advisory Group (MAAG), America's military gift to the Third World. A number very few Dominicans would dial, though I'd met Col. Blitzen socially. Even in my small way, I would be asking for U.S. military intervention. It made me weak, and if Mickey Alba found out he'd die of shame. On the other hand, Blitzen was a weapon of mass destruction I could drop directly on the heads of Dulce and Alejandro Baez and they'd never know what hit them.

Blitzen was a feared, sometimes hated, advisor. Much had been written about early military advisors in Vietnam and people often blamed the war on them instead of the politicians. Or at the very least, they were held in contempt. Men like Blitzen became 1970s bogeymen.

But my request, through Yancy, was unofficial and off the record. I'd owe a favor in return. So would Yancy. All of us sticking our necks out. For his part, Col. Blitzen was a son-of-a-bitch. But a powerful one.

I walked back to the love bed and dialed.

* * *

Colonel Blitzen insisted we meet at his home. It was secure, swept for listening devices twice daily he claimed. Though I doubted anyone cared what advice he gave Dominican military leaders, who didn't have the training, desire, or integrity to do anything with it anyway. I figured he was priming the Dominican Army, now crashing through the brush in search of Caamaño, to invade Cuba. The Army had more generals than privates and I suppose they needed something to do, but it was his extracurricular activities that kept us all in awe of him.

His house was palatial. The money was provided by his wife, Borneo, a whale who dressed like an exotic dancer and came from a family of Georgia rubber importers heavily invested in Southeast Asia. She once said her dad gave her a million dollars on every birthday. She was forty-six.

Borneo opened her own door wearing a halter top that failed to contain her or a roll of white doughy flesh curling beneath it. Otherwise she was naked, except for hot pants and high-heeled sandals. She had tiny feet.

"EJ! My God, how long has it been? You big Latin hunk!" She rolled me up over her belly and kissed me. "Blitzen's in the study," she said. "He can wait, we'll drink." She put me down.

Moments later she brought tall glasses of rum punch. "Come on baby," she begged. "Let's get drunk and screw."

"Bit early for me," I said, apologies to Buffett.

"For drinking, or fooling around?"

"As a Latino, it's hard to live up to either myth."

She stroked my hair. "Why don't you come by once in awhile when Blitzen's out in the jungle with the boys? We'd have a blast!"

"I don't know why I haven't thought of it?" I said. "You're such a kidder."

"Who's kidding?"

"Maybe I should see the Colonel."

"Chicken," she said, tossing back a mane of bleached hair.

Borneo was a legendary hostess, creating some of the best parties in the Capital. More international politics was resolved, business deals struck, and romantic trysts whispered around Borneo's pool, than in all the secret locations in Santo Domingo. Horny Borny was an institution. Her husband, Colonel Marcus Blitzen, was another matter.

When I entered his study, a room overloaded with furniture more suited to New England, he ignored me for some time, writing patiently at a polished desk. An average appearing man, medium height and physically fit without the over-developed physique common to body worshippers. His square face was composed and he could just as well have been writing the coverage options on my insurance policy. I tried to remember how dangerous he was.

At last Col. Blitzen said, "I greet you in the name of the United States of America. Sit down."

"Thank you Colonel. I'm already American by birth."

"Don't look it," he said. "But I did hear that somewhere."

"Maybe my mother," I volunteered. "You just danced with her at the Country Club Halloween party. She's from Minnesota. I think it's been a state there since about 1858."

"Is that some kind of joke?"

"No. I'm sorry." We'd known each other socially for years, though this was the first time I'd talked with him privately. Meeting me was always a fresh experience for him. "I bet you'd like to get down to business."

"I've got bigger fish to fry, Jones." He gnawed the end of his fountain pen. "Old Yancy lined this up for you, but you better know I'm not in the favor business. If this happens to fit with U.S. military interests I'm all ears. Otherwise, well, we pretty much leave the wogs to their own devices, if you get my drift?"

The chair I'd been ordered to sit in was leather and leather doesn't work in the tropics unless you leave the hair on it. I stood and paced, pausing at the window. "Colonel, I'm not crazy about asking. If there was a chance in hell I could solve this problem alone, I'd have done it. But this *does* involve U.S., and Dominican interests. Puts you in a position to alter history, at least in some way."

I believe Solomon wrote: *A fool takes no pleasure in understanding, but only in expressing his opinion*. Col. Marcus Blitzen had expressed his opinion again and again that the Dominican Republic should provide a training ground for another attempt at an invasion of Cuba similar to John Kennedy's Bay of Pigs fiasco. Like Cosme, but for different reasons, the Colonel displayed Kennedy's portrait. While it was true that many Dominicans were fond of Kennedy, especially after his assassination, they didn't want to attack Cuba. This didn't dissuade Marcus Blitzen. His opinions were becoming an embarrassment. That's the main reason, I think, he rose to the bait. Then again, he wasn't really a fool either.

"I think you're exaggerating my influence," he said modestly.

"Well, maybe," I muttered, knowing I still had to set the hook. "Mr. Yancy doesn't seem to think so." I wandered in the general direction of the door. "If I need to go further up the chain of command, that's fine." I stifled a yawn.

"You're about as high as you're going to get," he said. "Sit down."

I wandered back to the window. "This is highly confidential."

"I'm top secret, need to know." He narrowed his eyes. "Old Aussie seemed more cryptic than usual about this. We've worked together before, you know. He goes way back with The Corps. Back to the big war. Marines don't forget. Not even a generation later we don't forget. So what's this about?"

As an ex-Navy man I was wary of Marines generally. They're such zealous guards at Naval bases sailors tire of them quickly. Still, they're handy in a fight. "Did you know there's every possibility Ambassador Adam Quist met with foul play?" I told him.

Col. Blitzen, USMC, rose now from his chair and came out to stand eye to eye. "Are you that lunatic who said the Ambassador's a zombie?"

"Yes. That's me."

"You some kind of voodoo nut?"

I returned his stare. "I know this: there is a voodoo component to his death; a couple who worked for the Ambassador at his Residence tried repeatedly to kill me and a Lieutenant in the Policía Nacional; Quist's body is not in his coffin. These are facts. There is physical evidence, witnesses to corroborate them. I also observed the DCM, Duane Delbrick, in the company of the people trying to kill me. That's why Mr. Yancy called you. Which must mean that he holds you beyond reproach, because obviously, there's something going on in your embassy that no one knows about."

We stood nose to nose awhile but I could tell I'd won him over. He may have been an arrogant prick, but he wasn't stupid. I watched as the possibilities cascaded through his head. Finally, he said, "Okay. Sit down."

I walked over to examine his books. Nonfiction mostly. "I want something specific from you Colonel, or I wouldn't be here."

"What's that?"

"The names of the two people trying to kill us may be fake, but they claim to be Dulce and Alejandro Baez. Puerto Ricans. They were employed as servants at The Residence. They first tried to poison us, then followed me to Washington, D.C. and New York. Back here they machine-gunned Lt. Alba and left me for dead in a cave. The reason I need you is because they seem able to come and go from this island at will, and they are doing it at a time of tight security because of the rebels in the mountains. Now, how could they do that?"

He nodded. "Read about Alba in the papers. Obvious how they do it - by air with diplomatic passports."

"What can you do about it?"

"How sure are you that Duane Delbrick is involved?"

"I'm absolutely certain." I thought about giving him Pinhead's sleeping arrangements with Olivia, but passed.

"Why? What's he got to gain?"

"The ambassadorship. Power. Political advantage. Maybe he has personal reasons."

The Colonel chuckled. "That's even a poor list for a diplomat." He wiped his palm across his flat top. "If he's granting them diplomat status there's nothing you can do to stop their movement. Of course, there are other ways to stop *him*."

"I don't want Delbrick," I said. "I want the Baez couple."

"Suit yourself," he said. "But let's talk reality, okay?" He withdrew a silver .45 caliber automatic from the top desk drawer. "I hate working with civilians. This is a gun. A weapon that kills people. This handgun here isn't for sport or target practice. It's for killing, close up. Did you know that?"

"Yes," I said.

"We're at war all the time, did you know that? There is no peace. No love, peace bullshit. No hippie dream world. You come here, however well-recommended by a man I respect, you got to understand the realities. If what you just told me is true then you're at war just as much as your country's at war with Castro. I been trying to tell all these diplomats and other idiots that for years. Now they got this Caamaño over here trying to overthrow the government and Washington's all shocked they didn't see it coming. I told them, invade Cuba, kill that dumb bastard Castro. Caribbean, Central America, Africa, whole works settles down." He patted the weapon. "But they never learn, so you listen to me. I'll help you. But I play by my rules, not yours."

"What does that mean exactly?"

"If it's a rush job, I stick this .45 to their heads and blow their brains out. Messy in an enclosed space," he chortled. "Don't worry, I'll take 'em out in the country someplace. Take that bastard Delbrick out too, I suppose. He's a fellow Democrat though, I hate to do it. Car accidents are easy. You people got to learn rules of the road, you know? Bet I average two fender benders a year. Had to weld steel tubing to the front end of my truck, attach an I-beam three feet out the back." He grinned. "Público rammed it once and I drug him eight blocks - radiator pouring water, people inside screamin' and wavin' their arms out the windows, goddamn driver still blowin' his horn. Jones, you never saw a prettier sight in your life."

Much of what Blitzen said was not idle boasting. I'd seen his radiator buster. He was between wars, without command of armed troops, and in a banana republic where the State Department hoped to keep an eye on him. Even so, the grapevine said he'd killed two local communists. Nothing was ever proven and no one cared to investigate. Mickey told me once that Blitzen was a stone killer. Acted strange about it, like he admired it.

"I'd very much like to question Dulce and Alejandro," I said. "Forget Delbrick."

The Colonel straightened himself in his chair and held the .45 to the light. "There's that phrase we've all heard," he said, "*kill or be killed*. That's how it is in the end, just that. I don't question anybody. All I promise is you won't be bothered by the Baez couple again until you meet them in hell." He jammed the slide, swiveled in his chair and fired the empty chamber at his own reflection in the window glass. "Bang," he said, grinning.

"You're a dangerous man." I hadn't meant to say it aloud.

"Damn straight," he answered. "Did you want anything else?"

"No. I'd like to know what happened to the Ambassador. Ask them."

"Who knows?" he said. "I might do that."

The ease with which we finally came to the subject of killing troubled me. I knew we had no choice but I was ashamed. Dulce and Alejandro burned my father's barn where campesino kids often slept. They'd terrorized and tried to kill me. They'd hurt Mickey and killed one of his officers. So who's to blame for what happened next? You die if you hesitate and the enemy doesn't. Col. Blitzen wasn't going to hesitate. Was that so terrible?

"Fine," I said. "I'll leave it to you then."

He put the gun back in the drawer. "Keep your mouth shut. Yancy, you, me. That's the circle."

"Don't worry."

"I won't," he said flatly. "You worry. Now go out and have a drink with old Horny. She loves a fresh squeeze. I'm going to need time to think. Where can I reach you?"

"I'll reach you."

"Okay," he said. "I work alone anyway. Let me tell you

something. I'm not doing this for you. Don't give a shit about your problems. Yancy said help, I help. End of story. So you look out for your own ass. Start playing Macho Man, some other Dominican shit, deal's off. If these people are as well-connected and determined as you told me, then you best find another cave to crawl into for awhile. At least until I'm finished. Don't go home. Don't do anything you normally do, comprende? And make damn sure you got the lead in your pencil for what's about to happen."

"I found a place," I answered stiffly.

"Well, it better be good Zombie Man, because your life does depend on it."

That was something to think about, but not enough to make a drink with his wife sound appealing.

* * *

I waited for Olivia at the Mirador in Naco, an affluent neighborhood. It's high ground and the restaurant is on the top floor of the most prominent building, one of the tallest in Santo Domingo then - ten floors. The Mirador was expensive, no paper napkins.

I arrived before Olivia and nestled into the luxurious, velour seating and thick cabernet sauvignon carpeting, so new I smelled the glue. Give it a few years, I thought, it'll mildew and stink.

I chose the Mirador for its bar. Giant windows, cocked and leaning outward from floor to ceiling, faced south toward the Caribbean. The bartenders stood with their backs to the view and when they walked behind the liquor island it seemed they were about to step off into space. The bar itself was long, tall, and highly polished. Plush seats with executive backrests provided an ocean view that stretched half way to Aruba, and if you couldn't enjoy a drink here, you weren't likely to anywhere. One bartender and me. The place was deserted this early.

"Buenas tardes," he said. "What will you have?"

"Gin and tonic." I was thinking of Haiti and the veranda of the Splendid, maybe Johnson coming up to offer us a ride to the Iron Market. Johnson. Probably still sneaking around New York.

Olivia arrived ahead of the gin. I'd forgotten how tall she was, how lovely without being pretty. A smile broke out when she saw me - natural and seemly.

I just had time to stand before she threw both arms around my neck. "I wasn't sure until now," she said. "You're alive. I had to touch you and feel you to be sure. Those horrible people. I'm sorry about your friend Mickey. I never met him. I'm really sorry." She stepped back and caressed my cheek. "You have scratches."

"Sit," I said. My smile was feigned. If she was so concerned about my *scratches*, why hadn't she called? I made this appointment, not her.

The bartender flourished my drink.

"Oh, gin and tonics. I missed mine at the Spendid." She tucked her short checkered skirt between her thighs and slid back against the bar chair. "Can I have one now?"

"Of course." The bartender, a man of years, offered me a discreet, polite nod after seeing Olivia.

"It's pretty up here," she said. "Ocean waves look like ripples."

"How's the family?"

"Same."

"Almost packed up?"

"Almost."

"When are you leaving?"

Her eyes flicked from the horizon to me and back again. "Tomorrow."

"Ah. Well. Our last drink then." I hesitated. It wasn't the kind of conversation to plunge into without first getting acclimated.

"That wasn't why you invited me here though, was it? To have a last drink, I mean. Hold hands or something."

"I have to ask you a question," I said reluctantly.

"Ask it." She looked straight into my eyes as the bartender slid her drink onto the bar.

"At our bagel party in New York with your family, when I said your father was a zombie, did you tell anyone?"

"My goodness," she said and tried to smile but failed. "So that's what this is about. You think I ratted you out or something?"

"I have to be sure."

"Just when I think you're starting to trust me, even like me a little, you change." She sipped her drink and turned back to the windows. "I started this EJ. I went to Mr. Yancy. Now you think I betrayed you? Maybe I killed my own father or turned him into a zombie. This is why you asked me here? For this?"

"It's about the truth."

"Well, when you find out what that is, be sure and let us know."

"You haven't answered the question."

"No! No! No!" She glared at the bottles. "I didn't tell anybody."

"Look at me."

"No."

"Somebody in your family got Mickey shot, me in a hole left for dead. Olivia, I want the truth."

Her cheeks were flushed. "You go to hell! I'd never hurt you, or kill my father. Know what else? I wouldn't sell out a member of my own family if they *did* talk about it. Big deal! This conversation is really pointless."

"I thought you all just lived together like a school of fish."

"Why are you doing this?"

"I told you. I want the truth."

"A moment ago you were so sweet."

"You aren't stupid, Olivia. Someone in that restaurant in New York that day - you, your mother, your sister or brother - reported to whoever it is that pulls the strings on Dulce and Alejandro. Someone there told the U.S. Embassy in Santo Domingo, the State Department, even Dominican Secret Service that I said your father was a zombie. As a result Mickey and I almost lost our lives. So now you want me to do what, be too sweet to wonder why?"

"You don't know anything."

"Tell me the truth then. Please. I'm waiting."

Olivia glanced up at the bartender, who'd moved to the furthest corner of his space. "I may be younger than you." She gulped her drink. "But I know life doesn't always give you pat answers. You live and die and just never know."

"No," I said. "I will know."

"Well." She was calm now. "You've got all you can get from me." She emptied her glass. "Goodbye."

I clutched her forearm. "Wait," I said. "I'm not done."

"Did you forget who was with you in Haiti? Who sat next to you at the voodoo ceremony? Who listened to drums with you that night on the veranda?"

"No. I didn't forget." I eased her back into the seat. "I didn't forget you lived there when you were younger either. That you probably attended a hundred voodoo ceremonies. Kids you played with in the neighborhoods there, how many worshiped black magic? What's it like to be an impressionable teenager in a magnetic culture like that? Does it maybe draw you in? Kids that age sometimes blame everything on their parents. What happens if those parents are unloving? If the father is a diplomat who's never home to know his daughter?"

"He knew me. I was there when we saw the empty coffin and I understand how you add it all up and get me or my family, but you're wrong."

"Am I?"

"You're so smart. You've got it all figured out." She tapped her fist against her forehead. "Did you swear us all to secrecy in New York that day? Did it occur to you that maybe my mother sat frozen by decades of diplomatic politeness while you tried to convince her that her husband of thirty five years was a zombie? That maybe nobody believed you? Why wouldn't all of us talk about it? It wasn't a secret."

"I told you not to talk about it. I want to know. Did you?"

Olivia wasn't one to fuss with her hair but she ran both hands up the back of her neck, along her scalp and under her long chestnut hair, gripping it in her fists. "I don't know. I don't care."

"Did *you* talk about it? To your *friend* Delbrick, maybe?"

"Why?" she asked, releasing her grip. "Why are you saying these things to me?"

"I want the truth," I said and caught something in her expression, girlish contempt for adults maybe.

Olivia signaled the bartender and ordered both of us another drink. "You are the worst detective in Santo Domingo," she said. Her mood had lightened. "Maybe in the world. I'm nineteen not twelve. I can leave home whenever I wish. If I hated my father enough to kill him or hire Dulce and Alejandro to make a zombie out of him, why wouldn't I just leave?"

"Leave?"

"Like Sarah and David. Just pick up and go."

"Revenge," I guessed.

"Revenge for what? So we're not a Latino lovefest family. That makes us murdering scum? That how your mind works? Aren't you maybe suffering a little cultural prejudice?"

The drinks arrived and she stirred the ice cubes, slopping gin.

"Why'd you tell me all that about your family then?" I felt outmaneuvered.

"You asked," she said. "Whatever our family problems, my

father and mother were always cordial to each other and supportive of us. Whatever college I picked was paid for. I have a generous allowance and I told you about my own money. My father helped me accumulate that."

"If it's true."

"So now everything I say is a lie?"

"When you told me about how cleverly you accumulated your little fortune, you also said you hired Mr. Yancy to solve your father's murder. That's a lie."

"Is it?"

"Olivia, if you're going to lie don't lie about things that are easy to check. I talked to Mr. Yancy, of course, and he said you did *not* hire him. Maybe he's lying?" She flushed. I waited impatiently for her answer. When it didn't come I asked, "Having trouble thinking up a new story?"

"I lied because I didn't think you'd take my money for the exhumation otherwise," she said flatly. "I was pretty sure you didn't have it. I'm sorry."

I examined the large tinted windows. The air conditioning had created some condensation near the aluminum frames. How *do* you know when someone's lying? Especially when the lie is good? A lie about personal motives is good, almost impossible to disprove. She was smart enough to know that.

My mind raced. Olivia *would* lie to get me to take her money. A lie to save me from embarrassment and move things forward. The investigation she started by going to Yancy. Made sense. If I was wrong about this part of it, maybe I was wrong about all of it. Any of the Quists could've blabbed about the zombie theory I'd handed them. David was openly hostile. Any of their crowd would peg me as a nut case. Dr. Mercer warned me. Many people weren't prepared to accept zombies as anything but a joke. Half the time I didn't believe it either, but it was the only thing that answered all the questions.

If you're influential, surrounded by influential people, you don't need to say much to get action. If the Quists mentioned my zombie theory, even casually, powers might've been set in motion against me. Olivia did want me to get on with the grave digging. If she knew the coffin was empty she'd be foolish to pay for that discovery. Once again it seemed I'd gone up a dead end. But then, liars are often repeat offenders.

"Lying makes you look bad," I scolded. "Screws up what we're all trying to do - find out what happened to your father. Lies are clues. Even bad detectives like me know that."

"I really am sorry," she said. "I'm going to the bathroom." She left the bar. Through the glass doors I saw her reflection in the chrome elevator doors. A moment later she was talking on the pay phone.

"Let's change the subject," I said when she returned, waving the bartender over for another round. The late afternoon light, washed and golden, slanted through the windows and foamed in her hair. "You're not hard to look at," I said. "For a woman who seems to enjoy making me miserable."

"A woman? That *is* a compliment. A woman and not a girl," she smiled slightly. "If I could be like someone, I'd wish I was pretty like Sonja Cadavid."

I ignored the reference to Sonja at the moment, and might've been kinder to Olivia that afternoon, had I known what else was about to happen. But the cave left invisible marks too. The cuts and scabs were superficial but the inside marks cut deeper and were destined to fester much longer. Down there I'd gone where we all go when we look death in the eye, understanding again how insignificant a life can be. You aren't quite the same again.

Before long I was headed to an even darker place, but of course I didn't know that either and asked lightly about Sonja. "What do you know about her?" I laughed.

A fresh gin before her, she said, "Sonja came to see me."

"Really?" I shouldn't have been surprised by anything Sonja did, but this surprised me. "Really? What did you talk about?"

"Guess."

"I hope everyone was polite."

"She hugged me when she came in and she hugged me when she left."

"Sonja's like that."

"She loves you."

"Yes."

"I could fall in love with you myself." She faced me. Her eyes were moist but there were no tears. "Don't worry. This isn't the time for it. I'll go home tomorrow and find someone my own age and we'll probably never see each other again." She glanced down at the brimming drink. "I've got a favor to ask."

"What?"

"If we do meet by accident someday, like in an airport or someplace, I don't want to stare at you uncomfortably while you stare at me or look away," she said. "All I want is for you to hug me. Will you do that?"

"Promise."

"I want to say it right now though, again I mean. I didn't kill my father." She reached out carefully and touched my hair, her thin fingers slipping down to stroke my ear. "Can I have hors d'oeuvres too?"

"Hungry?"

"Empty. I need to put something inside me."

The bartender offered a wide selection and Olivia ordered the homemade plantain chips. We didn't talk much until they came and she munched a few, washing them down with her drink.

"Sonja's a little too possessive sometimes, I think. I'll have a talk with her."

"She was very nice," Olivia said. "We liked each other."

"What did she ask you?"

"Nothing. She told me how things were with you and that she didn't really mind that we'd slept together in Port au Prince as long as you knew enough to come home." Olivia shifted in her seat and crossed her legs. "We didn't raise our voices or anything. Aren't we all so terribly broad minded now?"

"Did you say we'd slept together?"

"No. I didn't deny it either."

"Why?"

"Let her wonder. Maybe it'll make her good for you."

"Now you know why you're a suspect."

"Excuse me?"

"That devious mind," I said. "It's older than you. Older than me, I think."

"Later, I told her the truth, that you didn't love me." She passed me the basket of chips. "If I were her, that's what I'd have come there to hear."

"You have everything figured out, don't you?"

She took the chips back and broke one in two. "Want to know what I can't figure out?" She ate half. "I can't figure out why I've never felt like that. So close to someone. I can't figure that out at all."

"I guess your time hasn't come yet."

"Guess not." She licked her lips. "It will though. Soon. Very soon."

There were clouds on the far horizon, stacking up to move ashore and shroud the mountains by nightfall. The sun, low on the water, caught them in its spotlight, burning white awhile longer before the richer colors rose to proclaim the end of another day. I reached out and took Olivia Quist's hand in mine. She rested her head against my shoulder and crunched down the rest of the chips in the basket.

To be kind, I said, "There's less between us than you'd like, but more than you think."

"Thanks," she said. "Keep holding my hand awhile and then I'm going to leave you here. Okay?"

"Sure."

Her head nestled against me. "I might write you a letter sometime."

"How are you getting back to The Residence?"

"I called the Embassy motor pool for a car."

"Good. Safer. I'll feel better when you're off the island tomorrow. I think this is going to get nasty."

We sat there and watched the sun drop into the sea and the sky grow more dome-like. On top of the world, we ordered another for the road, which we probably shouldn't have done, and conferred on the color of the clouds and debated how the tinted glass distorted our perceptions. I buried my mood of distrust there. That night I think we felt just a little better than anyone. That's what final nights do for you.

Olivia kissed me goodbye and sometimes I think I still taste it on my lips, but then I seemed able to feel her beside me long after she'd entered the elevator and the embassy chauffeur had whisked her away forever.

The bartender and I tried to spot her car, which I theorized would be the standard embassy Chevy Impala, black with rear window curtains. It didn't work. Traffic was heavier now with evening coming on. People returning from work and stopping for a drink or a loaf of bread like in any city, and so we guessed at a couple bigger cars but I don't think they were Olivia's.

The Mirador was on Abraham Lincoln above 27 de Febrero. Its mostly a north-south street and after the 27 de Febrero crossing it drops below one of the city's old limestone plateaus and heads for the ocean. The sun was just about a yard into the water when we noticed a plume of smoke puff up from below the ridge and then a boom sound, like cannon fire.

I didn't know then that it was Olivia's car. We were spectators up there on the tenth floor. The bartender thought it might be a fireworks explosion because we'd had one the year before and two people were killed. Christmas and New Years were times for fireworks. I told him it sounded too distinct and clear for fireworks, which would've exploded in a series as different rockets and things lit off. Maybe it did, he said, and all we heard was the one big sound.

After a few minutes, the plume joined the clouds and I finished my drink. Olivia Quist was dead, and unknowingly I smiled at what remained of her, a smudge of gray in a darkening Caribbean sky.

Chapter Eighteen

Arroyo Hondo is the other direction from the ocean so when I left the Mirador for the Sugar Shack that evening, I missed the accident scene and the skeleton of her smoldering embassy car. The driver was killed too in the explosion. A bomb they said later, fastened to the undercarriage and probably meant for someone other than the former ambassador's young daughter.

In Arroyo Hondo there was no television and for some unknown reason I missed the radio reports, which initially said Olivia Quist's body had been hurriedly removed by embassy officials. Her family was distraught - this coming on top of the ambassador's untimely death from heart failure. Sitting on the wooden porch of the Sugar Shack with a barber's daughter and a five-foot lizard, I knew none of this. We were drinking beer while Cosme plucked a chicken out back in a laundry tub.

Winter sunsets are colorful but this one was fading. Candles and cooking fires were being lighted in the barrio that surrounded the yard where we sat. The porch was narrow and we'd decided to sit on the floor and soak up the warmth of the worn wood rather than drag chairs out, so we had our backs against the building and the girl, Vivian, said, "Mi padre says you are from El Seibo. What is it like there?"

"Quiet."

"It's quiet here."

"Different kind of quiet. Here the city surrounds us and moments like this are few. In El Seibo, this is a way of life."

"Why then are you here?"

"I like both."

Vivian had a thirst for beer and guzzled while I sipped and smoked a cigar in memory of the living Olivia, who in my head, was back at The Residence sitting alone on an upstairs balcony crying softly as she thought of our last tender moments together. A comfort to know a young woman found me interesting, even briefly. I didn't relate her to the plume of smoke or imagine her body cooling in an embassy reefer.

"Señor Espinosa-Jones," Vivian began.

"Please," I said. "Call me EJ. *Señor* makes me feel old."

She giggled. "How old are you?"

"Never mind. What were you going to say?"

"Nothing. I just wondered what my father told you about me."

"That you were going to bring me food and take care of me. Here you sit drinking beer."

"What else did he tell you?"

"Nothing."

"That I was a virgin?"

"Yes."

"Do you have a wife?"

"Yes, an evil woman. She has gigantic thighs with varicose veins the size of small rivers. She's blind in one eye from a fight she had once when four young girls tried to steal me away. Her hair is spun steel and all eight of her teeth are filed to sharp points and when she bites you, the teeth remain in your flesh. Later she grows new ones."

"Are you making a joke?"

"Have you ever met a woman named Sonja Cadavid?"

She shook her head. Her eyes were wide and very black in the gathering dark. "Who is she?"

"The woman who should be my wife, and if she isn't busy with something else, she could very well be warming her backside at one of those cooking fires outside the fence, waiting to see what we're up to."

Vivian shivered. "But she doesn't have one eye?"

"She has many eyes."

The lizard stirred, swept the porch with its tail and stared at the wooden gate. "Someone's coming," the virgin said.

A dark figure slipped from shadow to shadow along the path outside the yard, moving stealthily toward us. "Go inside and get me the small gun," I told Vivian. "Hurry."

At the gate the figure paused, little more than a dark presence just outside. I waited there quietly until Vivian slipped from the darkened doorway and placed the cool pistol in my hand. "See him?" Her voice hushed, she pointed at the gate.

"Shh." I cocked the revolver, drew up my knees and rested it there. We were mostly hidden in the shadow of the porch. I could hear Cosme out back hacking the fresh chicken into bite-sized pieces.

We heard a long, low scraping noise as the gate was pushed open and the figure slipped into the yard. Carefully, I removed the lizard's leash.

Alberto leapt from the porch and hit the ground running. Iguanas stand up when they run, like crocodiles, and it's that extra few inches of height and the way they dash forward with their mouths gaping that paralyzes their prey. Nothing seems able to stop them.

When the figure saw Alberto lunging for him in the dark we heard him cry out and raise a stick above his head. "Are you in there EJ?" Mickey's voice. "Is this your damned lizard? Call him off or I'll clobber him with my cane."

"Here, Alberto," I said.

Vivian called him too.

Alberto stopped, confused. "Just walk around him," I told Mickey. "What the hell are you doing here?"

Mickey didn't answer but limped up to the porch where he could see us clearly. He was wearing his uniform but his left arm was in a sling. "Who's this?" he demanded, shaking his cane at Vivian.

"The landlord's virgin daughter," I said.

"Like hell."

"How did you find me?"

"Sonja."

I glanced at Vivian. "See?" I said. Her eyes got big again.

"You supposed to be in some kind of hideout here or what?" Mickey demanded.

"Nobody's found me yet."

"I've found you, Sonja's found you, the virgin of the plantains here found you, and you got a goddamn pet lizard in the yard." He sat carefully on the edge of the porch. "Any more of that beer around?"

I nodded to Vivian, who seemed relieved to go inside a moment. "It's Dulce and Alejandro I'm worried about."

"Your maid told me you left for Miami to go shopping." He chuckled. "That's a pretty dumb story. You're right in the middle of all hell breaking loose and you go shopping? Couldn't you think of a better one than that?"

"I was in a hurry. Why aren't you in the hospital?"

"I'm better."

"You don't look better."

"Can't wait anymore. Been over a week. Anyway, it hurts just as much when I lay around as when I move around. Don't you people have chairs?"

"We're very poor," I said, standing to fetch him a seat. "Did you just limp in here to order us around or do you have something on your mind?"

"Help me up," he said, extending a hand. "Muscles get mushy after so many days in bed."

Vivian pushed through the door carrying two beers and a chair. "Do you want a chair too?" she asked me. "Otherwise he will look down on you." Clearly, she didn't care for policemen.

"Yes," I told her, "but it won't stop him."

Mickey hobbled up the steps and eased himself onto the chair. "First beer I've had," he said. "Tastes funny. Thanks for calling in the troops. You got more pull with the Policía than I do." He chuckled. "Somebody owe you a favor?"

"Yeah, and I'm calling them all in," I said.

Vivian stood near the doorway and slightly behind Mickey where she could keep an eye on him. Mickey drank from the bottle, glanced at Vivian, and said to me, "Tell the virgin to take the lizard for a walk."

She left without a word.

"What's up?" I asked.

"Olivia Quist is dead."

Mickey liked to joke around, but I knew he wouldn't do this. "I just left her," I said.

"Just happened. Heard it on the police band and the regular media has it too." He reached a hand out and gripped my forearm. "Car bomb. She couldn't have known anything."

"She had an embassy car."

"Probably after somebody else. Violent new riots at the University. Army put some tanks into the streets near there but hasn't set foot on university property. That's wise, I think. Maybe things will calm down."

Mickey's voice droned on. Olivia and I wandered the streets of Port au Prince together, afloat in some timeless human current, dammed now by her death. Whatever spirit grafted us so strongly then, still remained. I didn't find this unusual though we'd known each other only a short while. It works that way sometimes. You know people a lifetime and don't really connect. Others come and go quickly and you feel like they've torn your heart out.

It was the hug. One of the first things she asked of me at the Splendid, the last promise she wanted yesterday before we said goodbye. Whatever we shared in so short a time, she needed physical proof to make it real. The child inside her, I supposed.

I tried to focus on Mickey's face in the darkness. He'd been shot, Olivia was dead, and I was hiding. There wasn't even time for grieving.

Mickey was still talking about rioting college students and I'd lost the thread of what he was saying. "Forget the riots," I said. "We both know who killed Olivia. Isn't that why you're out of the hospital?"

He stood up. "Hurts to sit too. Yes, I'm going to kill them."

"Colonel Blitzen's going to kill them for me."

"The crazy from MAAG?"

"Yes."

"EJ, he's an American military officer. What's the matter with you?"

"We can't get them by ourselves, Mickey. We can't get them with the entire Dominican police force. We can't even get them when we've got them. I know Blitzen's crazy - you ought to meet his wife - but they'll never suspect him and he won't hesitate. Dulce and Alejandro will be dead and we'll be safe." I sighed and thought of Olivia's body left along the road, white rib bones above charred insides like the studs of some gutted building. "I should've done it before. I should've listened to you when you wanted them in the Ozama. I should've quit being such a smartass and done my job. I killed her."

Mickey leaned on his cane and stared down at me in the dark. "We're still not safe and Olivia isn't dead because of you. Outside there," he said straightening, sweeping the darkness with his cane, "something we can't see. You were right from the beginning. It's voodoo."

* * *

After eating Cosme's chicken the fiesta fizzled. I explained about Olivia but didn't use her name - a family member, I said. It could just as well have been true. A recent acquaintance forever now in my life.

They forgave me. Mickey and Cosme went home.

I was tired and depressed. Olivia's death - my ultimate failure - tapped the last of my strength. I was no longer the objective investigator but the Grim Reaper's assistant. My God, they were dying in sight of me! I was tired enough to sleep sitting on the porch but the virgin persuaded me to come inside and lie on the bed. She crawled in beside me. I told her to go home but fell asleep before I knew her answer.

The drums were the first sound, the imperfect, hypnotic rhythm of that night in the hills above the Splendid with Olivia. Powerful cadences pressed in through my pores. Familiar, forceful. I surrendered and let them draw me in. Stronger now than in Haiti. I understood them, helpless to resist. Louder beats, compelling and persistent. I yielded to the magic darkness. The spirits mounted me and I could smell the cheap wine.

I looked down at my chest. A wound had opened, leaking tar blood, veins splitting, gushing red gas that was my spirit and soul. The drums filled me with powerful urges. Sweat poured out and wet the bed. I saw the firelight, the dancers moving in line outside the windows. Crowds circling the small house singing words that weren't words but moaning. Wood smoke drifted in dancing blue clouds. I heard the clicking and singing of a steel machete.

There was a thump on the porch.

I bolted upright in bed. The virgin was gone and the night quiet. I'd been dreaming.

One of the old palms close to the house was brushing its dry leaves against the metal roof like a wire brush on a snare drum skin and I rested back against the damp sheets. My breathing slowed as the dream faded.

My shirt was gone. Shoes and stockings too. The virgin, I supposed. And maybe she really was a virgin, since she left my pants on.

I swung my feet to the floor and went in search of a cigarette. Just before I struck the match a voice said, "Don't."

It came from the doorway, which I saw now was filled with a man's silhouette. "Would you like one?" I asked, not sure if he was a real man or a leftover from the dream.

"No. Thank you."

"Who are you?"

"You know me as Alejandro. That's not my name."

It was funny I thought then, that all this time I'd feared Dulce most. "Where's Dulce?" I asked.

"You're a hard man to kill," he continued. "I'm very curious about the hole where we left you. There was talk that you swam out."

"Yes. I did swim." I was thinking about how still he was, and about my shotgun.

For awhile he was quiet and I heard the frond leaves brushing the roof again. "You have weapons by the bed," he said. "If you move toward them I will cut you into two pieces."

I couldn't see his hands. They might hold a machete or a machinegun. They might be empty. But who woke you in the middle of the night to bluff? "I wouldn't mind a smoke," I said.

He laughed. "Go ahead. I'm going to talk to you for a minute."

"Then what?"

"You'll learn the answer to the age old question of resurrection." He chuckled again. "Or you'll find peace in oblivion."

"Great," I said, striking a match. "It's a good time for a smoke then."

"I like that about you," he said. "You're scared but you don't beg. You jumped into the hole. We didn't push you."

"Shame to kill a guy like that," I said. "Why not convert me to whatever evil drives you and your ugly woman? Maybe I'll be useful."

"Do you speak French?"

"No. Is that a requirement?"

"Does Sect Rouge mean anything to you?"

"No." I lied.

"Bizango?"

He might know of my visit with Dr. Mercer. "I've heard it."

"The red sects are secret Bizango societies that dine on human flesh and drink human blood," he said flatly. "I am a member. The woman and I. After you're dead I'm going to take you away and we'll eat your flesh and drink your blood warm. Your body will be preserved and the scrapings from your skull eventually used to make zombie powder."

"I'd rather be converted."

He took a single step forward and from the window pale moonlight set his grinning face aglow. "Goodbye," he said politely and raised a machine-pistol to my heart.

An eruption, like a large exploding pimple, appeared on his

forehead at the same instant I heard the report of a firearm. Alejandro's eyes glazed over. I didn't see the bullet, of course, but the bits of blood, bone, and brain tissue sprayed from the wound and across my face as it nicked my right ear. His head snapped like someone had slapped him hard and then he crumpled at my feet.

No more than ten steps behind, Sonja Cadavid lowered a large automatic. "We must leave immediately," she told me. "Grab your things."

I knew this side of Sonja existed, I'd just never seen it. She didn't speak until we were in the backseat of her car. Luis drove. "You're in over your head," she said, handing me a tissue.

"Thanks for telling me."

"I'm sorry about the girl."

"Did you do it?" I wiped the Alejandro mess from my face.

"Damn you, EJ."

"You're capable of it and I know you met with her."

"Yes, I met with her."

The car was speeding south, toward the ocean. The streets were slick and wet but I hadn't heard it rain. Undoubtedly she would take me to her place. Maybe to her bed. Now she sat in the dark corner of the backseat, her face visible only in flickers as the car passed under the streetlights. She was wearing black slacks, a thin black turtle neck, and her hair was tied back and held in place by one of those nets usually worn by old ladies.

"Why did you meet with her?" I asked.

"I don't like surprises."

"Or threats."

"Threats I meet head on."

"Like tonight," I said. She'd saved my life and I was ungrateful. "Her car blew up. You know about bombs, don't you?"

"Yes. I know about them."

"Deny it again."

"I will. I do." She stared out the window. "I liked her, EJ. You've had a bad time lately. Don't take it out on me."

"Oh, yes," I said. "I almost forgot for a moment that I was in over my head."

The car was a large Chevrolet, not a limo. No privacy glass separated Luis from our conversation. I guessed his ears were getting red.

"We can talk about this later if you like," she said, then changed direction. "The partner to this one. The Dulce woman. Where is she?"

"How should I know? I didn't even see this guy standing in my doorway. I don't know anything, really."

"And you haven't learned who is behind it? Who pulls the strings?"

"No. This Delbrick at the Embassy, maybe."

I expected a lecture but she only kept her face averted, staring out the window. Maybe she didn't want to look at me. After all, I was in over my head. I managed to keep my mouth shut.

Finally, she said, "I know you didn't want my help."

"Alejandro was going to kill me," I said, "so it's grand the Cuban Cavalry arrived in the nick of time. It's not the help, it's the condescension I dislike. The *I know best*. Don't you think I know how you and Luis here, and the rest of the gang, do things? I'm an investigator not an assassin. This is the first time I've carried a firearm since the war. We're not alike in that way, Sonja. I don't live on hate and I don't kill my enemies. I outsmart them."

She didn't look at me even once. She could've said I hadn't done a very good job of outsmarting anyone, but instead her right hand came up and she bit the nail of her index finger. We passed a set of streetlights and I saw a tear tracking down her cheek. Very softly she told me, "I'm a monster. Why don't you say it?"

This was not true. She was just the product of hatred. Castro won his revolution by destroying the hearts of its intended beneficiaries. Like dictators everywhere, Fidel held the land, but land has no respect. So the people he robbed, the remnants of those families he murdered, harbored his ultimate destruction. If they didn't kill him, all they had to do was wait. Revolutions are not economic or political in the end, but personal. "No," I told Sonja Cadavid. "You're not a monster. But I don't think you need to kill them all either."

"Someone has to."

"Someone had to tonight, I guess." I reached out and removed the hand from her mouth. "Sit next to me."

She slid into my arms. "You scare the hell out of me sometimes," I confessed. "Doesn't change my feelings for you."

"Gracias." Her head dropped onto my shoulder. "Luis," she addressed her silent driver. "I really love this guy."

Luis shrugged.

I grinned in the dark. Luis probably knew more about me than my mother.

Fifteen minutes later we passed inside the armored gate of Sonja's house and I wondered what Cosme and his virgin daughter would make of a dead Puerto Rican with a missing forehead. I wondered what they would think of me. I didn't want a new barber.

"Sonja, what about Alejandro? What can we do with him?"

"Luis will take care of it as soon as he drops us off. We'll need the body anyway to find out who he was."

"Of course," I said. "I'm such a dope. Where do you put a thing like that?"

"Isn't he cute, Luis?" she said. "And so sarcastic."

Luis could just as well be a post.

"Did you hear what he told me?" I asked. "Before you shot him, I mean."

"Just garbled words."

"He told me he's part of a secret red sect in voodoo. They drink blood and eat flesh."

"That's horrifying." Sonja "Widow Maker" Cadavid wrinkled her nose in disgust. "Guess I've heard talk. Mostly about Papa Doc, you know, that he welcomed important African visitors with a cup of warm baby's blood, things like that. Never gave it much credit. Always told to me by Anglos."

The car rolled to a stop, Luis hopped out and opened her door. "Sunrise soon. Come on," she said. "Let's see if we can't catch a couple hours sleep."

I followed her. Luis got back behind the wheel and drove off to recover the body of a blood-drinking member of the Sect Rouge. I prayed he would get everything cleaned up before Cosme or Vivian found out. The thought of Vivian made me smile. Not the least bit shameless, she'd undoubtedly crawled out of my bed the moment I fell asleep. I was very glad of it.

* * *

The next few days were anticlimactic and quiet. They set about the business of burying Olivia Quist. I went home and a U.S. Marine sergeant was sent from the Embassy to tell me not to attend the funeral or make an attempt to speak with any member of the Quist family. This request, demand, came directly from Mrs. Quist herself. I was provided with her telephone number should I doubt the messenger. I didn't.

Mrs. Quist had lost faith in me. Blamed me for Olivia's death, of course. I sat ten stories above in a bar while they blew her up. Just another dumb Dominican too lazy and cowardly to worry about anything but his own life, failing to protect the budding life of a nineteen-year-old girl. Who trusted a Dominican man with your daughter anyway?

I was polite to the sergeant. He had a job to do and performed it without emotion. He called me "sir" and didn't sneer. It still took me the better part of a day to convince myself that my odds of ever being vindicated were remote. I wanted to make the call. Explain myself to Mrs. Quist and her remaining children, but my only hope was to solve the crime. To solve them both, in fact. I knew Olivia's death was not political terrorism.

Meanwhile, I watched television in the hallway of my newly reopened penthouse. Carmen was called back from the country and daily routine gradually returned. I reasoned that without Alejandro, and with Mickey, Blitzen, and now Sonja's people in hot pursuit, Dulce Baez had more to worry about than me.

The U.S. Embassy bestowed on Olivia the same military honors as her father. Diplomats are a bit like royalty, if Americans had such privilege. On television, the honor guard moved with the same solemn precision as before. Olivia's flag-draped coffin carried to the waiting aircraft, a twin engine executive jet with the seal of the Department of State on its fuselage. Stars on the wings. But it wasn't with curiosity that I watched the tan shirts, the blood red stripes of the trouser legs, the small cluster of family moving out across the tarmac. This time I felt the loss of Olivia, the hatred of the Quist family, my own miserable failure. I'd known the dangers and given little more then cursory warnings and now another American body was carried to a waiting aircraft.

Carmen's hand was cool as she ran it gently along the side of my head and down to my shoulder. "Come," she said. "Stand up now."

I obeyed.

She hooked her arm through mine and walked me back through the living room and outside onto the veranda. "You haven't been eating," she said.

"I'm not hungry."

"You will eat now," she ordered. "I've made sancocho."

Five minutes later she sat me down at one of the outdoor tables and served the soup hot. It tasted good, though it was about ten o'clock in the morning and a hot day. "I'm sorry you had to come back from the country after so short a time," I said.

"Things go better there when I'm here," she said. "You're not to blame for this thing Señor EJ. That woman with the chicken the night of your sister's party. She's the one. I will get one pistola for myself and put an end to her."

A gun-totting Carmen was something to ponder. "Dulce. Her name is Dulce, and her life hangs by a thread now," I said. "She knows it too. Doubt we'll ever see her again."

This soon proved to be another monumental miscalculation.

Chapter Nineteen

Her shrill voice rose four stories in the pre-dawn light, passed easily through heavy glass patio doors, navigated the hallways and swept under my bedroom door. "The Policía Nacional is in my teléfono! I am tired of you! You are a lunatic!" La Doña Villacampa's proclamation sat me upright. "¡El Señor Campesino!"

I had another phone call.

"Mickey?"

"Why in hell don't you get a telephone or kill that obnoxious old cow? How can you stand it?"

I was barefoot. Mercedes was six inches away. "Please," I told Mickey. "State your business."

"I've got Dulce Baez."

"Where? In the Ozama?"

There was a pause while the great lieutenant drew a breath. "Well, I mean, I know where she is."

"So you don't really have her?"

"I have her surrounded. Thought maybe you'd like to be in on the kill. Your Colonel Blitzen failed. The old Policía Nacional from the old Banana Republic is poised to pounce on this international criminal."

"Okay, big shot. Where?"

"Alcazar."

"¿Alcázar de Colón?"

"Sí."

"I'm afraid to ask what this desperate international criminal is doing in the busiest tourist attraction in the city." The Alcazar is the house built by Christopher Columbus' son Diego in 1510.

"She works there."

"Pardon me?"

"She's a tour guide."

"So all the time we've been looking for her she's been walking around in plain sight with groups of tourists?" The Alcazar is a two minute walk from Ozama Prison. "How'd she get a job so quick?"

"We don't know any of that yet. Speaks English I suppose. Are you coming down to see the arrest or not?"

"So you have the Alcazar surrounded? Where are all the tourists?"

"It's 5:30 AM."

"I forgot. Give me half an hour."

"Hurry up. I'm not waiting. I'm going to kill the bitch."

I handed the phone to Mercedes who hadn't moved an inch. "Thank you very much," I said. "This was an extremely important call. A desperate criminal is hiding in the Alcazar surrounded by dozens of Policía Nacional. I must go there immediately."

"Ah, sí," she said. "A national emergency, then. All the República in your hands. It is a privilege for me, a simple old lady, the wife of a dentist, to get out of my bed in the middle of the night to assist you in protecting the nation. Muchas gracias!"

I left as quickly as I could.

The Alcazar was shot to pieces during the 1965 insurrections. A four hundred and sixty four year old national treasure nearly destroyed by the same foolishness that got it built. Anyway, it was restored with a sense of humor. Workers left bullet holes as a reminder, now part of the tour. I tried to imagine Dulce Baez, the Puerto Rican wife of a confessed Sect Rouge voodoo priest, pointing out the revolutionary indiscretions practiced by us bloodthirsty Dominicans.

The sun had cleared the eastern cane fields of La Romana and backlit the ancient limestone building as I pulled up to the police cordon and was halted by two policía with machine guns. I produced identification and asked immediately for Mickey. He arrived minutes later and walked me to a clear area inside the ring of police vehicles and armed men. "The building is completely encircled," Mickey said. "My orders are to shoot anybody who comes out unless they are surrendering to me personally."

"How do they determine that?"

"Dulce must say in a loud voice, 'I am surrendering to Miguel Alba.'"

"Why?"

"I want them all to hear it and I want her to say it."

"Great," I said. "If everyone knows their lines, can we begin?"

Mickey lifted a bullhorn to his lips and instructed the building to surrender in the specified manner.

We waited in silence.

I set the bezel on my dive watch.

Mickey repeated his threats and instructions.

A quarter of an hour lapsed. Mickey told the building that he would show no mercy. Within seconds the policia would storm the place and drag Dulce Baez out by the hair and most likely fill her body with holes.

There was no response.

"Now what?" I asked him.

"She dies," he said. "Stay here. This is police business." Mickey stepped out farther from the cordon and raised his voice. "Make no effort to take her alive," he shouted. "Shoot to kill! Follow me!" He drew his pistol and signaled the attack. The men shouted and rushed the building. Mickey limped after them.

In their dust, I managed a quick glance over my shoulder. If any tourists were up this early I prayed they'd think this was a reenactment.

The cops were inside more than an hour. No shots fired. Slowly, they began to dribble out and form up into squads on the manicured lawn. Their sergeants loaded them onto trucks and most were driven away. Mickey finally showed up talking earnestly with his two top investigators, who were nodding. When he got to me he was alone.

"How did she get out?" I asked him.

"Her boss saw her inside just before we surrounded the place." He ran his free hand down across his face and I knew how tired he was. "The reason we got on to her is because she's been living here."

"In the Alcazar?"

"Basement storage room. Her boss found out and got suspicious. Friend of his told him the police were looking for a heavyset Puerto Rican woman so he asked us about it last night and verified she was still inside early this morning, asleep in the basement. We were here a few minutes later. Now she's gone."

"Voodoo," I said.

"Bullshit."

"Well, maybe it wasn't her then. Some other woman."

"No. Her boss described her perfectly. It was Dulce.

I put my arm on Mickey's shoulder. "I didn't get breakfast. I'll buy."

"No time," he said. "I'm pretty sure I know how she got out. I just need to prove it to myself."

"No voodoo?"

"Ancient architecture." Mickey led me to his car, which was parked on the grass. "Those old Spaniards were cautious. With good reason. Everybody from Sir Francis Drake to various French fleets sacked the city for centuries. When they built Santo Domingo the Catholic archbishops insisted on catacombs and underground passages interconnecting most of what is today the Zona Colonial. They still exist."

"I've heard rumors since I was a kid. Who's really seen them?"

"Me."

"When?"

"Twice before. Once in '65 when I was a soldier. Once after. Both times I entered through the Cathedral, below where the bishops are buried."

"And they connect to the Alcazar?"

"Definitely. I've made the trip, but from the Cathedral end. Never went up into the Alcazar itself but the access is there. Somehow Dulce discovered the entrance from the Alcazar into the catacombs. We're meeting at the Cathedral in a few minutes." He fumbled with his sling to light a black cigarette. "You coming along?"

"Yes."

"Bring your pistol?"

"Forgot," I said. "Anyway, Carmen's threatening to use it."

"Now that *is* frightening. You can borrow one of ours."

"Do you think she's still in there?"

"Be the perfect hiding place, wouldn't it? Explain why we never found her before." He smiled for the first time that morning. "Bet she feels safe down there in the dark. Laughing now that she's fooled us again. The stupid old policía." He laughed aloud, blowing smoke from his nose. "I'm going to kill that bitch," he said. "She will not die peacefully." He smiled. "Or quickly."

We drove to the Cathedral and stood in the square with a dozen other policía in gray uniforms. I saw the shoeshine boys were up early this time and the dominos already cracking a table under one of the banyan trees. I inspected the restoration scaffolding and thought about Columbus' old bones piled in a steel box that resembled a treasure chest, hung between two giant elephant tusks behind the altar. Cities in other countries claimed Columbus was with them, but since local Indians killed him here in an age before refrigeration, I thought we had a pretty good claim. His bones were in our box but was Dulce Baez in our catacombs? Or had she used them to escape once again?

Half the morning wasted waiting for church permission to enter the catacombs through the Cathedral. So much for hot pursuit, I told Mickey. He's a good Catholic though and brushed my worries aside with assurances that Dulce felt safe below ground and would hardly come out until she knew we were gone. It seemed to me it was this kind of thinking that always kept her one step ahead, but I waited quietly.

A bishop's blessing on our heads, we abandoned the late morning sunshine and marched inside the ancient Cathedral. This church, the first and oldest in the Western Hemisphere, took more than twenty years to build and by anyone's standards is an impressive sight. The front door weighs two and a half tons. The inside was thickly plastered at some point in history, preserving the limestone rock beneath in almost pristine condition. Part of the present restoration was to carefully remove the plaster.

Mickey hushed us as we entered. They'd been holding church services here regularly since about 1530. Everyone genuflected except me, though I'd always thought genuflecting looked cool. We Lutherans wouldn't go in for anything that showy, of course. Most of the policía, about twenty-five men, carried flashlights. One clanged to the floor and drew a cold stare from Mickey. We moved forward, then turned right through an archway that led to a small door. There Mickey halted us.

"Listen," he said. "We enter the catacombs, the most holy resting place in the country. Archbishops, bishops, and priests have been interred here for hundreds of years. Be quiet and respectful."

Mickey opened the door and we descended a worn flight of circular stairs to a sparsely furnished room below. Again he assembled us, crowded together. "From here it's single file," he said. "Keep your lights down and your mouths shut."

He opened another door and we filed along narrow steps into total darkness. We held our lights down, their pale splashes lit ancient Christian tombs lining the walls. I remembered the story of one Archbishop of Santo Domingo, who somewhere in the 1580s had a disagreement with Sir Francis Drake, the English buccaneer pirate who sacked the city. Drake lopped off the Archbishop's hand. The Archbishop survived, but after his eventual death and burial in the Cathedral, the artisans making his crypt fashioned the lid into a sculpture of his body. It's there today in the sanctuary, and true to life, one hand is missing. We wouldn't do that today, I thought. A modern sculptor would replace the Archbishop's hand. Hide the truth.

"Watch your step," I heard Mickey say. "After we pass through the Mausoleum you'll see a platform ahead. Stop there."

Several of the men were coughing, muffling the sounds with their hands. The air was dead and smelled of bat dung and dust. I fished a handkerchief from my back pocket and tied it tightly across my mouth and nose.

On the platform, a stone island from which catacombs gave way to passages leading in all directions, Mickey assembled us into a tight semicircle. "There's no map," he said. "Ceilings are low. You'll be walking in water. There are large rats, black widow spiders, bats and scorpions, but the greatest danger is panic. Move slowly. Groups of three. First man in line holds the light, second man is the shooter, third pays out the string I gave you. When you find the woman make no attempt to arrest her, empty your pistol into the center of her body, tie her neck to the string and drag her out. That group gets a week's paid vacation and one hundred pesos. Questions?"

"Is that one hundred pesos each or one hundred split three ways?" a voice said.

"Each," Mickey answered. This created a murmur. Every cop there earned less than a hundred a month. "Just be careful. You can't spend it if she shoots you first. There's an accomplice too, a man named Alejandro. I'll give another hundred for him. This place is like an echo chamber. Be quiet as you can and don't talk. When she hears the footsteps, it will be more frightening if she doesn't know you're the policía."

The men began to tie their strings to a ring on the wall Mickey had pointed out to them. He assigned each group a passage to follow. "You and I go in alone," he told me and I knew then I should tell him about Alejandro but feared he would arrest Sonja.

"Great," I whined. "I've been yearning to get back underground."

Mickey got up close. "Am I going to have to watch you? All soft and weepy now because you spent a few days in a cave?"

"Screw you. Let's go."

"That's better," he said. Besides being a brilliant policeman, Mickey Alba fancied himself an expert in reverse psychology.

"Thought she was getting a slow death," I needled him. "Now they're going to empty their pistols into her."

"None of them can shoot straight. Noise should keep her moving until we can grab her. She doesn't know most of them never shot a pistol before."

As we walked, I made my mind up definitely not to tell him about Alejandro. Even if he didn't arrest Sonja, I'd never hear the end of it once he found out she saved me. Ahead, there weren't many cobwebs and it seemed reasonably dry. On the other hand, there were rats, bats, and spiders peeking from countless holes and crevices in the walls and ceiling just inches from our heads. I pulled my collar up to hide the exposed veins and arteries in my neck. Ahead of me, Mickey seemed oblivious, trudging along bent at the waist.

If ancient Europeans had eaten more fresh meat and vegetables they might've grown a little taller. We wouldn't have to stoop. My back spasmed and ached after fifteen minutes of hunched walking. Luckily, I didn't have to pay out string like the others. Mickey said it was a waste of time since he knew his way around. If he knew his way, I wondered why we stopped so often, shining a light into every crack and corner.

"Do you have any idea where we are?" I whispered.

"Shhh."

"Where do we end up?"

"Are you going to talk or sneak? We're sneaking. Be quiet."

We sneaked along for another fifteen or twenty minutes and nothing changed. The water deepened, a liquid containing urine and something thicker and more pungent. A bad smell I recognized but didn't remember. I'd foolishly worn sandals and tried not to think what I felt between my toes. I pretended they were someone else's feet. Eventually, the tunnel branched and I guessed Mickey would say "You go left and I'll go right," but he didn't.

Instead, we stopped and squatted to relieve the tension in our backs. Mickey played the light down both corridors. They seemed identical. Damp stone, lapping sewerage and darkness. Heavy air that tasted five centuries old. Mummy air.

"Now what?" I asked.

"Shhh. I'm thinking." He was panting and should've been in bed somewhere.

"Mickey," I began. "Nobody's living down here. Not even Dulce. She may have escaped through here, but I'm telling you, nobody is going to stay here any longer than they have to. Including me. Why don't we just turn back?"

Mickey shined the flashlight in my eyes. "You got me into this mess in the beginning," he whispered in a raspy voice. "Now you're going to see it through. We're going to find her and we're going to kill her. Right now."

One thing I've learned about cops, Dominican or otherwise, is that they're not innovative thinkers. They're plodders. We were going to tromp through every foot of this dank labyrinth until we found Dulce Baez or were introduced to every rat in Santo Domingo. "She's not here," I told him.

"We're turning right," he said, swinging the light down a misty shaft.

"At least limp a little faster," I told him.

"Shhh."

This passage was spacious. I listened, hoping for some sound from above. The rumble of a bus or beat of traffic. Nothing but the nauseating sound our feet made as they sloshed through the slime. With each step my toes curled against mushy solids floating in the gray liquid, collecting in sticky reddish-brown balls between each toe, sometimes fastening to my ankle hair. I prayed it was only feces, not something worse, and that I didn't have any remaining open cuts or scratches to become infected.

I sucked the mummy air in through my mouth, like drawing it from a snorkel filled with foul sea water. When it reached my lungs it felt heavy, greasy lumps clinging inside the air sacks. Inches above my head long bats hung upside down in rows. I'd been in caves where the bat urine formed something on the floor so thick and green you'd skate along it like icy syrup. If Dulce Baez was hiding here, she was welcome to the place. It made Ozama look good.

One of the policía had loaned me a pistol, which had been tucked into the small of my back but kept slipping down inside my pants. It was an old .38 long-barrel, more rust than steel. I hadn't checked to see if it was loaded, and had no intention of firing it. Few policía carried pistols. Most had ancient rifles for which bullets were no longer available. They often guarded banks and foreign embassies with empty weapons. That may have explained the missing toes. What a surprise when a weapon fired.

Mickey stopped again. "Now what?" I asked.

"Shhh!" he rasped. "There's something moving up ahead."

"There's something moving all around us."

"Quit whining. Got your gun?"

"Sure," I said. "I'm armed to the teeth."

We crept forward and Mickey kept us close to the left-hand wall so our shooting hands were clear. Cops think of such things. It was hard for me to see around him and I hadn't heard anything. If Dulce was down here she'd be running like hell, not sneaking around or sitting still in the slime. Since it took us half the day to get permission to chase her, why wouldn't she be at Vesuvio's having a pizza?

Mickey stopped suddenly and I crawled up his back. He stood frozen, steadying the light and pointing his pistol along the beam. Ahead, the tunnel came to a T. Sticking out from one corner was a naked human leg. It flexed rhythmically to the moaning song of its owner, still out of sight.

Mickey moved forward. I followed but kept my distance.

The mournful chant was clearer. Mickey's beam played along the leg as it moved in a rhythmic pulse to and fro in the gray water. The dirge had a sing-song quality, indistinguishable lyrics. A repetition of sound that seemed impossible to stop. An invocation or some sorcerer's curse.

The rusty pistol had gone completely down my pants. I drew it out and held it in front of me. If I pulled the trigger would it blow up?

Mickey dropped to one knee and jigged the light. The leg's rhythm continued as before, accompanied by the strange musical moaning. The leg was bare, the foot too, both dirty. Mickey's light was a lonely beacon in the darkness. Neither of us spoke. I wanted to tell him what I really thought - zombie. Maybe someone we knew. His wife. One of my sisters. Sonja. I hadn't seen her for a couple days. Not Sonja. She'd make zombies of them. I stared at the leg to see if I recognized it. Was it familiar? I wanted to tell Mickey to hold the light still so I could examine the feet. Feet are very distinctive.

Mickey sighed and stood up. "Come on," he told me in a normal voice.

We walked forward together. Around the corner a woman was lying on a bed of filthy rags and torn, soaked bedding. Nearly naked, she sat rocking a filthy doll and moaning a lullaby. "Pobrecita," Mickey said. "Una retrasada." A retarded person.

"How did you know?" I asked.

"My mother used to sing that song," he said. "Cover her with your shirt. We'll pick her up on our way back."

"What's wrong with your shirt?"

"You know how much these uniforms cost? Peach has never been your color anyway. Hand it over."

We buttoned her into the very crisp guayabera Mother had given me last Christmas. The retrasada smiled up at us and said, "My baby."

Mickey patted the doll's head. "¡Preciosa! You are lucky to have such a baby."

"Sí," the woman said.

"Is the baby hungry?"

"Siempre." Always.

"When we return we'll take you to where there's food for her. You too. Okay?"

"My baby."

"Yes," Mickey said tenderly. "Your baby."

We turned and started along the opposite passage. I heard the woman begin her moaning song again and it raised goose bumps on the bare flesh of my chest and back.

Neither Mickey or I mentioned the woman's plight. We knew it all too well. Our government had little money or motivation to help those like her. They were left to the streets and the charity of churches or individuals. Many lived their entire lives begging and homeless.

"Why didn't you ask her if she'd seen Dulce?" I asked.

"Would you believe whatever she said?"

"Guess not."

"We'll take her if it's not too late. She's so thin. God bless them, EJ."

Mickey had a big heart for a cop. "My mother does some charity work," I told him. "She might know someone in the city who can help."

"Your mother is a good woman," he said. "Her son is a dipshit." He said the word in English. A word I had taught him, of course. Loved the way it sounded he said. Unfortunately, I seemed to be the only one it fit.

"I'm following you through these miserable tunnels - shirtless - and now I'm a dipshit? It's your attitude that keeps you from making captain, you know."

"Oh, don't worry. I'm a terrible kiss-ass with my superiors. It's my friends with whom I'm honest." He chuckled. "Especially those who get me shot."

"Is this becoming another thing I'll hear forever? Aren't these people criminals? Isn't it your job to apprehend criminals? You should've been after them whether I was involved or not," I said. "If you don't shut up about it I'll shoot you myself."

"I saw that pistol you're carrying. Ramirez give you that? One of the seized up ones he carries around in the trunk of his car in case he needs an *armed suspect* after he's shot somebody. Is it loaded?"

"Cylinder's rusted shut."

Mickey laughed. "Dipshit," he said.

I felt foolish carrying a worthless weapon and tossed it behind me.

Mickey turned toward the splash. "What's the matter with you? Might've at least scared somebody."

"Yeah. Me."

"Come on."

This new passage seemed larger than the one before. The stagnant water was deeper, above my ankles. We saw holes and sometimes metal brackets in the walls where ancient torches had burned.

Our light reflected yellow from the water and walls. Had the torchlight been that color? Tunnels filled with black smoke? I thought of the blue smoke from Olivia's cigar drifting into the night while the voodoo drums beat in the hills of Port-au-Prince. Her father, then her. Both gone to smoke now.

"They wouldn't let me go to Olivia's funeral," I told Mickey.

"I know."

"Sometimes she was just a girl. But other times."

"I sent someone."

"Pardon me?"

"I sent someone to her funeral."

"In the States?"

"Yes."

"Who?"

"Carlos." One of Mickey's inner circle of investigators. "The funeral is today, in New York. She can't be buried in Arlington with her father. Carlos was going to New York anyway and the Quists don't know him, so I sent him."

"Why?"

He remained silent awhile except for the splashing of his polished boots against the water. "I shouldn't tell you."

"What's that mean? Damn it! Tell me."

He stopped and knelt down. "Okay," he said. "But I warned you."

"Fine. Talk."

"We had a guy there in minutes that day. Traffic cop. Heard the car explode. When he got there he was given a hundred dollar bribe from some *foreigners* to disappear."

"U.S. Embassy people. Didn't want him around to foul things up."

"Five bucks could've taken care of that, and how did they get there so quick, those Embassy people?"

"So what's all this telling you?"

"To look for a reason."

"At Olivia's funeral?"

"Was her papa in *his* coffin?"

"Mickey, she's in her coffin."

"Most likely. When Carlos calls me tonight or tomorrow, then we'll be sure. There's something with these Quists, man."

If Mickey had seen Olivia that day in the street in Port-au-Prince. Knew how close we were then. It made me secretly glad the Quists had banned me. Standing alongside Olivia's coffin was more sadness than I could take just then. Maybe she wasn't dead if I'd never seen her body.

"Did you hear what I said?" Mickey asked.

"I heard. I hope Carlos can't find her. I hope she's sitting on the balcony of the Splendid smoking a fat cigar."

"Sometimes EJ..."

"Yeah, yeah. Let's move."

We moved ahead again. A few minutes later our advance was halted by the largest rat I'd yet seen in the beam of Mickey's light. It hissed and stood its ground. Mickey was able to hold the flashlight with his sling arm and bring the pistol to bear with the other hand. The rat, almost as if he knew the threat of a firearm, backed away slowly, then turned and disappeared. I'd moved back several yards and covered my ears but Mickey lowered the pistol.

I was exhaling when a wizened hand shot from the darkness and clutched the soft skin of my bare armpit. Had that exhale not turned into an instant gasp I might've screamed and Mickey heard, but instead I was yanked into a near-invisible and narrow slit in the limestone. There I heard teeth grinding and smelled breath that I can only liken to the pus-filled abscess of a rotting tooth.

Chapter Twenty

"Follow me," a familiar voice said.

"Let go of my arm."

"Will you follow?"

"No. Let go!"

"Senor EJ." Her hand dropped away in the dark.

"Who are you?"

"Peor."

"What are you doing here?"

"I live here."

"That's too bad. Get away from me. You pinched me."

"I have to tell you a thing. Follow me to where I have a place. I mean you no harm. This will be important to you. Muy importante. Voodoo."

"Peor, I have enough trouble right now. Tell me about it later." Free of her grasp, I moved back to my left toward the place we'd entered.

"You won't find her," Peor said.

"What?"

"The woman you are chasing is gone. Hours ago. Why are you wasting time here when I have an important thing? The man Johnson. He is waiting now for you. He will tell you."

It was as if someone threw a pail of cold water on my bare back. "Johnson? How can you know that?"

"Follow me and see."

It occurred to me then that following people into dark caves hadn't been a successful strategy in the recent past and I hadn't forgotten her curse at Karin's. "I have a gun," I said. "If you're lying I'll kill you."

"Good," she said. "Let's go."

We felt our way back to the right another hundred feet or more. I cracked my head twice on overhead rocks. Peor moved ahead, invisible and silent. Only the clicking of her sandals, like clicking crabs, were audible against the rock.

The narrow passage led to a room about the size of a studio apartment. There was a nasty mattress on the floor, an assortment of cast-off chairs, boxes, a litter of clothing, and the little girl Peor used. The girl was on the bed, curled among dirty blankets and towels. Candles lit the space, their smoke drawn out a ragged break in the rock overhead. Faint sounds came from the hole. Traffic.

"Mi casa es su casa," Peor said.

"Great." The little beggar girl watched me. "Where's Johnson?"

"You don't have a gun." Peor smiled.

"How do you know?"

"I can see." The smile grew wider and I saw the source of the foul breath. "How about your wallet? Did you bring that?"

"What is this?"

"Business. Do you think I tell you for no money? No. You pay me cien pesos."

"A hundred bucks? You're crazy."

"I need to do some Christmas shopping."

I started back. "Goodbye."

"Fifty," she said.

I stopped and withdrew a money clip from my front pocket. Held up a twenty. "No bargaining. Twenty or I'm gone."

She shrugged, then reached for the cash. "Not yet," I said. "Talk first."

Peor moved to one of the chairs and gestured. "Sit. We will have coffee."

"I don't want coffee. I'm in a hurry. Tell me."

"You are in a hurry now? A minute ago you didn't want to talk to me. Now you're in a hurry. I make coffee."

"No coffee." I glanced around the cave. "Where do you get water?"

"Water? Water is running everywhere here."

My stomach tightened. "No coffee. Speak now or no money either."

Peor sat down. "Johnson. You know Johnson?"

"We're not friends but I know him."

"You want to find him? Talk to him?"

"Very much."

"If I tell you where he is you pay me twenty. If I take you to him, you pay twenty more."

"Fine," I sighed. "Forty. First you tell me how you happen to know Johnson, a jet-setting Haitian cab driver."

"Those are my trade secrets," Peor said. "I'll tell you if you give me the hundred."

"Forget it. Let's go."

Half an hour later, after walking some distance and crawling at least twenty feet along a stone airshaft we exited the catacombs and dropped into a restaurant wine cellar. Peor asked, "Do you know this restaurant?"

"No," I said.

"The Bodegón. I thought you ate here."

"Not in the basement. How am I supposed to know what the basement looks like?"

"It's the wine cellar," she said. "Johnson and his friend are waiting for you. Give me the money."

"How do you know they're waiting?"

"I told them you were coming. They are at the table next to the large wooden doors on the street side. Give me my money."

I peeled off the bills. "Aren't you coming up?" I asked.

"With you?" she said. "You have a naked chest. Your sandals are filthy. You smell like shit and the knees are out of your pants." With that she hopped into the airshaft and disappeared.

I'd been had. Johnson wasn't in the Bodegon. I was forty pesos poorer, the witch had got even and now I'd have to face Felix Maldonado, the best and most punctilious headwaiter in all the Américas. And Peor was correct, I smelled exactly like the sewer I'd crawled from.

I walked upstairs into the ancient restaurant, its walls part of the original Colonial city. I'd eaten there a hundred times. The stairwell lead to a hallway near the bathrooms. Felix was standing several yards away with his back to me.

"Felix," I called. "Buenas tardes."

He spun around. "I'm sorry, Señor Espinosa-Jones. I didn't see you come in."

"I entered discreetly," I said, smiling. "EJ, please. May I use your phone?"

"¿Como no?" He led me into an office. "Can I get you anything?"

"Cerveza."

"Pardon me," he said. "I was thinking of clothes. A shirt, perhaps?"

"You have shirts?"

"Sí. We spend our lives here. We are prepared."

"A medium then."

"Your trousers are dirty and torn."

"I'll brush them."

He was reluctant to leave on his errands and finally spoke with great humility, "Señor EJ. There is an odor."

"Ah. I apologize Felix. Is there somewhere I can wash up?"

"The bath for employees is through the door behind you. I will bring towels and clothes. And one cerveza." He smiled. "I have always known you to be an interesting man, Señor."

"More interesting then I'd like some days," I told him as he left.

The office was small but opened into a private courtyard, lavish with flowers and greenery. The Bodegón, with its secrets, its ancient Colonial construction, its hand-laid ceramic floors, was typically Dominican and seldom visited by tourists. The menu was small. Local. I ate there at least twice a month - usually alone, sometimes with Sonja. It was a place she preferred, and dined there as herself, which helped with Felix. They stocked a good selection of Spanish wine. She was fond of the heavy reds.

I found the phone and called Mickey's office. He wasn't in of course, but a sergeant said he'd pass on the message as soon as the lieutenant surfaced from the catacombs. He also predicted my ass was likely to finish up somewhere in the space between my ears. The radio chatter, he said, was pretty desperate. Mickey had called for reinforcements. Nearly one hundred men were now splashing through the catacombs in search of me.

Mercifully, the Bodegon not only had a shower, the water was hot. The shirt Felix left for me was more Hawaiian than Dominican. Two-tone green, a large flower blossoming on its front. I wore my sandals into the shower, they smelled nearly as bad as I did. The Presidente he'd wrapped in a bar towel. It was still cold and I drank half of it in a single pull.

After my shower I found my pants missing. In their place hung a fresh pair of black slacks. My belt and valuables piled neatly on the seat of a chair. Had I not lived so many years in the United States I might not have appreciated my own people as I do - their warmth and hospitality wasn't an act. This was the kind of service it pleased them to give, not just to a good customer, but anyone. On the other hand, Felix would've alerted every waiter in the place by now and they'd expect to hear my story, discreetly of course.

Freshly groomed, I walked into the restaurant. Peor had told the truth. Johnson and another man sat at one of the small tables along the wall. "Johnson," I said foolishly.

"That's not really my name," he answered, not the least surprised to see me. "Sit down."

"Well, I guess these days I can't be sure of anything"

Johnson smiled. "You're right about more than you know," he said. He gestured at the man across the table from him. "My cousin."

I recognized him as the guy with Johnson in New York. "Do I call him Johnson too?"

"You can."

"Good," I said. "I don't want to know your real names anyway."

"We'd like to talk to you," Old Johnson said.

"Couldn't you have just called me?"

"It's urgent. Anyway, we tried to call you. Some mad woman answers your telephone."

"That's my landlady."

"You should move."

"I like the view."

The Johnsons had been smoking cigars and sipping wine as they waited. "Looking for Dulce?" New Johnson asked.

"Before I answer questions I want to know how you got here," I demanded.

"We owe you no explanation," New Johnson said.

"Then you won't find Dulce through me."

"Relax, both of you," said Old Johnson. "We're on the same side." He shrugged at me. "We've been following you off and on. We were interested in your search this morning but we met the Peor woman and for a few pesos she divulged that it was in vain, since Dulce had exited the catacombs and disappeared before you entered. We sent her then to fetch you. Naturally, we wanted to talk to you without involving the policía."

"What is it with you people?" I sighed. "Can't you do anything without sneaking around? It seems like forever since I've sat down in a nice restaurant someplace and just had a normal conversation with somebody."

"This is a restaurant. Talk to us."

"Who in the hell are you people and what do you want?"

"Names aren't important. We're bokors from Cap-Haitien. The people you call Baez are dangerous. Before they came here they were condemned to death at home. We are the justice."

"You're voodoo? Vodoun?"

"Yes."

"I'm just interested in apprehending Dulce."

"So are we. Her real name is not Baez, it's Metraux. Her mother is Puerto Rican. Her father Haitian. She is a mambo in the Sect Rouge. You know what that is?"

"Blood drinking priests?"

"It's a bit more complex than that."

"Maybe, but I'm not interested in turning her over to you."

Johnson chuckled. "Don't you want to know why Dulce and Alejandro are trying so hard to kill you?"

"Alejandro's dead." I saw the surprise on Johnson's face.

"Ah," he said. "So you *have* killed him."

"Let's just say I was there."

"There are others. Dulce commands a large following. They are fanatically loyal and each one of them is assigned the job of killing you. Do you remember that Mr. Yancy told you to trust me?"

"He told me to trust Benwa."

"I'm Benwa's brother. We're members of the same organization."

"Some sort of Haitian Mafia? Maybe the damned CIA and I don't have a *need to know*? Everybody's a member of some secret society. You people are boring me."

"I'm not your enemy," Johnson said. "We were only protecting you in New York."

"Thanks."

Johnson had an open face and a youthful, almost impish, smile. His black eyes were clear. He could've sold health insurance to a Christian Scientist. "Will you listen to me for ten minutes?" he asked politely. "Then go on your way. Find your policeman friend. Chase ghosts. I wish to tell you something about our religion."

"I took Voodoo 101 at Columbia."

"Yes. Dr. Mercer. We're acquainted," Johnson claimed. "I admire his research, but voodoo is many things. The vast majority of us are no different from the average Catholic, Protestant or Jew. But some are fanatics. In voodoo, spirits physically touch the living. We forever seek charms and antidotes for the circumstances of our lives. This part of voodoo keeps our country poor, allows fanatics to frighten us. Some of us. Others band together to fight. We are a secret organization because if we were not secret, our enemies would quickly destroy us, just as Dulce and Alejandro nearly destroyed you."

"What's the name of this organization?"

"I can't tell you," he said. "We share the same enemy. Isn't that enough? Dulce Metraux is a high priestess. A strong mambo. She has many zombies to her credit."

"Ambassador Adam Quist?"

"Perhaps. That is why she seeks you. A grave mistake on her part, I think. No one else took your zombie talk seriously. We do, of course. Dr. Mercer might. Dulce and Alejandro saw the direction you were going and panicked. They are drunk with fanaticism and imagine all the world revolves around it. You are a lucky man."

"Yeah, I'm having a great time." Johnson had never been my favorite person and I hated it when he started making sense. "So you're just the good voodoo guys? The voodoo reform committee. Cleaning up after the radicals."

"Do we make fun of your religion?"

"Okay. Let's say I believe half of what you just said. Why are we talking?"

Johnson smiled. It seemed genuine, even warm. "You are half American. Not long after the American Revolution sent the British home, we Haitians rid ourselves of the French. We're not a new nation in this hemisphere, but one of the oldest. We share this island with you." He held up his hand. "I know. We've had our difficulties."

"They were a little more than that," I said. "You came over here and had a little trouble leaving for about a half century."

"Sr. Espinosa-Jones, I am not Toussaint L'Ouverture. Please. May I continue?"

I waved my hand.

"We believe Dulce Metraux and the man you killed are part of a sect within a sect. We think that this sect is not like any other, and not wholly Haitian at all. Perhaps even global in nature, with underground organizations in this country, Cuba, Jamaica, Puerto

Rico, throughout the Caribbean and very likely in the United States, especially New Orleans, Miami and New York." He sipped from his water glass. "Because voodoo has these two faces, the benign, and the one beneath, it often seems inoffensive, even humorous to some. The popular culture in America accepts the idea of voodoo people sticking pins in dolls to create pain. No such thing exists in voodoo. Only Hollywood. But it is accepted as fact. It's not difficult to believe that with some planning and effort, anything can be sold as truth. You understand that?"

"Of course, but my interest is Adam Quist, and now his daughter. I really don't give a damn about voodoo."

"But you think there is a voodoo component?"

"Obviously," I said. "Verve on the floor. Dulce and Alejandro. Quist was stationed in Haiti before he came here. It adds up. I just don't know what it adds up to."

Johnson looked at his cousin. The cousin sighed and Johnson said, "World domination."

"What?"

"This sect is dedicated to bringing voodoo to the world. Not so different from Christian missionaries, Muslims or Buddhists. They want voodoo to be accepted. They say it is the most misunderstood religion in the world." Johnson shrugged. "And it is."

"I can't see what Quist has to do with that. He was a diplomat, not a preacher. I doubt the Quists give a fig about religion. They're more into money."

"He was in Haiti a long time," New Johnson said. "Maybe he found out something, and you are not so far wrong."

While I mulled this over Old Johnson said, "I think you know something."

I called a waiter and ordered a Cuba Libre. Yes, I probably did know something, I thought. But what? The drink came and I drank before telling them straight out, "It's gone too far. I don't care anymore what I'm supposed to know. Dulce tried to kill me, burned by father's barn and machine-gunned my best friend. I'm tired. Alejandro got what he deserved and she will too. It's just gone too far."

Old Johnson rubbed at a spot on the table with his napkin. "Maybe we can help each other."

"How?"

"Your nation is Catholic?" he asked rhetorically. "The Spanish

Inquisition was not good Catholicism. Sect Rouge is bad voodoo. Muslims, Buddhists have their fanatics. These people share a violence. What they can't achieve by persuasion they try by force. You're right to protect yourself from Dulce but you must remember you're not facing a threat from one fanatic, but all the fanatics who believe as she does. Think of your family."

"The barn."

Johnson nodded. "They'll try again. But not the barn."

"What?"

"If they can't kill you, maybe other targets aren't so difficult."

I should've thought of this before.

"These people have no scruples," Old Johnson continued. "They wage total war and civilians bear the casualties. A Sect Rouge bokor is accustomed to superiority. Ours is a peasant society. Few of our people read or write. They're superstitious and fearful. Believe in ghosts, animals that are ghosts. Dulce and those with her don't lose such battles, they're used to domination. Powerful spirits direct their actions. If they can't defeat you personally, they'll defeat you through your family. Believe me, you must protect yourselves."

It hit me like something hard between the eyes. I was doing it again. Late again. "I'm a slow-witted fool," and rose to my feet. "I have to go home." I spun toward the door.

Johnson grabbed my elbow. "Wait. There's still time," he said. "You're family is in grave danger, but..." Johnson & Johnson exchanged glances. "We can use this."

"Use my family? Are you crazy?" I wanted to run but something held me back. "Tell me something. What do you really want?"

"Dulce Metraux."

"Why?"

"She's our door into their world. She knows the secrets."

"She won't tell you."

Johnson's eyes changed to something hard, but he grinned. "She will tell us."

"So that's your job?"

"Then to kill her."

"You're assassins. Poor Dulce. She's got almost as many people after her as I do." My palms were sweaty and I wiped them on the fresh loaner pants. "You or Yancy or somebody could've told me all this before. You've used me to get to her, and now you want to endanger my family even more."

"We need your help. Where you are, she eventually is."

"Fine," I said. They were right, I knew it, but family came first. In that instant I knew what had to be done. "You say you want to help. You know my family is in danger. I believe you. Okay. You want Dulce. I'll get her for you. I got Alejandro. But there is one important condition."

"Oh?"

"You protect my family. In return, I'll find Dulce."

"She will find you."

I nodded. "Sí, but this time it'll be different. Will you go to El Seibo and guard my family? I'll call my father. How many of you? Are there more cousins?"

"Just the two of us."

"The Johnson Gang," I chuckled. "Weapons?"

"Machetes."

"Dulce isn't quite so old fashioned."

"We are quiet."

"Try and be invisible too. Go to El Seibo? Agreed?"

"Okay," Johnson nodded. He didn't look pleased. "Two days. No more."

I stood and stretched my back, staring a moment at Old Johnson. "Remember Johnson, in Haiti, when you were still a cab driver? You met Olivia. Joked with her. Laughed. Saw us in the street together. What harm did she do to this Sect Rouge?"

He shook his head and repeated, "She knew what you know."

"I don't know much," I said. "But I know Dulce and I have a date." I borrowed a pen and drew a crude map to the farm. Father would have a fit when he learned two Haitian babysitters were on the way, but easier to send them than ask his permission. "I'll call you in a couple days. When I've got her."

They stood and Old Johnson took my hand in both of his. He kept silent and nodded his head. Some glint in his eye maybe or set to his shoulders told me I could trust him. He had been chasing Dulce a long time too, and he might've been as tired as I was. I never found out.

Later, I called Father from the restaurant and warned him. Explained it was too late to turn them back. The babysitters were on the way. He wasn't happy but he had the ashes of his barn to look at, and in the end, that spoke louder than any words of mine.

An hour later I caught up with Mickey. He was drinking a refresco at the Colmado El Conde. They'd gotten word to him that I was alive and well. He remained grumpy through most of my story about Peor and the Johnsons, as if everything was my fault.

"That's pretty much it," I finished up. "Wonder if I shouldn't head out there after them. Obviously Dulce has slipped by us again."

"Is that my fault?"

"Was I blaming you? You weren't far behind her."

"Far enough," he said. Traffic flowed steadily along El Conde and made our words sound strained. "We need a break."

"Like what?"

"Like if I could somehow get a piece of her," he said. "All the calls I made to Puerto Rico, FBI in the states, Interpol. Nothing. Like she's never existed. No passport, driver's license, Social Security. How does someone live these days without a number? All I need is a picture. I tried some drawings. They looked stupid."

"Could you get it in the press if you had a picture?"

"Are you kidding? The tabloids live for this stuff. I'd have every cab driver, poletero, vendor and lottery salesman in the country as my eyes. We'd have old Dulce locked up by six o'clock tonight."

I smiled. "So I guess her real last name might help."

"EJ!"

"Metraux. It's Metraux. Her mother was the Puerto Rican. Her father is Haitian. According to the Johnsons she's a big time voodoo priestess. A mambo of the Sect Rouge. She's made lots of zombies, they said."

"Yeah, well I'm going to make chicharrones out of her. If she's got any kind of criminal record, was ever arrested, there'll be a photo. Even if she's clean we might get lucky with a driver's license or passport. The *Listín* has a machine now that receives photos from anywhere across telephone lines in less than half an hour. What do you think of that? I better get back to the office. Sometimes EJ, you're almost useful." He slammed the glass bottle onto the wooden counter, red soda pop erupted from it and sprayed my new Hawaiian shirt. "Watch the morning paper. Adiós, amigo," he said over his shoulder.

I ordered a beer and some pickled pigeon eggs. It's the best thing I know for a hangover or to cheer you up after crawling through sewage. For some reason I didn't share Mickey's optimism. Dulce had a head start again.

Dulce Baez Metraux didn't look intelligent. Her broad face, small eyes and mouth, sloping forehead, black hair dyed golden brown in streaks, all etched in my mind. The thick, short body. She looked like a criminal. A deranged nurse's aide strangling old people in their beds to steal the gold in their teeth. A base, emotionless killer. How often our perceptions are wrong. Dulce was obviously very clever. Alejandro got himself killed because he came alone and I had Cuban cavalry. Would Dulce make such a dumb mistake? I'd bet my life she wasn't running like Mickey thought. She was planning her next attack.

I resolved then to call Colonel Blitzen again. Fill him in. Mickey thought he was a loose cannon but I thought his mind might track like Dulce's. The Colonel was clever too, in his way. A hunter. A foreigner couldn't move as freely but I knew he was deadly.

I'd parked the Jeep across the plaza from the Cathedral long before we entered the catacombs. Two barefoot street urchins were perched on the hood, guarding it.

"Gracias gentlemen," I said when I walked up. They jumped down. "Just for the record, did anyone come near the Jeep?"

"No Señor," one said.

I held out two, one-peso notes. "Are you sure?"

"Sí Señor."

After they ran off to spend the money, I thought if Dulce wanted to rig a car bomb, two easily bribed street kids wouldn't stop her. And if it wasn't a car bomb it would be a bullet or a hail of them. Someone would stab me or chop me with a machete. Johnson was right. War. From the minute she laid eyes on me at Quist's Residence she was consistent. Attack. Attack.

I held my breath and turned the key in the ignition. Nothing happened. Absolutely nothing. I popped the hood. The urchins had sold the battery.

I found a phone. Talked to Blitzen and my garage man. Blitzen said he had his own leads and the mechanic said he'd be right there with a tow truck. I didn't believe either of them, but the mechanic did show up an hour later with a new battery in the bed of his pickup.

Carmen greeted me at the door and begged me to take siesta, which I rarely did. "I'm tempted today," I said.

"Don't be afraid," she cooed. "I'll stand guard." She stroked the double knit fabric of the garish Hawaiian shirt. "At least," she said, "you're showing better taste in clothes."

"I got it from a waiter."

"Ah," she said. "that explains it. Come to bed."

I slept fitfully at first but finally fell into a deep and dreamless sleep that left me disoriented when Carmen shook me awake. "Get up," she said. "It's the teléfono."

"Mercedes?"

"Gone with Julio. Hurry, it's your policía."

I threw on shirt and pants, stumbling downstairs.

The maid, Luz, handed me the receiver. "Mickey?"

"You're taking siesta?"

"I was."

"This is slightly more important."

"You found Dulce again."

"No. We lost Olivia."

"Pardon me?"

"Carlos went to Olivia's funeral this afternoon in New York. He was standing by the coffin, you know, and he thought she looked kind of like wax."

"Mickey, are you drunk? Every dead person looks like wax."

"Sure. That's what Carlos thought. But he kept staring and staring at her until he convinced himself that maybe she was wax," Mickey chuckled. "So he took out his pocket knife and whittled out a slice of her cheek."

"Oh, shit!"

"EJ. She *was* wax."

I just hung up. There wasn't anything else to do. I didn't want to hear anymore. I stood there awhile and the phone rang again.

"EJ, Damn it! Don't hang up! Do you realize what this means?"

I couldn't keep the image of Carlos, a sly, shifty-eyed Dominican cop, slicing into Olivia's fine white cheek like it was the meat of a mango. "Didn't people notice?" I asked. "What did he do, just leave a big slice out of her face?"

"Told me he took it along the jaw line and rubbed a little makeup from the rest of her face over to cover the mark. He didn't take a meter of it, you know."

"Mickey, where do you find these people? Guys who slice up corpses because they think they look waxy?"

"Be thankful he did, Idiot. Means she's not dead. You should be dancing." He paused a moment. "Of course, may mean she's a zombie like her dad. Beginning to look like you were right about all that."

I had no response. Visualized myself standing before Margaret Quist trying to explain that now I thought her daughter was a zombie.

"EJ?"

"Give me time to think this over. I'll call you tomorrow." I went back upstairs.

It's a weakness, I suppose, thinking of Sonja at times like those. That toughness she has is overpowering. "I'm going to see Sonja," I told Carmen.

"Ah," she said. "Why not?"

I worried Carmen saw through me. Sonja's toughness was from childhood and she'd learned to turn fear into action. Part of me condemned her for that because I knew at the root of things she was the stronger for it, and I the weaker.

Independencia was busy. Públicos, trucks, buses. I switched off the Wagoneer's air conditioner and rolled down the window, inhaling the foul air like tonic. I wondered if Olivia was in her coffin, missing a wedge of cheek, or had she been replaced by a wax dummy?

Sonja's gate was locked and I waited some time before Luis came to open it. "Buenas tardes," he said. "Always a pleasure to see you."

It wasn't a day to be nice to Luis. "Screw you," I said when he opened the gate.

"Sí, Señor."

I stopped the Jeep alongside him. "Screw you, I said, you phony bastard. Say what's on your mind for once. Tell me to shove it."

The Cuban stood very erect and stared at a spot just above my head, a quiet note of satisfaction in his hooded eyes.

I drove on. I'd no reason to speak like that to a Cuban patriot, and later I'd apologize. Luis and I had known each other now for two years. Well, not known each other, and his disapproval had become a burden.

Inside, Sonja held her arms out to me. I hadn't called to tell her I was coming over. The dress she wore was one I particularly liked, a charcoal color with a sort of brocaded neckline that dipped temptingly. The remainder of the garment was simple and hung to the tops of her feet. She wore sandals. Her toes were painted red. So obviously ready.

"I think sometimes you're like a Boy Scout," I said. "So prepared."

"Ah," she said, reaching up to kiss both my cheeks. "A bad-tempered boyfriend."

"I'm not bad-tempered," I argued. "I did tell Luis to get screwed."

"Well, he's heard worse."

"Why are you being so understanding? Never mind. Don't tell me. I've been through a lot, and a guy like me, out of his depth, isn't expected to take that very well. I'm so completely in over my head."

"Don't put words in my mouth, Lover."

"Don't call me 'lover.' I spent most of the day crawling around in the catacombs under the old city. They're full of rats."

"Is that where you got that shirt?"

"I got it from a waiter."

"Are you mourning Olivia?"

"Aren't you? You said you liked her."

"I only met her the one time. You know that. I liked her fine."

"Well, she's not dead anyway. She's disappeared like the rest. Everyone is just disappearing all over the place."

"I think you better sit down and tell me about it. Drink?"

I told her the whole thing standing in the middle of the living room, I did take the drink, and another after it. "I think that woman is smarter than I am. She might be tougher too," I confessed.

"Olivia?"

"Dulce."

"Just because you haven't caught her?"

"No. She fools me. I don't like it."

"Nobody likes to be fooled, Eddie."

"Don't call me Eddie."

"*Don't call me Eddie. Don't call me lover.*"

"And don't mock me either. I'm not afraid of her, well a little. I'm just frustrated that she seems to be so damned good at everything. Some kind of primitive voodoo priestess, flying around, chasing me in airports, hiring limos in New York. Some kind of nightmare. Wants someone to disappear, they disappear. Wants me to disappear. I disappear."

Sonja munched an olive. "Can I say something without you biting my head off?"

"So long as it doesn't offend me in any way."

"Okay." She washed the olive down with a splash of gin. "If the tactics you're using aren't working, why not try something different?"

"How precise and military of you."

"EJ. Damn it."

"Okay. What do you suggest?"

"Oh, I don't know. What do you want?"

"I want to find her."

"Doesn't she have a habit of finding you?"

"Yes," I growled.

"Let her do it then. Only be ready."

This wasn't what I wanted to hear. "We've done that. It didn't work."

"Because you were all running or driving around," she said. "You need to be still."

"You have an idea I suppose."

She looked away then and I knew. "Sorry," she said. "I'm leaving in the morning."

"Time to piss in Fidel's rice and beans again? Why don't you just let him rot?"

"Well Genius, for the same reason you don't let Dulce make zombies out of everybody."

I threw my empty martini glass against a bust of Simon Bolivar she had there, since she didn't have a fireplace. "Come here," I said and took her in my arms. "You're the best damned woman in the world. I hope you shoot the son-of-a-bitch right between the eyes."

Sonja laughed out loud. She's a sucker for the macho stuff. She could be fiery herself if she wanted to, but that late afternoon she was gentle as a mother sponging a naked baby.

Chapter Twenty One

I concocted the plan flat on my back in Sonja's canopied bed, her snoring a soft rattle fanning the hairs of my forearm. Her hair - thick, moist black - forked across her face, stuck to a corner of her mouth, shuffling to the rhythm of her breathing. A stroke of genius, that plan. Best of all, I worked it alone.

Sonja and the Johnsons helped me discover Dulce's weakness, her soft underbelly. Dulce loved her secrets and there's no secret society if it's not secret. When the light explodes, the darkness dissolves as if it never was. That's why Dulce came after me - Johnson said it - to shut me up before I switched the lights on.

There was a feature writer at the *Listín* then, Bravo Benoit, who wrote a story about me every time I took him diving. Searching for fresh angles, he often delved deep into my imaginary life, pitting me against man-eating sharks or razor-toothed eels. Everything he wrote was a pack of lies. I saw no reason why a story of zombie-making voodoo mambos running through the streets of the Capital drinking the warm blood of newborn Dominican babies wouldn't appeal to him. Especially if Mickey came up with a photo of Dulce. I'd do an interview. Call her some names. She'd freak out and come after me. Of course, she'd probably come anyway, but this made it compulsory.

Always before I'd lost to Dulce because I didn't control the environment. Couldn't limit my exposure. Sonja was right about that. This time would be different. I'd stay home. Turn my apartment into a booby trap and never set foot out the door. Force her to come to me and take her on my turf, my terms.

I would kill Dulce Metraux.

I skipped the actual killing, in my mind, silly as that sounds since it was the whole object. But I've never killed. In fiction, or on the screen, hard-nosed detectives pack a weapon or an arsenal of them, never hesitating to pump lead through open doors, automobiles, and along busy streets. They often face off with their adversaries and fight to the finish - mano a mano.

In reality, such things are extremely rare. People are by nature backshooters, killing from ambush, for profit not honor. My motives weren't pure. Vindictiveness, revenge.

That worried me, justification being such an essential part of murder, or any other sin for that matter. I needed justification to plan Dulce's murder. I couldn't hesitate. I'd need to pull the trigger at the first opportunity. We wouldn't meet out in the street. No fair fight. I'd simply backshoot her.

Dulce tried to kill me. Killing her would be self defense. Dulce killed Adam Quist or had him made into a zombie. Then she did the same to his teenaged daughter. Dulce shot my best friend, Mickey Alba, an officer doing his duty. Dulce burned my father's barn and could easily have killed any number of innocent bystanders, even children. Dulce may have murdered dozens of people in her own country, according to Johnson. She deserved to die. She was a killing machine. It was irresponsible not to stop her. If she was caught in this country, or even in most states of the U.S., she'd be executed. What difference did it make if I happened to be the executioner?

None.

Except to me, of course.

That kind of thinking is how winners become losers, I thought. Just then Sonja awoke. "Hey," she said. "What time is it?"

"Early. Haven't heard the maids washing down the patio. Can't be more than five."

"Why are you up then?" She rolled toward me and swept her hand, gently, lazily, across my bare chest.

"What time are you leaving?" I asked.

"Early."

"Can we talk about something first?"

"I'd rather do something else," she said, biting me on the upper arm.

"No," I said. "I have to ask you this." I rolled toward her and brushed her hair back. "Please. When you shot Alejandro I know you did it to save my life and I'm sorry for what I said afterward, but what did you feel? After, and before."

She kissed my wrist. "Nothing," she said.

"You blew a man's head off and you felt nothing?"

"You mean like hate or anger, some great passion that helps me pull the trigger?"

"Something like that."

"No," she stated.

"What do you mean, *no*?"

"I mean no."

"Sonja."

She got up on one elbow. "This isn't about me is it?"

"I think I can get Dulce."

"But it means you will have to kill her?"

"Yes."

"Don't," she said.

"You tell me no? You do it all the time. You're leaving in a few minutes to do it again. I don't know how many people you've killed. Do you?"

"EJ. You don't know what I do when I leave here, and you will never know. Let me tell you this. I'm not in love with killing. If I could be you, I would. I'd turn back the clock, take back my innocent youth. Damn you sometimes," she said and fell onto her back, covering her eyes with her arm. "Do you remember when I told you long ago about Cuba? About the church?"

"Of course."

"Well, I skipped some parts. I didn't get away that night before my turn came to be raped by the soldiers. They came for me, one did, but my mother stood between us. I don't know why it was only school girls they were raping that night, other nights it was any age, sometimes even the men, but they had taken no older women from the church. Only girls. I watched my mother unbutton her blouse and entice the drunkard. 'Why do you want little girls?' she said. 'I can show you things you won't learn from little girls. Unless you're not a man. Maybe little girls are all you can handle.' He took her then, and after he raped her and shared her with his friends, he beat her and brought her back to us naked. You listen to that you think I'm after revenge. No. It's more than that. Something maybe you can't understand."

"Try me."

"I am the one who stops it from happening again. Fidel is my Hitler and like all madmen he knows I am coming for him. Not just me personally, but someone like me. If he didn't know that, the atrocities would worsen. Even in a society as controlled as Cuba today, without justice, free speech or press, there is always a way for information to get out. Fidel has to be careful. He can't go too far. He's forced to watch his back until the day he dies, even if he dies old in his bed. Then he can face God's judgement, if he escapes mine."

I never knew quite what to make of Sonja Cadavid. She wasn't like other women. "You were right before," I said. "About us doing something else instead."

"I'm out of the mood."

"Marry me then."

"You're always asking."

"You're always refusing."

She climbed from the bed, stood erect and gathered her hair together at the back of her head with both hands. "What do you think?" she asked. "A pony tail like an American?"

Sonja's hair was the luxurious black of her eyes. All her skin was white. No tan lines and barely a blemish, just a deep, warm cream scented with energy. She stood sculptured there in the gray dawn light, and all I could say was, "No pony tails, mi Cubana. Don't be American. Too many things are American already. Get in the shower. I've got to go and kill Dulce."

After she closed the bathroom door I lit a cigarette and flopped back onto the bed. Sonja was like this island, luxurious on the outside, fired on the inside by the same molten core that birthed it. Smoke curled up and billowed under the canopy. It reminded me again of Olivia and I snuffed it out in the ashtray by the bed.

If I got busy and Bravo Benoit needed copy, I could set my trap for Dulce by tomorrow night, or the next for sure. The rest was simple. Wait.

After that it wasn't quite so simple.

* * *

What if Dulce was one jump ahead again? What if instead of coming alone to my apartment she arrived fully prepared, backed by a squad from her voodoo army wielding AK-47s? They'd smash down my doors, storm the place and leave me and my great plan lying on the floor in a pool of blood. What if she stood out in the darkness across the street and lobed a couple grenades or explosive charges through the patio doors and blew the top off the building?

But what if I did nothing?

No, I thought, the plan is good. She'll come alone. It's personal, especially since Alejandro. She'll want me and she'll want me for herself. Once she read my quotes in the press she'd throw caution to the winds, because after all, the spirits she called from that other world would gather to protect her. On my side, it wouldn't hurt to tell Mickey about it just in case. Help coordinate our newspaper assaults anyway.

We met for lunch at the Flamboyant Cafe. That's not its name really. It has no name, no sign out front, and sits atop a hill in a residential neighborhood on a seldom traveled street. I call it the Flamboyant Cafe because there's a large flamboyant, royal poinsettia, tree growing in the yard. No one knows about the Flamboyant Cafe, literally no one. We've been going there for years and never seen anyone else there except the owner, and we don't see much of him.

The Flamboyant is a roof, supported by square concrete pillars spaced every ten feet, connected by a low wall three feet high. The concrete was once painted white, maybe a month or two after Columbus discovered the place. I don't know how the guy makes a buck.

"I don't like it," Mickey said.

"Of course," I responded. "I knew you wouldn't like it, that's why I almost didn't tell you."

"Well, I'm sorry you did. It's a bad plan."

"Because it's high risk? She'll surprise me somehow and kill me?"

"That too," he said. "You'll never see her. She'll smell it as a set up and stay a million miles away."

We were sitting at our usual table. I don't know why we had one, every table was available. We'd been there twenty minutes and the owner hadn't come to wait on us. Even when he did come he wasn't friendly, annoyed by the uncommon prospect of making money. The food was good though and the beer the coldest in town. He kept it in one of those old roll-top pop coolers.

"Where's the guy who runs this place?" I asked Mickey.

"Don't change the subject," he said. "I could use your help on the phones when these stories hit the papers tomorrow. We'll get hundreds of calls. Mostly junk, you know. Takes time to sort it all out. You'd be good at that."

"Locate a picture of Dulce?"

"Old one, but you can tell it's her. Wasn't any better looking when she was young. Of all the people, the German police had a mug of her. Did you notice her head? Cinder block with hair."

"Back to my plan."

"Forget it."

"You never like any of my plans," I complained.

"I liked the one where you got thrown in a hole and I got shot," he said. "Now I'm trying to be a little more discriminatory."

"Funny," I said. "Where is this guy? Waiter!"

He finally appeared from the back, wearing what had once been a white T shirt, a pair of baggy dark trousers with a towel of some sort tied around his waist. "Sí, Señor," he said unenthusiastically.

"Cold beer and a lunch menu, por favor."

"I have beer." He departed.

"Wasn't hungry anyway," Mickey said. "I'll drink one, then I've got to get back. Going to scrap this dumb plan?"

"No."

"Do me a favor then. Use the shotgun."

"I thought you said she wouldn't show up?"

"Probably won't. But if she does, she isn't going to make it easy. Something that shoots wide is better. You're a poor shot."

* * *

My trap was ready again a second night. The sun had set into a winter sky but we'd only had the usual afternoon shower around three thirty. The clouds on the horizon were red and burnt orange. I'd napped and felt some better than I had the night before. Waiting is stressful, especially when you're waiting to kill a woman.

I was disappointed Dulce hadn't shown the first night, though I hardly expected it. The stories in the newspapers that morning had been sensational. Dulce's picture didn't make it on the front page of the *Listín* as we'd hoped, but it did make it on the front of the *Última Hora*, a tabloid read by nearly everyone in town. I had eleven calls. I don't know how they got the number. I finally told Mercedes to ignore them. She wasn't grateful. She'd planned to do that anyway, and raise my rent. The quotes attributed to me in both newspapers were inflammatory. Among other things I called Dulce a fat voodoo puta and compared her religious beliefs to faith in aliens.

Carmen had been sent away again for a few days. I didn't want her in the crossfire. She had a "friend" to stay with, she said. A taxi came for her - purple and pink mood lighting around the windows, furry dashboard, extra caution lights and four mud flaps with rhinestone reflectors. It rocked with merengue. Carmen's view of Santo Domingo for the next three days.

There was one odd thing, the dog had gone too. Bill wasn't in the apartment. I guessed Carmen must've taken him somewhere. She left him with friends sometimes when we were both gone. I couldn't imagine him along for the cab ride.

I'd rearranged the apartment, cleverly I thought, using the furniture like the sides of a maze. The rear door was fortified so anyone entering was forced to use the front, where, as they maneuvered around the furniture, exposed themselves to my field of fire. Even if I missed and they ducked behind something they were trapped. No two pieces of furniture were close enough to offer sufficient cover.

I'd paced out and measured the distances to shoot any number of assailants from almost any angle of my reinforced position in the dining room where I built the bunker. I'd taken an old mahogany library table from my study and laid it on its side in the corner of the room so the large sliding glass doors of my veranda were on my right, the rest of the apartment and a wall to my left. The likelihood of anyone coming in over the veranda was remote. The roof had no access, except through my apartment, and the climb up from outside was suicidal. The concrete walls were smooth, challenging for a mountain climber, impossible for an overweight voodoo mambo.

At first I'd thought of shutting every door and window except the door by which I wanted her to enter, but it might look fishy, so I closed the bottom half of the jalousies and left the top halves open. The windows had metal security bars like most homes. Open, they seemed innocent enough and with the lower portion closed, you couldn't see inside. Dulce was short anyway.

My blind spot was the rear door and small maid's balcony, but it was also the most secure. The door itself solid wood. Outside was an iron door, and though I rarely used it, the balcony itself had another barred door on the end by the stairs. Since the apartment had originally been the Villacampas', it was built like a fortress. Mercedes was so paranoid she locked all the cupboards inside her own apartment and carried a set of keys around her humped neck. When her maid prepared dinner she had to come to Mercedes every time she wanted to dip out a cup of rice. Luz told Carmen once that the old bag knew exactly how many cups of rice were in a fifty pound sack and made a mark on a recipe card after each cup was dipped.

Another major concern I had was light. The main breaker was in a small hall closet behind some shelving and I switched on only certain parts of the apartment's power, then removed light bulbs from any lights that revealed my position. This controlled the scene like stage lighting.

From outside everything appeared normal. Open windows, light in some rooms and not in others. I'd even left the main veranda doors open part way, heavy sticks in the tracks to make sure they didn't open any farther. If Dulce shined a flashlight I'd have a target, but she wasn't likely to make that mistake.

Around my bunker I'd stacked most of the two thousand books I owned, two overstuffed chairs my sisters purchased because they looked like the kind of chairs city bachelors would sit in to read on long winter evenings in Vermont, a five drawer metal filing cabinet, and the mattress from a spare bedroom. Inside, I had the shotgun loaded and propped against a table leg. The pistol, a .38 snub nose made in Brazil, was also loaded and lying on the floor where I could grab it for close-in fighting. Ammunition was placed strategically alongside each. The shotgun was a 20 gauge with two boxes of ammo. Twenty four rounds for the pistol; twelve beside it, six already loaded, and six more in the right hand lower pocket of my dark blue guayabera. I was a little short on shells for the pistol but if things were so bad that I got down to reloading again and again, well, I'd probably be wounded, maybe dead.

I calculated all the angles, practiced the grab and shoot during the long night hours. Got it down to a second and a half. Two and a half if I was daydreaming. Five if I had my back against the wall. The pistol was hard to find in the dark so I practiced finding it with both hands and tossing it from left to right with my eyes shut.

I'd taken a full length mirror from the back of my bedroom door and propped it against one of the overturned chairs to my right. It faced out the open patio doors. Little chance anyone would come that way but I'd see them if they did. Redundancy is a comfort.

I didn't read or smoke, limited all sound and movement, crawled back and forth to the bathroom on hands and knees, then finally realized it was silly. Dulce expected a usual routine, so, after midnight I pretended I was going to bed and shut off all the lights except the one outside the rear entrance, then crawled back into my bunker.

Unlike country sounds, city sounds seem less stealthy and furtive. Traffic noise, slamming doors, music, voices, laughter. Later these diminish and quieter sounds - rattling palm fronds, pieces of newspaper scratching the street in the breeze, a howling cat, the rut of foraging rats - seem magnified, unexpected. I listened to separate these from the sounds a killer might make slipping along a sidewalk, up a stairwell, or working the lock on a door.

My ears were sensitive to even the slightest noise but I heard nothing that gave a warning. The only light in the room came from the street four floors below. Reflected light entered by the veranda and bounced from the ceiling, spreading on the tile. Santo Domingo had a critical power shortage. We experienced "apagónes" daily, usually eight to ten hours, sometimes twelve to sixteen. I wasn't surprised when the electricity failed. I'd expected it. I moved to the wall and stood up just long enough to glance outside and be certain all the other buildings were dark. They were.

Rich people installed small generators to maintain water pressure and flush toilets. The Villacampas weren't interested. Mercedes had Luz refill the toilet tanks after each flush. Luz hauled water in a metal bucket from a six thousand gallon cistern beneath the yard. The rest of us were welcome to do the same, up the stairs. I cheated and built a rain water tank on the roof. Carmen loved me for that. Uncommon she said, for a rich man to spend money safeguarding his servant's back. But then, I had foreign blood.

A small stairway down from the roof was secured by a steel trap door. It locked by means of two heavy metal rods, held tightly against a steel frame. You'd need a cutting torch. It was another of the many details I hadn't ignored in preparing my trap.

During the day, strong breezes gusted from the sea, but night winds from the mountains were light and cooling. I listened to the rustling of the bedroom curtains and the wind chime Carmen hung last Easter. Familiar sounds I'd heard often. The telltale sounds I waited for did not come.

Maybe I was napping a moment there on the floor. A light sound startled me. A tapping. I chuckled. Gently you came rapping. Tapping at my chamber door. "Darkness there and nothing more."

But it went on, insistent.

The pistol was easier to crawl with so I snatched it and crept through the living room into the dining room, pausing to listen. The tapping was through the kitchen, at the back balcony where everything was securely locked. My tension lessened. Someone must be knocking at this hour. A neighbor. I've seen Mercedes wander at night with her hair braided, wearing cotton gowns and wrapped in shawls.

When I stood up and approached the back door the tapping stopped. I waited a moment and listened carefully, wary of some trap or trick to get me to open the door.

Silence there and nothing more.

We have a long barred window there that looks out onto the balcony. I cranked the louvers open and peeked into the darkness. The balcony appeared empty.

The dead bolts squealed and screeched in protest as I drew them out to open the metal bars. I cursed softly but when I finally stepped out onto the concrete balcony it was truly empty. The wind chime trembled in the breeze and sang me a sweet, tinkling song.

Dark shapes of buckets, stacked cases of empty soda bottles, brooms, mops and cleaning supplies were smudged by shadow and there was the smell of amonia. The breeze was just enough to rattle the leaves of the large mango tree casting its heavy night shade against the side of the building. A small animal scrurried across the carpet of dead leaves on the ground far below but I saw nothing out of place. No movement in the shadows. Nothing sinister.

I decided to check the stairs as well. I walked across the balcony to the other door leading to the stairs and worked the locks. It took both hands and I stuck the pistol in my belt.

Like the other two doors, the inside door was wood and the outside thick iron bars. The wooden door swung in and I stepped around it.

The keys slipped from my grasp and clattered to the floor.

William the Conqueror's head protruded through the bars level with my own. His tongue hung limp at the corner of his gaping mouth. His throat was cut and dark blood ran down his black breast along his body to pool on the concrete beneath his hanging corpse. All four of his legs were crudely wired to the bars. Bill and I had our moments but this was the first time I'd ever pitied him. It was no way to die.

I knew who was next and slammed the door, snatched up my keys and ran back inside, locking the other doors. When I glanced down, by hands were trembling.

The next hour was the worst. Every sound was stealth. Every empty moment stiff with silence. No rest from tension, fighting every minute to free myself from new fears I'd conjured, cursing my foolishness, waiting impatiently for the honed blade to cross my throat.

All this time I'd sat on several of the couch pillows. The highly polished marble floor didn't offer enough friction to keep them under me, so finally I gave up and sat directly on the hard stone. At least it was cool. Something caught my eye as I slid the pillows against the wall. A shadow flickering across the night sky outside on the veranda. I grabbed for the shotgun, missed because I was looking over my shoulder, body at an odd angle. Reached again and had it by the barrel.

Outside, the formless thing materialized in the opening of the patio doors. A bulky figure.

The angle was poor and I held my fire, too close to the half open doors, shotgun pointed at the metal frames. No time to find the sticks inside the tracks to get the door open. I saw a muzzle now, I was sure. It crept slowly forward into the room like the hard head of a snake, sensing prey. Sniffing.

The 20 gauge had a push button safety. I applied pressure with my thumb, slowly, silently. The moment she followed her weapon into the room I resolved to fire. No hesitation. Apply steady pressure to the trigger.

The muzzle held steady. She was cautious. I was in the better position to wait, I thought. I held myself in check though I felt the shotgun growing slick in my hands, beads of sweat standing out on my forehead, creeping in small trickles along my spine.

No significant light. A glow from buildings below with generators. A dome of starlight. I listened to my own raspy breathing, amplified in the stillness. The snake head was motionless, stiff in the airless room. I blinked back a droplet of sweat from my eyelid. The angle was all wrong. Both sliding door frames blocked my view. I'd have to move left. But if the shotgun rattled or I bumped something, dragged a squeaky sole. Too risky.

I stayed quiet.

The dusky ghost, formless just outside the veranda door, seemed motionless enough to be illusionary. Was it the form of a woman? I couldn't be sure but someone had come for me. Did they hear my breathing?

The muzzle grew longer. If it was Dulce behind it, she'd abandoned her ancient black magic for what looked more and more like a small machine gun of some type. She was no more than ten feet away but I couldn't see her well enough to be certain it was even her.

I kept the shotgun leveled at the center of her shadow. My index finger ached against the trigger. All my energy flowing into one small extremity, begging to squeeze, like a pair of over-inflated lungs begging to explode.

White light flashed, detonating like a dazzle of pyrotechnics inside the room. The rattle of a machinegun. I covered my eyes, fell backward and accidentally fired the shotgun into the ceiling. Chunks of concrete and paint rained on my head. I smelled gunpowder, dust, the airborne wadding of the overstuffed furniture.

I cursed and brought the shotgun back down. She was gone.

My firing positions had all been created on the assumption she'd enter from the other side of the room. Now she was close. Behind something. But where? I didn't want to find out with the next burst of bullets.

Possibilities raced through my mind. She'd fired and stepped back outside. I saw nothing there. She'd fired and dropped behind some cover until she saw or heard me. She'd fired and gone to another part of the apartment, my bedroom maybe. Or she might be very very close, listening. What if she'd seen the overturned table and chairs, realizing what it was? She could be inches away now, preparing to stand and fire down inside. I was seconds from death.

A wall to my left, Dulce somewhere to my front, glass to my right. I jumped up, fired the shotgun into the patio doors and threw myself through the shattered glass, landing with a thump outside on the veranda. I recovered quickly and scrambled around the corner, slamming my back against the wall.

Four rounds remained in the shotgun. The pistol I'd forgotten on the floor inside. For the moment I was safe. She was inside, I was outside. The element of surprise was gone. No backshooting. Mano a mano.

I edged to my right until I touched one of the patio chairs with my foot, then ducked behind the table, not for protection but to avoid being silhouetted against the bare concrete wall. If she followed me outside she'd have nothing clear to shoot at and maybe I'd recover the advantage and put a few pellets in her before she fired again.

Time dragged. She'd seen the trap. I'd fired twice so she knew I was armed. If she checked the doors she'd soon learn that being inside was no better than being outside. All were key lock deadbolts. She could pick them, of course, but did she have time? Could she do it without making a sound?

The light was slightly better on the veranda. I saw something leaning against the wall behind me. I couldn't make it out and crawled over for a look. A small steel ladder leading down from the roof. I moved back to the table. Heard nothing from inside.

It was a standoff until someone did something. Made a move, or a mistake. What if I just leaned around the corner and pumped three of my remaining rounds in an arc across the living room and the dining room? I might not kill her but if she came up or moved to a safer place I'd still have one shell left to finish her. She might right now be planning the same thing. A quick dash through the smashed doors, spraying machinegun bullets at everything on the veranda. I was bound to take a couple. Better to strike first. My mind seemed razor sharp.

I took a deep breath and stepped square into the opening, oblivious to my own silhouette against the night sky. The shotgun fired left, center, right. The sound was deafening. Glass shattered into silver shrapnel and filled the air, smoke poured from the muzzle and hung in the room, I heard the explosion of my display case filled with signed baseballs. Paintings and hand carved wooden masks flew from the walls. I stepped back around the corner, shocked that I could still stand, that I was still alive.

Dulce didn't make a sound.

From far below, like a voice in a dream, I heard, "Idiota Enfermo! Espinosa-Hones." Mercedes Villacampa never pronounced the American "J" sound, always the Spanish "H" sound. I hesitated, wondering if her voice could be heard by Dulce inside. It might panic her. Someone now to call the cops.

"What are you doing, hombre loco? Idiota! Why is there a dead fat woman in my garden?"

A flashlight beam jerked about below, shining in the trees and flashing against my veranda. "Señor EJ!" It was Julio's voice. "Are you alive? Did you kill this woman? Is she a ladróna?" A robber.

Moving cautiously, I edged to the railing and looked down. Julio, Mercedes and Luz were standing several feet from Dulce's twisted corpse. "I don't see any blood," Luz said.

"You will see blood," Mercedes promised her. "This time I will involve the doctor, my husband himself. He will deal with this maniac."

"Julio!" I shouted down. "Shine the light on her face."

He obeyed. It was Dulce. I hadn't shot her.

"Call the policía," I told him. "Tell them to find Lt. Alba wherever he is. It's important. They must go to his house and get him if necessary. Hell to pay if they don't. Understand?"

"Sí, Señor," he said. I could tell he was excited by his role in this drama, an event that would be talked about in the neighborhood for years. He would tell how he summoned the police, instructed them on how to proceed. An important witness as well.

"Señora Villacampa," I said. "Go inside and wait for the police. There may be more ladrones in the building."

She looked frightened enough to obey, I thought. But what on earth had killed Dulce?

The mirror. I found it shattered, its thick wooden backing contained an almost even line of machinegun bullet holes. Dulce had shot her own reflection as she crept through the door, and then confused or struck by shards of broken mirror or frightened by my shotgun blast into the ceiling, ran back too far or stumbled over the railing to her death.

It hit me then. I was free. Dulce was dead. My family was safe. It was over.

I wandered back inside. The lights came on just then and I saw the wreckage. I flipped up one of the chairs, filled with shotgun beebee holes, and dropped into it, too tired to think. I laid the shotgun across my lap and lit a cigarette. She was dead.

I might never know what happened to Ambassador Adam Quist, or to Olivia. Surely, the Quist family would never speak to me again. Maybe they'd take comfort from hearing that both Dulce and Alejandro were gone. Maybe they'd already flown home to forget Santo Domingo. They'd want to forget me - the man who said the Ambassador was a zombie and got Olivia killed. They didn't know Olivia was missing, a wax dummy buried in her place. And what difference did it make?

With Dulce, died any link to Delbrick. Whatever his role, he'd landed safely behind the line. I could do nothing more. But then neither could he. Any further interest in pursuing me would only draw negative attention to him. He was, after all, in my town.

The cigarette tasted fine. I closed my eyes and exhaled. What on earth would I tell Mr. Yancy?

Chapter Twenty Two

Mr. Yancy was in Santiago for a few days so I decided to drive out and relax awhile in El Seibo, put my family's fears to rest and brag about Dulce to Johnson. I'd tried to call earlier that morning. Phone rang but no answer. This nagged me because my sisters received calls by the hectokilo, but Dulce was dead, the danger past.

Once again I summoned Carmen back, cutting her vacation short. She didn't seem to mind and arrived early that morning with her skirt on sideways, zipper down, bare-bellied below an ill-fitting, soiled pink tank top. Hair flat as a chopped cane field. She'd returned or lost the rental teeth.

I was drinking coffee I made myself. Carmen stood by the door and admired the destruction in the living room, dining room and veranda. She stared empty-headed, like she'd had exactly the same kind of a night. "Welcome back," I said. "Sorry you missed the party."

"I didn't miss it," she said, scratching herself.

"The kitchen's okay," I told her. "No shooting in there."

"What a relief," she said.

"I haven't eaten yet. Just coffee."

"Eat out." Carmen shuffled to the kitchen and returned with a cup of my coffee. Did nothing to fix her clothing. Her plastic thong sandals were on the wrong feet.

"So," I said. "Did you get to take a ride in the taxi?"

"Sí, mucho."

"Great. Guess I'll call Mickey and go out somewhere, if you're not going to fix breakfast I mean."

"I'm going to my room and lie down," she said. "I'll clean later."

"Fine. It's only your job. I'm heading home for a few days."

"Bien viaje," she said, stumbling toward the rear of the apartment.

"An amazing woman," I said to myself.

"Gracias," I heard her say as she turned the corner, coffee slopping from her cup.

I was in the mood for a large breakfast. A heaping plate of scrambled eggs, tostónes, fresh Sosua sausage, lots of fruit and a giant glass of papaya with milk. Mickey could always eat so I drove to his office through light morning traffic.

La comisaria where Mickey worked was one of the oldest buildings outside the Zona Colonial. A couple guys there didn't like me much. I didn't belong to the club. Cops are the same all over. But the Colonel in charge, Negro Guzman, thought I was muy gracioso. I liked him, too. He protected his command by doing his job and taking only enough payoffs to satisfy his family's needs, and shared with his troops. He was the blackest man I'd ever known. At birth he said his parents agreed negro he was and Negro he would remain.

That morning he put his arm around my shoulders and hugged me close to his massive chest. "You should've been a policeman," he said. "I heard what you did last night. Poor Mickey didn't get much sleep and since about six o'clock has been writing reports." He nodded toward Mickey half way across the room hunched over his desk. "Have you come to take him to breakfast?"

"Yes. Would you like to come along?"

"Ah, no. I have a meeting," he said. "This Dulce woman. What a bruja! As a Catholic, I find this voodoo business very strange. What was she afraid of?"

"The light, I think." I stared up at him. "You wouldn't want me as a policeman. I'm almost giddy this morning because I didn't kill her."

Negro hugged me once more and turned me loose. "Thank you Senor EJ," he said. "I am serious now. Thank you. How about I tell you a secret? Our amigo Colonel Francisco Caamaño Deno has been found."

"Dead or alive?"

"Alive yet for awhile but soon dead."

"Is it wise to make him a martyr?"

"He is Castro's man." He shrugged. "One little island. Centuries of outside influence. Spanish, British, French, Haitians, Americans - now the Cubans? I don't think so. We thumb our nose at them all. Castro too. We are Dominicanos. Not a rich country, but a rich people." He smiled and reached out for me again. "This is what I like about you. You struggle always to be Dominican. You are typical of us, yet you are half American, no? Maybe it's this struggle that makes us strong." He rubbed my head and let me go again. "One half-and-half, one negro," grinning, he raised his voice to attract Mickey, "one mulatto? What are you Mickey, huh?"

"Hombre."

"Ha, ha!" Negro said. "Bueno. Go to breakfast." He turned toward his office.

We drove separately and met at the Jaragua Hotel on the Malecón and ordered breakfast by the pool. The hotel was rumored to be Mafia owned and the food was excellent. Mickey always said it was a good place for a policeman to eat.

"So, you are going home?" he asked.

"Just for a few days."

"Aren't your Johnson boys still with them? Why worry?"

"I'm not worried. Something with the phone. Common enough." There were gulls and pelicans squawking for garbage in the low surf. "I don't see them often."

"What's the matter with you Norte Americanos? Appreciate your family."

"Why is it that I'm an 'Americano' when I do something you don't like and a Dominican the rest of the time?"

"Shut up and eat. Do you want that last sausage?"

"Keep your hands off my food."

"Damn greedy Americano."

We ate in silence awhile. Mickey drizzled ketchup on his tostónes. From the pool bar behind us I heard the radio playing Feliz Navidad. They played it about a hundred times a day. I still had Christmas shopping to do.

"You have the eating habits of some kind of predatory beast," I told Mickey.

He paused and looked up, ketchup filling one corner of his mouth. "Yeah? I like to eat. Never grew one of those little bellies under my belt though, like you've got."

"I do not."

"You will. Half breed Americanos always have those."

"If you don't shut up you'll end up like Dulce."

Mickey smiled and wiped his mouth. "You mean I'll look in the mirror, scare myself so bad I jump backwards and fall down four floors and break my neck?"

"You're funny."

"Just because Negro thinks you're a hero. When I examined Old Dulce, she didn't have a shotgun pellet in her. You shot up the furniture, the ceiling, the glass doors. Never touched a hair on her head. Total damn waste of ammunition. You have a desperate criminal five feet away, and what do you do? Shoot up the chairs in your own apartment. Un detective muy peligroso. Ha!"

"For that, you're buying this breakfast, fuzzball."

"Fuzzball?"

"Yeah, fuzzball. That's what we Americanos call the policía we don't like. Fuzzballs."

"Fuzzball," he said thoughtfully. "Fuzzball," he repeated slowly. "I like the way it feels in your mouth. It's not like baseball?"

"No." I knew that by the end of the day half the policía in Mickey's squad would be calling each other fuzzballs. "I'm sorry I ever brought it up."

His eyes on my plate, he says, "Are you sure you're going to eat that sausage?"

"Fine. Take it."

"Hey. Where's your woman?"

"Sonja?"

"Of course, Sonja."

"Gone. Making the world safe so you can stuff your face."

"Ah," he said. "She made a very clean shot with Alejandro, and in the dark too. With a pistol. You could learn from her." He grinned at me. "Don't look so shocked that I know your little secret. She called me herself. Told me where she moved the body and that she was available for any questions I might have. There were none, of course."

"Think you know everything don't you? I'm going to the desk and see if the *Última Hora* is out yet."

The Jaragua was an old hotel. Once owned by the government and allowed to run down, now renovated into one of the most desirable properties in the city. The small casino across from the lobby was very chic and always crowded in the evenings. I found the *Última Hora* on a stack by the reservation desk, its entire front page consumed by headlines that the Army would soon surround Colonel Caamaño in the mountains and kill him and his band of revolutionaries. I took the paper back to the table and showed it to Mickey. "Bueno," he said. "Things will soon get back to normal. No more double shifts." Having cleaned his plate, he was stabbing my sliced fruit with a toothpick.

"We shouldn't kill him," I said. "Just creates more hatred, more violence."

Mickey finished chewing a mouthful and kept a toothpick dangling from his lips. "That's why I like you," he said. "The impossible is not impossible to you. Violent people are apprehended without violence. Hatred is washed away by love. I like you for that." He tossed the toothpick onto his empty plate and drank the remainder of his orange juice. "Sometimes though Amigo, I think you believe that shit."

"I do."

"And you wonder why Sonja won't marry you."

"I'm too kind hearted?"

"Blind. Without sight. In the dark. A puppy waiting for its eyes to open."

"You're starting to piss me off now Mickey. Why don't we drop it?"

"Sure," he said. "I'll say one thing more. Nothing good in this world is born without pain and violence. When the Jews got to the Promised Land flowing with milk and honey, what did they do? Took it by killing the inhabitants. And Christ? Was his kingdom not established by suffering? The Renaissance, your great Americano democracy, all born by violence and war and death of innocent people. This is the way of the world."

"Maybe," I said, "but it doesn't have to be all that's in our hearts."

Mickey Alba toyed with his fork awhile. "Sometimes, when I'm knee deep in the shit of this city, I think how we do the same job, see the same things, but with different eyes. I don't understand it."

"As long as we stay friends," I said. "You had me worried when you got shot."

"Good." He smiled. "It was all your fault."

You only get maybe one or two good friends in your life. The kind who stick with you from beginning to end. Who don't judge you. My best friend was a crooked cop named Mickey Alba, a cynic. "Who's paying?" I asked.

"Don't be stupid. Cops don't pay here."

"So the Mafia is taking us to breakfast? You got no problem with that?"

"Better than having them take us for a ride." He laughed. "Relax. I catch them bringing in drugs or stealing, I drop them in the Ozama myself. No problem."

Talk about naive. What did he think they were doing here, body-surfing at Boca Chica Beach?

Our cars were parked behind the hotel. We strolled casually around the pool. The morning trades were light and cool yet, coming up from the southeast fragrant with the sea. In the parking lot, fresh smells were overpowered by a kitchen dumpster.

"Thanks for breakfast, Godfather," I said, tossing the *Última Hora* on the front seat. "Can I ask you something before we go?"

"What?"

"Is it possible that Sonja had anything to do with this Caamaño's hunt?"

"Personally you mean?"

"That, or some other way."

"I've never lost my country," he said. "I don't know how a Cuban feels, never able to go home again. Like Negro said, Caamaño is Castro's man. Sonja is Castro's enemy. But if I were you, I'd forget about it. You're confused enough. Go see your mother. Try to behave yourself."

I climbed in behind the wheel as he walked away. It felt like we were parting.

* * *

We'd lingered over breakfast. It was mid-morning before I drove clear of city traffic, happily picking my way along country roads in and out of potholes so large the Jeep went down one side and up the other. When I was at college in Minnesota and they complained about road conditions there, I'd tell my pothole stories. Always told with humor because people can't accept any truth too far outside their own experience.

In fact, giant Dominican potholes start out small, a break or crack, like potholes anywhere. The pavement wears year after year and no one ever comes to repair it. Rain washes it, traffic tries to avoid it and soon wears new tracks. The edges break down. The hole fills with water, dries out, always growing. Eventually, it's a smoother ride to drive directly into it than to avoid it. After that it wears more quickly and before long it's large enough to swallow a truck.

In the States I felt insulted when people didn't believe such things, although truth is often veiled because some mental or emotional blind eye won't allow us the vision to see it. Therefore, we can't accept monster potholes - voodoo mambos, or zombies either.

The death of Dulce and the promised death of Caamaño were a somber duet in my mind. Both lives threatened me and my way of life. I was relieved one was dead, another soon to be, but not joyful - pain poorly remembered. What remained was nagging doubt.

It was a hot day and my back had created a soaking oval of sweat against the seat and I guided the vehicle to a level patch of grass alongside the road and stopped. I lit a cigarette and got out to stretch my legs. In an overpopulated country there are always people. People in the mountains and valleys, along roads, rivers, beaches. I saw here a barbed wire fence, evidence of goats. No people.

My gaze swept the hills and fields and I was restless. My greatest fear has always been the unanswered question. I love a mystery only if I solve it. Garrett Yancy hired me to find out what happened to Adam Quist. No one had seen him since the day he died and the daughter who wanted his mystery solved was now a mystery herself. Some threats removed by death, others flickering only in the ardor of a restless mind as the detective Edgar Espinosa-Jones stood smoking alongside a country road where there might be goats.

Clouds drifted in from the northeast and gathered in the mountains. Rain. Maybe several days of it. Some of the clouds were already dark. Down along the valley road the sun was shining. I had beads of sweat on my forehead and was thinking about somewhere to find a cool drink.

In many parts of the world strangers are treated with indifference or hostility. The DR is warm, its people too, and welcoming of strangers, often inviting them home for coffee or a cold beer. The spirit of "mi casa, su casa" is even more pronounced in the country, the campo. If I didn't spot a colmado or small cafe, I'd pull over by somebody's house and see if they had something to drink.

The cigarette tasted hot. I flipped it into the road, slid back behind the wheel and drove on at less than thirty miles per hour, dust boiling up alongside the truck.

Another quarter hour passed before I spotted a small wooden shed with three open sides, dirt floor, thatched roof, and a weather-beaten sign - *Coca-Cola. ¡Bien Fría!* I pulled up and parked.

Inside, I found a patch of shade, a small wooden counter, canned goods, a very old woman without teeth. "Buenos días," I said. "Do you have any cold drinks?"

"Of course," she said.

"Refrescos?"

"Refrescos, cerveza, jugos, whatever you want."

"I think I would like the Coca-Cola," I said.

"Of course." She hurried out the back door and disappeared along a trail into the brush and trees.

I waited several minutes but she didn't return.

There were chickens in the side yard and pigs. Farther back, a fenced goat. The place smelled of dust and dung. Impatient, I walked behind the building and followed the path she'd taken. It led to several small thatched homes with swept dirt floors and children playing. An older girl, thirteen or fourteen, covered her mouth with her hand and ran away into a grove of bananas.

I asked the younger children, three girls and a boy, if they had a mother or father around. They shook their heads shyly and went back to batting a round stone at each other with long sticks. In the doorway of the middle house a naked baby sat alone in the dirt, drooling.

I turned to leave just as the old lady came at a trot, shaking a key in the air. "La llave, la llave," she announced.

I followed her back to the tiny store. "I'm sorry to put you to so much trouble," I said.

"No problem, Señor. My cousin Gloria's husband Dajer is in Higuey today to sell four goats. He usually leaves the key with Gloria but she had to go to her mother's, who is sick with a discharge of the liver. She gave the key to Rosaángela Ricart because it was her turn to watch the store today but I changed a day with her because I can't do it next Sunday when my granddaughter will receive her Bible storybook from the priest. I'm sorry, Señor. I forgot Rosangela had the key."

"The key to what?" I asked.

"The refrigeration device where we keep the refrescos. This is the property of Dajer. The merchandise belongs to Consuelo and her son Raúl. Mario Montes buys the refrescos."

"What is your part in this cooperative?"

"The store. It is my house."

I looked around. "There's no place to sleep."

"At night I drop the sides down and sleep on the counter. I have a mat. It is good someone is here for the rats."

Dominicans are very resourceful and often pool their assets. In a remote fishing village, Mickey and I rented a small boat once to go diving, one guy owned the boat and two others the motor. We quickly located the man with the motor in his house, but waited several hours before finding his partner with the spark plug.

The old lady unlocked the cooler, uncapped a Coca-Cola and collected my fifteen centavos - a transaction now of approximately thirty minutes. My American friends never understood why things took so long to accomplish here. You had to understand the complexities.

"Are you traveling far?" the lady asked.

"Another hour or so."

"There is a cock fight this afternoon, which is a thing that interests men. Only a short walk. You can leave your guaguita (little bus) here. I will find a boy to watch it."

"No," I said. "I'll just drink this and get back on the road."

Later, I ate some canned sardines, crackers, drank another Coke. We talked. I switched to beer and walked back with her to the cock fight. Drank some rum not to hurt people's feelings, lost twenty bucks and most of the afternoon.

When I got back on the road the green hills had dark shadows. Clouds had massed above the mountains and begun to descend, cool and gray, toward the valleys. My mood was light. Most of the men at the cock fight knew each other and were pleased to have a stranger in their midst. Someone nicknamed me Canelo (cinnamon) because of my skin color and the road dust in my hair. I told them it was a girl's name and instantly attracted bettors to whichever chicken I picked. "¡Canelo! ¡Canelo!" they shouted. It was the first time I'd relaxed since before Thanksgiving.

The boy who watched the Jeep had also washed it. Even the seats had been wiped clean. I leaned back and drove the remainder of the way home in dreamy contentment.

* * *

Night crept down the mountains, extinguishing twilight with thin layers of wet clouds. I plunged into the valley with the radio blaring and a cigarette between my lips, gray fog mist blanketing the hills, dampening the valley, cloaking me in darkness as I sped toward home.

The night was coming early and my thoughts went back to New York, the "Zombification" paper Dr. Mercer had slipped into my hand before I left his office. What is it about scientific language that can transform black magic into sterile fact? A zombie was exciting and bone-chilling. "Zombification" wasn't.

Dr. Mercer's paper outlined the steps in Zombification. First the poison. A mixture of things that often included the glandular secretions of a particular toad, soaked for about a month in menstrual blood and dried to a powder. Then came the tetrodotoxin of the puffer fish, which made one of the most lethal poisons on earth, more deadly than cyanide. Lesser ingredients, the preference of the particular bokor making the zombie, might include a little ground spider, some poisonous leaves, and the all important scrapings from a human cadaver. Fresh skull scrapings were preferred, sometimes cooked together with bits of rotting flesh stolen from a recent grave at a nearby cemetery.

This pestilent brew was combined in exact amounts to simulate death by inducing the zombie-like catatonic state when applied topically. You didn't drink a potion like in movies, all this stuff needed to do was touch you. Dr. Mercer said a favorite trick was to dig a hole in front of some intended victim's hut, place a candle inside the hole and spread the poison on the ground around it. When the victim came out and stepped over the candle the poison entered his body through the bottoms of his bare feet. Intense pain and hours of suffering followed.

I remembered too, Dr. Mercer wrote there was always an antidote. This wasn't created for the zombie but the bokor and his assistants who might accidentally touch the poison during preparation or administration.

Gruesome ponderings I thought, cruising up the driveway toward the house. My headlights were absorbed by the fog and I slowed to a crawl. The last of the rum seemed to snap from my head and my senses spiked.

The house was dark. No welcoming glow from windows or porch lights. Immediately I jerked my foot off the gas petal and let the Jeep coast to a stop. I couldn't remember the house dark in the evening. When we were gone, the maids were home. When the electricity failed, we lit candles. Lights were left burning for anyone out late. Even after we were all in bed there was light from a fixture on the end of Tobacco Barn Number One. That, of course, had burned out.

I killed the engine and headlights, rolled down my window and listened. No door banged, no laughter or music, only the mist, cool and damp on my arm and cheek, thickening in the trees. I stepped out onto the gravel drive and quietly closed the door. I was gripped by an acute sense of foreboding. There was a flashlight in the glove compartment but I felt safer moving in the darkness alongside the road.

Where were Pulga and Pest, the two English Setters? They often followed Dad or one of the girls to the sheds or out in the fields, but this time of night they should've been here. And where were Johnson & Johnson?

In the ninth grade I took a class in agriculture - my father had insisted - and for a final project I planted fifty-two royal palms along our drive. Twenty six trees on each side of the narrow gravel road. One died and was replaced. I picked it out in the gloom, slightly shorter than the rest. I knew then I was almost to the front yard.

Hotel properties sometimes have the trunks of their royals painted white and ringed with wide strips of tin to keep rats from nesting or eating the fruit. Ours were left in their natural state; rough, circular bark below a long section of smooth green skin near the top just beneath the fronds. It's almost as if they were purposely trimmed to achieve this odd shape. I kept to their shadows, walking silently on the wet grass. Above, the fronds hung in listless curls, dripping in the mist.

The house was a dark shape ahead. The mist slid from left to right rapidly but there was no discernible wind. I shivered and dropped to one knee, studying the house. I wasn't close enough to see clearly and each moment that passed brought more darkness as the vanquished gray sun, lost somewhere beyond hills, sea, and mist, died out completely. Fear crept out from deep inside and my shivering became like a palsy.

I listened. Stood up and took a few steps toward the porch. My foot struck something soft and heavy. It bounced from my toe and rolled ahead in the grass. I bent down. It was Johnson's head.

He must've been in a state of panic when it was severed. His eyes were wide and wild. His lips curled in what I imagined was a final shriek.

I tore my eyes from him and looked from side to side. I saw his body then across the road, chest down. He must've been running away from the house.

My thoughts were not of Johnson. Everything I held dear was inside that house. I was going to open the door on a butcher shop. The chopping of machetes, the bloodletting of vengeful Sect Rouge deviants, devouring my sisters, mother, father. I fell to both knees, my breath came in sobs. I wanted to run to the house. I wanted to run away.

I staggered back up onto my feet, trembling. Fear boiled inside, alive, tearing at my stomach with snappping teeth. I lurched to the nearest tree and hugged its wet, rough bark, choking back sobs. My stomach cramped by pain and nausea. Eyes screwed shut, I fought hard to control my breathing. There wasn't time to panic.

A moment later tears broke from my squeezed eyelids and rolled along my cheeks. They broke the grip of hopelessness and I inhaled the taste of salt from my lips, palm bark and damp smoky air. Now was not a time to weaken. I inhaled a deep breath and pushed myself erect and backed away from the tree.

Something struck me in the head. I spun around and faced a naked foot. Above, the other Johnson hung garroted by wire. An iron stake had been driven into the tree to hold him out away from the trunk like a swinging sign. I saw where the garrote wire was wrapped around the iron. His eyes looked remarkably like his cousin's.

I knew then that everyone was dead. The murderers gone away in the mist.

Only I was left. Unarmed, impotent.

I dropped again to my knees in the gravel and cried to God in a voice so hoarse I didn't recognize it, "Don't make me see this. Don't make me."

I hadn't expected an answer so quickly, but a voice said, "Stand up."

I hadn't been alone on the road. People surrounded me, materializing in the mist. How could such a crowd have been so quiet? Many of them were armed with machetes. "My family," I said.

"We have waited for you," the same voice said. It belonged to a small thin man. His accent was Haitian and he wore a yellow baseball cap that said Hotel Splendid, and instantly I remembered him in white and gold, our waiter at the hotel. Hollow-eyed women stood on either side of him.

"Where is my family?"

I heard the sound of some sort of rattle. The women chanted a phrase in Creole and the small man poked his head toward me like a black gargoyle and said, "We came for you. Enemy. Enemy." He was wearing sunglasses in the dark.

They hadn't denied the death of my family and neither did they seemed interested. I turned to push away but more people had moved in behind. "¡Mi familia!" I screeched at them.

My arms were pinned back and tied at the wrists and elbows. Several of the women moved in close and rubbed themselves slowly against me, wiping me with their breasts and bellies. One of them told me she was absorbing my power.

Still more of them appeared, ghostlike from the mist, quiet as the dead. Whatever they did now wasn't going to be quick. A slow death, or worse. I wasn't going to talk myself out of it or swim to safety.

They took me by the arms and started pulling me along. I struggled. "Show me my family," I demanded.

"You have no family but us," the man answered. I guessed he was the bokor or houngan. He looked like a farmer.

They led me behind the house, through the back gate and into the savanna that made up the land between a large hill or small mountain we called De Poco Pecho, which means flat-chested. Farther up the slope trees and vegetation thickened, but we moved along the narrow dirt road that led toward the valley's baseball stadium.

Some lit torches now and I heard drums ahead.

I guessed at least twelve or fifteen in our party. How many more waited? Would I discover the dismembered bodies of my family around some voodoo campfire? Bizango priests drinking my mother's blood? Maybe Dulce's spirit had come back for me, or she'd risen from the dead like a zombie and waited to take me by the hand and lead me into hell. It didn't matter. I was miserable beyond caring. There's no destitution greater than the loss of family. I was worthless without them, a wretched man who stumbled along toward a hell where even fear is barred entrance.

Alejandro would've been disappointed in me if Sonja hadn't killed him. He said he liked it that I faced danger with panache. Now I'd lost it, no élan, just despair. I thought of a morning long ago when I was sixteen. My mother awakened me as usual but I flew into some adolescent rage. "Leave me alone!" When she refused, I shouted "I wish your were dead!" I sobbed silently in the mist and begged my mother's spirit to forgive me.

We came finally to the stadium, pride of the valley, remodeled last year at considerable cost and the only lighted stadium outside a major city. Tonight it was menacing - a dark steel voodoo church. Between second base and the pitcher's mound, two fires burned inside a line of torches. To my right, at the end of the infield, someone had tied flashlights to poles and stuck them in the ground. The beams of light traveled only a few yards into the air before being lost in the fog, which had thickened here closer to De Poco Pecho.

The drum sounds originated from the visitor's dugout where the drummers sat. The remainder of the field was hidden in total darkness. They threaded a wooden pole through my arms so two men could grab its ends and stand me up, sit me down, direct me as they wished. While they held me, my shoes, socks, and clothes were stripped away. They left my underwear and I felt relieved. Why, I don't know.

I quit struggling. My heartbeat slowed and my mind cleared. I wasn't afraid of this evil little farmer. His power extended only to my body, they'd destroyed me when they killed my family. Soon I'd join them, eagerly. "You people have to quit taking my clothes all the time," I said. My voice sounded hollow but tolerant in the close air.

"You must be cleansed," my little gargoyle explained.

The women returned, some brandishing whips made of leafy branches, others doused my body with what smelled like a citrus oil. Several of the women rubbed it into my skin with their hands. Others whipped me until I was cleansed. The whipping stung but didn't draw blood. The citrus smell wasn't offensive either, but I had the distinct impression of being marinaded. I knew from Dr. Mercer that the Sect Rouge drank warm blood but I didn't think they ate you first.

The waiter-turned-farmer-bokor said something that sounded to me like a Creole limerick and then I was led between the two fires. "You are enemy," he told me. "You have not kept the secret."

"It's not my secret," I explained.

"Do you know what is going to happen to you?"

"Go to hell," I said.

He struck me across the face. "You will become a zombie slave in Haiti." He smiled. "Your mind will be taken from you and you will obey. You will obey."

His hands were hard and I tasted blood. "Zombification," I said to the waiter, who glared back blank-faced. "You the head sorcerer, or is the head chef still telling you what to do?" If they did make me drink anything, I resolved right then to spit it on as many of them as possible. I knew if it was topical there wasn't much else I could do.

He didn't answer. Ordered me dragged beyond the fires to a grassy area of outfield between first and second base. He drew a flashlight from his pocket and pointed it at the ground. A fresh grave was dug there and a rough coffin lay open beside it.

"Mine?" I asked needlessly.

"Making a zombie is bokor magic. You must be buried before you are raised from the dead."

"Can't we skip that part?"

This earned me a trip about three inches off the ground by means of the pole which bent my arms back, stretching my shoulder muscles in a manner so painful I howled and tears sprung to my eyes. Grace under fire didn't seem much appreciated in the voodoo experience.

They dragged me back to the fires.

"Ti bon ange," the bokor said. Theft of the soul by power of the bokor. "The mambo comes to capture your ti bon ange."

Why did he need a mambo to help him? Then it struck me. Dulce wasn't dead.

The drums surged, intensifying, amplified by the weight of darkness and fog. I inhaled heavy oily smoke from the torches, and the flashlights pointing in the air seemed to crack the earth and release the demons of hell, crawling out like insects. Across the infield, behind home plate, another group moved slowly toward our fires. They were led by a willowy mambo who moved like sea grass. Olivia.

Her face appeared greasy when she got up close. Her hair tied back under a scarf. She wore a simple cotton dress with a pinched waist and buttons down the front. She was barefoot.

Olivia's eyes were wide and unfocused. My first impression was that she'd been possessed by a loa, mounting her to assist in the theft of my spirit. "Olivia," I said.

She ignored me and spoke instead to the bokor. The Creole sounded hollow and flowed from her mouth like black water from a fountain.

The bokor laughed and came close to my face. "A white mambo to take a white man's soul," he said.

"I'm really a half breed," I explained, my eyes on Olivia. "This is all a joke right? Olivia? I used to play third base on this field. You can't be taking all this seriously."

Olivia's head jerked slightly several times and her eyes rolled up under the lids until only white shown in the flickering light. She moaned and spasms seized her body in waves that were almost like a dance of frenzy. She bridged the gap between the living and the dead. Nothing could touch her in that state.

Other members of the sect moved in around her, their faces glowing in the firelight. Drums sounded louder and I heard the rattle again. The mist was cool on my skin but my body burned with fever.

A moment later Olivia seemed to gain control and stayed still. She gathered her full skirt with both hands and stuffed it into her crotch. "I'm hot," she said in English.

I was close to her and I knew from her face there was no hope. When she'd slipped from the car in Port au Prince and led me into the pressing crowd, people touched her like an icon, stroking her pale skin with their soft black hands. Somehow they must've known. I should have. Now it was too late. She was not pretending. She was a mambo. A member of a Sect Rouge.

"Do you drink blood, too?" I blurted.

An odd, almost secret smile, creased her lips. "In your house I have been drinking this very night."

At that moment I overcame my fear. The pit of my stomach was no longer hollow, its emptiness replaced by a heavy stone. "Then this very night you will die," I said.

Olivia's smile widened. "My father was the most powerful man on this island. Where is he?"

"You killed him? Zombified him? You're crazy."

"Loa protects us." She moved closer, the wadded dress forcing her legs apart so she walked on the sides of her feet. Her mouth seemed slack and her lips moist. "He came into me when I was nothing but a small child. When loa mounts us we are protected from the evil of Adam and from the evil of any who would destroy us. You are a destroyer."

"Loa didn't protect Dulce," I said. "Alejandro died when his head exploded. It won't protect you. If your father molested you why didn't you tell someone? Tell your mother."

"She couldn't force herself to believe me. Why do you think she drank? The spirit world has great power," she said. "Don't be afraid. The zombie is a bridge between this world and the next."

"You turned your father into a zombie. Maybe it was a just punishment. Why involve Yancy or me?"

"The fool doctor," she said. "He missed the pulse."

"If he hadn't you'd be in jail now where you belong."

Her smile was chilling. "You are a foolish and weak man. Do you think the magic of the poison makers is our own, or the spirits we bring into us? A nonbeliever can't accept the existence of zombie. The doctor saw nothing. Had he felt the thread of life in the monster who was my father, what could he do? Say the Ambassador is a zombie? What happened when you said it? And now you see, you selected your own fate."

"How can you believe in this nonsense?" I asked her.

"Voodoo saved me. Can't you feel its power, transcending all power? We are the power. I am the power." The little smile returned. "You know it's true. I see it in your eyes. I feel your fear. Some say it's better to be dead than to be zombie but a zombie lives. There is a plantation south of Cap Haitian. You will work there and be useful cutting cane with the other zombies. There are many. More than anyone could believe. If my magic is too strong you may die."

Olivia Quist stepped back and spoke softly to the waiter. "Strike his wound so it opens to bleed freely."

He used a closed fist, striking me twice in the mouth. The lip split wide and blood streamed from it, dripping along my chin onto my naked chest. The drums beat and the women chanted.

Olivia unbuttoned the top two buttons of her dress and reached her fingers inside between her breasts and drew out a Q-Tip. A crude cup was brought to her by one of the other bokors. The cup was suspended inside a long piece of mesh plastic, like the sacks used to hold onions. A cup of poison. They held it carefully because even a single droplet was lethal.

Painstakingly, Olivia inserted the Q-Tip between the mesh and into the cup, drawing forth just a tiny amount of the zombie poison. "This will work quickly in a fresh wound," she said. "I promise to awaken you to new life. There is a certain malaise to the spirit of a zombie that must be a comfort from the evils of ordinary living." One of the guards held me by the hair as she dabbed the Q-Tip into my wound.

"There. It won't take long now." She carefully wrapped the Q-Tip in a thick oily rag, then quite suddenly smiled like her old self and gently stroked my cheek. "Goodbye EJ."

She stepped back and one of her assistants handed her an old rum bottle filled with some liquid and she drank. Her "protection" bottle, the antidote, in case she'd slopped some of the poison on herself. This didn't seem likely. Anyway, the antidote was useless. I knew that. Ground up aloe and other plant leaves which offered nothing strong enough to counteract the deadly poison. Sometimes it made you vomit or worked like a laxative. This was of little help unless taken soon after you ingested the poison. Mine was introduced to my body through my wound.

Depending on how Olivia mixed her zombie powder, it might also contain datura, a mixture of scopolamine and other drugs that were violently psychoactive. I'd go nuts within a very short time. I was already confused and weak. My mind wandered, recalling a story of medieval European witches who used datura as a body rub. Broomstick as an applicator, they rubbed it across the moist tissue of their vaginas. Witches did ride broomsticks. They just didn't fly, except in their hallucinations.

Everything depended on Olivia's expertise. The usual poisons were all deadly. The amounts were critical. I could expect anything from a Mickey Finn to instant death. Or just maybe zombies are more common than we believe, and I might stagger through the remainder of my days and labor under the hot sun, the walking dead.

I lost track of time. Minutes, hours, I didn't know. The pole had been removed and my arms untied. I was lying on my back and people had gathered around me and they seemed very tall. I studied them. They were on the ground and I was below it in my new coffin, which seemed to crowd me at the shoulders. I was free to move but powerless. Uncaring. I didn't want to move. I did want to speak but no words formed and all the functions of my body seemed to be shutting down in the manner of some mechanical device, which though it was switched off, continued to cycle awhile like a spinning wheel, until it ran out of energy.

Olivia stood at the foot of my grave. "I might have loved you," she said.

I wanted to tell her that I did love her and that I was happy to be a zombie but that my skin was beginning to burn and I had the feeling that the flesh beetles that eat cadavers were already crawling beneath my skin, gnawing at me. I didn't want that. I didn't want to see Baron Samedi coming through the cemetery for me either.

The burning worsened. Olivia smiled at me. I tried to smile in return but my facial muscles were frozen.

The voodoo men brought a lid for my coffin and stepped down inside the grave to nail it. A shallow grave, I thought. The easier to dig up. Good news. Someone was going to come back after I'd been turned into a zombie. There was some talking above but most of it was in Creole. Part of the ceremony or magic being done to me. I felt very special and could see just a little through the cracks in the coffin lid.

Before long I heard the sound of a hammer and felt the vibrations. They were nailing me in. I monitored their progress along my body, beginning at my feet. When they reached my head I saw one of the nails come through. It was dangerously close to my left eye but sank painlessly, harmlessly just below into the soft flesh of my cheek. Perhaps it would release the beetles. A hole for them to escape. Surely they were trapped. They didn't eat you until you were dead. But did we know when we died? Or did we simply remain exactly the same but without the benefit of a body to carry us around?

Maybe cemeteries really were filled with the spirits of the dead. Imprisoned in their coffins until the end of the age. I was lucky. I was going to be a zombie.

A rattle. Thudding. Dust.

The burial, of course. I knew that. Shovelfuls of dirt thudding above my head, sifting inside through the cracks. It didn't choke me. My breathing seemed to have stopped. I remembered some poems and silently recited them. Then something reminded me of Poe's *Tell-Tale Heart*. At the beginning of the story the murderer is wondering if he's mad. It's a problem, you know. The point at which we are separated not only from life but reality, sanity. If we can't consciously make the transition how can we know? Really, isn't madness not knowing?

I didn't know.

For the first time everything was total darkness. I knew there was a space between my body and the dirt but I wanted to rise above it nonetheless, and be free, so I did. I floated like gas. I filtered up through the ground and came to rest just above the sod that had been so carefully replaced, covering my fresh grave between first and second base.

Above the earth something restricted my vision, like I was wearing my oval, black rubber diving mask and the only direction I could see was down. The grass, sod, dirt, didn't impede my vision. I saw myself quite clearly lying there in the coffin with my hands at my sides. Weren't they supposed to be across my chest?

I studied myself carefully. I was dead.

I had a new understanding of death. All the other corpses I'd seen were just that, others. It's not the same as experiencing it yourself. My body wasn't going to rot like other peoples bodies did, because I wasn't going to remain dead. Olivia promised. I was going to work on a plantation.

I was lucky. I was going to be a zombie.

Chapter Twenty Three

Normal awakening is a passage from trance to reality. The shell of insensibility cracks and the sensory world returns. Awakening from zombie death is slightly more traumatic - it's rebirth. The pain and travail is all yours. The awakening pushes you forth not in regular contractions but explosive thrusts, bullying you toward consciousness, where you arrive in a placental ooze of confusion, thick enough to paste your senses with the slick mud of disbelief.

I strained to blink my eyes, webbed with a sticky yellow slime through which I saw Olivia. The ground had opened and she was singing a bokor song. Drums and rattles sounded in the fog all around.

The crowd grabbed me up and beat me with their leafy whips. I was tied once more and wrapped into a dark cloth that they wound round and round me, tight like a mummy. I was standing with two men on each side to support me.

"Zombie," Olivia commanded. "Walk."

Muscular control was spasmodic and weak but it existed. The muscles in my face too, had come to life. I didn't think I could talk and I felt the malaise the waiter bokor had promised. This then, was being a zombie. A man without will.

I wondered why they had me tied. Didn't they have faith in their magic? Would I suddenly bolt from the stadium and disappear?

We were still in the stadium. Had many nights gone by? Or just hours?

It was darker than before. Most of the torches were gone or extinguished. I felt the people still, the ghouls, gathered around in the dark awaiting my first lurching steps or some guttural noise from my parched throat. Maybe for some of them it was their first zombie. I wondered if I could break from the black cloth, stretch my arms out like a sleepwalker and moan a little to please the crowd. I smiled to myself - my first zombie joke.

Someone slipped a rope around my neck and used it to drag me along. We passed the pitcher's mound and headed for home. I felt grass under my bare feet and it thrilled me. I had feeling.

My memory was returning too. I knew where we were going. To the plantation where I would work with the other zombies cutting sugar cane. It wouldn't be so bad, I thought. Maybe they'd let us sing. I might sing even if they didn't let us. I might lead a zombie revolt. *Revolt of the Zombies*. The old Realto on Independencia had black and whites like that when I was a kid and we'd go there for the Saturday matinees - fifteen cents and popcorn a nickel.

The pain high on my left cheek was resurrected too. The coffin nail. I was beginning to remember everything, or almost everything. I was thankful to Olivia for mixing the zombie powder just right. I remembered about the poison makers and their mixture of faith and science. I had no faith in voodoo, and perhaps Olivia had enough faith in me to cut the dosage. Maybe she would come to the plantation sometimes and we could talk.

There was an explosion just then. A silent explosion of light.

We froze.

Someone had turned on the stadium lights. A voice from the outfield screamed, "Let's rock and roll you voodoo bastards! The Marines have landed!"

I turned to see Colonel Blitzen standing in center field in full camouflage, complete with helmet, face paint, M-16 resting on each hip. As we stood rooted, he fired both machine guns into the air and with a blood curdling scream started running toward us.

My captors scattered.

A moment later Blitzen roared past me, changing clips and firing again. He didn't stop or even acknowledge me. Seconds later I was standing five feet in front of home plate, still on the grass, all alone. Fog drifted across the face of the light banks. It was perfectly quiet for a time, then more machine gun fire, more distant now. Those bokors must've been running for their lives. I looked around for Olivia but she'd disappeared too.

"EJ, baby!" A woman's voice called. Dawn Blitzen, dressed like a fat whore, lumbered out onto the field from the service door near the home team dugout.

"Did you turn on the lights?" I asked. My first audible words. I talked like a man with a mouthful of peanut butter.

"Marky showed me where they were. We planned it together. Ain't he just a hunk?"

I heard more machine gun fire. "He's about my favorite guy in the whole world," I confessed. "How did you know where to find me?"

"Don't ask me, Baby. You know all this isn't my style." She shook her shoulders, setting massive breasts in motion. "I was born to party!"

"Can you get this cloth off me?"

She began to untie the portion of material which held the rest in place when she suddenly stopped and leaned very close. "That may not be such a good idea, Hot Stuff." She kissed me lightly on the lips. "I've sort of got you where I want you."

I returned the kiss. "Yes, but all we can do is kiss until you get this stuff off me."

"Ooo," she said. "You Latin men make me so horny." She went on with her work.

"Hurry please. I have to find my family."

She stopped again. "They're at the house."

"Alive?"

"Sure. What'd you think?"

"There were two dead guys in the driveway when I drove up."

"Did you know those men?"

"I think so. Much as I know anything."

"They sent your parents and sisters – all of us – way into the fields. Hid us in the tobacco. Lying in the rows. Tell you the whole story later. Now they're more worried about you."

The last of the black cloth fell to the ground. I stepped away from it and threw both arms around Dawn Blitzen. "I've never felt this good in my life," I said, kissing her hard on the mouth.

She pushed me away. "Hold on there Romeo. I was just kidding around."

"Let me lean on you at least," I said. "Take me to the house." We heard more machine gun fire. Barely audible. "You wouldn't happen to have a cigarette?"

"Where would I keep 'em?" She wore only a purple tube top and pedal-pushers.

"Let's go."

We headed for the exit. "That was the Ambassador's daughter, wasn't it? Olivia? The one supposed to have been killed in the car bombing?"

"Yes."

"Is she like a Patty Hearst?"

"It's complicated," I said. "Did you see where she went?"

"I couldn't see good from where I was."

"She won't get far," I predicted. "Sorry if I'm heavy. Unsteady on my feet yet."

"Isn't every day you get stripped naked and turned into a zombie. Aren't you cold?"

"Sort of drugged up yet. Don't suppose you'd consider keeping all this zombie stuff to yourself?" I begged.

"Are you kidding me?"

Dumb question. "Never mind." My knees had been replaced with swivel joints and I clung to her.

"You're about to become the most sought after dinner guest in Santo Domingo," she whispered in my ear. "You're going to be famous."

"I can't wait."

Better to be called a zombie than be one, I guess. Mother would insist I see a doctor, but I felt that the zombie powder had worn off because Olivia mixed it light. Brain cells are all different. Some survive awhile without oxygen, others only seconds. If the tetrodotoxin was mixed perfectly, approximating death, but not excessive enough to cause permanent brain damage, then a full recovery was likely. Had Olivia mixed it on the strong side I'd be dead or a zombie forever.

As it was, it knocked me out and gave me pretty extraordinary dreams, hallucinations, raging emotions, out of body visions, but didn't kill me or destroy brain cells in large numbers. I wasn't a vegetable. So I got lucky, or she did have some feeling for me. Or a week from now my eyes would roll back and I'd swallow my head.

Olivia. Poor broken child. She'd mixed her father's dose too. Was he dead or alive? If he was alive he knew her power and she would've wanted him to feel it, like she wanted us to feel it. Not just the power but the justice it brought her. More vindication than revenge, I thought. She might find absolution now for her own sins with him, or sins she imagined in her child mind to have done.

I staggered on.

Back at the house it was pandemonium. Lights blazing, hugging, laughing, crying. Two whole hours passed before Edwina called me EJ her darling little zombie. It would take months, maybe years to outlive it. My mother made a fuss over the coffin nail track in my cheek, but my father, in a rare moment of wit, said I shouldn't even have it stitched up. "Imagine that scar," he said. "A woman asks where you got it and you say quietly 'coffin nail.' Hijo, they'll drop into your lap."

"Sonja won't," I said.

"Then that's the one you should marry."

"I'm trying, Dad. I'm trying."

My mother said, "You will do nothing of the kind. Dr. Ruis will sew you up."

Dawn drank a sizable dent into my father's liquor cabinet and Blitzen arrived and joined in. Crazy kind of party. It was four-thirty in the morning someone finally told me. The Colonel had chased the terrified voodoo sect into the surrounding countryside. "Nicked one or two," he claimed. "Raised all kinda hell down at the cop house. Got a bunch of 'em loaded into pickups to scour the hills. Never find a thing I'm sure, but it'll keep 'em running all the way back to Haiti."

Johnson & Johnson were packaged inside old bed linen - the first Johnson's head under his arm - and stored temporarily in the cookhouse cooler. We listened in rapt silence as Blitzen told how he'd followed them here the day before and called Dawn to bring his equipment. "I just knew it," he said. "Like being back in-country. Followed them after I saw the three of you in the Bodegon. Didn't see me there, did ya? Never saw two more guilty-lookin' beggars in my life as those Johnsons. After that they never left my sight. Damned if they didn't turn out all right though. Sent me and Horny into the field to protect your people while they took the heat. Of course, we had no idea there was so many of the bastards. I wish I'd killed some of 'em."

I realized then how lucky I'd been. Blitzen's success owed to following the wrong guys after stumbling across them talking to me in the Bodegon where he'd gone to take a leak. The Johnsons weren't so lucky. They guarded the road while Blitzen, finally clued in about who was who, covered my family far away in the field.

Around sunup we all wound down. For once, my mother said, no one had to stand guard. We slept well. My last thoughts before I drifted off were of Olivia. Not Olivia the mambo but Olivia the little girl molested by her father. Like Sonja, her innocence stolen early. I wanted to tell her how I understood about the hole left in her heart, and what she'd done to her father to fill it. I wished to see her just once more. A rooster was waking the farm to a new day as my mind gave up to sleep. I would've asked her too, where is Adam Quist?

* * *

I didn't get back to my apartment in the Capital until after Christmas. Carmen had bought an amulet from some supposed wizard she found in a barrio along the Ozama. Instead of wearing it around her neck, she'd hung it above the patio doors to protect the whole apartment. When I asked what was inside she said, "Chicken entrails."

"Great," I said. "Now I'll be able to get some sleep."

The first party of the new year was held at Dawn and Marcus Blitzen's. I was guest of honor. Sonja made an ass of herself by talking incessantly and somehow Dawn had found out about Duane Delbrick's role in the Quist affair and invited him too. He showed. More out of bravado than anything else, I thought. His career hadn't been damaged. He was confirmed as the new United States Ambassador to the Dominican Republic. I drank too much and called him Pinhead. He left early.

Olivia, after disappearing into the fog that night, was never seen again. There were rumors of "white zombies" and I wondered if that wasn't what had become of her. Maybe she'd dedicated her life to making zombies out of men like her father, if there were any in the hidden mountain villages of northern Haiti where a white mambo might be welcome or feared.

My problem was an old man named Garrett Yancy. I'd avoided him as long as possible but the time had come. He'd hired me to do a job and I'd failed. That morning I made an appointment to see him in the afternoon. I wasn't looking forward to it, and couldn't think of any time I'd failed him so miserably.

"Did you read the letter from the bank?" Carmen asked before I left.

"Yes."

"What did it say?"

"Mind your own business."

"It's my business to know if you're going to have enough money to pay me. I've been thinking about a raise."

"You're not getting a raise. You get paid more than any maid in Santo Domingo. If anyone ever found out how much I pay you I'd be better off as a zombie." I had zombie headaches still but Dr. Ruiz reasoned too that the poison in Olivia's mixture was weak, explaining my near total recovery.

"I could learn how to mix that zombie powder," she said. "Shake a little in your chivo."

Wouldn't hurt, I suppose, to bump her up a few pesos. She was better with her money than I was, maybe I could borrow some of it back.

* * *

December can be chilly sometimes, nighttime temperatures dipping into the upper sixties, but January is often the most pleasant month of the year. Dry, less humid. The kind of weather that makes you want to work. But that afternoon outside Mr. Yancy's house it was hot, airless, and oppressive.

I glanced up at the sign, the winged passport with its inscription Yancy Tours, SA, and I thought it looked a little predatory, and was glad it didn't have a beak. This meeting had already been postponed too long but I could've turned around and jumped back in the Jeep without much encouragement. Mr. Yancy and I enjoyed a relationship that had never once included anything but cordiality. I couldn't help wondering if it could survive such total failure as I was about to deliver.

Ethel opened the door. I knew they had servants but never saw any. Ethel smiled. "Mr. Espinosa-Jones. Please come up. How are you feeling?"

I was asked this often now. "Not bad for a zombie," I said.

She led me upstairs as she always did, though I'd been there dozens of times. She had admirable legs which were today encased in nylons. A little formal even for her, I thought, especially in the heat.

Mr. Yancy was at his desk. No oxygen tank in evidence. His color looked better too, but I was pretty sure you didn't recover from emphysema. "Buenas tardes, Mr. Yancy," I said respectfully. "I'm glad to find you looking so well."

"I have energy today Mr. Espinosa-Jones," he said. "You always cheer me up. An old man must live vicariously. Please give me a full report. I've been impatient for every detail."

"Every failure, don't you mean?"

"Please," he said pointing to the chair alongside his desk. "Just the facts. It's my job to decide what is failure and what isn't."

So I told him. Started from the beginning and went through it all again. I was tired of telling it by now but he had a right to the full account, and I gave it. Sometimes when people questioned me at parties and social functions, I embellished the details slightly to keep myself from looking like a complete idiot, but Mr. Yancy got it straight. He was my employer after all, and deserved an undoctored report. That's what he paid me for, though I'd decided not to accept payment this time.

I finished up by saying, "I think Olivia came to you in the very beginning because of how mad she was to prove her power. Voodoo, and her own personal power too. Suffering from childhood. Her innocence stolen. Voodoo saved her she said, and it was the weapon, the sword of justice she swung against those who preyed upon her. It gave her power to seduce Delbrick and use his power to keep Dulce and Alejandro one step ahead. Always beyond our reach. Victimizing your children, or your citizens, doesn't bring peace. She just found power in the wrong place."

I paused for awhile and then told him, "If there was a success, it was that your client didn't get stuck with a large bill to exhume an empty coffin. I'm thankful for that."

"Why did she pay for that do you think?"

"May never know for sure, but I think it was because of a short gray skirt. The one she wore to her father's burial. When I made mention of it she claimed it was for me, so I'd admire her shapley legs. I never believed that. She was showing off. She dug her father up to show off again. Probably thought you wouldn't pay, so how could she show off if nobody knew the coffin was empty?" I shook my head. "She must've been confident I wouldn't get it anyway. And I didn't.

"From the beginning I was hung up on details and didn't see the big picture. I told you about Mickey's cop with the pocket knife," I continued. "Well, he squeezed the mortician - same guy did both the Ambassador and Olivia - and finally learned they used a two-headed wax dummy made in Haiti. First it was Quist, then they switched heads, changed clothes, added some little breasts, and it was her. That's why Quist's coffin was empty. Simple. Clever. I never caught on. Delbrick told the mortician it was a matter of national security. Didn't even have to bribe the guy. Details. I couldn't get past them. Make sense of them.

"Mickey's guy thinks Olivia had it all planned from the beginning, first her father then her. Fake her own death as an escape, but delayed it awhile to see what I was going to do. To play with me, he said. It worked. I was suckered."

He didn't interrupt my narrative, and when I finished ignored my obvious confusion, then asked, "What about the Johnsons? Were their bodies claimed?"

"No," I said. "Mickey Alba used up all his contacts in Haiti, admittedly not many, and never heard anything. Finally he had to do something with the remains. My father insisted they be buried at the finca, in the family plot. His story of how they saved our family is worth hearing. Ask him about it. Anyway, we had a nice funeral."

"I contacted my sources in the voodoo community as well." He shrugged. "No response. I'm interested in men who give their lives to save a family, and their religion from this blood sect." He glanced around for Ethel and lit a cigarette. "I will talk with your father."

Ethel had a nose. I heard her heels on the granite. Mr. Yancy quickly handed me his cigarette. I don't think we fooled her but she set a tray containing two ice cold bottles of Presidente. She poured, and wrapped the glasses in folded paper towels. She smiled at the cigarette in my hand. Not my brand.

"I'm sorry about Olivia," I said when Ethel left.

"A tragedy almost worse than her father's," he said. "Must've made it back across the border somehow. I was fond of her too, you know."

"Yes sir."

He stared rather pointedly at me. "This has been hard on you. Zombie jokes aside. I feel awful about the dangers that I've exposed you to. I'd like to apologize."

"Mr. Yancy, I'm the one who owes you an apology. I don't know any more about what happened to Adam Quist today than I did the day you gave me the assignment." I stood up, wandered the room awhile to collect my thoughts before sitting back down. "I thought he was dead. I thought he was a zombie. He turns out to be a child-molesting creep who was obviously dealt with by his own child. And she destroyed herself in the process. That's not how I define success."

"The man was dealt with, was he not? What should we do with child-molesters?"

"I don't know," I said. "Dominicans aren't very tolerant of crimes against children. If Mickey Alba arrested such a person, well, their death would be painful and their trial probably delayed until Judgment Day."

"Yes," Yancy agreed. "But this molester would most likely have escaped unscathed. Diplomatic immunity."

"I suppose, but his daughter didn't escape him." I took a long drink of the beer. "I'm still a little mad at Olivia for Dulce and Alejandro."

Mr. Yancy nodded. "Must be tough though," he said, "being a sorcerer."

"Sir?"

"Like a famous actor. The moment you're on top someone tries to knock you down, don't they? Your magic has to keep improving. Don't you think there are many more of Olivia's followers like this bloodthirsty couple? Even now she must be creating some new magic."

"That thought gives me the chills."

Mr. Yancy smiled at me and sipped his beer. Finally he said, "She could've killed you quite easily."

"I know." I tried to return the smile. "Anyway, she scared me half to death."

Mr. Yancy got up from his chair and led me by the arm out onto his veranda. "What do you think of my garden, Mr. Espinosa-Jones?"

"It's very private. The flowers are well tended."

"Everything has a place in nature," he said, "but in this garden I decide what grows and everything is in the place I put it. Someday soon someone else will come along to tend it, so my garden may be completely different. Won't make it any less lovely. Someone else's idea of beauty."

I thought this over. "So you think what happened to Quist is someone else's idea of justice?"

"You'd like a neat ending. The law and all that." His eyes scanned the rich colors, the expanse of clipped grass, the swaying palms. "But aren't laws next to useless? Mostly obeyed by those who agree with them? Anyway, we answer to a higher law, my young friend. I think justice was done."

I felt the heat of the sun through the soles of my shoes. "It's left me a little empty, like I'm still waiting for something."

"You did the best you could." He smiled. "I've been authorized to include a little bonus with your usual fee."

"You owe me nothing," I said, embarrassed.

Mr. Yancy turned and leaned his back against the iron railing. I suddenly saw him as a young man, lanky and loose. I felt a twang of nostalgia from the loss of never having known him then. "There'll be no more such talk," he said. "I take it as a personal insult. Our business has been the business of life. Not so? Our usual arrangement always good enough. So it shall remain."

I didn't argue.

He strolled to his desk, picked up an envelope and started back. "Thank you," I said, taking it from his hand.

"I missed my siesta today," he confided. "I'm going to rest now. Ethel is taking me to Vesuvio's for pizza tonight. I haven't been out in a long time. Do you know the Vesuvio's?"

"Yes."

"Someone has told me they have a pizza there made with fresh lobster."

"I've eaten it. Well worth the trip."

"An unobstructed view of the ocean too," he said. "I'm not fond of this new construction. Hotels. Condominiums. Spoils the country. What's the matter with these developers do you think?"

"Someone else's idea of progress, I suppose."

"Greed, more like."

We stood a moment longer and I knew it was time to go, but there was just one more thing. "Mr. Yancy," I said. "Please. You have to tell me. Who is your client?"

He placed a gentle hand on my shoulder. "Is that so important now?"

"Sí, Señor. Now more than ever."

Mr. Yancy's complexion was strengthened by a faint glow of freckles strapping his nose and cheeks. He patted my shoulder in his absentminded old man way and brought his hand back down. "You have a right to know, I guess." He spoke in a low voice. "My client is Adam Quist."

"He's alive?"

"No," he shook his head. "No. Adam is dead. He must be, and I'm not sorry about it."

"I don't understand."

"In 1942, I was an Australian coast watcher on a desolate island in the South Pacific. It was overrun by the Japanese. Adam and his squad rescued me." He shrugged. "We managed some other adventures during the war as well. Both of us wounded. And we drank together. Even pursued the same women once or twice. The friends you have at times like that are never forgotten, never forsaken. If someone kills one of them you avenge them. You can understand that, I think."

"Yes Sir."

"Life is long." He grinned. "If a man is lucky he has a friend or two that walks part way with him. My friend Adam was less a perfect man than I imagined. But still and all my young friend, I would not be standing here if it weren't for Sergeant Adam Quist, USMC. You see why I didn't want to tell you? Does it help?"

"No," I said. "It's only a loose end. People hate them you know. Helps to explain Olivia's behavior. I failed to reconcile Olivia the kid, with Olivia the mambo. Just too incredible. She knew her father wasn't in his coffin yet paid to have it dug up. She was a fine actress and fooled Delbrick her lover and me her stooge. But then, I suppose she's been acting all her life. How can you be a real little girl when your father is doing things real fathers would never do?"

I read the same confusion on Mr. Yancy's face, and he saved us by saying, "I hate those hotels." He sighed. "But not to worry. I won't be around to see it all grow into something greedy and homogeneous. Goodday Mr. Espinosa-Jones."

"Good day, Mr. Yancy." How politely I was always dismissed.

Ethel appeared and lead me out. Such wonderful old fashioned manners, I thought, but the moment we were out of sight around the corner she did something strange. She took my hand and held it tightly until we reached the bottom of the stairs.

"I appreciate your kindness," she said. "See how good he looks? I heard him singing this morning after he heard you were coming. Thank you."

"He's a lovely man," I answered. "One day I'm going to take you to the Vesuvio's myself."

"At your service, Señor."

You never knew with Ethel, she kept such a straight face.

* * *

A few weeks later, in February, the *Última Hora* covered its front page with Colonel Caamaño's head. A nice looking middle aged man, about three days growth of beard on his face, firm chin below slightly parted lips. His eyes were open slightly too. Just above his left eye, somewhat off center on his forehead, was a very neat bullet hole. The headline read: *What do you say Mamá Caamaño? Where is your boy?* Colonel Caamaño's head was lying in what looked like dried grass, and I don't know why, but the first thing that came to mind was Sonja.

Olivia Quist and Sonja Cadavid might've been sisters. They had much in common, and I don't mean me. They were both damaged from youth, irrevocably changed by their suffering. Both were dangerous and slightly mad. But only slightly, the rest became poise and action – a means of converting determination into savagery and setting them apart from any other women I'd ever known.

The death of Caamaño closed a door for me. I was done with it all and thought it a sad ending. Would the mambo half of Olivia gain supremacy and devour her? Some toothless hag, mad for blood? And Sonja? What if Castro lived on? Could she pursue him relentlessly, until she too was consumed with hatred? Mickey was right no doubt. This was the way of the world – the damaged and the dead. And while I condemned myself as a fool, I knew that road led to perdition, and I would never take it.

Chapter Twenty Four

Children can be cruel. When I first saw the graffiti, that came to mind. Kids painting 28 where they knew I'd see it on the wall surrounding the apartment building, then again on a tree across from my veranda. Twenty eight refers to one thing here, kilometer marker 28 on the Santiago highway where the insane asylum stands. My zombie fame had spread.

Neighborhood kids tagged me Zombie Man. Whenever I came near they walked past with their arms out, heads thrust back, moaning. Bravo Benoit wrote another sensational feature story - I got crackpot letters and crackpots at my door. I was glad *not* to have a phone, or use of one if Mercedes Villacampa kept her pledge. Not to be outdone, my friends and family took pleasure in relating the trials of their relationship with a zombie. Every memory lapse, trip on a stair or garbled sentence grew my reputation as a lunatic zombie who might crack at any moment and attack the innocent or run screaming into the streets.

The teasing would eventually run its course. Meanwhile in my apartment, I studied the lettering. It didn't look like graffiti to me. Carefully painted. No dripping or haphazard colors. Nice curl on the 2. Kids weren't that careful. The more I thought about it the more it worried me.

What if an adult had painted it? Might be a threat or a message from some criminally insane lunatic seeking a soul mate. I was now well-known and this was a large city after all. And if the poison makers had returned, vengeance was at hand. The 28 on the tree was very near the spot Dulce and Alejandro had stood with a beheaded chicken.

These are not the kinds of things a person needs to sit in his apartment and ponder, so I left for Arroyo Hondo. When in doubt, get a haircut.

I'd seen Cosme the barber only twice since Christmas. Sonja's man Luis had cleaned up after Alejandro, but Cosme said nobody wanted to sleep in the Sugar Shack again. I kept apologizing. He was just glad, he said, that neither he or his daughter had been present at the time of the shooting. There were stories in the papers, and though he hadn't been mentioned, he knew he was part of a larger story that included Ambassador Quist's death. (The official story never changed. Adam Quist died of a heart attack.) I'd told him my side of it but wondered if he believed me.

John Kennedy, like a faded saint, hung in his place of honor. The mirror was still cracked. The pig curious. It was dry again and I asked Cosme to close the door to keep dust out.

Behind me he picked up his scissors and said, "I think you are a different man now."

"Oh? Why do you say that?"

"Because you are wearing shower shoes and short pants in a business district."

I tried to imagine Arroyo Hondo as a business district, miles from downtown or anywhere else. "I left home in a hurry," I told him. "Somebody painted 28 on the wall around my building and even on a tree."

"They are making a joke for you?"

"About me." The day was warm. The closed door made me sweat. "Started to imagine worse things, you know? Needed a change of scenery."

The snip of his scissors cut slices from his voice. "The Veintiocho has been a fearful place the whole of my life," he admitted. "I think of it like I think of hell. There it is, but who has ever seen it?"

"We've all seen it," I corrected him. "It's right along the road."

"Sí. You see parts of some buildings. Trees. Barbed wire. A parking lot. What else?"

"What else would you want to see?"

"Nothing. I'm only saying we see, but we don't see. Who knows what hell is like until he dips his toes into the burning lake?"

"You know it's hot," I said. Barbers. What goes through their minds all day standing with their noses in other people's hair? "How's your sweet virgin daughter?"

"She's very well. I think she liked you."

"One day when there's more time I'll walk back and see her."

"She would be pleased." The scissors paused for a few moments before he asked, "Do you think someone wants you to visit the Veintiocho?"

"To make fun of me, you mean?"

"Or for another reason."

"There isn't any other reason," I said.

After the haircut I went home for lunch, rather than appear at a restaurant where I might know someone. Carmen gave me rice and beans, all she had, then I changed clothes and drove down to the Malecón. I wanted to be close to the ocean.

What Cosme said made a kind of twisted sense and stuck with me. They painted 28 where I could see it clearly day and night. Was someone trying to tell me something? I left the Jeep and walked awhile. Only two surfers beyond the small breakers, straddling their boards talking. The sea was calm as a lake.

January was almost gone. Mr. Yancy hadn't called again. Didn't need me or didn't want me. A dive shop in New York wrote to say they wanted me to handle their diving for at least a week when they came down. Their advance money saved me from begging my parents for rent.

On the ocean side of the street, all along the Malecón, a concrete wall separates the jagged limestone cliffs from the broad sidewalk where citizens of Santo Domingo make their evening promenade. It doubles as a long bench, extending the entire length of the street.

It's unpopular when the sun is hot, but Peor didn't seem to care. I spotted her and the child climbing the wall, then angling through traffic to intercept me as I walked along the other side.

I'd seen enough of Peor.

"Señor EJ!" she shouted as I turned to duck away.

I faced her. "What do you want?"

"Have I asked for anything?"

"You will."

She stroked the child's expressionless face in a loving manner. "Heaven forbid I should ask for a peso or two so this innocent might eat today."

"No."

"As you wish." Peor wagged her head. "Zombie Man they call

you now."

"So?"

"Maybe they're trying to tell you something."

"Maybe."

"You should listen."

"Pardon me," I said, starting to move around her. "I'm on the way somewhere."

"Maybe they're trying to tell you to go to the Veintiocho."

"What? I don't think so."

Peor shrugged and pushed the child ahead of her along the sidewalk. "Too bad," she said. "You are a fool."

The woman was crazy. A beggar. Worse. An exploiter of children. What was I doing talking to her? Had she been by my building and seen the letters? Or painted them? Had she delivered a message for someone? Why hit me over the head with it?

An hour later I was sitting in the outdoor bar at the Jaragua. It shouldn't have been a tough decision but a weak stomach and a vivid imagination worked against me. An insane asylum in those days was not something I needed to see.

I called Mickey from the lobby and invited him for a drink. It took him an hour to get there. The surfers gave up and paddled ashore, climbing up from a tiny beach among the rocks. They drove away in a green pickup with some sort of writing on it.

Mickey barely had time to flop into a chair before I asked him, "Do you think you can get me into the Veintiocho?"

"Without a doubt," he said. "As one of your oldest friends, I think I speak for everyone when I say we've all been wondering how to bring up the subject."

I closed my eyes and listened to the hum of traffic. "Thank you," I said. "I was hoping you'd take me seriously. You've no idea how relieved I am that you, my very best friend, haven't fallen into the insipid, vacuous sport of humiliation which has become the mainstay of my current existence. Think what it would be like if even your best friend offered nothing but shopworn 28 jokes!"

"Man, you sure got the idioma, you know? So you're telling me you really *want* to go there?"

"Yes."

"And I'm not allowed to laugh?"

"No."

"Are you driving, or is the wagon picking you up?"

"Mickey! I'm losing my patience."

"The first thing that goes after your mind."

"Your death is imminent."

"Okay, okay. I'll make a call. They'll want to know why."

I told him about the graffiti. Not about Peor. "I'm at loose ends now anyway. Got a New York group on the way down. Nothing else doing."

"So why not visit a nut house?"

"Will you just make the call?"

"Cigars on the veranda later this week. Got a good one to tell you anyway about that beat cop I sent to the airport last fall, remember? They're still working on the immediate report I asked for and they're still looking for Dulce and Alejandro. Tell you the whole story. Can't imagine all the paperwork it's generating. So, let's say Friday, cold beer, quiet candlelight dinner - lobster would be nice. Some of that expensive cognac you keep in the back of the cupboard."

"There's nothing worse than a crooked cop," I said. "Bring your wife at least so I've got somebody intelligent to talk to."

The Veintiocho was a nut house, an insane asylum, a hell hole from all I'd heard. Rumor was the Ozama Prison paled in comparison. Instead of relief now, I was filled with dread.

* * *

The Veintiocho was a nondescript cluster of buildings along a busy highway. Beyond the chain link and barbed wire, motorists granted it the same respect they did road kill. Inside, a place where devils lived and hope was abandoned. The barber was right. You don't know hell until you dip your toes into the burning lake.

One hand covered my nose and mouth. The other gripped the shoulder of a man who'd introduced himself as Elvin Mendez. We were several feet apart when we left the reception area and moved through the first unlocked ward. He hadn't warned me when we stepped inside. Maybe he was immune or insensitive or rankled because he had to waste time showing me around the place. I don't suppose it would've helped if he *had* warned me. Anyway, he didn't seem surprised that I clung to him.

The smell was putrid. Feces, urine, vomit - other unidentifiable odors, ripe with eye-stinging rot, neglect, total disregard for cleanliness.

Inside the first doorless room on my left, one man alone. He appeared unconscious, lying naked on the concrete floor facing the wall. For some time he'd been defecating in neat piles throughout his space. Pools of urine evaporated in the intense heat, stinging my eyes and nostrils. I first grasped Elvin by the shirt and gagged. "My God," I said. "What's wrong with him?"

Elvin shrugged. "He doesn't speak."

The man had feces smeared on his legs and buttocks. There was no evidence of bedding or a toilet or scrap of furniture. "Can't you keep him clean?" I asked.

"Someone comes through with a hose every few days," he said. "These people are lunatics, you know."

"Where does he sleep? He's naked?"

"He sleeps there on the floor. How can we give him clothes? See the mess he makes? It's much more sanitary to leave him naked so he can be thoroughly hosed."

We moved on and I felt my head sinking into my shoulders. I breathed through my mouth and thought maybe if I only looked left I'd see only half as much.

In the next room we found several people, partially clothed. Both men and women. They were more aware of us and stared at me particularly.

"They like strangers," Elvin said.

Another bare room with concrete floors, walls, ceiling, an emptiness broken only by banks of metal jalousie windows on the far side opposite the open doorway. "They live here together?" I asked.

"Yes."

I counted four men and three women. All stood mute except one of the women. She screamed, "Ah, ha!" and ran toward us, halting close enough for me to smell her breath. "You come to copular!"

I stepped back from the doorway. "What does she mean?"

"People stop sometimes," he said, waiting for me to catch on. "There are men who come here. Even lunatics know some things."

"Are you trying to be funny?"

Elvin looked hurt. "What did you expect to see here? Do you think this is the Santo Domingo Country Club? Maybe we have a pool?" He laughed. "No one comes here without a good reason. Why did you?"

I moved several feet along the wall and fumbled for a pack of cigarettes. Elvin helped himself and we smoked. It didn't kill the smell, but helped a little. "I'm not sure why I came here," I said. "What did Lt. Alba say when he called?'

"He asked us to cooperate with you in every way possible." He crossed his arms and stared up at me. "This is a dangerous place. I can only warn you. What more do you want to see?"

I couldn't tell this man I'd dropped in because someone painted 28 on my wall or because of feelings I had. "I'm a detective," I said, hoping the man would be impressed. "It's something I needed to see."

Elvin smiled. "Nobody needs to see this."

We smoked in silence awhile and then I flipped my cigarette on the floor. The woman who'd asked about sex sprang from the doorway and snatched it. Before she could take a drag the others were on her, biting, swearing, punching, struggling. "Stop it!" I shouted.

Elvin tossed his butt a short distance away and said, "Here!"

Several of them scrambled toward it, leaving the woman to fight only two of the men.

I took out my pack and shook it in the air. "Here! Here!"

Elvin grabbed my hand and pushed it back toward my shirt pocket. "Most of them will only eat the tobacco anyway," he said. "Let's go."

He led me farther along the hallway and I didn't pause until we exited into an open courtyard. I drew in the fresh air. The courtyard was mostly overgrown except for an area the staff used for cooking and eating, a corrugated roof held up by chain link fence at one end and two poles on the other. Beneath was a place for a charcoal fire, a large table and some mismatched chairs. We walked to it and sat down.

"Are all the wards like that?" I asked.

"Pretty much. The ones that hurt themselves are there," he pointed to the next large building beyond the eating area. "The next one after, to the left, is for cripples."

"Why?"

"They are insane or have been brought from the streets."

I thought of the woman with the doll in the catacombs. No wonder she preferred to live underground. Thankfully, Mother's missionaries had moved her to a private hospital. "How long have you been here?" I asked.

"About eight years."

"Is the pay good?"

He laughed. "You must be as crazy as these."

"Then why stay?"

"Benefits."

I didn't ask. I didn't have to. There would be food and clothes sent in. Maybe some families came for a visit or wanted to give a gift, pay for extra care or to assuage their consciences. Always, there were benefits.

I'd seen enough. "Take me back," I said, standing. "Through the courtyard not the ward."

Elvin didn't need encouragement. Only too glad to be rid of me. We picked our way through the brush, broken concrete block and trash until we struck a path that led both ways.

"Left?" I asked, turning. I'd lost sight of the buildings behind the tall grass.

"Yes."

"What's right?"

"Buildings for the criminally insane. You can't go there. Too dangerous."

I stopped. It hit me then. This was what I came for. "Cooperate in every possible way," I said, quoting Mickey.

The little man patted my arm. "You didn't like seeing the least crazy, now you want the most? These aren't the foolish. They're killers. We have them separated. Isolated. Even so, two guards have been injured this week alone. Some are very clever. Last year one escaped and we never found him. Another was shot in the city, but not until he raped a little girl. You will excite them."

"Nevertheless," I said.

"Listen to me," he said, drawing closer. "We have a man there who drinks human blood. Sediento de sangre. Vampiro."

"I've met those kind before," I said. "Please. Let's go."

Elvin turned, shaking his head, and I followed him down the path. We passed a large mango tree on our right and I heard lizards scampering in the dried leaves. The winter had remained dry. Grass and thorny brush grew to shoulder height along the path and we didn't see the buildings until we were almost on them.

"There," he said, pointing.

Each cell, rows of metal boxes set down in a small open field, had its own door. I doubted a six foot tall man could've slept stretched out in them even corner to corner. I counted twenty two. Fourteen in the first bank, eight in the next. All occupied. And Elvin was correct. I did excite them.

They had come to the small windows to stare. I saw the madness in their eyes. Whatever else was there I didn't think about. "What are their crimes?" I asked.

"Murder and rape mostly. Child molestation, and the cannibal I mentioned. He bites himself, if you'd like to take a closer look."

"No," I said. I walked along in front of the cages and examined each man's face. Some spoke but most watched in the same manner a shark watches before thrusting his tail and rolling back his lips to expose his gums and teeth. I was glad of the bars.

"Ready?" Elvin asked.

"Yes," I said. "I didn't recognize any of them."

"Who did you expect to find?"

"I'm not sure."

"Well, you've seen it all now. Except the zombie."

"Zombie?"

"Came in last year, just before Christmas."

"Where is he?"

Elvin pointed behind the cages. "No more room here. Come, I'll show you."

We started back behind the cages. "What's his name?" I wanted to know.

"No name. He can't speak."

A short walk brought us to the fence and alongside it was a bus sitting on its axles in the tall grass. Wide streaks of rust ran down from the roof between the windows. The windows were barred on the outside and screened with flat wire inside. The bus had once been blue and someone painted Casa del Zombie on the side, below the roof line.

I didn't see anyone behind the bars and the path leading around to the door was barely worn. "How often does someone come here?"

"Just for feedings, but he doesn't eat much. I've heard him laugh in the night. He likes the night."

"Can I get a look at him?"

"Why not? Anyway, he isn't aggressive."

I walked around to the door, surprised to find it open. I climbed the steps inside. A sturdy cage was welded across the width of the vehicle. Some seats remained. In the cage, half way back, sat Adam Quist licking his fingers. He'd practiced this, because he put them in his mouth quickly and in order, beginning with his thumb, sucking all ten in quick succession, smacking loudly.

"He does that," Elvin told me. "Cleans his fingernails. Don't come just after he's been to the bathroom."

"There's a bathroom?"

He pointed to a small jagged hole in the floor. "Better for him, better for us. Someone comes back here and shovels under the bus every week or so. Cook uses the shit for her tomatoes."

I stared at the former United States Ambassador to the Dominican Republic, his face gray and swollen, bathed in sweat, I saw his rags and the vacant, puzzled stare as he examined us with the same enigma he must've found in everything that surrounded him. I felt no pity. If anything, I was relieved that his daughter had failed with me and succeeded with him.

"Have you seen enough?" asked Elvin Mendez.

"More than enough," I said, "but I want to talk to him. Can you unlock the gate?"

"He won't answer you."

I placed a hand on Elvin's shoulder and stared hard at him so he'd know I was serious. "He really is a zombie, you know."

Elvin chuckled. Life in the Veintiocho. "There's always room here for one more," he told me.

I'd learned not to press the point. "Open the gate. I'll only be a minute."

Elvin shrugged. He was tired of me. The gate swung open.

When I stepped inside past the hole in the floor, I realized the week had passed. I fought a gag reflex, moved closer to the Ambassador. "Mr. Quist," I said. "My name is Espinosa-Jones. I'm a detective hired to find you. Do you understand what I'm saying?"

Adam Quist hung his head and hunched his shoulders in preparation for a scolding.

"Listen to me," I ordered. "I saw your wife in New York. David and Sarah too. They think you're dead."

His lower lip trembled.

"Olivia," I said suddenly. "Remember Olivia?"

Gradually the shoulders relaxed and the eyes lifted from the floor to stare, vacuous, out the barred window of the bus. Twice his lips moved as if to form words. I couldn't tell on what level of consciousness he existed. Maybe some image came to his poisoned mind and he saw her, the sorceress, the little girl who once crawled trustingly onto her father's lap. I looked carefully for some spark in his eyes, some hint that his spirit was more than a memory. Some sign of cognizance. I saw nothing. Adam Quist lived alone inside his own tortured reality, securely imprisoned. It was in my power to bring him home.

I hesitated.

* * *

Friday I caught a lobster out on the sand at La Caleta. He weighed in at 8.5 kilograms. Carmen boiled him live but I found his flesh chewy, dry. Mickey got pictures of me though, holding him by the antennae, tail dragging. I'm going to blow it up and frame it.

Sipping rum on the veranda that night, Mickey finally asked me about the Veintiocho. I told him I'd gone there looking for Quist but he wasn't there. "¿Verdad?" he said.

I pretended it was no big deal.

"Funny though," he remarked later. "Someone painting 28 outside your apartment like that."

I'd had the numbers painted over. "Yes," I agreed. "It *was* funny." You had to be careful with Mickey. He was no fool. "I guess we'll never know about Quist," I said.

"Maybe not."

He was looking away. I wanted to tell him, but the Veintiocho created a dilemma for me. Justice or truth. Could both be had? My hesitation grew from the calculation. The remaining Quists would pay the price for truth. I'd be proven right and everyone else would suffer and be shamed. Quist, of course, might be upgraded to a better nut house. "Anyway Mickey, I'm glad it's over. I'm tired."

"It's all over except for one thing," he said. "Who did that, do you think? Painted 28?"

"Get off it. Maybe you did."

"If you had any brains you'd know how stupid that is. Think now."

"I give up."

"A certain woman you know maybe?" he said.

"Sonja?"

"Why not?"

"You're wrong but I'll ask her," I said. "She talks to me. She doesn't have to paint stuff on my wall."

"That's one terrible mujer, my friend. Nothing about her is what it seems."

"Watch out," I warned him. "You're talking about my future wife."

Mickey laughed. "Bueno. You're both crazy, but you should ask her."

Carmen had candles on the outside tables and they danced in the night wind. Cigar smoke wavered under the veranda roof until the breezes released it into the darkness. My hesitation was hardening into resolve. Mañana, I thought. I'll worry about it tomorrow.

Acknowledgments

Santo Domingo, Port-au-Prince, Washington, D.C., and New York City were all different in 1972, and I've done my best to portray them as they were then. Any imperfections and opinions are mine alone, since most research was done in my own memory. Exceptions to that rule include the fascinating book by Wade Davis, *Passage of Darkness: The Ethnobiology of The Haitian Zombie* and Philippe Girard's *Paradise Lost: Haiti's Tumultuous Journey From Pearl Of The Caribbean To Third World Hotspot.* Recommended reading for anyone sympathetic to the Haitian plight.

On the other portion of the island is the Dominican Republic, birthplace of one of my children, setting for numerous short stories and several upcoming novels, and how can I thank an entire people? Until I find a way, know that I am one Norte Americano who has never forgotten the generosity and sympathy of so many Dominicans who spent years showering my family with sunshine and love. And I'll never trade a good Dominican cigar for a Cuban.

There are people here too, who helped in making *Poison Makers* a joy to write. Dr. Thomas Satterberg, M.D., had more fun concocting E.J. and Mickey's cocktail then I did, selecting the most likely compounds used in 1972. Thanks Tom. Kristin Rothstein was a gift from Heaven and a joy to work with, since she likes to laugh, even at my jokes, and takes me by the ear whenever necessary. My editor, Joan Tapper, is the consummate professional. And a fine writer in her own stead. Mike Hamilburg, my long-suffering agent, came up with the series concept while floating in his pool.

Thanks always to my wife, Camille. My son Matthew for keeping me humble. And eldest daughter Christy, who works without pay, offering hope, bilingualisms, and her very special brand of humor that's kept me laughing for years. Often at my own expense.

Finally, thanks to my students at Carol Morgan School in Santo Domingo. It is from you that I drew the character who became my protagonist Edgar Espinosa-Jones. The blending of Dominican and American genes and culture creates a most intriguing and sympathetic character. But of course, you know this much better than I. Gracias.